Elisabeth Luard has spent much of her life on the move – which may explain her appetite as a novelist for exotic locations. A diplomat's step-daughter in the post-war years, she enjoyed a peripatetic childhood, but finally settled in London during the swinging Sixties until, in 1963, she married novelist and conservationist Nicholas Luard, co-founder of *Private Eye*. When four children appeared in quick sucession, she followed her own lead and took them off to be educated in Spain and France. The story of their wanderings is told in her most recent book, *Family Life: Birth, Death and the Whole Damn Thing*, an autobiography-with-recipes, which was widely praised and included a moving account of the loss of a beloved daughter to AIDS.

Marguerite, the story of a child brought up in a Roman Catholic safe house in the uplands of Provence, is Elisabeth Luard's second novel. Her first, *Emerald*, the fictional story of the illegitimate daughter of the Duke and Duchess of Windsor, was chosen for the WHSmith Thumping Good Read award in 1995.

As a prize-winning food writer she is the author of a number of successful cookery books, including the modern classic, *The Rich Tradition of European Peasant Cookery*. She has a weekly column in The *Sunday Telegraph* and contributes regularly to *House & Garden* and *Country Living*.

Also by Elisabeth Luard

Non-fiction

EUROPEAN PEASANT COOKERY
THE PRINCESS AND THE PHEASANT
THE BARRICADED LARDER
EUROPEAN FESTIVAL FOOD
THE FLAVOURS OF ANDALUCIA
FAMILY LIFE

Fiction

EMERALD

Marguerite

Elisabeth Luard

CORGI BOOKS

MARGUERITE
A CORGI BOOK: 0 552 14320 0

First published in Great Britain

PRINTING HISTORY
Corgi edition published 1997

Set in 10pt Sabon by
Phoenix Typesetting, Ilkley, West Yorkshire.

Corgi Books are published by Transworld Publishers Ltd,
61–63 Uxbridge Road, London W5 5SA,
in Australia by Transworld Publishers (Australia) Pty Ltd,
15–25 Helles Avenue, Moorebank, NSW, 2170
and in New Zealand by Transworld Publishers (NZ) Ltd,
3 William Pickering Drive, Albany, Auckland.

Reproduced, printed and bound in Great Britain by
Cox & Wyman Ltd, Reading, Berks.

For my father,
Richard Maitland Longmore
1917–1943

Acknowledgements

My heartfelt thanks, as always, to my husband Nicholas for soothing the troubled brow in time of need. To my children, Caspar, Francesca, Poppy and Honey, for feeding in love and laughter. To Broo Doherty and Ursula Mackenzie at Transworld for advice and support. To Edward Leeson for giving the manuscript the necessary trim and shave. To my agent, Abner Stein, for care and attention beyond the call of duty.

Part One

1940–1945

Part One

I

The Hermitage

It is a secret place, the Hermitage of the Rock.

Its location is marked on no maps. Its function has never been known to more than a handful of outsiders.

High in the rugged hills of Upper Provence, no casual traveller would fall on it by accident. The citadel grows naturally from a rocky outcrop tip-tilted from the earth's centre by some prehistoric upheaval, the building-blocks so cunningly matched to the boulders that the edifice blends seamlessly into the russet-patterned cliff. The few visitors who follow the narrow road along the ridge which flanks the valley on the far side, linking the little village of Pernes-les-Rochers to the market-town of Valréas, might travel on without ever being aware of its existence.

So miraculous is its construction, so skilful the blending of man's work to God's, that the passer-by who is not of the Faith might think it simply a work of nature, one of many in these deserted canyons. All the country people thereabouts know of it, either because they hold their land on ecclesiastical tenure, or because their ancestors have been associated with the place in some way.

Thérèse Leblanc, a young woman just over thirty, with a strong, intelligent face and the bright dark eyes and straight, almost blue-black hair which characterizes the people of these parts, was well aware of its location and, to some extent, its function.

As she came within sight of the tall tower – all that was

visible of the Hermitage as she rounded the curve of the mountain – Thérèse set down her bundle, a hand-stitched sailcloth knapsack which contained all her worldly possessions. Her muscles ached. It was evening, and she had been on the road since dawn.

The footpath which gives access to the citadel meanders down the steep slope on the far side of the canyon and stops abruptly at the line of water-polished stepping-stones thrown casually across the river-bed. The river, an all-important resource in the bleak uplands and harnessed for irrigation at its source, swells to a torrent in winter, but now at the end of summer it is a fine thread of glittering spring water. On the far side a broad flight of steps hacked casually into the precipice rises to the ochre-coloured citadel.

The water and the walls were once indispensable to the inhabitants of the valley. In the old days, the Hermitage, as with all such establishments, provided a livelihood for the village which came into being to service it. In return, the Hermitage maintained the irrigation system designed to water the hand-hewn terracing. Nowadays, only the few remaining *paysans* have any use for the land, and the stone conduits which harness the waters have long since been left to their own devices.

The villagers have the right of sanctuary within the walls, although it has been many years since anyone has claimed the ancient privilege. Yet sanctuary was one of the practical considerations which, on this particular autumn day of 1940, brought Thérèse to the Hermitage. There were other reasons, less easily defined. As one of those blessed or cursed with that disturbing ability to see ghosts, both of the past and of the future, Thérèse knew that she had no choice. This was where her child was to be born.

The child would be a daughter, Thérèse knew, although she had not yet even been conceived.

Wise women, or witches, whether wise by divine

authority or taking their powers from the moon, are no strangers to the Hermitage. The cave and the wellspring which rises inside were once sacred to Aphrodite, goddess of love, whose likeness, complete with scallop shell, has been long since transferred to the museum of antiquities in Avignon, safely out of harm's way.

The early church fathers went to considerable trouble to eradicate any reminders of the old gods, replacing pagan myth with Christian legend. In this instance, legend has it that the cave served as a refuge for the Blessed Mary of Magdala, beloved of Jesus. The story goes that the Magdalene, with two other wise women, fled the Holy Land and miraculously crossed the Mediterranean to seek sanctuary here. The trouble was – and the Magdalene was never anything but trouble – that the legend also had it that she brought the bones of the Virgin Mary with her. A little embarrassing in the light of later years, when the church fathers declared it a tenet of faith that the mother of God was carried body and soul to heaven. The story persisted, as such stories always do among the flock, even though it was strenuously denied by the shepherd. One bag of bones is much like another.

The Magdalene has always been something of an embarrassment. Neither virgin nor wife, she belongs to that other category of women – the ones against whom he who is without sin may cast the first stone. Vows of celibacy are hard to keep; it is a matter on which even popes have not always been infallible.

Fallen women have never caused anything but trouble to the Church. Still more so when it is the priests themselves who are the cause of their fall. Fallen women were the reason the sanctuary was built. The initial purpose was to provide a safe house for the female dependants of the Knights of the Rock, a celibate order of Richard the Lionheart's crusaders based in Avignon. During the turbulent years of the first Crusades, the stone citadel acquired a watchtower and became a fortress manned by soldier-monks. Tolerance ruled in those days – men will be men, and soldier-monks more so than most.

This was all very well while Rome held the only key to St Peter's gate, but in the less tolerant climate of the Reformation the Vatican thought it wise to be a little more circumspect. The Hermitage became a place of incarceration for the Church's little embarrassments – pregnant nuns, the discarded mistresses of senior clerics, women who aspired to the priesthood.

In modern times, its use has broadened to provide sanctuary for those who, because of the power or influence they wield, qualify for Mother Church's protection. And protection against secular retribution, the paying of society's price for wrongdoing, was what was guaranteed. For as long as necessary – until storms had blown themselves out, or (as most often in the case of the female supplicants) the nine months had run their course. Rome has always been eminently practical in her choice of those who receive her charity.

Every parish priest knows of the existence of such sanctuaries – although only those higher up the ecclesiastical ladder are aware of their location. In the case of the Hermitage, the most ancient of these, application was made directly to the warden, a senior prelate based in London, who judged each case on its merits.

Whatever the sins committed, the price of admission is – and always has been – full confession made to the resident priest. Absolution is within the priest's remit. Evil is a matter for God. The confessions, transcribed into a ledger, are locked and stored on shelves in what was once the crusaders' refectory. Just a precaution naturally. No-one has to labour the point that the confessions serve both as a receipt for favours granted and as a proof of wrongdoing, guaranteeing the Holy See good friends in high places.

It was a cardinal-librarian to one of the Borgia popes who, charged with the disposing of a love child inconveniently delivered to the Supreme Pontiff's young mistress, first realized that here was a valuable thread which might be unravelled from the ledgers in the Hermitage.

With the utmost delicacy, the cardinal-librarian brought the information he had gleaned to the attention of His Holiness. While the official records of marriages and births told one truth, human frailty ensured that it was not by any means the only truth. Powerful men kept mistresses. Wives as well as husbands stray. The entanglements lead to the inevitable, particularly when both the erring partners obey the Catholic rule forbidding contraception. The true parentage of the resulting love-children does not appear in any document. None, that is, except the records so conveniently stored in the Hermitage.

His Holiness, always keen to extend his temporal power, took the point.

In time, the information extracted from the ledgers provided the great Catholic families of Europe with the only true record of blood-lineage – information impossible to obtain in any other way. Its authenticity unquestioned, it provided a fail-safe when dynastic alliances were contracted, ensuring that – as could easily happen in the circular marriage-go-round of such an enclosed world – half brother was not matched with half sister, or worse.

It could also, discreetly, be brought in as evidence in disputes over property and rights of inheritance – sometimes even, blood being thicker than water, preventing the outbreak of minor wars.

The information could also be used – perish the thought – to further the Holy See's private agenda.

Thérèse, who did not approve of popery, would not

have been surprised by any of this when, refreshed by her brief rest, she picked up her bundle, slung it over her broad countrywoman's shoulders, and set her face to the path which led across the stream.

At the moment of crossing, she was aware that she had officially left French soil. It had been so for five centuries – a consequence of the secession of the country of Venaissin to the papacy when the Holy See took temporary residence in Avignon. At the time, the Hermitage with its dependent village and valley became sovereign territory, the property of the Vatican – and so it has remained ever since.

The revolution in France, which led to the outlawing of priests and the destruction of the monasteries, caused a moment of concern. Then responsibility for the Hermitage was transferred to a warden in London, where it became customary to offer the warden's post to a distinguished member of the English-speaking Catholic clergy, chosen for his worldliness and his ability to move easily among the rich and powerful. That the Hermitage was run from Britain and not from Republican France was a convenient arrangement. The secular French state which was effectively its landlord had no desire to take responsibility for the place.

The warden's duties were not arduous. They were limited to checking and approving the credentials of those who asked for refuge in the sanctuary, an annual visit to Provence to check that all was running smoothly, and providing the relevant names and dates for the Vatican's genealogical files.

To maintain distance between those who take decisions and those who carry them out, the day-to-day running of the Hermitage was left in the hands of the resident, a glorified housekeeper, an ordained priest who could hear confession and give absolution, who could write in 'a fair English hand', and whose ambitions were unlikely to come into conflict with his position – that of trust rather than power.

Discretion was of the essence at the Hermitage. It was another reason why Thérèse Leblanc had chosen the place.

Father Patrick O'Donovan, the incumbent resident on that autumn day in 1940 when Thérèse walked up to his door, was, in spite of a somewhat Irish penchant for stretching the rules and bending the regulations, absolutely discreet.

Discretion had not come easily to Paddy O'Donovan. He had had to learn it the hard way – down the barrel of a gun.

2

Meeting Father Patrick

'Devil take ye, ye greedy little bastard!'

With an unpriestly curse, Father Patrick O'Donovan aimed a kick at the vanishing backside of a large black rat.

At the moment Thérèse Leblanc was making her way across the stream and up the rough steps which led to the heavy iron-studded oak door of the Hermitage, Father Patrick was contemplating the ravages wrought by a regiment of rodents on the debris of the previous evening's supper. Although, in all honesty, they were welcome to it. A hunk of mouldy cheese and a handful of sprouting potatoes scarcely justified the rendering of thanks to the Lord for His bounty.

The place was going to rack and ruin, no doubt of that.

For seven years now he'd been resident of the Hermitage, but it was not an appointment Paddy O'Donovan would have chosen for himself. It was too lonely for the Irishness in him. There was an elderly widow from the village who came to cook and clean for the visitors, but as the supply of these had almost dried up, and the widow's knees were giving her trouble with the climb, it had been many months since the place had seen a woman's hand.

It was time he found himself a housekeeper, a sturdy countrywoman who knew how to keep a place in order. It was only proper, even if the wages came out of his own stipend. The Hermitage had empty henhouses and

18

abandoned sties, and terraces which might easily be planted up with vegetables. He himself had plans to establish a good Irish potato patch, a lazy-bed, on the ridge above, and thought there might even be some peat to be cut.

On the day, that bright day in the autumn of 1940, that Thérèse walked into his life, Father Patrick was a year away from his fifty-fifth birthday and thirty years from the day he had taken his vows.

Born at Ballycannock in the county of Cork, in an Ireland which in 1885 was still suffering from the effects of the famine, he had the toughness and physical confidence of a countryman born and bred. He was still a handsome man, not tall but sturdy, after the breeding of the Celts, and much like that of the Provençaux themselves.

In his youth, Paddy O'Donovan had been a firebrand radical, constantly in trouble with his bishop for preaching militant sermons.

He was indeed, as his bishop suspected, actively involved in the struggle to free Ireland from the English colonizers, and proud to count the poet William Butler Yeats as his friend. He took part in the Easter Rising of 1916. His activities caused his superiors considerable embarrassment, and he was soon moved from his parish in the rougher end of Dublin to a rural living on the southerly island of Valencia, as far from the source of the Troubles as possible.

Even in the country parish, Patrick managed to get himself into trouble. In 1931, when the *taoiseach* declared the Irish Republican Army a banned organization and set up a tribunal to investigate 'treasonable activities', it was discovered that Father O'Donovan had allowed his church's crypt to be used for the storage of smuggled arms.

His bishop declared that enough was enough. The priest was intelligent – no doubt of that – which made him doubly dangerous. He would be sent to Italy, to the Vatican. He could occupy himself with clerking in the Curia, where they always needed literate priests to translate papal documents into good English.

Patrick had no choice. The truth of the matter was that the move had come as something of a relief. He was beginning to sicken of the violence in Ireland. He had seen too much of the sufferings of innocents, there had been too many killings over too many years, and he was no longer proud of his part in it.

Rome was not much to his taste. Too much pomp and circumstance makes a man soft. The work in the Vatican's offices was repetitive and concerned more with the shepherds, the maintenance of rank and the conferring of privilege than with the pastoral care of the flock. Had it not been for his friendship with one man, he might have lost his faith – if not in his God, at least with those who spoke for Him on earth.

His friend's name was Albino Luciani, a priest who, like Patrick himself, had been born in poverty. Luciani shared the Irishman's view that it was the business of the Church to involve itself in secular matters when those matters threatened the poor and those who could not fight for themselves.

The two men sat on either side of the same desk, each engaged in his own task. At midday they ate together in companionable silence in the staff refectory. But every evening, both billeted in the Augustinian residence beneath the Vatican's walls, they escaped into the maze of Rome's ancient streets, searching out the little trattorias which served honest food and country wine in convivial company. Here they talked far into the night, comparing their experiences: Luciani's in the little village in the north of Italy where he was born, and his first ministry among the poor of Naples; Paddy's fermenting revolution in the slums of Dublin.

Later, Father Albino was to become Patriarch of Venice, the pagan city which no bishop had ever been able to tame. In time, although then there was no hint of the possibility, he was called to fill the shoes of St Peter. His reign was the briefest and most turbulent of all, but it was to be by his hand that the Hermitage was changed for ever.

Patrick O'Donovan's time in the Holy See was never meant to be more than a temporary secondment, and when the post of resident at the Hermitage of the Rock in Upper Provence fell vacant Father Patrick qualified on two important counts: he could write in English 'in a fair round hand', and he was not an Englishman.

The lack of Englishness was an important qualification because the Vatican's efficient intelligence service anticipated war. In March 1933, Adolf Hitler declared the Third Reich, and the Vatican could see that the new political movement could be turned to its own advantage. Fascism, after all, was infinitely preferable to communism, and its aims were by no means incompatible with the Holy See's political views.

Closer to home, Pius IX had no difficulty in coming to terms with Il Duce's family values; Mussolini, declared the Holy Father, was a man upon whom the Almighty might be expected to look favourably.

If anyone was likely to rock the boat, the Vatican's intelligence warned, it would be the bloody-minded British.

The Vatican paid heed and quietly began to put its house in order. The Curia was nothing if not thorough. The appointment of an Irish national to the residency at the Hermitage was part of that thoroughness. Since the Irish Free State was no longer under the British colonial thumb, it was likely that with a little encouragement the staunchly Catholic Irish would remain neutral in any war.

France had been a battleground before. She would become a battleground again. As an Irishman, Paddy

O'Donovan would prove an excellent choice should the Hermitage once again revert to being a fortress.

Father Patrick packed his bags and made his way to the uplands of Provence. Once installed in the Hermitage he put the library in order, tidied up the ledgers and settled down. He learned the language of the country immediately so that he could attend to the spiritual needs of his flock. It was not hard since he already had the Latin, and his Italian was quite colloquial enough for Rome's taverns. He also had the Gaelic language from childhood, a tongue which had much in common with the ancient Provençal language.

Nevertheless, Patrick O'Donovan was lonely.

He might be in heaven or in hell, but he might just as well have been transplanted to the moon. The harsh uplands, with their baking summer heat and icy winters, their steep valleys clad in thorny scrub, lacked the gentle greenness of his native countryside. His faith wavered again, buffeted by the barren land and the loneliness. He was homesick not so much for the green pastures of Ireland as for the people. He longed for familiar voices, for that odd elliptical Celtic humour, that appetite for living, loving and laughter which is the birthright of every Irish man and woman – even though, as he knew well enough, it can slide into drink and black despair.

It was even something of a relief when, as the phoney war turned to reality, the armies of the Third Reich pushed south to the Mediterranean. France fell with astonishing speed. Britain had withdrawn to its island fortress to rearm and regroup. No-one knew what would happen next.

At the Hermitage, confirmation that the Vatican's diplomacy had paid dividends came when a polite young German staff officer followed the path to the rocky walls. On gaining admittance, he presented his Führer's compliments to the resident, cast a cursory eye over the

brothers who do not relish the company of our uninvited guests.'

She waited, looking for some sign from the priest. Receiving none – Paddy O'Donovan knew better than to give anything away – she added: 'Since I have ceded my rights of inheritance, I am homeless. Since I am homeless, I am ready to begin my duties immediately.'

Again the joyous smile. 'You will find me diligent, honest, hard-working, and as good a cook as you might wish. I can assure you, you will have no reason to regret your decision to employ me.'

'I suppose I have no say in the matter?'

Thérèse laughed. Her eyes danced. 'You are a man, for all that you are a priest. Men have no say in domestic affairs. Besides' – a mischievous note crept into her voice – 'doesn't the Bible advocate the conversion of the heathen? I may be fertile ground . . . *mon père.*'

For the first time, she had given him his clerical title.

The priest frowned. 'Conversion's a serious business, daughter.' He glanced up, and Thérèse saw that there was a twinkle in the blue eyes. 'However, I doubt not the Lord might grant His grace.'

Father Patrick hesitated for a final instant. There was one further question to be asked.

'Mademoiselle . . .' His voice was hesitant. 'If there is anything you would like to tell me? Anything at all which might lead to . . .' He fumbled for the word. 'Consequences?'

As a priest, he had to know.

Thérèse flashed her white teeth and shook her head.

'No, monsieur, there is nothing – unless it be that your fears are groundless. I am a virgin, and for the time being I intend to remain so.' The bright dark eyes shone with amusement. 'I will of course inform you if the situation alters.'

His face reddened as it had not since he was a boy and

27

had taken a few too many liberties with Kate Kinnahan, a bright-haired colleen, at the country fair.

'Of course,' he muttered. 'My apologies, mademoiselle.'

My, but she was a fine-looking colleen. Any young man would be proud to court her. He shook his head. It had been so long since he had had such thoughts.

After all these years, his vows of celibacy no longer troubled him. But sometimes, late at night, when the moon hung low and pale over the horizon, he wept for the women in his life: the sister he had lost, the mother he had left behind, the wife he might have won, the child he would never hold in his arms.

As yet Thérèse Leblanc was none of these things to Patrick O'Donovan. But, as time went on, in the secret depths of his soul she was to become all of them.

3

Wartime at the Hermitage

'I'm not a fool, Thérèse. Sure and it's time you told me what you're about.'

It was not long after Thérèse took up her post that Father Patrick noticed that his housekeeper was spending an unusual amount of time scrubbing out the cellars. He also observed that the freshly cleared and planted vegetable patch appeared destined to feed a small army. Not only this, but the egg-laying capacity of the twenty-two hens now pecking around in the yard far exceeded the modest requirements of the Hermitage's two residents. Finally there was the stocking of the pigsty. A pig was proper for any household, but Thérèse had installed no fewer than four little piglets in the sty, where she was fattening them up on mysteriously acquired grain.

All these things suggested that Thérèse had plans. She had already spoken of her brothers' sympathies, and he knew that the people of the high valleys who were of Cathar stock were reputed to be setting up a resistance movement. There was much to resist. Every day came new rumours of mass executions in the countryside, reports of atrocities in the towns. Fear fed on rumour. Rumour fed on fear. Young men had been taken for forced labour in the munitions factories of Germany, and there had been reports of gypsies and Jews being rounded up.

'Well?'

'I can't imagine what monsieur means. Are my activities

affecting the discharge of my duties? Is monsieur finding himself neglected?'

'You know very well, Thérèse' – Father Patrick patted his stomach ruefully – 'I have had to let my belt out at least two notches since your arrival. And, as for the house-keeping, the place shines like a new pin.'

'Then, I can assume monsieur is satisfied with my work?'

'You know well enough 'tis not what I'm asking.'

'Nevertheless it is my reply.' She hesitated for an instant. 'For the present, *mon père*.'

'For the present?'

'There may be . . . *developments*.'

Patrick looked at his housekeeper, his blue eyes level. 'I see. I take it that, as with that other matter, you will inform me of any change in the situation?'

'In all things, monsieur.' Thérèse's eyes were steady, her guardedness an acknowledgement of the boundaries which governed what he might or might not wish to know. Nevertheless, the more she knew of the priest's radical past, the more she knew that she was on safe ground. Because of this, Thérèse understood that she would not be able to leave the priest in ignorance for long. Her preparations were almost complete. There would soon come a time when he would have to know everything. Her mention of the anti-Nazi sympathies of her brothers was merely to plant the notion in his mind – to elicit any unfavourable reaction.

Since there was none, she had proceeded with her plans.

For herself as well as for her brothers, there had never been any question of where their loyalties lay. The Cathars, egalitarian nonconformists, did not easily accept authority from anyone – let alone from an occupying power. Five hundred years of religious guerilla warfare had honed their skills in opposition. There was much to oppose. Five centuries ago, the iron fist of the English

Simon de Montfort had smashed their citadels. But nevertheless the nonconformist English were the Cathars' natural allies, just as they had been of the Huguenots seeking refuge from the consequences of the Edict of Nantes.

Father Patrick's sympathies were confused.

It took the Irishman a little longer to accept that the old arch-enemy was now the last defender of freedom. The moment for his change of heart came when a family in the nearby village of Souligny received the attentions of the SS.

Souligny was not one of the Cathar strongholds. It was a village on the lower slopes of the hills, prosperously surrounded by ancient vineyards which had once produced fine wines for the Pope's table in Avignon. The wine was still good, even though it was four centuries since the popes had returned to Rome. The merchant vintners of Souligny continued to find a ready market for their goods; and, as with all tradesmen, it was not their business to question the politics of their customers. They were as happy to supply the officers of the occupying army as they had been to supply the burghers of Avignon, Lyons and Paris.

The particular family which received a visit from the men in the grey uniforms had done nothing more subversive than make a deal with a wholesaler for the sale of the year's vintage. The wholesaler had a rival, who accused the family of harbouring Jews. The accusation, delivered anonymously to the military authorities, was neither investigated nor accurate.

The male members of the family – grandfather, father and his two young sons – were lined up against the wall of the Hôtel de Ville and shot at point-blank range. The murders were committed quite casually, as if the matter was of no more moment than the price of a pound of grapes. Yellow stars were pinned to the bodies. For three days the corpses, the blood congealing on the ragged *bleus*

31

de travail which scarcely covered the torn flesh, were left slumped among the rubbish and rotting vegetables. It was intended as a warning to those who might have similar intentions, and as an encouragement to those who might feel inclined to inform on their neighbours for personal gain.

The villagers locked their doors, hammered down their shutters, and waited, paralysed with fear. By the end of the three days, most of the flesh had been torn from the victims' bones by scavenging dogs. On the fourth day the soldiers returned, poured petrol on the bodies and set them alight.

The black stench of roasting flesh curled round the shuttered streets. The women of the family – mother, grandmother and two young daughters – came out into the market square to protest at this final indignity. For answer they were raped repeatedly and publicly against the same bloodstained wall.

Still the villagers cowered behind their shutters.

After a week the bolder of the frightened populace unbolted their doors and sent for the priest to bury the dead – or what was left of them after the rats and blue-bottles had had their share.

Father Patrick was the priest they sent for, their own being fearful of the consequences of administering a sacrament which might be taken as giving the lie to the executioners. Paddy O'Donovan's anger at the massacre was matched by his rage at the timorousness of his colleague in the priesthood.

After that he had no choice.

'Thérèse. You will know that until now I have turned a blind eye to' – he hesitated – 'certain activities in which I know well enough you and some of my parishioners have been engaged. I would like you to know that in the future I shall render you and your friends whatever assistance is needed.'

Thérèse looked at him speculatively. 'You know what you're saying, *mon père*? What you may be required to do?'

The reminder of his priestly calling was unmistakable.

Patrick O'Donovan stared at her for a moment. Then he grinned broadly.

'I have some experience in that line. There was something of the kind in Dublin around 1914. Though I say it as maybe shouldn't, I doubt ye could find a man in the green island to say I was found wanting.'

Thérèse's gaze met his own, level and direct as always, but with something else there, something which he had last seen in the eyes of Kate Kinnahan, his childhood sweetheart.

After a moment Thérèse lowered her gaze, a faint smile on her lips.

'Welcome to the organization, Father O'Donovan. We'll be glad of your help.'

The Hermitage proved ideally suited to its new purpose.

The heart of the building was a warren of interlinking cells and rock-hewn corridors designed by the crusader knights for ease of access – or, when necessary, escape. The hidden exits and entrances were camouflaged on the outside among the narrow caves which honeycombed the limestone precipices of the valley.

Within the Hermitage, the access-tunnels had been walled up since the time of the Revolution. It had been a time of great difficulty for the monastic communities, whose buildings were confiscated and brotherhoods disbanded. The Hermitage's isolation and secrecy, as much as the ancient papers which made it sovereign territory, saved it from physical destruction. But its activities had been suspended for fifty years, and afterwards the tunnels remained closed.

Once the walled-up corridors were unblocked, the

Hermitage was the safest house in France. The Resistance took over the wine cellars to store their weapons and explosives, converting the old ice cellar – when not filled with snow, the warmest place in the subterranean labyrinth – into a hospital ward. Here Thérèse used her knowledge of herbs to supplement the lack of conventional medicine.

Paddy O'Donovan found that he had lost none of his old skills. Now he added several new ones. His parishioners would no doubt have been astonished to find their father confessor turning his hand to the packing of explosives for home-made bullets and the conversion of alarm clocks into detonators.

God's house indeed had many mansions. What mattered for the moment was to get the gelignite load weighed accurately, and the fuse-length right.

The Allied forces landed in Marseilles on 16 August 1944. The landing forced Thérèse to look to the future.

It took three weeks for liberty, in the uncertain shape of a ragged detachment of British Tommies, to reach the valley. The final days had been hard at the Hermitage. As the Führer's garrisons prepared to withdraw, the Nazis panicked, destroying evidence, settling old scores, looting and killing as they pulled back to their own borders. There was a new influx of wounded to tend. Thérèse and Father Patrick had scarcely a moment to draw breath.

Thérèse was the first to confirm that the war was finally over. In a brief lull she had made her way up the steps of the tower for a little air. From the tower's vantage point she noticed a small squad of soldiers toiling up the valley. For an instant her heart leaped into her throat, fearing that the retreating German soldiers had finally decided to raid the safe house.

Then she recognized the uniforms and ran to swing the heavy ropes which set off the bell.

Father Patrick, for the first time since the start of the war, immediately dressed the altar in all its finery of scarlet and gold, and set the Lord's table for a Mass of Thanksgiving.

Throughout the years of occupation, the Hermitage had served not only as headquarters and hospital for the Resistance, but also as a staging post for escaped prisoners of war who were given sanctuary in the cave which had once been Aphrodite's lair. There were some who were guided to safety across the Pyrenees, and others who, through betrayal or chance, came to grief.

It was one of the fortunate of these escapees, Tom – for safety's sake, Christian names were all that anyone ever used – a young lieutenant of the élite Coldstream Guards, who led the liberation party. Tom made his way straight through the village with its flag-waving children and cheering adults, and took the narrow footpath which led alongside the water-conduits up to the Hermitage.

'Thérèse!'

Thérèse, busy in the hospital cells, suddenly found herself enfolded in strong arms.

'Remember?' The young soldier stood back, waiting for her smile of recognition. 'It's me – Tom!'

She had not at first recognized him. There had been so many who had passed through the Hermitage, so many who had sworn undying gratitude – some who had even sworn love.

But the face was so flushed with delight, the blue eyes so sparkling, so eager for her recognition, that Thérèse could only laugh and nod.

'Of course, Tom. Of course I remember you!'

'Really? You do? Everything?' To Thérèse's surprise, Tom's face had gone scarlet with embarrassment.

He searched in his pocket and held up a scrap of metal, a flattened bullet. Then Thérèse did remember.

Tom had been wounded in the thigh. The bullet had

35

passed cleanly through the flesh to lodge just below the left testicle. Thérèse had dressed the wound with home-distilled white brandy – conveniently the monks of the Hermitage had been enthusiastic distillers – and poured a generous measure down her patient's throat. Then she had made a neat incision and removed the bullet head-first.

'An inch to the left, *mon brave*, and you'd have lost *les bijoux de famille*, the family jewels.' She had held up the lump of fused metal. 'Here. Keep it.'

Afterwards, each time she dressed the wound, the young man had, then as now, been embarrassed by his body's all too evident reaction. She knew he was watching her now, remembering.

'You did a wonderful job,' said the young man.

'Are you so sure?' Thérèse's eyes sparkled mischievously. 'I might have to find out for myself.'

'Yes.'

She looked at him more shrewdly now. The strong affirmative was undeniably an answer to her unspoken invitation.

It was the young man's innocent blue eyes, so trusting – so like Father Patrick's must have been in youth – which had moved Thérèse to choose him. And it was indeed a choice. Thérèse could have taken her pick from any of the young men that wild night of the Liberation.

She was still a little doubtful, anxious that he might swear undying love for her. But then he showed her the crumpled photograph – and the agreement, though silent, was made as clearly as if it had been written and witnessed.

The photograph was of Tom's girl. Her slender figure was tightly belted into the unbecoming uniform of a land-girl, but she was standing in front of the grandest house Thérèse had ever seen. Her hair was as fair as Thérèse's was dark, and she was smiling straight into the camera, her hand extended to display a ring.

'She's lovely,' said Thérèse.

36

'Her name's Rosie,' said Tom proudly. 'We got engaged on the day I left for the war. We are to be married just as soon as I get home.'

This avowal had not come between them; it was merely a declaration of a prior commitment – a prior commitment which suited Thérèse's purposes perfectly.

Thérèse examined the dog-eared photograph more closely.

'It's a fine house – a château. Your people must be very wealthy.'

'I suppose so. The house has been in the family since the Domesday Book. I've always lived there, so to me it's just home. Some day it'll be mine – and Rosie's, of course, as long as she hasn't forgotten me.'

'I doubt that – if she has any sense.' Thérèse smiled up at him and tucked the photograph back into his pocket. 'She's safe enough in there, close to your heart.'

She turned her dark eyes on him, lifting her hand to the neck of her blouse, toying with the buttons. She took his hand and guided it until his palm cupped the curve of her breast. Pressing herself against him, she was in no doubt of the response.

She laughed, and lifted her lips to his, exploring his mouth, her arms round his body, feeling the ropes of muscle through the thick stuff of the uniform, the rising and hardening of him.

Her eyes danced as she pulled away.

'A complete recovery, I hope. But we have not yet put it to the test.'

He pulled her towards him, held her again until she broke free.

She whispered: 'Not now, soldier-boy. I'll come for you.'

Thérèse Leblanc was not a sentimental woman. She had seen too much sorrow and pain, the dark corridors which

37

led from life to death, to have room for such a useless emotion. Compassion she had in plenty, but not sentimentality.

Sentimentality did not produce babies. Nor, indeed, did love.

She, too, had found love – but not for the young soldier. The love of her life was Patrick O'Donovan. Her own father had been killed in the trenches of the Somme. She had never known a father's love, so it wasn't surprising that she should choose to love a priest. She had known it as soon as she had looked into those blue eyes, shared the first laughter, felt the need he had of her – emotional as well as practical.

Patrick had known his own feelings, and he feared them. He had not felt such feelings since he held his childhood sweetheart in his arms. Kate Kinnahan had been all he had ever wanted, more even than his priesthood. He knew that now, now that it was too late.

And now this woman, so many years too late. The fire of her was Kate's, and she had Kate's gentleness. Above all, it was her bravery which made him love her. Her staunchness over the years of that terrible war, the war fought in darkness against the forces of darkness, when discovery meant death. The sharing of fear in the underground cavern where the casualties were brought, the harshness of the moment when deliverance from pain was all that could be hoped for from battered bodies. All these things bound them to each other with hoops of steel.

Now it was over. Their nearness, their shared experience would once more become a distance; he would no longer be a man but a priest.

Naturally enough, choice, the rational exercise of free will, had nothing at all to do with the matter for either of them. In reality, as with all such things, she and he had no choice, no choice at all. She knew, they both knew – from the quickening of the blood, the secret joy brought to each by the presence of the other – the nature of their feelings. Nature will not be fooled.

Patrick O'Donovan knew it in his heart, but his head would not let him admit it. He was old now, too old for such feelings. Yet, whatever his head dictated, his obedience to his faith demanded, his duty as a priest required, his heart felt for Thérèse the love a man feels for a woman.

It was not the greatest of sins. Yet to Father Patrick, flawed and human as any man, this was forbidden territory. Paddy O'Donovan knew too well the price to be paid. Forty years ago, in Ballycannock in the house where he was born, he had not been the one who paid. For Paddy that would have been the easy thing, but he had had no choice, and nor had she. This was the thing which had formed him, which had led him to the priesthood, which he could never chase from his dreams.

But Thérèse, misreading the signs, despaired of the love of a priest. So she held her peace and laid her plans.

The victory celebrations went on through the night.

'Come, soldier-boy. We have work to do.'

Thérèse's voice was soft in the young man's ear, her breath warm on his cheek.

In that black darkness which comes before dawn she took his hand, feeling the urgency which matched her own. She led him through the olive groves and into the meadow where the grass provided a soft bed. They made love and slept, and made love again and slept, and woke at last when the sun was high in the sky, and were glad to find each in the other's arms. They awoke in joy, with the scent of the bitter fruit in their nostrils and the bright wings of summer butterflies overhead.

'So sweet, such sweetness,' he whispered.

'My soldier-boy,' she said.

She watched him walk naked among the ancient olive

trees, so young he was, his body so pale among the silvery trunks with the shadows of the leaves dappling his skin.

She lay there, all shimmering in the sunshine, with the pollen gilding her skin. She stretched out her hand towards him, pulled him to her, caressed him once more.

'Show me again,' she said.

That third time, with the sun warm on their bodies, she could feel her body opening to him, closing round him, drawing in his seed, small seed, precious seed. She was a fisherman trawling the seas, the sea-scent in her nostrils, her net cobweb-fine, pearl-smooth. She caught his seed and swallowed it inside her womb. She felt greedy, guilty, like a thief.

They dressed, laughed, kissed and parted.

In the time to come, in the darkness of the night, Thérèse treasured the memory of that carefree coupling. There was so much laughter in the lovemaking, so much joy, there was no possibility it could be wrong. It was inevitable, complete and perfect. Neither he nor she could have any regrets.

By sundown the soldiers had gone. There was a rogue detachment of German troops giving trouble in the hills – the news of surrender had not reached them.

She did not know it then or ever, but the young soldier never returned from the war – his only legacy the child he had given her.

And one other thing. 'Keep this to remember me by.'

He tugged at a ring on his little finger, a fat ring with a crest, the kind of thing noblemen once used to seal letters. 'You must take it. For my sake. I can offer nothing else.'

'I know that well enough,' she said. But she was glad that he wanted her to remember him. She took the ring and slipped it on to the chain she wore round her neck and tucked it next to her own heart.

'Be happy,' was all she said as he left her.

Afterwards, Thérèse was not the only unmarried

woman in those valleys to find herself with child. 'Liberation babies', they were called – and the villages were glad of them when so many of their young men had been taken.

And Patrick O'Donovan – would he welcome the child?

How could he not, when she had done it for him as much as for herself?

4

The Spoils of War

When she was absolutely certain that she was with child, Thérèse chose her moment to break the news to Father Patrick.

No doubt he would feel it his duty to scold her, but she was certain that deep inside himself he would be joyful. It would be her gift to him, a gift for the vocation which forbade him a wife and children. There would be no blame. Many children had been conceived in the frenzy of freedom. No-one would know or care who the fathers were. For many of the women who had lost their men, any child was better than none at all. The children at least were innocent of who or where or why. A new generation of young men would grow up to replace those lost in battle.

Thérèse chose a Saturday evening to speak to Father Patrick. Saturdays were quiet now that the secret affairs of the Resistance no longer had to be dealt with. On Saturday, Thérèse busied herself with her mending, and the priest looked over his sermon for the following day. More often than not, the pair of them would get to arguing over theological matters, and the debate would go on far into the night.

This particular evening they had taken their meal in the cool of the courtyard in the shade of a mulberry tree which had once provided the Hermitage's silkworms with sustenance. The air was heavy with the scent of summer flowers: jasmine, roses and blossoming thyme.

The priest was sitting at the table sipping a glass of lime-blossom tea. He glanced at Thérèse and smiled contentedly.

He had many reasons for contentment, most of these due to the young woman who had come into his life as his housekeeper, but was now, he told himself, the dearest friend he had ever had. Friendship had become his way of telling his heart to keep its emotions within bounds – and, after a fashion, it had worked.

Thérèse was a wonderful cook, and even under the restrictions of wartime Patrick's wiry Irish frame had filled out remarkably. Today he had not been able to resist a second helping of *pot-au-feu*. Thérèse had made an especially good one: the soup rich and fortifying, made with an old hen past her laying, onions and carrots just pulled from the garden, flavours of sarriette and juniper. Thérèse had simmered them all in a fine strong broth made with an ox-foot begged from the Valréas butcher.

For the first time since Liberation, market-day had been festive. Everyone had dusted off their prettiest hat, and even the babies in their pushchairs sported the tricolour ribbon in their topknots. Babies were coming to mean happiness to Thérèse.

Now, bursting with her news, Thérèse set a dish of lemon tarts by the priest's elbow, with two plates and two little forks.

Father Patrick glanced up, sighed, and patted his midriff. 'You spoil me, Thérèse.'

Thérèse laughed. She took a lemon tart for herself, set it carefully on its plate, and sat down. She bit into the crumbly pastry and then put down the fork absent-mindedly, composing in her mind what she needed to say.

The priest watched her.

'What is it, Thérèse?'

'Monsieur, I told you I would inform you if my situation

changed. I keep my promise. I am happy to tell you I am with child.'

Thérèse waited.

Slowly the priest removed his reading-glasses and set them on the table with a little click. His silence should have screamed a warning. Thérèse noticed nothing, waiting patiently for the scolding which must surely come. And then the happiness which would surely follow.

After a moment he said: 'You are telling me you were forced against your will?'

Thérèse shook her head vigorously.

'No.'

'How? Who? What? Where?'

His voice echoed, hollow and irrelevant.

Thérèse was too wrapped up in her joy to notice. She had told him. She felt nothing but happiness – and Patrick, her Patrick, was asking the most absurd questions. He needed reassurance – time to get used to the notion. She decided to treat her news as lightly as possible.

'As for the how, I don't think I need to explain the mechanics to you, *monsieur le curé*. As for the who and what and where, rest assured there was no question but that the young man, the father, was happy to be of service and has no intention of laying claim to the child.'

Patrick stared at her, his mind in turmoil.

'You are telling me you did this deliberately?'

'I was never more deliberate in my life.'

'And you – you thought this news would *please* me?'

For the first time, Thérèse hesitated.

'I thought . . .' Her voice was uncertain. 'I thought you might get used to it. Might even consider it a chance of happiness . . .'

'A chance of *happiness*?'

The outrage in his voice surprised even Father Patrick.

Thérèse was bewildered now. She would have to explain. He must listen. Nothing was so terrible after all.

44

'But, Father, it is a child. Conceived out of wedlock, to be sure, but a child, none the less. A child to share this place, for me, for us both. A gift—'

'A gift? *Whose* gift?'

A dark cloud of fury descended on him, engulfing and chasing out all rational thought. He recognized the emotion. He had felt it once before, on that fearful night when his sister Sinead had told him what his father had done to her. Then it had been his father he had struck. This time there was no such outlet, and no such reason for righteous anger.

Hard on the rage came something else. This time it was unfamiliar. Patrick O'Donovan had never before felt jealousy – the jealousy a man feels when he knows his woman has betrayed him. But Thérèse, *his* Thérèse, was telling him she had wilfully chosen another. That she had conceived a child – *his* child – with a stranger.

He had never thought he might feel these things. He had no defence against this terrible madness, this whirlpool of love and fear which sucked him into its depths, obscuring all sensible thought – everything except what he suddenly felt as a man.

He was on his feet, his face wild, peering into the corners of the courtyard. Surely he must be still there, the intruder, the stranger. Then he let out a great cry of pain and anguish. He picked up the heavy wooden table and heaved it on to its side. The lemon tarts rolled across the flag stones, splattering golden juices. Plates and kitchen utensils clattered to the floor, shattering as they landed.

He swung round to face her, his fist clenched.

'What have you done to me, woman?'

Thérèse gazed at the priest. She felt no fear for herself. She had expected reproaches and then, as good sense prevailed, acceptance. After all, his religion was quite clear on the matter: children were a blessing, in or out of wedlock. She had thought he would be content. She had expected any reaction but this unreasoning anger.

'Patrick, I did it for us – a child for us.'

'For the love of Almighty God, woman!'

Thérèse backed into the doorway which led to the kitchen. There she turned and held her ground, feet planted firm, hands on hips. Her dark eyes blazed. She, too, was angry.

'Do I take it that you wish me to pack my possessions and leave?'

The priest shook his head wildly, unclenched one fist and pushed his fingers into his thick shock of grey hair.

For an instant, as his hand came up, Thérèse thought he was going to hit her.

It was her gesture in response – stretching her open palms defensively towards him – which brought the priest sharply back to his senses.

'My God! My God!' He slumped back into the chair, his face white, his body trembling, his eyes tight shut. 'Thérèse, Thérèse, how could you do this to me?'

Silence filled the room. With the silence at last came understanding.

When Thérèse spoke her voice was gentle. 'Patrick. You must understand. I did it for you, for us. I did it because I love you.'

The priest opened his eyes.

'Because you love me?'

He shook his head. Not that. Not the one thing that he had expected never to hear again. The forbidden thing which no priest could ever hope to hear.

'Of course.' She was certain now. She came towards him. Her fingers stroked his cheek. 'It was because I wanted this for you, for us both.'

'It is a mortal sin . . .' His voice was a whisper.

'A mortal sin for you, not for me.'

He caught her hand and pressed his lips to her palm. 'To

think I might have raised my fist to you. You, of all people . . .'

She cupped his face in her rough and work-worn hands. 'Tell me,' she said.

It was Thérèse – wise woman or witch – who coaxed it from him, the events of the terrible night which led him to the Dublin seminary where he had taken his vows.

In the dawn of that night of all nights of his life, Patrick told the story to the first living soul who had ever heard it. It had been buried in the depths of his soul for so long that his heart might once again be broken with the telling. Yet in the telling he found peace.

'Patrick Michael O'Donovan, where the de'il are ye hid?'

On that particular Saturday night his father had been drunk, as always; and, as always, he was looking for his eldest son to pull off his boots.

Crouched in his usual hiding place in the hayloft, the boy shuddered – from fear less for himself than for his younger sister Sinead, shivering beside him in the hay.

'Paddy, I'm scared.'

Patrick squeezed his sister's hand. The noise of the man when the drink was on him would have woken the dead, had they not been tucked up safely in their cold beds in the churchyard on the other side of the wall.

The drink was a terrible thing. In 1910 the cluster of terraced houses which ringed Ballycannock Bay boasted four drinking dens. Being no more than a front room with a few wooden chairs and a rickety table to serve as a bar, none of them could be dignified with the name of public house.

Ballycannock was a whaling station which had fallen on hard times in the wake of the Great Famine. Depopulation rather than outright starvation was the reason. Lacking the four grown men needed for each boat to put to sea, the wooden fishing smacks in which the whalers once braved the Atlantic had been drawn up on the shingle until the winds and tides turned them to skeletons. The backbones of whales, huge bleached lumps of calcified bone, littered the shore.

These days the village lived as best it could. The rent was hard to come by, and Paddy had not had an easy childhood – although there was no child in the village who could claim otherwise. But at fifteen, and the eldest of the O'Donovan children, Patrick Michael had had it harder than most.

The O'Donovans' cottage was set well away from the village, shunned by the villagers because it stood beside the old plague burial pit and was held to be haunted. Father Sam Murphy, the parish priest, lived next door, handy for the church. He was a good man and a vigorous preacher, for all that he liked a drop of sloe brandy in the cold weather after a Saturday's fox-hunting – but not so much that it would interfere with his delivery from the pulpit on the Lord's day. He was also something of a militant on the matter of Home Rule.

'Fight the good fight,' he would admonish his congregation at the end of each sermon, and everyone knew which fight he meant.

He was good with the children, having the gift of patience and a gusto for country pursuits. There was many a child who, later in life, acknowledged that it was to Father Sam he owed his skill in poaching.

Young Paddy O'Donovan was a favourite of Father Sam. The boy was quick and sharp; and the priest, mindful of his duty to the Lord to nurture fresh talent, thought he might go far – provided that his lout of a father let his eldest son follow the path the Lord had mapped out for him. Father Sam intended Paddy should be free of the bounds of his upbringing, and bury his nose in the books in the university city of Dublin.

Paddy wasn't so sure. It was not the vocation to serve

the Lord he doubted, but the vow of celibacy which troubled him. For a year now, since his fourteenth birthday, he had been courting young Catlin Kinnahan from the next parish. Kate was pretty enough to win the heart of any man, with her slender figure and full breasts. She had the red hair, deep and full of golden lights, and the green eyes and fierce temper of the Irish colleen. But she could be gentle when she had a mind to it, and she played the harp like an angel, singing the old songs of love in the melodious Gaelic which lends itself so naturally to such tales.

Above all, Paddy liked the womanliness of her, the scent of her hair, the curve of her cheek, the sweet passion in her lips. When the time came, his mother said with a laugh, it was surely set to be a fierce battle between Kate and the Lord for Patrick's soul – and, if his mother had any say in the matter, Kate was set to win.

There was not much of an example for marriage to be found at home. Paddy's father was a wastrel, and every Saturday he drank such of the family income as he chose, returning home well after midnight, shouting for his eldest son to pull off his boots.

It was on just such a night that Paddy left home for good.

'God's bones! Is it myself must fetch ye out?'

Paddy squeezed his sister's thin shoulder reassuringly. What he had just heard from her own lips had made his blood boil. The worst Paddy might expect at his father's hands was the strap or a fist; but he had learned a few moments earlier that Sinead, his junior by two years but womanly for her age, could expect far worse attentions.

'He does *what*?'

'He puts his thing in me,' the young girl repeated, her voice a terrified whisper. 'You know. Like he does to Mother – except that she won't let him when he's with the drink. Then he comes to lie with me. It is most terribly that it hurts me, and his face goes all purple and I can't breathe because of the weight of him.'

Sinead's eyes were huge and glistening. 'Don't be angry with me, Paddy.'

'Why should I be angry, my bird?' The boy forced his voice to be gentle, but he could feel the anger rising – a blind anger which threatened to overwhelm him. '*How many times?*' Sinead shook her head miserably. 'What does it matter, Paddy? I'm in a state of mortal sin.'

Paddy stared at her, knowing his clamped fingers were hurting her to the bone.

'No you're *not*, Sinead. It's not your fault!' He was almost shouting. 'God knows that. And so will Father Sam. He'll know what to do. We must go to him at once.'

Sinead shook her head. 'Paddy, I'm scared. I haven't had the bleed for a month. Does that mean I'll have a baby?'

Paddy was silent. Silent and angry. The man now bellowing in the yard was his father, and he hated him with all his heart.

'Is there no mercy in your black soul, Paddy boy?' The voice, slurred with sentimentality, rose. 'Come out of there and lend me a hand, y'hear?'

Paddy could hear his own heart beating so loud in his chest it sounded like the drumbeat of the dreaded Black and Tans. Even the British mercenaries would have been welcome if they could have stopped the noise of his father's voice.

'Hell's bones!' This punctuated by an explosive belch. 'I'll have the hide o' ye yet!'

The two children burrowed deeper into the pile of hay. The boots clumped over from the cottage on the other side of the yard. The hinges of the heavy door creaked.

'Sinead! Ye'll not be denying your old da' his comfort . . .'

Comfort! Paddy clenched his fists. At this moment Sinead let out a frightened sob.

The footsteps stopped, and then resumed in the direction of the loft.

'So that's where the pair o' ye are. Rats in the haybarn.' The voice was coming closer. Paddy held his breath as the first rungs of the ladder shook.

'Beelzebub take it!'

The crash of timber told the two shivering children that the rickety ladder had jumped off its hooks.

'God's bones!'

The ladder banged back into place. The boots recommenced their ascent.

Paddy took his decision. He let go of his sister's hand, pushed her back into the hay until she had disappeared, and stood up.

'Looking for me, Father?'

'So there ye are! Both o' ye!'

Paddy stared down at the red face beneath him. The rising stench of the poteen almost made him giddy. So this was how he came to her, to his own daughter, stinking with the drink.

'Bastard,' he said quietly.

'*Bastard*, is it? How many Hail Marys would ye have to pay for that?'

The father lunged upwards, grabbing his son's ragged shirt and pulling him downwards. The weight of the two bodies was too much for the woodwormed ladder. It crashed downwards into the churning mud of the yard, carrying its double burden with it.

Paddy was the first to his feet, in his hand a broken strut. He stepped back, the weapon clasped in his fist.

'I'm telling ye, Da'. . . .'

'*Telling*, is it?'

The last thing he saw was the red face whiten. It was the first time he had ever hit his father – indeed, that he had hit any man in anger – and it was to be the last.

Father Sam dipped into parish funds. Paddy entered the

seminary, and Sinead was given over to the care of the Poor Clares, who ran a hostel for girls such as her who found themselves in trouble. Sinead's small body was too young, too unformed for the birth of a child. The baby, a tiny girl Patrick could cradle in the palm of his hand, was stillborn three months before its time. The mother survived the birth by no more than a few hours.

When Paddy buried the two of them his heart hardened. There was no outlet for his anger except to channel it into the fight against the English colonizers.

Paddy never returned to Ballycannock. He never spoke to any man or woman of what had happened. Until now. Now he spoke. And in the telling of it found the love he had never thought to find.

'Do you understand, Thérèse?'

'Hush, don't speak.'

She traced his lips with her fingertips, laid her lips on his.

'Patrick,' she murmured. 'My beautiful love.'

She touched his closed eyelids with her mouth, tasting the salt tears on the lashes.

In her soft French, she said: 'Now. Just this one night. This one night for a lifetime. Is that so much to ask of your God?'

His voice came back to her, gentle and sure.

'One night, Thérèse. One night for a lifetime.'

The baby was born in the month of May, when the first fruit was forming on the olive trees and the bees were already gathering nectar in the flowering sagebrush.

The child was a daughter, perfect as spring blossom. After the child was washed and wrapped and laid in the cradle, and the mother slept at last, Father Patrick walked alone in the morning dew.

Among the twisted trunks of the olive trees on the mountainside he gathered meadow daisies, choosing the ones with the snowiest petals and hearts as bright as sunshine. He tied the flowers with a twist of grass, and laid the posy, neat as a wedding bouquet, on the pillow where mother and baby slept.

Thérèse smiled when she found it, an earnest of love, a secret shared. She kept the posy as a talisman. Her daughter would be called for the daisies. She would be Marguerite Dieudonnée – gift of God.

Father Patrick wrapped the child in a shawl and took her to the font himself, his heart filled with love.

'Marguerite Dieudonnée, ego te baptiso. Mary, mother of God, bless this child of my heart.'

It was done. The child was safe. As for himself, the priest knew he was not in a state of grace – at least, as far as his church was concerned.

In the fair round hand required for the ledgers, he made confession of his sin, that weakness of the flesh, to his companion from his days in the Vatican. Albino Luciani was now a force to be reckoned with in the Vatican's labyrinthine corridors.

Receiving the letter, Luciani prayed for all three – the mother, the child, his friend. Ego te absolvo – as long as the repentance is real. All sinners come to judgement in the end, and true repentance is a matter between a man and his Maker. Whatever the catechism demands, the Lord's mercy is beyond reproach.

The result was that a candle was lit for Marguerite Dieudonnée Leblanc in St Peter's church by the man who was in time to occupy St Peter's throne. Suffer the little children to come to unto Me, for of such is the kingdom of heaven. Better still for her earthly welfare, the child's name was written on the papal heart.

Part Two

1955-1962

5

The Ledger

'Are you ready, Marguerite?'

'Oui, mon père.'

Marguerite Dieudonnée Leblanc, her chestnut mop of hair gleaming in the shaft of sunlight from the arrow-slit window, settled herself on the tall stool which had been set ready for her in the writing cubicle. Her green eyes, so unusual among the dark-eyed children of the village, were bright with excitement.

Even if today had not been her tenth birthday, it would still have been the most important day of her life. Today was the day when for the very first time she was to be allowed to help Father Patrick with his work. He could no longer see clearly enough to make the entries in the ledgers himself.

The ledgers were books bound in scarlet leather embossed with a gold crest, in which the stories of the visitors who came to the Hermitage were recorded. Father Patrick called these stories 'confessions', and they had to be written down, as sometimes happened in school when someone did something wrong and they were given lines to copy out. Pierre the butcher's son was always having to write out a hundred times, 'I must not blow my nose on my fingers.' Although Father Patrick said it wasn't quite the same, because the confession was a kind of payment for being allowed to stay at the Hermitage. Afterwards the confessions were locked away and kept, just like money.

He said that people were usually unhappy and in trouble when they made their confession, but this made them feel much better, and she was not to worry about it.

It all sounded very exciting and rather mysterious.

There was a little brass key, very old and worn with use, which was used to lock up all the ledgers and which was kept in a drawer in Father Patrick's desk. Once a ledger was complete, it was set alongside the others in the room which had once been the crusaders' refectory but was now where Father Patrick heard confessions.

Specific rooms in the Hermitage were set aside for the visitors' use, and they stayed for as long as they needed to, with her mother to cook and clean for them. Sometimes babies were born, and that could mean a long stay and a great many comings and goings. Sometimes they only stayed for a short time, a week or two, but mostly they didn't have anything to do with Marguerite, because they lived in a separate cloister of the Hermitage.

The writing-room was in the main part of the building. Lit by a single arrow-slit open to the four winds, it was a shadowy little cubicle which led off Father Patrick's larger room. From her perch on the stool which made it easy for her to reach the writing-shelf, Marguerite was screened by a heavy curtain, but she could hear Father Patrick next door, busy with his rosary, making ready for Miss Belinda Fitzherbert, the visitor who was coming to make confession.

She tucked her bare toes under the parallel strut of the stool. She didn't wear shoes except when she went to Mass, which she sometimes did to please Father Patrick, even if her mother didn't approve of her going at all.

Father Patrick had told Marguerite to be sure to get into her place well before it was time for the confession to begin, so no-one would guess that she was there. It was very important. No-one must know how blind he had become.

'So, mavourneen, are your hands clean?'

Marguerite wiped her hands quickly on her shirt-tail and tucked it back into her shorts – an old pair cut down from the dungarees she had worn through the winter.

Fortunately there was plenty of tail on the shirt, as it was one of Father Patrick's old ones which her mother had darned and patched for her. As today was the second week of the Easter holidays, she didn't need to cover her clothes with the *tablier*, the front-and-back pinafore which all French schoolgirls wear as their uniform. Marguerite did not like uniforms any more than she liked wearing shoes.

'Oui, mon père,' Marguerite called back cheerfully.

Her mother didn't call him 'mon père' because Thérèse Leblanc was a Cathar, and the Cathars didn't believe that priests were fathers. Her mother called him 'Patrice' or 'Paddy' in private and 'monsieur' in public, which was only good manners because he paid her wages. But Marguerite called him 'mon père' because, in every way which mattered to her, that was what he was.

'Let me see.'

The curtain was pushed aside.

Father Patrick had to put on his spectacles to inspect her palms – and even then she did not think he saw them clearly. Indoors you would not have guessed how blind he was, although when he went walking on the hills without Marguerite skipping in front he took his olive-wood stick so he could push it into crevices which might make him stumble.

Father Patrick was probably the kindest person in the world, even if he did get a little muddled sometimes and forget to tell her mother when new visitors were due at the Hermitage. He called Marguerite *petite chouette*, 'little owl', which she liked because she herself had a pet owl, Abelard, which she had reared from a chick after he fell from his nest in a hollow tree.

In fact Father Patrick had saved the baby owl. He fed it initially with bread soaked in soured milk, and soon the owl was eating worms which Marguerite dug up for him in the midden outside the kitchen door. You could say that Father Patrick had reared Marguerite from a chick, too, even if she had not actually fallen out of a nest. Except she nearly had, because it was well known in the village that she had no father. Unless you could count Father Patrick as her father – which of course he was, but he was for everyone, not just for Marguerite, even if she was special for *him*.

Some of the village children were beaten by their fathers – which seemed like a good reason to be scared of fathers. Some of the children were scared of the priest as well, partly because he would give them plenty of Hail Marys for their wrongdoings, but mostly because they were frightened of hell-fire, which was the place where the wicked people went, according to Father Patrick.

Marguerite did not go to confession and did not expect to be sent to hellfire because her mother was a Cathar, and therefore, in Father Patrick's view, a heathen unbeliever and not subject to the same rules.

Even if Marguerite had gone to confession, she still would not be scared of Father Patrick. How could she be? Father Patrick had never said so much as a cross word to her all her life – although he argued all the time in his soft Irish voice with her mother.

Her mother was not scared of Father Patrick, either. Thérèse Leblanc was scared of nobody. She held an important position in the village. She was not only Father Patrick's housekeeper; she was also the village healer, the person who knew all about the herbs which could be gathered on the hillside and their curative uses. Of course, you could go to the doctor who held his weekly surgery down the mountain in Valréas; but he was a busy man, and had no time for anything but the most serious and profitable of physical ailments.

Birth and death were Thérèse's specialities. She dealt,

60

too, in those things which were part of everyday life. Cradle-cap, snake-bite, measles, the curing of warts and the alleviation of the discomforts of the monthly cycle, all were brought to Thérèse Leblanc, just as they had been brought to Thérèse's mother, and to her mother before her.

It was not only the villagers who needed her, either. Father Patrick had good reason to be grateful that Thérèse was a healer and a skilled midwife. Quite often the guests at the Hermitage needed her ministrations, too. Thérèse was sometimes kept busy all through the night, and would have no time to do anything in the morning but set out a mug of *café au lait* with bread for dipping, make sure Marguerite was wearing a clean pinny and her dinner-canteen was in her hand, and shoo her out of the Hermitage on her way to school.

'Off you go at *once*, or mademoiselle your teacher will scold me,' she would say.

Marguerite had been going to school for four years, although she had been reading quite difficult books and doing joined-up writing for much longer. Often she managed to be late for school, but Mademoiselle was never really cross because she had further to come than any of the other children – right down the steep path and all the way along the cobbled lane which followed the irrigation channel.

The real reason she was late was because there were such interesting things to do on the way, like watching the snails climbing up the broom branches, or chasing the big blue lizards which lived in the cemetery wall.

Marguerite was more interested in wild creatures than in humans. Once she had found a double butterfly, with two bodies and eight wings, hanging upside-down on a leaf. She had picked it up and taken it to school, and Mademoiselle had gone pink and explained that it was not a double butterfly at all, but two insects making babies.

Making babies and its associated activities were a favourite subject among her schoolmates. The boys were as rude as you might expect. They would tease her and pull her ponytail and pinch her bottom when they got the chance. They did it to all the girls, particularly the pretty ones like Marguerite.

Marguerite could always give as good as she got.

When she reached the village, she had to climb up the steep narrow street to the school building which was by the Mairie at the end of the market-square, and then everyone knew that *la petite* from the Hermitage was late again.

The village did not have a church because it had the Hermitage; and it did not need a priest because there was Father Patrick to say Mass. The villagers respected Father Patrick. They knew that the Hermitage was an important place whose affairs took precedence over everything else, including getting to school on time.

Marguerite knew that important people came and went at the Hermitage, although she did not understand why they should be important. The visitors spoke English. Marguerite could speak and write in English, too, because Father Patrick had made sure that there had never been a time when she had not been able to do so.

There was another language, too, which Marguerite could understand, even though she could not always find the words herself. It was her mother's language, the language which Father Patrick called heathen, the language in which Thérèse did her healing. Her mother said it was very ancient, more ancient than the French Marguerite learned in school, or even the English which Father Patrick taught her in his soft Irish accent.

To Marguerite, Father Patrick had always been old, but even she could remember a time when his blue eyes had been as bright as the sky, and not pale and a little milky like they were now, although his hearing was as sharp as ever. Later she realized that, if she crept around as quietly as one of the mice Abelard was so fond of catching, Father Patrick would not know she was there, unless he was wearing his spectacles.

Soon afterwards Father Patrick decided to teach her to read and write – not as she learned in school in French, but in English with joined-up writing. It was the exercise of the skills she had learned which had made today such an important day, a day she had been working towards for months. She felt very special and privileged because Father Patrick had made sure that she understood that the work was important.

In a way the confessions were magic, like spells.

Marguerite had to keep out of the way of the visitors, but she loved to watch the ones who were young and fashionable, like Miss Belinda Fitzherbert. Even though their clothes did not look as comfortable as Marguerite's, there was no doubt that some of them were as pretty as the picture on a most expensive box of chocolates. The notion of chocolates reminded her of the chocolate cake which had been ordered for her birthday from the patisserie.

She looked up into the rafters to make sure Abelard was in his usual place. The owl roosted by day in the embrasure of the arrow-slit which lit the writing cell. The arrow-slit was handy for hunting because there was no glass and only a bit of curtain, which he could easily push aside.

Abelard was her guardian angel, since as a Cathar she was not allowed one. In a way he looked like an angel, what with his wings and the speckled feathers on his head which he could fluff up to resemble a halo.

Father Patrick had named the owl, explaining that it was because he had such a woebegone expression. Abelard, Father Patrick told her at some considerable length in words she did not entirely understand, was a very important philosopher-monk who had sacrificed every-thing for love – including those parts of himself whose mention was probably worth at least three decades of the rosary.

Marguerite giggled to herself when she thought about Abelard's namesake's parts, even though it was a very serious matter and it must have hurt terribly at the time.

You could tell when Abelard did not like people because he fluffed up all his feathers to make himself look bigger, picked up his feet one at a time to show his sharp talons, and clicked his beak as loudly as he possibly could.

While Marguerite awaited the arrival of Miss Belinda Fitzherbert, her mind wandered back to what she might expect for supper. Her mother was acknowledged as the best cook in the village. She was also very frugal – and frugality was a quality much admired in the women of the valley. Everyone knew whose mother was a good cook because each child came to school every day with the midday meal in a canteen – a little metal pail with a clip-on lid.

The contents of Marguerite's canteen always attracted interest and not a little envy, since many children had to make do with plain vegetable soup with barley. Sometimes she had a spoonful of Sunday *cassoulet*, a thick bean stew with a scrap of pickled goose, or a *daube* with meat and carrots flavoured with home-pickled olives and red wine. The hors d'oeuvre was her favourite: it was carried inside the canteen, in a little metal dish on top of the stew. It might be a sliver of salty pink ham with sweet butter, or maybe a hard-boiled egg with the yolk taken out and mashed up with a whiskery-boned anchovy, or cheese with a pickled cherry, or, in summer, a fat red tomato, sliced and dressed with chopped garlic and olive oil.

The children used to leave their canteens with the dinner-lady to be warmed up in the big steamer – lowered carefully into boiling water, but not before Marguerite's little dish of hors d'oeuvre had been taken out and set ready on the table.

Abelard also liked to eat his dinner warm. Mostly he ate mouse. Abelard certainly thought mouse was delicious. He would put one foot firmly on to the wriggling body, spearing it with his talons and paying no attention to the squeaks, and pull it to pieces with his beak. When he had finished eating everything he shut his eyes and rocked back, as if he had just eaten the most exquisite meal – maybe a dried plum stuffed with marzipan, or a sugared almond.

She sometimes collected the pellets he spat out afterwards. She soaked them in clean water, and took them apart with two darning-needles from her mother's workbox. Wrapped up in the fur were the tiny skulls and bones of the wild creatures Abelard had eaten. She had a natural-history book with black-and-white drawings of the skulls of mammals and birds, so she knew what they all were. Abelard did not only eat mice. He ate shrews and water rats, robins and tomtits, and lots of insects like crickets and grasshoppers, and the greeny-gold beetles which ran along the bottom of the wall, although all that was left of them were shining scraps of carapace.

As Father Patrick told her, one could learn lessons from Abelard. One was that prettiness and colour made people notice you – they helped the owl spot the beetles – and that it was not useful to be noticed. Another was that it was natural for the strong to gobble up the weak.

When she grew up, Marguerite intended to be strong. Not soft-bodied, pretty and brightly coloured like Miss Belinda Fitzherbert, whose high heels she could now hear tap-tapping on the stone staircase which led to Father Patrick's room. If Miss Belinda had been a beetle, Abelard would have had her in no time. Snap, clatter, gulp.

Marguerite took up her pen expectantly. A commotion on the other side of the heavy curtain had warned her that her duties were about to begin.

6

Miss Fitzherbert Makes Confession

'Forgive me, Father, for I have sinned.'

Marguerite knew confession always started like that. People who came to confess had to do penance, depending on how bad they had been.

'Make yourself comfortable, daughter.' Father Patrick's voice was gentle and reassuring. The scrape of wood on stone told Marguerite that a chair was being set in place.

'How long since your last confession?'

'Three months, Father.' The young woman must be nervous because her voice was very quiet.

'Speak up, daughter,' said Father Patrick. 'I'm a little deaf.'

Marguerite knew that Father Patrick was not deaf. He was just saying that to help her. She waited for the words to be repeated, her hand poised above the page. Father Patrick had taught her some signs which meant that she did not have to write out all the ritual phrases, and would have time to transcribe the important parts.

'Three months, Father.' This time the answer came loud and clear.

Marguerite could not resist a little peep. The young woman had a pretty, rather silly face – in Marguerite's opinion. This face was framed in tight golden curls, and today there were neat little pearl studs in the ears, whereas yesterday there had been diamond drops. Miss Fitzherbert was dressed most fashionably in a summer frock with a stiff petticoat underneath, a nipped-in waist topped with a smart little jacket made of sky-blue polka-dotted silk.

'What have you to tell me, daughter?'

All at once came the sounds of muffled sobbing.

'There, daughter. Take your time.'

After a few moments, the patient voice of Father Patrick rose again. 'Have you committed any grave sins?'

'Unkind thoughts . . .' The girl's voice was high and nervous.

This sin did not seem very serious. Marguerite often had unkind thoughts, most of them towards her teacher at school when she was given too much homework, or towards Marie-Pascale who was the daughter of the mayor and therefore the richest person in the class, and who teased her about her clothes being patched and mended. Unkind thoughts were perfectly natural. Abelard was guilty of unkind thoughts towards mice all the time.

'Towards whom, daughter?'

A silence. Then, quietly: 'Towards many people, Father.'

There followed a list of names – mother, father, grand-parents, aunts, uncles.

'Anything else?'

'I have committed the sin of disobedience. I have not respected my parents' wishes . . .' The girl was whispering again.

Marguerite was not impressed. She disobeyed her mother – and Father Patrick and mademoiselle the schoolmistress – all the time.

'With what consequences, daughter?'

Marguerite could tell from his tone that Father Patrick thought there was something interesting coming. She had noticed that it took a long time for people to say what they really felt bad about. Sometimes these things were quite exciting because they had to do with love. Marguerite was

67

curious about love – not the kind Father Patrick recommended, when you were supposed to forgive your neighbour, but the other kind, the one where you kissed boys.

It seemed there was a young man Belinda wished to marry, so she must certainly have kissed him lots of times, but her parents did not approve of her marrying him.

'Whatever they say, Father, I do so love him – and he loves me.' The muffled sobbing started up again.

Marguerite began to feel sympathetic – more so than Father Patrick, who was far too old and, anyway, was not allowed love because of the vows he had made. Marguerite was quite sure that falling in love was the only good reason for marrying someone – and in all the fairy stories the more important you were, the more unsuitable the person you fell in love with. If you were a princess, you would almost certainly fall in love with a swineherd. This was quite understandable, considering that you would then be able to eat all the pork you wanted. You could have a slice of ham every day for your canteen, and probably roast pork with cream sauce on Sunday as well.

All this time, Marguerite was writing down what Miss Belinda was saying, together with Father Patrick's replies.

'Your own feelings are not sufficient reason, my child, to disregard the commandment to obey your parents.'

He was saying this, but even Marguerite could tell that Father Patrick's heart was not in it. Perhaps he did understand about love after all.

Marguerite's hand was aching. She hoped the confession was drawing to an end. She wrote in long joined-up sweeps, just as she had been taught. She was writing with a goose's flight-feather, sharpened and shaped into a nib. After every other line, she dipped the pen in a dense black liquid which smelled a little of fish, which was not surprising because Father Patrick said it was made in

China from the little glands in cuttlefish. Chinese ink sounded suitably exotic for the task. Every now and then she reached out to scatter the page with a handful of sand, disturbing Abelard, who flicked open one eggshell-blue eyelid in protest. He had double eyelids anyway, so he could do this without waking himself up.

Then, just when she was getting so tired that she thought she would have to stop, the young woman began to explain something which was so interesting that Marguerite almost dropped the pen.

'There's worse. Much worse.'

'How worse?'

'Unclean thoughts, Father. And . . . and . . . unclean deeds.'

Unclean thoughts, everyone knew, meant one decade of the rosary and were not particularly bad. Marguerite had a loose grasp of what thoughts might be considered clean or unclean. Unclean deeds sounded much more educational. She waited expectantly.

'Don't be scared, daughter,' Father Patrick's voice encouraged gently – a sentiment with which Marguerite heartily concurred.

The voice started up again. Marguerite's hand flew over the page. Miss Belinda Fitzherbert had clearly done much more than kissing. She had done a great deal that the unsuitable young man had told her to do instead, including what Abelard had done with Héloïse, but without the bits being chopped off after it was all over.

But, when it came right down to it, Miss Belinda had done no more or less than let the young man have his way with her. No worse and no different from the kind of thing that went on in Pernes-les-Rochers all the time. There had never been a time when Marguerite had not known how the reproductive machinery worked – what bits went where and how and why. Every country child knew about the mechanics of sex almost as soon as it could toddle. You could not get away from it. In every farmyard there were bulls covering cows, buck-rabbits jumping on their females, cockerels climbing on hens.

And, if she had been in any doubt of the connection, her classmates, who shared their parents' sleeping-quarters until they were of school age, were only too pleased to tell her all about it. She had seen enough human babies born, too, when she fetched and carried for her mother, to know that there was no real difference between her own species and every other warm-blooded mammal.

True love was different.

What she needed to know was what made the difference – how such things were transformed into the thing her mother's troubadours sang of. The things Miss Belinda Fitzherbert had first spoken of before she got all muddled up with the machinery.

Marguerite gathered from Father Patrick's questions that there were rules which governed when you did it, and what might and might not be considered the right way to do it.

Right and wrong. It was all a puzzle, but she wrote it down just the same. Some day she would fall in love herself, and then she would know.

At last the voices ceased.

'That's all?'

'Yes, Father.'

'And do you truly and earnestly repent?'

'Yes, Father.'

'You will not see the young man any more?'

'No, Father.'

'It seems to me you have been punished enough, daughter. Ego te absolvo in nomine Patris, et Filii, et Spiritu Sancti. Go, my child, and sin no more.'

So that was it? Sin no more. Sin did not seem so extra-ordinary. It was simply a matter of machinery.

The chair scraped back.

'You may spend the rest of the day in prayer and contemplation.'

'Yes, Father. Thank you, Father.'

After a moment Marguerite heard the click of heels, and then silence.

She stretched and sighed. She blew off a little cloud of fine sand which had settled between the pages and shut the heavy leather covers. Then she dipped the pen into a pot of water she had set ready earlier, dried the nib carefully on a special scrap of white linen, and set the pen back in its holder.

It was all done, and done well. Even if she had not understood all the words in the machinery section, Father Patrick would be pleased with her.

She glanced up at the owl.

'Mouse, Abelard,' she said in a conversational tone, just to reassure him she had his best interests at heart.

The owl fluffed out his feathers, blinked, then hopped down on to his mistress's shoulder. He nibbled her ear, which tickled and made her giggle.

'*I'm* not a mouse, stupid.'

With the owl bobbing against her cheek, she pushed aside the dividing curtain and entered the larger room.

The priest was alone again, seated in his usual place, which was a wooden rocking chair set beneath an arched window with a view right across the valley. His face was turned towards the rays of the sun slanting through the panes. Anyone who did not know the meaning of the lowered lids might have thought he was taking his afternoon snooze, rather than resting his tired eyes.

'Mon père? C'est fini. I can go now?'

Father Patrick turned towards her, but he kept his eyes shut.

'That's how it is, is it, *ma petite*? Such impatience. You managed to write all that down?'

'Oui, *mon père*.'

'Speak in English, mavourneen. So?'

'Most of it, to be sure.'

'The quill is washed and put away?'

'Oui, mon père.'

'Good. Now read it over to me.'

In a clear voice, Marguerite read out what she had written.

The priest nodded in satisfaction. Marguerite's grasp of the language was remarkable. She had only the faintest trace of accent – and when it came it was the Irishness of his own voice that he heard. Father Patrick had set about the task of teaching her when she was scarcely able to lisp her own name.

Bearing in mind that an Irish accent, while delightful on the lips of a colleen, might be something of a handicap when she needed to earn her living, he had invested the year's Easter offering (which the priest was permitted to keep for himself) in a radio on which it was possible to receive the BBC World Service. Then, through the long winter evenings, the child and the old man would listen with passionate intensity to reports of delays to the Green Bus route through the Mendips, news of the latest exhibitions in London's fashionable art galleries, warnings of storms over Tiree and cricket rained off at Old Trafford. Sometimes there was a play to listen to, or a comedy series, or an interview with a popular musician. This was Marguerite's favourite, because sometimes they played the musician's songs.

The result of all this listening was that Marguerite not only acquired the finer nuances of the language and was able to speak without the Irish accent, but also in the process acquired an intimate knowledge of places and events and cultural preoccupations which had nothing at all to do with life in a valley in Upper Provence.

That evening her mother prepared a special meal of all her favourite things – eggs fried in very hot olive oil so that the edges were lacy and crisp, a thick slice of pink salty ham, and a big slab of yellow cornbread. To drink there was a glass of the special syrup made with an infusion of water-mint sweetened with honey from the hive in the Hermitage's orchard. To finish, and best of all, was the shop-bought cake, ordered specially from the *pâtisserie* in Valréas, with shiny chocolate icing and tiny silver balls, with *Meilleures voeux* written on it in white icing.

Father Patrick had picked a bunch of meadow daisies to put into a jam jar on the table for decoration. He always did this on Marguerite's birthday, explaining that this was because they were her name-flower; but Marguerite knew from the way her mother looked at him and smiled that they represented a secret between him and her mother.

7

Growing Up

In spite of her pleasure in being useful to Father Patrick, Marguerite was happiest when there were no confessions to be transcribed, no school to go to, and she was free to roam the hills.

'I'm off now, maman,' she would call up the stairs as soon as she had finished her breakfast bread and milk.

Sometimes Abelard would consent to accompany her, and sometimes she was all alone – except that on the hillsides she was never really alone.

The soles of her feet were as tough as leather, and she could move as quietly as the wild creatures with whom she kept company. In the spring she knew where to find the downy nests of the plump little partridges whose babies scurried around catching insects in the sagebrush; in which particular cliff the jewel-feathered bee-eaters reared their young. One day she even found a shrike's larder – fat caterpillars and shimmering beetles spitted on a thorn-bush, ready for a rainy day.

When she was little, she had always noticed smells and sounds and the texture of things. The smell of milk and running water, the powdery smell of pillows stuffed with goose-feathers. Above all, she noticed kitchen smells, because that was where her mother and she spent most of their time.

When visitors came, Marguerite could bury her face in her mother's skirt or in her white petticoats which smelled of carbolic soap. Over her skirt her mother always wore an apron made of dark cotton printed with tiny bunches of flowers, which she would take off when she answered the door. The apron had a yeasty smell of bread put to rise by the fire, and the nutty smell of baking.

The kitchen mostly smelled of the herbs her mother distilled for her medicines: camomile for burns, clary for infections of the eyes, lime-blossom for the fits, foxglove for wounds, hyssop for the toothache. And in autumn the kitchen smelled of thyme and rosemary and peppermint all simmered in goosegrease to make an ointment to rub on people's chests against the winter chills. But in summer it smelled of lavender and rose-petals to be dried to scent the rooms in winter, and to stuff into little muslin envelopes to tuck into the linen-cupboard and the wardrobe.

Marguerite knew that she was not beautiful like her mother. She was not curvy like her mother, either. Her legs were too long for her body – like a little goat, said Father Patrick. Her skin was honey-coloured like her mother's, but her nose went freckly in the sun. Her mother wore her hair braided into a long plait which she wound round her head and covered with a dark cotton scarf knotted at the nape of her neck. Little wisps of hair would escape, and Marguerite would tuck them back under the folds when her mother carried her up to bed at night.

Marguerite knew many secrets. The borie village was the most treasured, an abandoned village high above the olive groves.

This particular village had once been a Cathar stronghold, although the little beehive-shaped dwellings were far older than that. Her mother told her that the bories were the oldest dwellings on earth, and it was there that she went to gather her herbs, although no-one else in the village ever went near them.

Marguerite's schoolmates said that the bories were haunted by the ghosts of the Cathars who had been killed there many years ago. Célandine, who shared a desk with Marguerite, told her that her mother said the Cathars were the Devil's own.

Marguerite's mother said that the herbs which grew in the bories' little enclosures were special, they only grew there, were very ancient and were the most useful of all for her healings. Marguerite weeded the stony little patches which the borie people had used for their gardens and made sure the herbs had plenty of room and sunshine to grow.

In the middle was an ancient mulberry tree. The fruits were small and creamy pale, and Marguerite knew that the colour and size of the fruit meant that the mulberry tree was there for the silkworms, and not for the making of cordials and conserves, or the distillation of the white brandy which the farmers made each autumn with walnuts, wild plums, brambles or sloes.

'The silkworms were our corner-of-the-apron money,' said Thérèse.

Corner-of-the-apron money was the few sous which the women could earn for themselves to pay for their necessities – such as ribbons and laces, and the ministrations of a wise woman like Thérèse.

'You got the eggs from the silk-merchant,' her mother said. 'In the warmth of the kitchen, the eggs hatched into little caterpillars. They ate all day and all night – and we children always had the responsibility of gathering the mulberry leaves and keeping the worms clean and fed. It was a very important task, looking after the silkworms. When they spun their cocoons you had to hang them in the rafters; and when they had finished you could sell them back to the merchant. And then you could start all over again.'

Knowing this, Marguerite searched the leaves for the

little worms, but even with Abelard's help she never found any. She had, however, found a cracked wooden bucket, a wooden scrubbing-board and a tin bath in a patch of nettles.

One day, she dreamed, this would be her home. If she shut her eyes, she could hear the sound of little children, *her* children, playing. She would have lots of children, so that they had brothers and sisters. They would look after the silkworms, and there would be plenty of corner-of-the-apron money for everyone. Marguerite would have a husband who would live with her. Naturally, he would be tall, strong and handsome. He would also be kind and wise, like Father Patrick, but Célandine would not be able to take him away.

The thought of Célandine made her frown.

It was not until she first went to school that she knew that Father Patrick was not her father at all, but the priest, and just as much everyone else's father as he was hers.

One morning, Célandine, who had a real father as well as a mother, told her she could not even call him Father because the Cathars do not believe in Fathers.

'Liar!'

'Ask anyone,' said Célandine. She tossed her head, and her blond curls bobbed around in what Marguerite considered a particularly stupid way. Célandine's mother put her hair up in rags at night so that it curled in long ringlets, and in the morning she undid the rags and tied the curls in bunches with red ribbons bought from the ribbon-man in Valréas. To Marguerite's mind, the bunches looked silly sticking out of the side of her head, like the ears on a donkey.

'Célandine, you don't know anything.'

Célandine dropped her voice so no-one else could hear. 'My mother says you're the priest's brat.'

Furious, Marguerite pulled Célandine's hair because it was easy to grab hold of the bunches. She did not know what being the priest's brat meant, but Célandine had on her mean face, so she knew it must be a horrible thing to say.

'Stop that, girls!' Mademoiselle always blamed Marguerite when she got into fights, particularly with Célandine. Mademoiselle picked up a bucket of water and threw it over them both. The water was as cold as ice, and they separated immediately.

'I don't know whose fault it was,' said Mademoiselle, 'but I'm sending you both home in disgrace.' This was unusually fair, because Célandine was the apple of the teacher's eye.

While her mother dried her and gave her some clean clothes, Marguerite told her what Célandine had said. Then she put her face very close to her mother's, so that she could see right into her eyes.

'It's not true, is it? I'm not the priest's brat, and Father Patrick is truly my real father?'

Her mother's eyes went so dark that they were quite black, and she thought for a moment her mother was going to cry.

Instead she said quietly: 'No, Marguerite, Father Patrick is not your real father. He's the priest, and priests aren't allowed to marry and have babies. He's called *mon père* as a courtesy – to give him the proper dignity. Just the same, Célandine shouldn't say such things. She's a naughty girl, and you're not to think any more about it.'

Her mother did not send her supperless to bed, but let her play in the stream all afternoon with the terrapins which lived under the big stones. And for supper she had a bowl of bread and hot milk with almonds toasted in sugar sprinkled all over it.

The almonds were a special treat, and made Marguerite absolutely sure that something was wrong. She went up to bed as usual, but crept back down when she thought the coast was clear. There was a place on the staircase where,

78

if she put her ear to the wall, she could hear people talking in the kitchen.

'It's only hearsay, Paddy. Village gossip.'

'Gossip can do harm. I don't want her hurt for my sake. Or you, either, Thérèse.'

'You're a good man, Patrick. No-one begrudges us a little happiness.'

'You've certainly given me that.'

Father Patrick's voice was very gentle and soft, and Marguerite felt a bit jealous of what Father Patrick felt for her mother, just as she had done when she was a baby and she had watched him brush her mother's hair by the fire. She tried to forget what she had heard, but it gnawed away inside her like a worm in the core of an apple. If you had cut her in two, you would have seen all the little wormy tunnels. You had to be careful with apples which had worm-holes. One bad apple in a barrel turns all the others bad.

8

Meeting the Monsignor

'Excellent,' said Monsignor Charles Melton to himself, stepping back to admire his appearance in the full-length mirror.

Monsignor Melton, the newly appointed warden of the Hermitage of the Rock, was preparing to leave his suite of rooms in the private Mayfair hotel for his morning stroll.

He smoothed his new soutane, enjoying the softness of the wool. He did not wish to be thought vain, but there was no doubt that one had to look the part.

Modernists might choose the business suit worn with bib and clerical collar, but he preferred the full-skirted monkish soutane. Modernity was not for Monsignor Melton.

The monsignor – the courtesy title came with the appointment – felt that his tailor had been perfectly right to recommend the vicuña; it was certainly expensive, but the luxurious fabric was light, showerproof and, the cutter had assured him, durable. Naturally he had himself tailored in Savile Row rather than resorting to the clerical outfitter in Victoria Street where his colleagues shopped.

Finally he slipped his feet into a pair of exquisitely crafted black brogues. He had a particular passion for shoes. Black for town, brown for the country. No gentleman ever wore brown shoes in London. He put the finishing touches to his toilette, adjusting the purple-piped monseigneurial cummerbund round his expanding waist.

In spite of his expensive tastes, Charles Melton not been born into luxury. He had had to pull himself up by his bootstraps. Although he came from a respectable Catholic family-tree – a Melton had been implicated in the Gunpowder Plot – his particular branch had withered somewhat over the centuries. By the time young Charles had made his way into the world, there was little enough to pay the rent, let alone educate a son, however promising.

So young Charles had had to earn himself a church scholarship at one of the great Catholic public schools, where the scholars were expected to serve as altar-boys and general dogsbodies to the other boys. This experience taught him that the poor might well be blessed, but the inheritance of the earth must come from other sources. He made himself a small but useful income selling a modern form of Indulgence – forging school reports for those whose parents' expectations exceeded their sons' achievements.

When the time came for him to enter university, he applied to read theology at Christ Church, Oxford, where once again he was beholden to Mother Church for his daily bread. It was a tribute to his embryonic powers of persuasion that he managed to convert his course to politics, philosophy and economics – a subject which, unlike theology, brought him into contact with the future leaders of his country.

A respectable second-class degree – he had been viva'd for a first, but somehow had managed to fall at the final fence – led to four apprentice years in the Special Administration of the Holy See, the banking arm of the Vatican. Here he acquired a powerful patron, the Sicilian-born Bishop of Palermo, Guiseppe Navarino, a man who, as head of the Vatican's highly efficient secret service, was always on the lookout for bright young men.

Under Navarino's patronage he took holy orders

before returning to England to take up an appointment as chaplain to Christ Church. His duties here were not arduous, being principally the cultivation of those students, whatever their religious denomination, whose friendship might be useful to his masters in the future. It was at this time that he learned the most important lesson of all for those who seek reward in this world rather than in the next. Some might call it flexibility, a willingness to bend with the prevailing wind. Others might call it the opportunism of the born scavenger. Whatever it was, Melton appreciated that the end can always be made to justify the means, that ruthlessness is not listed in the canon of deadly sins. It was a lesson he never forgot.

Among the undergraduates he drew into his orbit was Catherine Cuthbert, only child of a devout and ancient Catholic dynasty. On her recommendation, Melton became private chaplain to the Cuthberts of Minton Mallet, a position which carried few responsibilities but confirmed him as a high flier and gave him a small private income. New horizons opened up for the ambitious young priest.

The Cuthberts soon had good reason to be grateful to their chaplain for his timely intervention in a domestic matter which concerned their headstrong young daughter. Catherine was not the first young woman to fall for a scoundrel, but it was somewhat unfortunate that the young man of her choice – although of high birth, and destined for an earl's coronet – was not even a Catholic. Fortunately their father confessor was able to be of practical assistance through the offices of his Vatican mentor, now elevated to the College of Cardinals, a man who knew the value of silence and the price of a favour.

'The Hermitage, I think. I'll put in a word with the warden.'

'The Hermitage?'

Swiftly his patron outlined the function of the one-time crusader stronghold. 'A service to the beleaguered, dear boy. A convenience for the faithful. We look after our own.'

This was the first time that Melton had heard mention of the sanctuary or had knowledge of the unique service it offered. That this timely intervention had tragic consequences could scarcely be blamed on the young chaplain. Unless, like Navarino, you knew quite literally where the bodies were buried. In this case, one body – but not one which was likely to tell tales.

Melton glanced out of the window and sighed, putting such appalling memories to the back of his mind.

The summer of 1955 was late in coming. Even though it was nearly summer, the avenue of plane trees which marked the edge of St James's Park was misted with drizzle. It was high time the Lord did something about London's dismal weather. He folded his showerproof cloak neatly over his arm, taking pleasure in the texture of the silk twill which lined the finely woven gabardine. Charles Melton did not deny himself any of life's small pleasures. He prided himself on the excellence of his claret, and had an arrangement with the management which permitted him to maintain a private cellar.

He did not entertain ostentatiously, preferring small gatherings in the private dining room. Two or three guests chosen for their importance, wit, or value to each other and naturally to himself. The menu was always simple, but chosen with exquisite forethought – oysters delivered direct from Brittany, smoked salmon flown down from the Shetlands, a leg of mountain lamb from a Welsh upland farm.

This lifestyle did not come cheap, and had his yearly stipend not been supplemented by several more of the private chaplaincies it would scarcely have covered a month's expenses.

With the single exception of what he preferred to call a youthful error of judgement, Charles Melton's progress through the labyrinth of church preferment had been as smooth as cream. Even so, that error had almost cost him his career. Even now, sixteen years later, beads of sweat broke out on his forehead at the memory of his superior's reprimand.

'The sin of arrogance. Sinning against your brethren, you sin against Christ. Tidy it up, my son.'

Tidy it up was precisely what he had done. And, if his conscience occasionally troubled him, that was a cross he had to bear. Yet even that he had managed to turn to good account. He reflected that his association with the Cuthbert family had done him no disservice in the long run.

He picked up his second-best hat – no sense in ruining the best one – and went downstairs.

He made his way to the concierge's desk.

'Morning, Wilberforce. Any post?'

The concierge reached into the line of pigeon-holes. Monsignor Melton was one of half a dozen distinguished permanent residents, men whose domestic arrangements made the hotel's services a convenience.

Melton sifted quickly through the bundle.

Three circulars, a subscriber's copy of the *Catholic Herald*, and several typed envelopes which bore the logo of one or other of the City's most respected stockbrokers. Melton's preferment owed a lot to his financial acumen: the Church rewarded those who filled her coffers.

He thrust the bundle into his pocket.

'Cab, sir? Weather's a little changeable.'

Monsignor Melton peered through the glass doors. The fine drizzle had stopped, and he had not far to walk.

'Unnecessary, I think.'

He placed his hat on his head and descended the broad steps with regal dignity. He was conscious of the admiring glances of passers-by. He trusted he cut an elegant and romantic figure in his full skirts and wide-brimmed clerical hat.

The hotel, a discreet conversion of one of London's great ducal residences, was most conveniently situated both for the shops of the West End and for the City of London.

His morning routine never varied. He breakfasted lightly at Fortnum & Mason on a perfectly acceptable *café crème* and the best Viennese pastries in town. Regretfully he limited himself to only one of the buttery morsels. His Harley Street doctor had warned him against over-indulgence. At just turned fifty, Melton had no intention of exchanging the fruits of his earthly labours for the uncertainty of heavenly reward. Particularly not now that he had been offered such golden preferment. Had it not been for the moisture trickling down the back of his collar, he would have felt himself blessed indeed.

He walked quickly, holding his skirts clear of the puddles. Fortunately it was only a short walk from Fortnum's to Trumper's, the gentleman's hairdresser in Curzon Street. Here, in company with half the Cabinet and several of the City's most powerful money-brokers, Melton anticipated the pleasurable ministrations of his barber and the enjoyment of a little harmless gossip. So useful, a gossip. Politics, money, sex – there was nothing a man did not discuss with his barber.

'Morning, George.'

'Good morning, sir. Be with you shortly.'

'No hurry.'

Today, as it was the rush hour, all the chairs were full – which was pleasant since it gave Melton a moment to catch the mood of the morning. He settled down content-edly in one of the snug leather armchairs provided for customers waiting their turn.

George was just finishing off a junior minister at the

Home Office. Melton watched as the barber pommaded the man's sideburns, finally holding up a mirror. The minister preened, turning his head this way and that.

'Sir will notice I left a little more on the back.'

The vanity of politicians never ceased to astonish Melton.

'Good. The ladies like it.'

George assented. The ladies did indeed like a curl on a gentleman's neck.

A tip changed hands with a conjuror's sleight of hand.

One final attention. 'Something for the weekend, sir?'

'Good idea, George.'

Melton listened to this exchange with professional interest. The minister's affirmative was entirely predictable. The politicians were as randy as cats. Bankers, on the other hand, rarely took up the discreet offer of contraceptives; either they were as cautious in private as in their public life, or they went quietly home to their wives.

Celibacy was not something which gave Melton the slightest difficulty. He neither sought nor desired sexual entanglements. He found women neither interesting nor trustworthy. Naturally, as a young man, before he took holy orders, he had felt it necessary to boast of his female conquests to other young men who might otherwise have thought him queer. Society did not tolerate queers – in either sense of the word. Celibacy was so convenient. Unlike the politicians, no-one was ever likely to catch *him* with his trousers down in a tart's bedroom.

If the sixth commandment was a matter of supreme indifference to Melton, the seventh was another matter. If Melton had a besetting sin, it was that of covetousness. He was not alone in this. It was known that the Holy Father himself agonized over the definition of what was and was not moral behaviour in the matter of worldly goods. 'Thou shalt not steal' was open to so many interpretations.

With these thoughts in his head, Melton took the minister's place in the chair, noticing that the man in the next chair was an eminent Cambridge scientist who also happened to be a member of a well-known banking family.

'Morning, Victor.'

The scientist glanced across. 'Good day, Charles. Congratulations. Saw the announcement in the *Jewish Chronicle*.'

'Did you indeed? Didn't know your lot reported on the enemy.'

'A broad church, Charles. We're all in the same business.'

Victor Goldberg always kept his finger on the pulse. But, still, it was flattering to be noticed. Melton felt the warm glow of acceptance.

'Talking of business, how's the world of academe?'

'Selling well, I'm told.'

Both men laughed comfortably at this reference to a recent scandal involving the head of the university's arts faculty. It appeared that the professor had augmented his salary with a kickback from a well-known firm of architects who had been engaged to build a new library.

Melton felt good about this exchange. He felt part of the family. Unlike most dons, Victor Goldberg did not need to raid anyone's petty cash. His considerable private means enabled him to entertain lavishly at his house on the outskirts of the university city, and Melton hoped his preferment would earn him an invitation.

'Your charming wife? Well, I hope?'

'Shopping.'

The single word said it all. Victor's third wife was young, pretty and, it was said, wildly extravagant.

'Ah, the ladies. What would we do without them?'

'Indeed.' The voice was dry – managing to imply in the lengthening of the two syllables that a celibate priest could scarcely be expected to know what to do with or without a lady.

The scientist stood up. 'Mustn't keep the fair sex waiting. Good to see you, Charles. You must come down for the weekend. Ernestine does so enjoy the Vatican gossip – says you Catholics have all the fun.'

'I'd be delighted.'

'Good. Give my best to the cardinal-banker. Gather he had lunch with my brother last week. But no doubt you know all about that, Monsignor.'

With a nod he was gone. Melton stared after him. Victor's brother was the head of the family bank, but he himself knew nothing of a scheme which might involve Navarino and the Istituto per le Opere di Religione – more familiarly known as the Vatican Bank – with Goldberg's. But, then, the Holy See was so hedged about with secrecy that it would have been surprising if he *had*. The left hand never knew what the right hand was doing.

With this thought, Melton turned his attention back to the gathering of political tittle-tattle which was the main business of the morning.

Anthony Eden had called an election, although only weeks earlier he had succeeded Winston Churchill as premier after the old warhorse had thrown a tantrum over Washington's issue of confidential documents to do with the Treaty of Yalta.

'Hope Eden's up to it.'

'Anthony's always been a ditherer.'

'Never trusted the man. Bit of a limp-wrister, if you ask me.'

'Thank God for Rab.'

This reference to R. A. Butler, Eden's new chancellor, acknowledged the traditional pre-election tax-cutting budget.

'Good man, Rab. Knows what's needed.'

'Middle classes like him. The stuff about a property-owning democracy goes down well in the shires.'

The chair vacated by Goldberg was now occupied by the Honourable Member for Nottingham Potteries, who was grumbling to the Scottish Member for Fife that he would be obliged to endure the discomfort of the provinces for a few weeks.

'Bloody baby-kissing. The wife's furious.'

'Och 'tis nae so bad, laddie.' The Member for Fife affected a broad Scots accent south of the border – in spite of the public-school drawl which was his birthright. 'The beer's drinkable.'

So absorbed in this exchange was the monsignor that he scarcely noticed that the shave was over and the haircut was about to begin. With it came those small additional attentions which could only be enjoyed on a morning at leisure. You could always tell a Trumper's customer by the discreet scent of lime aftershave which hung about their person.

'Friction, sir?'

He refused George with regret. The soothing rub with cologne was an attention which he usually enjoyed, but today he couldn't afford the time. He had travel arrangements to complete. Melton, too, had to visit what might be considered his constituency: a valley just as inconveniently situated in the wintry uplands of Provence. It was expected of him, and any delay in visiting his new responsibility would be unseemly.

It was a bore naturally. The journey would be uncomfortable and exhausting; and, in common with the Honourable Member for Nottingham Potteries, he, too, expected to suffer – mercifully somewhat more briefly.

It was also damned inconvenient that he would have to drag his godson Ben with him, but there was no help for it. The young rapscallion had been rusticated again, and the grandparents were no longer capable of anything unexpected in the domestic line.

Taking responsibility for Benjamin Catesby was a cross he had to bear. Part of the price he had had to pay for that youthful error of judgement which had so nearly cost him his career.

It was his reward, well deserved and hard-won, that the cardinal – now in charge of the Vatican's London offices – had recommended him for the wardenship.

Both men were agreed that the Hermitage's services were under-exploited. The modern church had to survive in the market-place; it could no longer run on charity and hope. Faith must earn its keep.

The two discussed, in strictly general terms, what might be done to maximize profitability. In the right hands, Melton was sure, the place was a potential goldmine.

'I like your ideas, Charles.'

'I'll need a free hand, your Eminence. Sometimes one has to seize the moment.'

'I see no difficulty there.'

'I take it I shall report directly to you?'

'Naturally.'

'No need to trouble the Holy See with the fine print?'

'I think we understand each other.'

'Indeed we do, Giuseppe.'

And, indeed, Melton's understanding of Navarino was as perfect as twenty years could make it.

All was well in the new warden's world. All but one thing. Young Ben, the wild card in his personal pack.

If he had not believed that the Almighty took no more than a passing interest in the affairs of men, he might have thought it a celestial trick, a divine dig in the ribs, that the first time he visited the Hermitage after all these years he should have no choice but to take Benjamin Catesby with him.

9

The Monsignor Visits the Hermitage

'Marguerite, lève-toi!'

Marguerite opened her eyes in her little bedroom tucked away in a turret of the Hermitage. She closed them again tightly, pretending she was still asleep and today was yesterday, which would mean that there was no visit from the monsignor to be endured, and no boy – the monsignor's godson, it seemed – to be entertained.

'Slug-a-bed!'

Father Patrick was after her as well.

'Moles' skulls and newts' toes,' said Marguerite crossly. These were spells, the standard equipment of all self-respecting witches. Marguerite had every intention of becoming a witch when she grew up. She would be a black witch, not a white witch – which was more or less what her mother was. Abelard would be her familiar. Owls would be better than cats at that kind of thing, what with the flying around which had to be done.

Feeling a little more optimistic at this prospect, she swung herself out of her warm bed and began to pull on her clothes.

The monsignor – the new warden of the Hermitage of the Rock, to give him his proper title – had been due last night off the Avignon train. He was bringing his young godson, Benjamin Catesby. She had heard the clattering and the fuss when they arrived, but she had been half-asleep by then anyway.

Marguerite was supposed to entertain the boy while the monsignor and Father Patrick saw to the affairs of the Hermitage. Father Patrick was worried that the new monsignor would guess that he could no longer see well enough to write up the confessions.

The worst thing that could possibly happen as a result of this was that the warden might decide to replace Father Patrick as his resident. This would be terrible, because they were a family, she and her mother and Father Patrick, and the Hermitage was their home.

All this made the household anxious. Knowing she was late already, Marguerite tumbled downstairs and hurled herself through the kitchen door, her hair unbrushed, her shirt-tail flapping. She was in such a hurry she nearly tripped over the monsignor, who was just getting up to refill his coffee cup.

The monsignor was quite stout although not very tall, with pale skin and pale eyes of no particular colour. All over the top of his head was a fuzz of very fair hair which made him look like a monk with a tonsure, or as if he was nearly bald. He had a nose which looked more like a beak than a nose, and a very stern expression.

'Well,' said the monsignor, peering at her.

'Excusez-moi, monsieur – monsignor . . .' Marguerite was confused. She wondered if she was supposed to kiss something. A ring perhaps.

'Bonjour, mademoiselle. Vous vous appellez?' The monsignor had very bad French, and used the formal plural form of address, not the *tu* which was normally used to a child. This pleased Marguerite, even if he did not know what he was saying. She felt grown up and important enough to reply in English.

'My name is Marguerite, monsieur. Marguerite Dieudonnée Leblanc.'

'Is it indeed? Well, Marguerite Dieudonnée Leblanc, I'm delighted you speak such good English. Most remarkable.'

Marguerite did not quite know what to make of this. Why should it be remarkable? Lots of people learned different languages. It was not so difficult. She was saved from questioning this by her mother, who was bustling around setting out home-made bread and apricot conserve.

'Tiens, petite. Mange.'

Thérèse pointed firmly to a place on the bench at the far end of the table and handed her daughter a steaming bowl of hot chocolate.

Gratefully Marguerite cupped her hands around the bowl. Hot chocolate was a treat. It was too hot to drink straight away, so she began to dunk bits of bread in it and eat them with her little finger crooked in exaggerated daintiness.

The monsignor waited for a moment, then said in English, very slowly and loudly: 'This young man, mademoiselle, is my godson, home from boarding school. I am hoping you will be gracious enough to entertain him.'

'Oui, monsieur,' she said politely. Gracious and entertaining sounded a most superior thing to do. She stole a look at the boy. She was surprised that he had to go away to school. It meant he must be stupid. No French child ever went to boarding school, not unless their parents were very rich and they were stupid enough to need special attention.

While she ate, she inspected him out of the corner of her eye. The monsignor's godson was drinking black coffee rather than the delicious *chocolat chaud* her mother must have made as a special treat. *Tant pis*, she thought to herself. Clearly he did not know a good thing when he saw it.

Another thing. He had the longest eyelashes she had ever seen, the sort of eyelashes which would have looked acceptable on a girl, or even on a baby goat, but were ridiculous on a man – or even a youth. The eyes were half-hooded, but she could see they were not blue or brown, but a kind of grey, like storm clouds with sun on them. His hair was yellow and very curly. In fact he was probably very good-looking, if you liked that kind of thing, which Marguerite did not. Not at all. She liked brown people, with brown eyes and brown hair, like her mother and Abelard. She did not much like her own coppery hair and green eyes, because they made her look so different from everyone else.

She guessed he was about sixteen, which seemed a bit old to be still at school, even if he *was* stupid. The village boys would expect to be working men by then, although those who were clever and whose parents could afford to do without their help in the fields might go to the senior school at Valréas to take their *baccalauréat*, and some even went on to university in Avignon.

Meanwhile the monsignor was talking to her.

'I hope, mademoiselle, you will be good enough to encourage my idle godson to practise his French.'

'Oui, monsieur, voluntiers . . . monsignor.' She was saved from a fit of the giggles by the arrival of Father Patrick.

He was looking very smart. Her mother must have given him a proper shave because you could not see any of the little tufty bits he normally missed when he did it himself. His cassock was clean and brushed, and his shoes were beautifully polished. He was wearing his spectacles, which made him look as if he could see perfectly well through them, which Marguerite knew he could not really.

'Top of the morning, your Eminence. And you, too, young man.'

A silence greeted this.

'Both of you slept well, I trust?'

'Up to a point, Father.'

Father Patrick looked worried. 'To be sure and perhaps

94

it might not be quite what your Eminence is used to, but we have had no complaints from the visitors.'

'A little primitive perhaps. Rustic. But these days good servants are hard to find. I imagine your housekeeper comes of what is known as sturdy peasant stock.'

'You can say that again,' said the youth.

Marguerite stiffened. Her mother did not understand English, so she would not know what was said. But Marguerite did, and she did not like what she heard. Quite apart from the terrible rudeness of the youth, there was nothing primitive about the Hermitage. There were jugs with water for washing in all the rooms, and each person had his or her own chamberpot in a little cupboard by the bed. And a prayer book, too, and a picture of the Virgin on the wall, and clean sheets and soft blankets.

The monsignor smiled, shrugged and spread his hands, which were white and bony, with very clean nails. Then he added: 'I expect you do your best.'

'Of course, your Eminence,' said Father Patrick politely. Marguerite knew that he would not like her mother being called a servant, either; but, then, he had to smile and nod, and not say anything which might upset the warden.

Marguerite consoled herself with the thought that, if the monsignor considered her mother to be a servant and a peasant, he would never in a million years guess that it was her daughter who was writing up the ledgers. It would not occur to him that a servant's child could even read, let alone write everything down in a foreign language in the clear, rounded copperplate which was almost indistinguishable from Father Patrick's own.

Marguerite decided that she did not like the monsignor much. There was something about his eyes, which were small and never seemed to blink. They were the kind of eyes which belonged to a lizard, one of those with greeny-blue scales and pink insides to their mouths who lived in the wall of the cemetery.

There was also something about the way the monsignor looked at her mother – or, rather, *did not* look at her. He sort of *overlooked* her. It was as if she was not a person at all, maybe a cat or a dog. This made the hairs on the back of Marguerite's neck stand up, like Abelard's when he was trying to scare someone.

But Father Patrick had laid his hand on her arm.

'Marguerite, Master Benjamin might like to help you pick the peaches,' said Father Patrick in English. 'They're already dropping from the tree.'

'Charming,' said the monsignor. 'I'm sure Master Benjamin will be enchanted.'

Enchanted, was he? *Master* Benjamin, was it? It was too bad. She was going to have to put up with this stuck-up youth all day. The only consolation was that, in contrast to the village boys, he was highly unlikely to try to see her knickers or pinch her bottom.

'Run along now, both of you. I'm sure Master Benjamin is very good at climbing trees,' said Father Patrick, still smiling politely.

But the youth was paying no attention to anyone. He had finished his coffee and had gone over to the window, so he had his back to the room. There was a sulky look to his back, as if he wanted everyone to know that he was far too old to be given into the care of anyone, let alone a girl like Marguerite.

'Eh!' she said, loudly and not at all politely. 'Vous là! Vous venez?'

The young man straightened up. She could see now he was very tall and lanky.

'The name's Ben. Benjamin Catesby. Not *vous là*.'

'Eh bien, toi. Oui ou non?' she added hopefully, just to give him the chance to let her off her duty.

'Benjamin!' The monsignor was frowning.

Ben shrugged. 'OK.' He still did not look as if he wanted

anything to do with Marguerite, let alone be taken to pick peaches with her.

'On y va,' said Marguerite, marching towards the door without looking back, hoping he still might change his mind. But she could hear his footsteps behind her as she pattered on her bare feet through the long corridor and down the steep steps which led to the yard, and from the yard down a steep path to the cemetery where the peach tree was, right at the end by the gate which led into the heretics' graveyard, the meadow where all the people who were not Catholics were buried.

She had to stop several times for him to catch up. She had already decided that once she got well away from supervision she would not speak French, but only patois.

The patois, the dialect of the valleys, was not a patois at all but a proper language, the ancient *langue d'oc*, the tongue in which the troubadours sang their songs. In the *langue d'oc* the word for 'yes' was *oc*, whereas in the *langue d'oïl* the word for 'yes' was *oui*, and her mother said it had been spoken in these parts since the beginning of time. Or at least since before the Pope's army came and put to the sword all the priests and important people whose religion was different from Father Patrick's.

This ancient rivalry, Marguerite guessed, was the reason why Father Patrick and her mother had such furious arguments over matters which were of very little interest to her.

But of great interest were the songs which her mother sang to her, which the troubadours had sung. In the village they did not think it was quite right to sing them. The village really belonged to the Hermitage, and everyone was careful not to offend Father Patrick's Catholic sensibilities. But Marguerite knew from the arguments he had with her mother that Father Patrick's Catholic sensibilities were a lot harder to offend than *that*.

Marguerite particularly liked the songs about beautiful ladies who were rescued by gallant knights. They were quite rude, full of the kinds of thing which were to be heard at confession, but not nearly as delicately put and using what Father Patrick said was very explicit language.

'Listen,' she said in the patois, 'I shall sing you a song.'

And so she did, pulling faces and making the gestures the bad boys in the village made to accompany a very rude song indeed. She extracted some of the ruder words, just to give extra emphasis.

'Bottoms,' she sang, confident he would not understand. 'Bottoms and belly buttons. Willies and fannies.'

These last, she knew, were worth a dozen decades of the rosary at least.

Marguerite stopped and looked back to see if she was having the desired effect, which was to shock him without giving him any ammunition for telling tales on her.

The youth was right behind her, scowling at her even more ferociously. She was pleased to see that he was in no doubt that what she was singing was rude.

'Girls' bottoms,' she offered, this time in French. 'Fuck and shit.'

'Bet you don't even know what that means . . . *girly*.'

Marguerite stopped abruptly. *Girly* was the worst insult anyone could hurl at her.

'Coitus interruptus,' she trilled.

This was something Miss Belinda Fitzherbert had said she practised with her young man so as to avoid having babies.

Then the boy did something very surprising and most humiliating for Marguerite. He burst out laughing – and then he went on laughing until his face went almost blue.

Her cheeks quite pink with annoyance, Marguerite scrambled up into the tree and began to pelt him with the squishiest of the fruit. Splat! they went, all over his beautiful clean shirt and his pressed linen trousers.

Splat! like little yellow bombs.

'More!' shouted Benjamin into the branches. 'More!'

At that moment Marguerite hated him more than she had ever hated anyone. She could see that she would get into trouble for what she had done, giving Father Patrick more trouble to pile on his worries over the ledgers.

'Take that! And that! And this!'

When there were no more peaches within reach, she swung herself out of the branches on to the top of the wall which divided the cemetery from the heretics' graveyard. Quickly she jumped down on the other side. The boy would surely not follow her there, not if it meant scrambling over the wall.

She heard the sound of a key turn in the lock. She had forgotten that the gate had a key.

'Girly?'

She withdrew rapidly to the far end of the meadow where the stream bathed the roots of a particularly luxuriant clump of willows. Here, in the damp grass, she hollowed out a nest for herself. After she had stayed hidden long enough for the boy to go away, she cautiously raised her head.

But he had not gone away. Instead he seemed to be taking a great interest in one of the rough-hewn stone slabs which were all that marked where the heretics were buried. He was scraping and scratching at a cushion of moss which had grown over one corner. After a moment he stopped, keeping very still. From her hiding place, Marguerite could see that he was frowning, as if what he saw there surprised or shocked him.

Whatever it was he had found, he stood up suddenly, pushed his hand into his blond hair and disappeared through the gateway into the cemetery.

More secrets, thought Marguerite. But this one looked like something really important.

10

Someone Else's Secret

When Marguerite was quite sure that the young man had gone, she crept over to the stone slab to find out what had so interested him.

She stared down. On one corner of the slab, neatly etched into the rough surface, was a monogram, a set of entwined initials like something which might be embroidered on the corner of a lady's handkerchief, and underneath was a date, very faint but just decipherable.

Marguerite had never noticed the marks before, probably because of the thick cushion of moss. She did not recognize the initials, let alone why they might be of interest to the young man. It was curious.

Curiosity, Father Patrick was fond of saying, killed the cat.

'Got you!' said a voice behind her, and Marguerite nearly jumped out of her skin.

The boy had her wrist firmly behind her back, so she could not move without it hurting. Marguerite, used to the rough and tumble of the schoolyard, twisted round like an eel. She managed to get her knee into somewhere soft. The young man let her go immediately.

'Jesus,' he groaned. 'Where did you learn to do a thing like that?'

'Bugger off!'

'I wish I could,' said Ben. 'But since I can't, and nor can you, perhaps we'd better declare a truce.'

'What would you be thinking that might be?' asked Marguerite suspiciously, what Father Patrick called the Irishness of her coming back under the strain.

'An alliance. We'll join forces.'

Marguerite shook her head. 'First, you should be apologizing.'

'Apologize? What the devil for? You've probably crippled me for life, you little bastard.'

'That I'm not,' said Marguerite crossly, with the irrationality of one who knows the insult to be accurate. After a moment she added: 'Sure and your godfather was very rude. He called my mother an ignorant peasant. The Hermitage was primitive, he said. And it's agreeing with him you were.'

'He said it first. You can't blame anyone for a godfather. It's not a blood relation.'

Marguerite considered this. She had no direct experience of the process of selecting godfathers. She did not think she had any, being a Cathar, unless Father Patrick had sneaked some in when her mother was not looking.

There might be another reason for the disclaimer. 'Is it that you don't like the monsignor, either?'

'I don't know if I like him or not. He's all I have.'

'Don't you have a mother and father?' Marguerite persisted.

'You ask too many questions, miss.' The heavy lids descended over the grey eyes so that Marguerite could not see what he was thinking any more.

'Would you be going everywhere with your godfather? Is that why you came?'

The young man shrugged. 'I got rusticated.'

'Rusticated?'

'Sent home from school for bad behaviour.'

'What kind of bad behaviour?'

'Nothing much. A girl.'

'A girl?' Marguerite was impressed. She was also curious. 'Did you do things with her and get her into terrible trouble? Will you make confession for the ledger, like all the other visitors?'

'What's that?' Ben's eyelids flicked open. 'What ledger?'

'Nothing.' Marguerite stared at him, aghast. 'I didn't say anything at all.'

'Of course you did. You said there was a ledger. You said the people made confession for it. So that must mean it's all written down.'

Marguerite shook her head frantically. 'No. Not at all.'

'If you *don't* tell me,' Ben said triumphantly, 'I shall tell my godfather *and* Father Patrick that you *did*.'

This was the meanest trick that anyone could play. She would have to strike a bargain. 'Only if you promise not to tell. Cross your heart and hope to die.'

'Good. I promise.' He made the gestures.

'And only if you tell me what the marks mean.'

But he just shook his head, the grey eyes hooded once more.

Marguerite persisted. 'Is the person under the stone a relation of yours?'

'Shut up, girly.'

Once again this insult struck home.

'I'm *not*.'

'Prove it.'

He towered over her. The yellow hair was like a halo round his head – which only went to show that, as Father Patrick was also fond of saying, appearances were deceptive. The eyes really were very odd when you looked into them. They were not grey at all, but one was brown with yellow flecks, and the other was blue with green flecks. They looked wicked, but rather exciting. She felt a funny feeling in the pit of her tummy, as if something was tugging at her and making her feel as if she was not really in control of herself.

Marguerite was so confused by this that the truth came out all in a rush.

'The ledgers are where the visitors' confessions are written down, and they're bound in red and they have a big gold crest on them and they're all locked up and there are simply thousands of them. There,' she finished triumphantly, knowing she had not told him the dangerous part – the bit about who was doing the writing. 'Now you know.'

'Show me.'

'I can't.' Her voice rose to a squeak.

'You're scared.' The voice was scornful.

She shook her head. 'No. I mean, they'll catch us. They're kept in Father Patrick's room.' She cheered up suddenly. 'The monsignor will be there, anyway, with Father Patrick. And we'd disturb them. So we can't.'

Silence descended as both contemplated the consequences of disturbing the monsignor and Father Patrick.

Then the young man said: 'I'd make it worth your while.'

'How?'

'Whatever girls like. Chocolates. A new dress.'

Marguerite considered this new notion. There were practical difficulties. The monsignor and his godson would be gone tomorrow, so there would be no time to go shopping. But he could give her some money, and she could buy these things for herself. Money was the most difficult thing of all to get hold of.

Meanwhile Ben had wandered back to the stone slab. She trotted after him and tugged his sleeve. 'I've had an idea. We could say I was taking you to see Abelard, if we were caught.'

'Who's Abelard?'

'My owl. A *chouette* – a tawny owl. He's mine – well, more or less. Nobody owns an owl really. He only hunts at night, but in the day he roosts in the writing-room,

103

which is right next to where the ledgers are. There's a thick curtain between. We could say we're going to visit him, and then wait till the coast's clear.'

Ben frowned and then shook his head. 'Too dangerous. They'd know we were snooping. My godfather's strict about things like that.'

'So's Father Patrick. Discretion in all things, is what he says.'

Marguerite gave the problem some more thought, and then brightened.

'Tonight. Surely we can do it tonight, when everyone's gone to bed. We can get a good look, even inside. There's a little clasp so they can be locked and put away, but I know where Father Patrick keeps the key. It's in a secret drawer in his desk.'

'Good,' Ben said firmly. 'It's a deal.'

He held out his hand for her to shake. Then he spoilt it completely by adding: 'And if you don't keep your part of the bargain I'll tell about the rude words and the peaches.'

She hit him then, punching with her small fists as hard as she could, with the thumb outside the knuckles, just like a boy.

'Steady on! That was a joke!'

He was laughing at her again, and holding her wrists. He could do this quite easily because he was much stronger than she was.

'Bugger off!' she yelled.

She was humiliated by this show of physical superiority, and so cross with him for thinking that she might *not* keep her side of any bargain that she ran away for the rest of the morning, leaving him to his own devices.

She appeared for the midday meal naturally, and was relieved to see that Ben had changed his clothes so that the peach-splatters did not give her away.

Ben grinned at her all through the meal, but she ignored him. No-one noticed anything – except her mother, who frowned at her warningly as if to tell her not to be so rude.

Rude, thought Marguerite. That was a good one, considering.

In the afternoon she picked the remaining peaches for her mother, while Ben sat on the wall, not saying anything, just swinging his long legs and watching her and sometimes looking at the stone again.

She wondered about the stone, and the marks on it; but the young man looked so thoughtful, and even a little sad, that she suddenly felt sorry for him, and did not want to bully him about what the scratches might mean.

She hoped it would all be explained by what was in the ledger.

Marguerite went to find Ben in his room just as soon as she was sure all the grown-ups had gone to bed.

The clock had just struck midnight when she crept down from her bedroom in the turret. A full moon illuminated the balconied courtyard where the visitors' rooms were. Ben's room was number seven. She knew that because she always helped her mother with the sweeping and polishing of the rooms for the visitors.

She opened the door very quietly, so that the hinges did not squeak.

'Ben? Are you awake?'

'Of course.' She could see his tall figure now, outlined in the moonlight from the window. He was fully clothed, and she was glad to see that he was wearing plimsoles. She herself was barefoot as usual.

'Viens alors.'

To his surprise, she led him downwards, rather than upwards to where the library, the refectory and the kitchen were situated, and into the bowels of the building.

There was another way up to the writing room which

meant that you did not have to go through the main part of the building at all. A kind of secret staircase had been tunnelled out of the rock, narrow but leading from the bottom to the top, with secret entrances all the way up. At the top was a door which had once led out on to the battlements, but this was now securely locked since the wooden platform which gave access to the roof had long since crumbled away in the weather. Immediately below was a secret entrance to the writing room. The staircase itself descended right down to the cave where the wellspring rose. In places the roof was so low that you had to duck your head, and at other times so narrow that you had to turn sideways.

Marguerite had discovered the entrance to the secret staircase by accident, the first time she had come into Father Patrick's room, before she had things to do like writing up the ledger. All the ways in were different, although you could work it out once you were inside. From the writing room, access was gained by putting light pressure on an iron nail head set flush to the wall which activated a pulley which moved one of the flagstones to reveal the entrance.

To reach the staircase from below, you had to go through the cave, the ancient sanctuary which was the real heart of the Hermitage. It was always very dark in there, even if you lit the oil lamps, and Marguerite was always a little scared. The place was certainly thoroughly infested with ghosts and the kinds of thing with which she would be familiar when she grew up to be a witch, which she fully intended to be.

The doorway, although it was more of a deep fissure in the rock, was right at the back, near the wellspring.

Marguerite was usually too frightened to venture into the cave, but it was all right with Ben close behind her. They moved quietly up the staircase until she stopped and felt with her fingers for the little iron handle which controlled the pulley. The stone swung up, and they were in the writing room.

Because everyone else had secrets and she had so few of her own, she did not tell Father Patrick or her mother what she had found. It was her secret. Hers and Abelard's. And now Ben's.

She could hear his sharp intake of breath as he came out suddenly into the cold air.

The moon was very bright through the arrow-slit, and the little room was flooded with light. The night air smelled fresh and clean after the stuffiness of the stairwell.

Marguerite glanced upwards into the rafters. Abelard had not yet gone hunting. The owl clattered his beak enquiringly, then coughed three times and brought up a neat little pellet of bone and fur, dropping it with perfect accuracy at Marguerite's feet.

He peered down, his huge dark eyes glistening. Then, noticing the unfamiliar figure behind his mistress, he hissed and rocked from side to side, as he always did when he was warning off an intruder.

'It's all right, Abelard. It's only me,' whispered Marguerite.

Abelard hopped down on to the writing-ledge, on the edge of which happened to be the silver inkwell. This tipped over, and the ink from the bottle splashed all over his beautiful speckled feathers.

In an instant, before she could save it, the inkwell fell on to the stone floor. The owl screeched and launched himself into the air, scattering droplets of ink. Marguerite watched in horror as the bird swooped around the room once, twice, and then headed out through the arrow-slit into the night.

'Now look what you've made him do!'

Marguerite and Ben gazed round at the mess. There were little glistening drops of ink all over the stone floor, and a large inkstain all over the writing shelf.

'Now what?' Ben whispered.

'Hush. Listen.'

The sound of footsteps echoed on the main stairwell. The door to Father Patrick's room opened. Marguerite and Ben froze.

'Who's there?' Father Patrick's voice floated through the curtain.

Marguerite was almost paralysed. Another moment, and Father Patrick would discover them both. She motioned to Ben to get back into the hidden passageway, and stepped boldly towards the curtain.

There was no help for it. She would have to sacrifice herself. There could be no possible explanation for nocturnal ramblings with Ben, even if she said it was to visit Abelard, who was not usually at home at night anyway.

Father Patrick would not be able to see clearly enough to know what a mess Abelard had made, so she could safely come back later and clean it up before the morning.

All these things went through her head as she stepped out through the curtain, nearly colliding with Father Patrick.

'Marguerite!'

'Only me, *mon père*.' Marguerite tried to make her voice as casual as possible.

'What ever are you doing, child?'

'Just checking up on Abelard. I was worried he might have been scared by the monsignor.'

'In the middle of the night?'

'I couldn't sleep.' She had taken his hand and was drawing the old man gently away from the danger area.

Father Patrick hesitated, moving back towards the curtain. 'But I heard a noise, *petite chouette*.'

'It was only me, *mon père*.' With her free hand, she crossed her fingers behind her back. 'I just stumbled on the stool.'

'Are you sure?' Father Patrick was peering at her. He fumbled for his glasses.

She squeezed his hand reassuringly. 'Of course. I'm going right back to bed now. I'm sorry I woke you.'

Father Patrick sighed. He seemed to accept this explanation. 'Off you go, then – and be quiet. The visitors are asleep.'

'Oui, *mon père*.' She crept back up the stairs and dived under the covers.

She left her curtains open so that she would wake with the light. At dawn, she crept back down to the writing-room, righted the inkwell, wiped it on her shorts – she would have to take them down to the stream and give them a good scrub – and set the inkwell back in its place on the writing shelf. Then she stripped off her cotton vest and carefully mopped as many as she could find of the tiny drops, drying now in little blobs of dark pigment.

The pigment lifted quite easily in little blisters, leaving no marks at all.

A thought struck her then. What if Ben had not gone back to his room, but waited until the coast was clear and done the deed without her? She went through into Father Patrick's room, moving as quietly as one of Abelard's mice, and opened the little drawer where the key which opened the ledgers was kept. The drawer was empty.

This meant either that Ben had it or that Father Patrick had thought it wise to remove it.

That morning she did not have an opportunity to question Ben, and all her attempts to get his attention in public were met with a raising of the eyebrows as if she was the village idiot pulling faces at the schoolmistress. After that it was too late, because the taxi arrived to take the visitors to catch the Avignon train.

There was a great fuss when the key was discovered to be missing, and Father Patrick suspected that it was she who had taken it. For the first time in her life, he was angry with her and sent her supperless to bed.

Most inconveniently, Father Patrick had to send to London for Monsignor Melton's key, and this Father Patrick kept on his rosary which was always either in his hand, or on his belt, or under his pillow at night. So that, for Marguerite, was the end of that.

She would never be able to learn Ben's secret now. And the worst of it was that he had not even handed over the bribe. It was too bad, too bad in every way.

Two weeks later an enormous parcel was delivered by the postman. Inside was the most beautiful box all done up in scarlet ribbon, and inside the box were chocolates, a huge quantity of them, some with little candied rose petals on top and others with tiny silver balls, and all of them perfectly delicious. Some of them were made in the shape of letters wrapped up in gold paper, and these had been used to spell out her name.

After that she had quite a lot of difficulty convincing both her mother *and* Father Patrick that she had done absolutely nothing to deserve it.

The arrival of the chocolates marked the start of all the trouble.

11

The Coming of Winter

Ask anyone who lived through the winter of 1956 in the uplands of Provence, and you will be told tales of the harshest winter in living memory. Perhaps the harshest there has ever been, since the sap froze in the taproots of the thousand-year-old olive trees, the earth turned as hard as iron, the shadows of wolves were seen in the forests, and birds which had not migrated to warmer climes were turned to stone where they perched. Nowhere was it harder than in the valley of the Hermitage and the village of Pernes-les-Rochers.

That same year, as the leaves fell and autumn turned to winter, Father Patrick had been concerned for the health of his beloved Thérèse.

He showed this in small ways. Even Marguerite, who was usually far too busy to pay attention to the doings of the adults unless they directly concerned her, noticed that her mother and the priest no longer argued so long and so hard. She noticed, too, that Father Patrick often tried to stop her mother going out on the night-calls which were most frequent when the autumn mists filled the valley. But her mother would smile and shrug and pack up her medicine basket just the same.

Marguerite added a new responsibility to her clerical duties: helping her mother with her ministrations. She was good at those small emergencies which needed quick neat fingers: stitching up a cut, finding the grit in an injured eye.

She did not yet have her mother's skills, but she was learning fast.

Thérèse's illness had not been a sudden thing. For some years now she had had trouble with her lungs. The story was all too familiar in those parts. There had been tuberculosis in the old days, and then there were new drugs to cure it. But during the war, when Thérèse had not looked after her own health as well as she had the health of those in her care, it had returned. There were others to treat; she had not had enough of the drugs to cure herself. A scarred lung made her vulnerable to winter's ills. Many of the villagers were prone to bronchial troubles, and each year some new infection was almost impossible to avoid.

Although Thérèse could cure others, she knew in her heart that she could not cure herself. Her lungs sometimes felt as if they would suffocate her, and there were times when she coughed blood.

Thérèse knew in her soul that she would never again see the spring. She had seen the hooded figure waiting in the shadows.

'Not yet,' she pleaded. 'The child's too young. It would be too cruel to take me now.'

The Hermitage was cold and damp in winter. Although the guest quarters were comfortable enough, and the kitchen was warmed by the range, the rest of the place was impossible to keep warm. The monsignor kept a tight purse string, and the landlord was reluctant to pay for repairs. In the village, too, the houses were damp and the roofs often leaked – although Father Patrick fought long and hard for each small concession for his parishioners.

The first snow fell in the week before Christmas, a scattering of feathery flakes floating down from a sky as blue as a blackbird's egg. The crystals settled as prettily as a lace handkerchief on the village's russet rooftops, tipping the Hermitage's ramparts with little caps of white.

The children were happy with the snow, building snowmen and tobogganing down the village streets.

Then the wind came, as sharp as steel, slicing the drifting snowflakes into an icy blizzard. Finally from the mountaintops a grey wall descended, as heavy as lead, rolling off the ridges into the valleys, dragging its blanket of whiteness, drifting across the narrow tracks which criss-crossed the high slopes, blocking the winding road which crested the ridge. Finally it reached the valley floor, freezing the water in the wells, icing the waterfalls, stopping the streams in their beds.

More snow fell, and froze, and fell again.

It happened so suddenly that there was no time to make preparations, no time to herd the animals indoors, or fasten down the shutters, or scatter salt in the streets.

For the first few days there was no communication between the Hermitage and the village – there could be none, since the snowdrifts were twenty feet deep. Finally a path was carved out, and Father Patrick and Thérèse could reach the villagers. Each morning the snow had to be cleared anew.

At the end of the third week the snowfall ceased, but still the wind did not abate. The icy tempest merely seemed to pack the snow more thoroughly into the corners and crevices.

Father Patrick opened the barns to shelter such of the village's domestic animals as had not already been herded inside, but there was little fodder with which to fill their bellies, and their bleating and crying grew weaker by the day.

The villagers themselves, shocked and battered, did what they could to help each other. Many of the families lacked food, and the Hermitage reverted to its ancient role of provider in times of need.

Fortunately Thérèse was a provident housekeeper. Each autumn she stocked her cellars with bacon flitches, salt-cured hams, sacks of dried beans, jars of olive oil, milled flour stored in big wooden barrels tarred to keep out the weevils. The cellar shelves were stacked with jars of preserved vegetables and fruit grown in the Hermitage's *potager*. Even so, Thérèse's generous storecupboard was soon emptying fast.

Each day, as long as the light lasted, Marguerite and her mother toiled up and down the cleared pathway between the Hermitage and the village, carrying bulging straw baskets of stores and medicines, slipping and sliding in the unaccustomed leather boots on the icy slabs, noses blue and faces numb with cold.

Marguerite was young and strong, and her body quickly recovered. Thérèse was not so resilient. So each evening, when it grew too dark to follow the path, Marguerite stoked up the kitchen range, melted snow for the drinking water, and set a pot to simmer on the hob.

'Can I bring you *la soupe*, maman?'

'A little, maybe.'

More often she was too tired to take more than a mouthful, so Marguerite ate her meal alone. By the time Father Patrick returned from his day's labours she was already fast asleep, curled up on a corner of the settle which flanked the fire. Father Patrick would carry her up to her bed, and was gone again by the time she woke.

Then one morning, as suddenly as it had begun, the snow vanished, the olive trees put out their fragrant little blossoms, and the whole world sparkled in sunshine.

Marguerite knew that something was wrong as soon as she came close enough to the Hermitage to smell the burning bones. Her mother always took great care not to waste anything, let alone burn good food.

She had been so sure that her mother would be better now, with the sunshine to warm her bones, that she had left her in the warm kitchen and had gone out into the olive groves with Abelard to pick the newly formed buds of dandelion for a fresh salad – the first of the year. Abelard had hopes of a meal of young dormice or maybe a baby rabbit.

Already the earth was preparing to put out new growth. There was a faint mist of green on the terraced wheat-fields, and the lapwings had returned from their southern quarters to pick over the winter plough. The first yellow brimstone butterfly floated past, and there was a hatch of water-boatmen on the stream.

Abelard was the first to tire of the amusement, lifting himself from his mistress's shoulder and swooping low over the valley on his way back to the Hermitage.

Marguerite followed him down, her tummy telling her it was time for her dinner.

The kitchen was warm and comfortable, and Thérèse had covered its stone floor with rag rugs made of little strips of cloth cut from the good parts of dresses and shirts and aprons which were too patched and darned to hold together any more. She made them in the winter evenings, and each rug reminded Marguerite of something or someone.

When Marguerite reached the kitchen, the pan on the stove was belching smoke. The stench was horrible. She dropped the basket of dandelions, tight little rosettes which rolled over the stones like fat green spiders, and pulled the pan away from the fire.

She looked around for her mother; and then she saw her, and understood why she had not seen her immediately. Her mother was sitting in a corner on the floor, looking like one of the rag rugs.

'Maman?'

It frightened Marguerite to see her mother sitting there, with her skirts spread all around her, like a scarecrow which has been blown over by the wind. Thérèse started coughing into her apron, coughing and coughing.

'Maman, maman, what's the matter?'

As she bent over her mother, Marguerite could see there were dark patches of blood on her apron, and her face was white and her eyes were as dark as mud.

She put her arms around her mother and held her tight to stop the shaking and the terrible coughing.

'Don't do that, maman. Please, maman.'

She was really scared now. Her mother usually smelled of lavender and wheatfields hot from the sun, and the herbs she used for her healing. But the smell rising from her mother's skin was thin and sharp, like a sick animal which is too weak to suckle. When you smelled that smell, you knew that in the morning there would be a little body stiff and cold in the straw.

Marguerite had seen dead people in her life. When people died in the village they were put into their coffins and brought up to the chapel. The dead people were always neatly dressed and looked comfortable in the buttoned satin, and very peaceful, with their eyes closed as if they were sleeping, and pink cheeks which were a bit brighter than they should have been because Madame Blanchette, who did the laying out, had been a little too lavish with her paints.

Before then, she had never thought her mother would die. Dying was something which happened to infants who were too weak to live, or when people were old, as old as Father Patrick. Not when they were young and strong like her mother.

When young children or babies died, people made the excuse that Mother Mary wanted them with her in heaven, or Baby Jesus wanted them for a playmate. When old people died, people said they had had a good life and it was a merciful relief that they were taken. In Marguerite's mind there could be no possible excuse for anyone taking her mother.

*　　*　　*

The day of the burned saucepan was a Sunday. Father Patrick said Mass early and took the village taxi to Valréas to fetch the doctor.

As soon as he arrived, Marguerite kept out of the way in a corner of the room so that she would not be noticed and could watch what was happening.

The doctor was old and whiskery, and smelled of *eau-de-vie*. He had striped trousers and a black coat, and a waistcoat with a watchchain with a big gold stopwatch, and when he took off his top hat there was a stethoscope curled inside.

'Well, well. What have we here?'

He tapped her mother's chest and listened. Then he put his fingers against her neck and pressed all round.

'Just as I thought. Bronchial pneumonia, complicated by residual tuberculosis. Keep the air circulating and the patient warm. One each of these three times a day.'

Father Patrick nodded but did not say anything. Marguerite could see his hands were trembling when he took the little bottles of pills.

'Beyond that,' said the doctor, 'I have no need to advise you of the efficacy of prayer.' Without even glancing at Marguerite in the corner, he added: 'And the girl. She must be removed from the source of infection.'

In spite of her protests, Father Patrick bundled her across the valley to sleep at mademoiselle the schoolmistress's house, which was cold and very tidy and very lonely. Not even Abelard would go with her.

For a little time after the doctor's visit her mother got better. But then she began to get worse again. This time it did not improve, not even when the doctor came from Valréas to give her a new kind of pill. She got weaker and paler, and her cough was thin and mean, like a little cat with croup.

Marguerite used all her knowledge to make her mother better. She rose early to gather the herbs which were good for the lungs – fennel and lungwort, the young leaves of pennyroyal and rue, mustard roots and nettle tops – and made them up with spring water, according to the proper recipes.

Her mother took small sips, and smiled at her. Then she would send her off on errands to keep her away as much as possible. Maybe to take her medicines to someone in the village, because there were others poorly with their lungs.

Father Patrick made up a bed for his housekeeper in the kitchen by the range, which was kept banked high all day and all night. He slept in the rocking chair just in case her mother needed him. Marguerite knew this because she always found him there when she came over to the Hermitage each morning.

Marguerite spent the nights at Mademoiselle's because the doctor said so, and her mother would not let her disobey him, but no-one was going to keep her away in the day, not the doctor from Valréas, not Mademoiselle, not Father Patrick, not God or the devil himself.

'Better today, maman?' Each morning she asked the question, although both of them knew the answer. It was their secret that they knew. So her mother would smile and nod. She smiled at Marguerite all the time because talking made her tired. The smiling made Marguerite feel both happy and sad. Happy because the smile told her how much her mother loved her, and sad because she knew nothing was doing any good.

Then Marguerite would chatter on about things which were happening in the valley, the young fruit forming on the olive trees, and how the daisies would soon be in bloom for her birthday, and there would be the posy from Father Patrick like always.

The moment that she knew for sure was when her mother took off the gold chain with the ring on it which she always wore round her neck. She did not wear a cross on the chain like all the Catholics did, but Marguerite knew that the ring was important because it had something to do with the man who was her father.

When her mother gave her the ring and chain, she knew that there was nothing she could do about what was happening. She took it without saying anything and slipped the ring from the chain.

Her mother's eyes were gentle with love.

'Shall I put it on my finger, maman?'

She knew by her mother's smile that that was what she had to do. It felt very loose, so she put it on her middle finger, the fattest one.

The hardest thing for Marguerite was not to cry. She knew that her mother did not want her to be sad; and she did not want Father Patrick to be sad, either.

Marguerite could not let her mother see her thinking sad thoughts because her mother could read them in her face. Humans show their thoughts on their faces with the little wrinkles and the way the mouth and eyes move. You never could tell what Abelard thought.

As the days passed, it seemed to Marguerite that you could get used to anything; as long as it happens slowly, you scarcely notice any difference. It was just that every day her mother seemed a little weaker, her body a little thinner, which was not surprising because she ate like a sparrow. She would take a little soup, if Marguerite coaxed her.

'Here, maman. A spoonful – just a spoonful.'

But the mouth would not close properly, and the liquid trickled down her chin.

Soon her skin, which had once been all gold and pink, was like transparent white silk, and you could see the shape of the bones. To Marguerite she was still as beautiful as she had always been. But it was as if she was a tree in autumn, slowly shedding all its leaves and sucking back the sap into its roots.

Her mother died in the night, just in the dark time before dawn. That was always when sick animals died. It was a bad time for all living things, even hunters like Abelard.

It was Abelard who came to tell her that her mother was dead. When she came down to make herself breakfast very early, when the schoolmistress's curtains were still drawn across the window, Abelard was there, on the window sill, waiting.

So when Father Patrick came to fetch her she already knew.

The anger was easier than the hurt which sat just behind it like a big black crow on a fence.

'I'm ready to come home now,' she said to Father Patrick very coldly.

Madame Blanchette was in the kitchen with her colouring-box in her hand.

'Bonjour, Madame Blanchette,' Marguerite said quite calmly.

'Ma pauvre petite . . .' said Madame Blanchette, putting down the box and holding out her arms.

But Marguerite walked straight past her to where the bed was by the kitchen range. There was something ugly in the bed. Not beautiful like her mother, but ugly.

'Don't be frightened, *ma petite*,' said Madame Blanchette. 'You can touch her. You can kiss her.'

Madame Blanchette had no business to be there. But, then, the thing in the bed had no business to be there, either.

Just the same, she did as Madame Blanchette suggested. She looked at it and touched it. She even kissed it. But the thing which was in the bed was not her mother at all. It was no more her mother than a dead goat which has fallen into a ravine is anything but meat for the crows.

'What have you done with my mother?' Marguerite asked Father Patrick.

He looked at her with a worried face. 'She's sleeping with the angels, *petite chouette*.'

'Then, get her back,' Marguerite said coldly.

Madame Blanchette was fussing around the thing which was not Marguerite's mother. Father Patrick was on his knees now, the rosary in his hand.

'Holy Mary, pray for us sinners,' said Father Patrick. But Marguerite knew that her mother was not a sinner.

'Your mother is in heaven now,' said Madame Blanchette.

'You're lying, Madame Blanchette,' Marguerite said with icy accuracy. 'My mother's a heretic and she can't go to heaven. Father Patrick said so himself.'

That was when she laughed, loudly and horribly, so that the noise bounced around her head, and off the walls, and set Abelard in a terrible fluster on his perch in the rafters.

'Hush, girl,' said Madame Blanchette, and Marguerite could hear how shocked she was, and she did not care.

'Marguerite, child!' Father Patrick stopped clicking his rosary, came to her and put his arms round her. He meant to embrace her, to hold her close and comfort her, but the cloth of his robe was wet and rough and smelled of blood. Marguerite could smell the blood and the fear, and it made her angry.

The anger was against the trick they had played on her. Father Patrick with his praying, and Madame Blanchette with her paints.

She was certain now that the thing in the bed was not her mother at all, but an imposter, a changeling like the goblin babies who were slipped into the cradles of unwary mothers.

Did they take her for a fool?

At that moment Marguerite hated Father Patrick. She hated him with all her heart. She fed the flames of her hatred with little twigs of anger, remembering small things done to thwart her, to trick her, to cheat her out of what was rightfully hers. Like sending her away at night to sleep with Mademoiselle. And surely her mother would have called for her, would have cried for her at the last?

She could have held her mother, rocked her, sung to her. The songs came so easily to her lips, the cradle songs from her childhood. Such comfort in the hands which say this is love, this is truth, such sweetness in a kiss.

And now it was too late. The thing which looked like her mother, but just as clearly was not, was not something she could take into her arms and comfort.

She could have done something that they could not. She was a wise woman, too, wasn't she? A young one, to be sure, but she had knowledge they did not. There were spells to be said, even if she had not yet learned the words.

If she had been there, if Father Patrick had not sent her away, this terrible thing would never have happened. Someone or something had stolen her mother and replaced her with a thing which had nothing to do with her mother. That at least was perfectly clear.

It was also perfectly clear that that someone was Father Patrick.

12

The Resurrection and the Life

On the day of the burial of Thérèse Leblanc, the sun rose as scarlet as a ripe strawberry, as ripe as the rage in Marguerite's heart.

The rays of the sun spread like a great crimson stain over the dripping slopes of the valley, and in the village of Pernes-les-Rochers life began again.

Children came out to play on shining cobbles. In back-yards, mothers hung out washing. Grandfathers dragged chairs on to new-washed stoops. There were solemn faces as the people exchanged news. There were three new widows in the village, and two more in the outlying farms. There were always more widows than widowers. The women lived longer, were tougher than the men.

When Father Patrick came out of the dark chapel into the rosy morning, his heart was as heavy as the lead which lined the coffin. All night long he had prayed for guidance, hoping for a sign.

His Catholic conscience told him that his beloved Thérèse must be buried outside the wall, where the heretics were laid to rest. His heart dictated otherwise. The thought of eternity without her was too hard to bear. It seemed that heaven had no intention of offering an opinion.

The Lord helps those who help themselves, thought Father Patrick. Thérèse had served the Hermitage well. These were circumstances under which rules might be bent. If he explained the situation to the warden, it was possible that an exception might be made.

He telephoned the monsignor's London number early, catching him unawares just as he was collecting his letters from the concierge's desk on his way to the barber.

'Out of the question,' said the monsignor. 'Rules are rules.'

This was an easy answer, costing no intellectual effort. But it was also true.

'Perhaps a special dispensation—'

'My dear Father, they're defrocking bishops for less.' This was also true. After eighteen years on the papal throne, that same Holy Father who had taken such a liberal view of the Führer's activities was in a mood to put his house in order, and that would not include sharing eternity with the riff-raff.

Unfortunately the call drew the monsignor's attention to practicalities.

'This housekeeper . . . I recall a daughter?'

'Indeed.' Father Patrick's voice was cautious.

'The child's of the Faith, I trust?'

Father Patrick breathed again. 'On that I can set your mind at rest, monsignor. I baptized her myself.'

'Excellent. Makes it so much easier.'

'Easier?'

'To make the necessary arrangements.'

'Arrangements?'

'My good man, the Hermitage is not a refuge for waifs and strays.'

Father Patrick digested this news with some surprise. He had rather thought that such indeed was the purpose of the sanctuary. However, discretion as always being the better part of valour, he held his tongue.

Worse was to come.

'You surely did not expect us to house the girl ourselves?' The clipped English voice did not hide its irritation. Such a situation might be considered at best unsuitable, at worst immoral. 'The Poor Clares run an orphanage in Avignon for deserving cases. As a Catholic, the girl will qualify. I'll have a word with the Mother Superior.'

Patrick O'Donovan's blood ran cold. 'Sure and that won't be necessary, your Reverence. There's her own flesh and blood will surely take her in.'

This was only half a lie. Many years had passed since Thérèse's brothers had last been in touch with their sister, and he had no idea what their views on their bastard niece might be, but family she certainly had.

'Family, eh? I see. In that case, we must pray your optimism is not misplaced.'

Remembering the women in his life whom he had lost, Patrick O'Donovan had no intention of breaking faith with the child he considered his own. Marguerite Dieudonnée Leblanc was no waif or stray. She was the child of his heart, and it would take more than the power of the Church to take her from him. As long as he had breath in his body, he would protect her, whatever the cost, even if he had to perjure his immortal soul to do it.

He did not yet know how high the cost would be.

At ten of the Hermitage's clock on the morning which followed Father Patrick's conversation with the warden, the funeral procession set off.

The line of mourners all in black made its way past the marble angels who kept watch over the cemetery, stepped through the gateway beneath the peach tree, and entered the heretics' graveyard.

Marguerite watched the coffin being lowered into the ground. The coffin looked very small and not very heavy because the thing inside was not her mother, but a changeling left by goblins.

A picture popped into her head. The picture was not her

mother; but it was not *not* her mother, either. It was something of its own, like nothing else she had ever seen or ever wished to see.

It sat on the edge of her mind, just out of her sight, but there just the same. It was something which looked quite like her mother, but was bony and hard, not curvy and soft. The colours of the thing were not the soft colours of flesh, but the yellow of mustard and blue like ink. There was red, too, fiery red, on the lips and the eyelids.

To get rid of the terrible thing which was not her mother, but was becoming more like her every second, Marguerite felt nothing, nothing except the sharp points of Abelard's claws digging into her shoulder.

Madame Blanchette had tried to persuade her not to bring the bird, but Marguerite had paid no attention. She never meant to pay attention to anyone again. Not to Father Patrick or the schoolmistress, or the mayor or the baker's wife, or any of those who had come to pay their last respects to the thing who was, had been her mother.

Father Patrick had decided that, whatever the warden's decision concerning the last resting place of the body, the spirit would come well recommended. Heretic or not, Thérèse would be blessed in Catholic language.

Marguerite, her head filled with nothing, listened to Father Patrick telling lies. They were like spells, Father Patrick's sayings. The words had no more meaning than newts' toes and moles' paws.

For behold I am the resurrection and life, said Father Patrick.

But Marguerite knew better. There was resurrection all right. But not for her mother. Resurrection was for the mourners all in black, and for the man who dug the graves but who otherwise kept the road verges neat. For the schoolmistress and even Célandine, whose bunches were done up in black silk ribbons as a mark of respect.

Yea, though we walk through the valley of the shadow

of death we shall fear no evil, said Father Patrick. But Marguerite knew perfectly well that everyone was scared out of their wits by the valley of the shadow of death, including her. You could see it on their faces, the faces of the mourners all in black.

Death was not what Father Patrick said it was. It was the thing which sat on the edge of her mind, and the sooner you got rid of it the better.

'Ashes to ashes, dust to dust,' sang Father Patrick as he threw a handful of earth on to the coffin. Small stones tinkled on to the brass fittings like little cymbals. One by one the mourners filed past, and more handfuls of stones rattled and bounced. Marguerite threw in some, too, but only because Madame Blanchette pushed her forward. Soon the coffin began to disappear beneath the black earth.

All the while the thing was still sitting there, just beyond her mind's eye, waiting. This time there was a difference. Now she knew for certain who it was. But now, instead of wanting to hold it in her arms, she wanted it to go away with all her heart.

Father Patrick made a long speech in which dearly beloved brethren, reconciliation and redemption featured strongly, ending in further assurances that Thérèse was a good and honourable woman, and the burial outside the wall did not preclude her admittance to heaven.

This was another of his lies. Even Abelard knew more than he did. Dead meat was meat. If you were Abelard, and it was dead, you ate it. If you were human, you buried it and put a stone on it to keep it down. This was the only difference. Worms ate the dead people, Abelard ate the worms, and then he spat out one of his pellets.

It was a comfort to think of her mother as an owl pellet – the first comforting thought she had had since her mother died, not least because she knew that the idea would horrify Father Patrick, let alone Madame

Blanchette. It was certainly an improvement on the thing which still sat just at the edge of her mind, waiting to pounce.

Back in her mother's kitchen, instead of hot chocolate and newly baked bread, there was Madame Blanchette's special orange brandy and a tray of hard little biscuits.

'Prends un peu. Ça fait du bien,' said Madame Blanchette, pouring out a little glass and offering it to Marguerite. Marguerite did not know if it did her good or not, but it certainly made her dizzy.

The mourners all came in and ate the biscuits and drank the brandy.

'Go with God,' said Father Patrick, which was his way of saying the party was over. And then everyone nodded and looked at Marguerite. Some people kissed her or squeezed her hand or said something about her mother being a wonderful woman and she could be truly proud. The women's faces were warm and smooth, the men's were scratchy and hurt her cheeks.

'*Pauvre petite*,' said the people, 'she's just a child. She'll soon recover.'

Neither of these things was true. Marguerite was no longer a child, and she had no intention of recovering.

Gone were the childish thoughts of yesterday. Yesterday was a hundred years ago. Today was today, the day her mother was buried in the heretics' graveyard under an unmarked stone.

Today was the first day of the wall.

Marguerite built her wall with care; brick by brick, reinforcing the ramparts until nothing and no-one could touch her.

The Hermitage had survived all through the centuries because it was a fortress, and Marguerite was a child of that fortress.

Father Patrick had once told her that the strongest walls were in the mind, so her walls were not built of bricks and mortar, or even of hewn stone. You could climb a real wall, or knock it down, or put a doorway through it. This wall was a citadel. She took her rage with her, for a hearth-fire, to warm her cold heart.

Father Patrick laid siege with gentleness. 'Marguerite, the Bible tells us to forgive one another.'

'Bugger the Bible,' said Marguerite.

Bugger the Bible or not, thought Father Patrick wearily, the visitors still had to be looked after. He set about putting his household in order. Madame Blanchette was engaged on a permanent basis to see to the cleaning and the cooking for the visitors, and, naturally and very discreetly, to help in the care of the orphan.

He wrote a letter to the warden, explaining that Marguerite had gone to live with her relations, so the orphanage would not be necessary.

At first Madame Blanchette tried to make friends with Marguerite. She hugged her and kissed her, and called her 'little darling' – which, in Marguerite's view, made her either a liar or a fool.

There was nothing darling about Marguerite Leblanc, particularly not what she felt about the housekeeper.

Madame Blanchette did all the things Marguerite's mother had done, except that everything she did came out wrong. She could not cook like her mother, or sew like her mother, or even sweep the floors like her mother. Let alone polish them to a shining brightness with wax which smelled of honey and spring flowers.

'I like everything neat,' said Madame Blanchette.

Neatness had never been a preoccupation of Thérèse Leblanc. Good food and clean linen, but not neatness. So Marguerite deliberately left trails of dirty clothes all over the stairs.

When Madame Blanchette had tidied the Hermitage from top to bottom, she did her best to tidy what remained of her predecessor.

'No sense in reminding ourselves,' said Madame Blanchette as she bundled up petticoats and handed them over to the rag-and-bone gypsy in exchange for a handful of clothes-pegs. Even the birthday daisies, all carefully pressed and tied with blue ribbon, only just escaped incineration in a bonfire.

Marguerite did everything she could to disrupt the household. Although Madame Blanchette soon ran out of patience, Father Patrick never did, and this was the most frustrating of all.

The only task she continued to perform, although with the worst possible grace, was the writing up of the ledger. Had Father Patrick but known it, this was the most gigantic concession she had ever made in her life.

She only did it because confession was very strong magic, and she was frightened that the thing which was not her mother but she now accepted was not *not* her mother might come back if she neglected her duties in that respect.

Father Patrick could only pray for the Marguerite he loved to be returned to him. But, even so, there were moments when he was at his wits' end.

One of these moments was when she insisted on attending a confirmation class for the younger children. The mystery of her religious fervour was soon explained.

'Excuse me, Father Patrick, but if the angels don't have willies how can they pee?' was followed by 'Excuse me, Father, but if St Joseph wasn't the baby Jesus' papa does that make Jesus a bastard?'

If her mother was a heretic, she was a heretic, too, and these were the most heretical things she could say. She was a little frightened that she could be so bold, but she did it anyway.

Célandine told her that her mother had said she had gone to the devil. 'Like mother, like daughter,' said Célandine's mother.

The villagers, particularly those parents whose youngsters bore giggling witness to Marguerite's scandalous behaviour, agreed that allowances had to be made.

'She's taking it hard,' said the baker's wife, who had a forgiving nature.

'Deserves a spanked bottom,' said the mayor's wife, who did not.

'Wait till I get her back in the classroom,' said Mademoiselle.

Father Patrick half-expected Marguerite to refuse to go back to school. But Marguerite never did what was expected. She returned to the classroom, but not because it was what she wanted. She did it to get away from Father Patrick and Madame Blanchette, and that was all.

The schoolmistress soon noticed that Marguerite was making no progress at her lessons. In class she was silent, in the playground withdrawn, and when the mothers of the village tried to include her in their family celebrations her refusals were downright rude.

'Fuck off,' said Marguerite.

Things did not improve in the summer, when the holidays came. She would come down to the kitchen early in the morning, cut herself a big slice of bread and cheese, and then vanish into the hills until sunset.

In the evening she refused to eat her *souper* with Father Patrick, but filled a bowl for herself and immediately took it up to her room.

'Can't we be friends?' pleaded Father Patrick.

'I can't imagine what you mean, *mon père*,' was Marguerite's reply, but the green eyes glittered.

When the autumn term brought no improvement in her schoolwork, Father Patrick began to despair. Perhaps he had been too hasty, too confident in thinking he could provide what the young girl needed. It seemed as if the healing would never begin – as if the child had abandoned everything, as if the loss of her mother had sapped her strength, destroyed her will.

But Father Patrick could not have been more wrong. Marguerite had never felt stronger. Her will had never been firmer. Her wall had never been higher.

And now Christmas was coming, and for the first time in all her life she would be truly alone in her citadel.

Alone, that was, if you did not count Father Patrick, whom she hated, and who was anyway kept very busy with Mass and paying visits to the old people with Madame Blanchette's horrible soup; and Abelard, who was not at all interested in Christmas; and Madame Blanchette herself, who fortunately would go home to her family for the Gros Souper of Christmas Eve, which meant she would have a terrible headache for days.

This year Marguerite did not want Christmas to come at all.

13

The Night of the Réveillon

'All ready for the Réveillon, *ma petite*?'

'To the devil with the Réveillon,' said Marguerite. But she said it under her breath, so Father Patrick could not hear.

This caution was necessary because Madame Blanchette, finally tiring of her rudeness, had told her that the punishment for insolent children was to be sent to the orphanage.

'You be careful, my girl,' warned Madame Blanchette, 'or it'll be the convent for the rest of your days.'

To prove her point, and in the strictest secrecy, she had shown her a paragraph in a letter from the warden she had found while tidying up Father Patrick's desk.

Marguerite stared down at the terrible words.

'On that other matter which concerns us both. Should there be any further problem with the child, I have secured an assurance from the Mother Superior that a place can be made available at the orphanage.'

Further problem? Orphanage? Little shivers of fear ran down her spine. The fear was even greater than the anger she felt against Father Patrick.

This was not an auspicious beginning to the feast of Christmas.

'It'll be a grand time, surely it will,' prophesied Father Patrick with an optimism he was far from feeling.

'It won't,' muttered Marguerite, but under her breath. Just the same, she volunteered to help Madame Blanchette in the kitchen with the fasting supper of salt cod and sage broth which they were to eat before Midnight Mass. In Provence the Réveillon came in two parts, the fasting supper before and the feasting dinner afterwards, and salt cod was essential to any fast.

'Hurry up, girl,' said Madame Blanchette, well satisfied with herself for taking matters into her own hands. The poor Father had been planning the celebration for weeks, making secret preparations and laying in stores. The girl would just have to mend her manners now, take what was given and be grateful.

There were garlands of ivy and yew bound round the beams. The table had been polished and laid. In the hearth, an enormous pine-log smouldered.

Father Patrick was bustling around the dining table when Marguerite had finished helping in the kitchen and Madame Blanchette had gone home. There were three places laid at the table, the third being for the stranger who must always be expected at the Réveillon.

'Just in case,' said Father Patrick with a cheerfulness he was far from feeling.

'Oui, *mon père*,' said Marguerite. But her face told him that that stranger was a lie, just as angels were a lie, just as Christmas was a lie.

Father Patrick sighed. It seemed that nothing which had anything to do with the Réveillon, or anything else for that matter, could bring a smile to her sombre little face – not even thoughts of the feast which was to come after Mass when the Advent fast might be broken. Not partridges stuffed with raisins and roasted in butter, nor the anticipation of the cinnamon-scented apple pie which was to follow. Not even that the copper kettle had been polished and set on its tripod ready for the wine to be mulled with sugar and spices.

Father Patrick missed his beloved Thérèse almost as much as Marguerite. Not a day passed in which he did not feel her loss. Not a day passed in which his beloved child's pain did not cut him to the quick. But he hoped and prayed that this night would mark a new beginning for them both.

'Candles. We must light the candles.'

The old man bustled around with a taper. Marguerite, her green eyes glittering, watched him with hate in her heart. Because he could not see very well, Father Patrick kept missing the wicks, but she did not offer to do it herself.

It was ten months and five days since her mother had died. She could not help what she felt, the little burning core of anger inside her, now further fuelled by what she had read in the letter. Anger and fear.

The Réveillon fed her anger, which blazed anew as the tapers were touched to the wicks and the great refectory blazed with light.

Father Patrick chattered and smiled, pretending everything was as usual.

'Have you set out your *sabots*?'

'Non, *mon père*.'

Her *sabots* – the wooden shoes which everyone wore in winter to work in the fields – were supposed to be set ready by the hearth for the presents to be tucked inside. There were always three gifts for good children: something to wear – a new woolly hat or a warm pair of mittens; something to use – a box of colouring crayons or a pencil case for school; and something nice to eat – a bar of chocolate perhaps, or a bag of sugared almonds.

'Why not, Marguerite?'

'I'm too old for that kind of thing, *mon père*.'

Marguerite had always loved finding the presents when she came back from Mass, but now she wanted nothing at all.

She knew that Father Patrick was only pretending that he did not hear what she said. He could hear perfectly well – almost as well as Abelard, who was keeping well out of the way. Abelard did not like candles and tinsel and noise.

'Anyway,' she went on, as if it was the least important thing in the world, 'I don't believe in the Réveillon.'

She knew that Father Patrick was longing for things to be as they were, and she was having none of it. Just the same, she had had enough of a fright to change into the velvet dress Madame Blanchette had made for her and to wear her shiny new shoes, and this reminded her of the new betrayal.

'Or the *candelou*.' This was the log in the grate which was supposed to smoulder all through the year. She kicked it, just to explain what she meant.

'Or the stranger at the feast.'

She paused.

'And I don't believe in angels, either.' She added that last bit to remind him that she had not forgotten the day her mother died.

Father Patrick looked at her quietly, his face very serious. Then he rummaged in his soutane and found a stub of candle. He lit it and set it in the window.

This, too, was an old custom. It told the dead that they could depart in peace, and the newborn must be made welcome.

There was a prayer which went with it. It was usually Marguerite's special duty to say it, but tonight she was silent.

Father Patrick waited for her to do so, and when she did not move he said himself, very deliberately and slowly:

'Grant to us mortals a child at the door,
That we be not less, that we be not more.'

Then he motioned to Marguerite to take her place at the table so that he could say grace.

After that he said a short prayer for the dear departed. Marguerite thought how stupid this was. She knew now that when people were dead they were not dear at all, but a bundle of bones which could not depart anywhere.

They ate the fasting meal in silence. Afterwards it would be time for Mass. Marguerite had not been to Mass to please Father Patrick since the day of the funeral. And then it was not a Mass, not a proper one anyway.

When they had finished the meal, she watched the old man as he fussed around the table opening paper bags and boxes to fill the dishes which made up the thirteen desserts. These were little treats which were not to be eaten until after Mass was over.

There were twelve, one for each disciple, and the thirteenth, the *fougasse*, a sweet bread flavoured with orange-blossom and shaped like a big flat leaf, for the Enfant Jesu. Deliberately, knowing Father Patrick was waiting anxiously for her approval, Marguerite examined each of the little dishes in turn. Sultanas and raisins, almonds and hazelnuts, two kinds of nougat – one white, one black – yellow apples and fat speckled pears whose stalks had been sealed with a little cap of scarlet wax, oranges from the Marseilles market, bunches of little shrivelled grapes saved from the harvest, thick apricot-fleshed slices of winter melon made up eleven of the dishes.

The twelfth depended on the village – each had its own speciality, and a woman who came from another village always provided her own. Thérèse's village, being on the edge of the high forests, specialized in *marronettes*, chestnuts candied in honey.

You could not buy them in Pernes-les-Rochers, or even in the market at Valréas. The candying took three days: the chestnuts were scalded, skinned and threaded on button twine, and each day they were dipped in a pan of boiling honey till they were as shiny and brown as conkers.

All through Christmas week, when her mother was

there and not Madame Blanchette, the kitchen had been filled with the perfume of the candied nuts. Her mother said they were a labour of love, and to Marguerite they tasted of love – sweet, fresh and perfumed as her mother's kisses.

Eagerly she sought the twelfth dish. Most terribly, most poignantly, it was heaped not with the honeyed nuts, but with sticky golden dates. Marguerite could feel the misery rising in her throat.

'No chestnuts,' said Marguerite.

As soon as the words escaped, she wanted to bring them back. They were such small words, yellow and mean, that even Marguerite was ashamed of herself. Like little yellow scorpions they scuttled across the flagstones and were gone.

The tears began then. The tears of grief and anger. The tears which were too grievous and angry to share with anyone.

Her heart beating so loud that she thought it might burst, Marguerite ran from the room, her shoes clattering on the stone stairwell, down through the empty rooms and through the echoing hall until the cold air of the night rushed at her like a wave.

It was approaching time for Mass. The bell tolled.

Through the darkness she could hear voices, see the torches and lanterns swaying as the villagers made their way up to the Hermitage. Soon they would all be in the church, celebrating the miraculous birth to a miraculous mother of a miraculous baby.

That, too, was a lie.

She must find somewhere to hide. In the dim moonlight, she made her way through the cemetery to the meadow beyond, the meadow where her mother's body lay. She was not scared of ghosts. If there were no angels, there were most certainly no spirits to haunt her. Things which were dead were dead and never came back.

At the end of the meadow was a stone-built barn, empty through the summer but used to store hay in winter. Ever since she could remember, it had always been Marguerite's haven, her refuge in times of trouble.

The barn was huge and cavernous, stacked high with hay-bales. She crept into the hay, pushing her body into the depths like a rabbit burrowing into a hedge. She needed to feel the sharpness of the thorns among the dried stalks of grass. There were herbs which smelled bitter when she rolled the leaves in her fingers.

She remembered the bitter stench of the burning bones on that day when she first knew her mother was going to die.

Her rage was replaced by hurt, not for her mother but for herself, for the terrible loneliness of having no-one and nothing to love. Her body felt all hot and steamy like the earth before a thunderstorm.

Célandine's father had said her mother had gone to the devil. If that was so, Marguerite fully intended to join her.

She closed her eyes, tasting the saltiness of her own tears. Merciful oblivion descended on her misery.

14

Meeting the Devil

Marguerite woke suddenly. Something or someone was breathing very close to her.

She could smell goat – not the stale goaty smell which hung about Father Patrick's skirts when he had been out visiting certain parishioners, but a mixture of warm fur and fresh milk.

The moon was shining through the narrow vents which kept the barn aired, and she could see the devil quite clearly.

He was leaning on one of the wooden cattle-stalls, the lower part of his body out of sight so that she could not see the furry legs, the cloven hoofs and the tail.

'So you're awake, are you?' said the devil, for it could only be he, with his horns buried in his curly hair.

'If I wasn't, I would be now,' said Marguerite curtly, to show he could not scare her. The devil did not frighten Marguerite at all. She was quite beyond fear and quite happy for the devil to pick her up and carry her away, just so long as he took her to her mother.

'There's my girl.' The devil spoke in the patois, which did not surprise her. The only thing that *did* surprise her was that the devil was not an old man, but quite young – a bit older than her, but not much.

The devil came out from behind the stall, so that she could see him properly. He stopped a few yards away from her, and squatted down on his haunches, like a wild animal which likes to keep its distance.

His body was one-sided; he had funny eyes, of a golden colour with dark flecks, and a terribly dirty face. She could not see if his legs were hairy because they were covered by rolled-up trousers several sizes too big – presumably to accommodate his tail. Out of the trousers stuck not cloven hoofs but very dirty feet which were all crabby and cracked from going barefoot, with toenails which turned over like a donkey's which needed clipping. A goatskin vest with the fur turned inwards completed his apparel.

The devil fumbled in a bag on his belt, pulled out a battered tin and took out a lump of tobacco and some papers. Neatly for someone who looked so clumsy, he rolled himself a very thin cigarette. When he licked the paper to close it, Marguerite noticed that his tongue was pink, whereas she had half-expected it to be black.

The devil examined his cigarette with approval. Then he looked inside the bag again, found a flint, a little wheel and a bit of cotton wick. He struck a spark and lit the cigarette.

'Like a puff?'

'No, thank you,' said Marguerite politely.

This was temptation, or so she thought, and she was not such a fool as to give in to it.

'Suit yourself,' said the devil. He shrugged, and she could see that one shoulder and one leg were withered and very thin, which was what made him look lopsided.

'What's your name and why were you crying?' asked the devil.

She remembered immediately that it was Christmas and she was all alone, and she could not stop a small sob.

'There, there,' said the boy-devil, and he darted forward and wiped her face with the back of his hand, which smelled of hot tobacco and goat. The boy-devil put his face very close to hers. Under all the dirt, it was a surprisingly nice freckled face. She still could not see the horns, although she knew they must be there somewhere.

'I can't d-do anything', said the boy-devil, 'if you won't t-tell me what's the matter.'

Marguerite stopped crying, partly because she was surprised that the devil had a stutter, and partly because the devil must already know all about her.

'You should know without me telling you. You should be *glad* I'm crying.'

The boy-devil looked at her with his head on one side and his eyes all yellow and narrow. After a moment he said: 'Who d'you think I am?'

'The devil of course,' she answered indignantly.

The boy-devil threw back his head and laughed. He had long white teeth, and a very loud laugh which ended in a belch and a hiccup.

He said: 'I'm sorry to disappoint you, mademoiselle.'

'Who else could you be?' Marguerite asked crossly, and then listed all the reasons why he could only be who she thought he was. 'So, you see, you can't fool me,' she finished in triumph.

The boy-devil stopped laughing and made his face serious.

'Would you be d-disappointed if I told you I'm only the g-goatboy?'

'No, because I wouldn't believe you.' She had a vested interest in his being the devil since she was just about to bring up the matter of her mother, in the light of Célandine's words.

'Suit yourself.' After a moment he added: 'I c-can be very wicked.'

He sucked hard at the cigarette and puffed the smoke out in three or four perfect rings, like a line of little haloes.

Seeing that Marguerite was still doubtful, he added: 'If you d-don't believe me, ask Babette.' He chucked a grimy thumb towards the far corner of the barn, where the cow-stalls were.

'Babette?'

So that was it. The boy-devil had a girl-devil certainly. And no doubt they had lots of baby devils.

'Babette. See for yourself. She won't bite you.'

A faint moaning rose from the corner. Whatever it was, it did not sound dangerous.

Marguerite scrambled out of the hay-bale, dusted down her velvet dress, and went over to see what was making the noise.

'Oh!' Marguerite began to giggle.

An elderly nanny goat, clearly in the final stages of labour, peered up at her from the straw.

'What's so funny?'

Marguerite stopped giggling immediately. 'I'm sorry.' She hesitated. Then she blurted out: 'It's just – I thought she might be your girlfriend.'

The goatboy burst out laughing. He had a lovely laugh which made his eyes go crinkly. 'Did you indeed? I don't know what Babette would have to say about that. She's certainly in the family way, if that's what you mean. But it wasn't me who g-got her there. She's t-too old for me, for a start.'

Marguerite giggled again. The village boys always made rude jokes about goats and goatherds, but this boy did not seem to mind. She thought she might like him. He had broad shoulders, even if his body was lopsided; and if he had a good wash and brush-up he would really be quite handsome. She even liked his stutter.

He smiled at her. It was a nice smile. He held out his grubby hand. 'I'm T-Tonin.'

She shook it, feeling a little silly at the formality of it all. 'And I'm Marguerite. Marguerite Dieudonnée Leblanc.'

'I know. You're the princess in the tower.'

He had it all worked out, it seemed: the party dress, the

no-longer-clean white socks, the ribbon in the hair. He added: 'I'm afraid we – Babette and me – we d-disturbed your Réveillon.'

She shook her head. 'Not at all. I always come here when I want to be by myself.'

She waited for his apology. After all, *she* was at home, and the goatboy and his charge most certainly were not.

She did not get it. Instead the goatboy – clearly she could hardly argue with that now – was busy with the nanny goat. The animal's flanks were heaving, and her breathing was quick and harsh. She was clearly in trouble.

Marguerite squatted down in the straw beside the labouring nanny.

'There, there, Babette,' she said.

She put out her hand, following the curve of the belly. At her touch, the animal's breathing calmed. She moved her hands expertly, pressing here and there, assessing the position of the unborn kid.

Usually Tonin would not have let anyone else within a mile of his precious flock – let alone a female. But this one was clearly different. There was a wiry strength in the slender fingers as they worked over the distended belly; more than strength, there was knowledge.

Tonin knelt down beside her.

She said: 'A breech.'

She could hear the goatboy's sharp intake of breath. A breech-birth was bad. It meant that, even though the contractions were fierce, the head had not engaged in the pelvic girdle and the mother could easily bleed to death. If the unborn kid was not pulled out, it would certainly suffocate.

She said: 'Have you tried to turn it?'

'N-no.'

'Look, goatboy' – her voice was impatient – 'if this was a *human*, you'd have to turn the baby. Show me your hands.'

He spread out broad dirty fists. She shook her head. 'Too big.'

Marguerite was already rolling up her sleeves.

'I've done it masses of times – for humans, of course. You'll have to help. It'll scare her. Hold her here – round the haunches.'

Tonin obeyed. Without a moment's hesitation, Marguerite plunged both arms up the exposed birth-channel. The nanny heaved in protest. Tonin found himself struggling with the plunging goat.

'Good girl, Babette, good girl.' Marguerite's voice was as gentle, as soothing as if she had been talking to a human mother. 'Patience, my beauty. We're nearly there.'

Blood and mucous spurted. The goat gave a cough, a heave, and surged over on to her side.

'That's my girl. . . .' She talked on softly while her hands worked steadily upwards.

It seemed to Tonin an age until the young girl's wiry arms emerged – and when they did they were streaked with dark red blood and a gluey white liquid. But gripped in her strong fingers were four little hoofs, transparent and per-fect. Just behind, a damp furry body slid smoothly through the narrow opening – until it could slide no further. The oversize head had caught in the cradle of bone.

Marguerite tensed her muscles again and pulled with all her might.

'I can't!' she gasped.

Her face was beaded with sweat, and Tonin could see the neck-muscles knotting under the strain. He put his arms around her waist and added his own lopsided strength to hers.

For a long moment they struggled, locked in the battle for birth. Just then, the nanny gathered herself for the final contraction. Such was the force with which the kid was ejected that the two midwives fell backwards in a tangle of glistening membrane.

Of the four of them, the kid was the only one who was not in the least surprised. While Marguerite and Tonin rocked with relieved laughter and the nanny bleated weakly, the tiny creature climbed on to spindly legs and began to nuzzle its exhausted mother for the teat.

Marguerite settled back in the straw. It was good. She had not failed. It was Christmas. A new creature had been born. And she might have found herself a friend.

She watched with a professional eye while Tonin tied the kid's umbilical cord and pulled out the afterbirth – a tangle of blue-black veins in a shining caul. This he laid by the new mother's head. The nanny sniffed at the glutinous mess and then began to nibble at it hungrily.

Marguerite watched this development with interest.

'What's she doing that for?'

'It's g-good for her. Like medicine.'

Marguerite looked at Tonin with new respect. He had not been much good as a midwife, but he certainly knew things she did not. Other people, she thought to herself, might consider such an issue as eating an afterbirth perfectly disgusting.

She could not imagine why, but she knew they would – particularly Madame Blanchette. She wondered if it would be good for humans to eat their afterbirths. The goat certainly seemed to enjoy her meal. After all, it had kept the baby goat alive, so it must be full of everything you needed.

'Animals are such sensible creatures,' she said thoughtfully. 'They know exactly what they should do, and they just do it. Not like people.'

'That's why I prefer goats to people.' Then, seeing the green eyes narrowing, he added hurriedly: 'M-most people, that is. One or two are all right.'

'Like me?'

Tonin grinned. 'Like you, M-Marguerite D-Dieudonnée Leblanc.'

'Tonin?'

She was going to say it would be so much more sensible if people behaved more like goats. Then no-one would have to mind so much about things, or blame people, or be anything except exactly who they were. Except it was not quite like that. People needed friends as much as they needed families. People needed companionship and someone of their own age to mind about whether they lived or died.

That was it, then. The goatboy certainly had a family and a home and brothers and sisters and a father and mother.

She said: 'You'll be going home now. To your family. As it's the Réveillon.'

'No.'

'Why not?'

'I don't have a home. Just a place where I live, where I look after my goats.'

'I don't mean that,' Marguerite persisted. 'I mean your real home. The place where your mother lives – and your father and brothers and sisters, too, of course,' she added hastily.

He did not answer immediately, but made a fuss rolling and then lighting another cigarette.

When it was properly lit, he said: 'I'm a kind of orphan.'

'You're either an orphan or you're not,' Marguerite said sharply.

The boy blew another perfect smoke ring. 'Half-orphan anyway. My father died when I was' – he counted on his fingers – 'eight. We had no money, and my mother had to sell our house to buy food. She took my little sister Annie and went away to find work in a big house down on the plain. I've never been there. I'm a cripple, so they wouldn't have me.'

Marguerite did not quite know what to say about this, but the boy went on: 'What about you? You should be having your Réveillon at the Hermitage. Everyone knows Father Patrick looks after you now your mother's dead.'

Dead. *Yes*, she thought, *my mother's dead*. He had said the word perfectly naturally, so it sounded quite ordinary. People did not use words like 'dead' or 'death'. They said 'passed on', or 'departed', or 'late lamented'. But *dead* was quite right. At least it was not complicated with who was or was not to be saved, who might or might not be buried where, or heaven or hell, or all the stuff that people had in their heads and – worse still – tried to push into hers.

She made up her mind.

The goatboy did not have anywhere to go, so the goatboy could be their stranger, the stranger that Father Patrick was waiting to welcome to the Réveillon. It was as plain as the nose on your face that it was meant to be.

'Tonin?'

The odd eyes met hers. He had such a nice look in his eyes now. It was a kind look, a look which made her feel all soft inside, so that she blushed a little. Confused, she said it all in a rush.

'I just wondered – would you like to share the Réveillon with us? With me and Father Patrick? Mass will be over now, and we have roast partridges stuffed with walnuts, and apple pie. We can bring Babette and the baby; I'm sure Father Patrick won't mind.'

Tonin smiled at her. 'I'd be honoured, p-princess.'

It was the first time a boy – a young man even – had ever called her anything as nice at that. It was not as if he was teasing her, but as if it was a natural thing to call her. So perhaps he knew that she was special, might be willing to make her his friend.

'You bring Babette,' she said happily, 'and I'll carry the baby.'

In a little glow of excitement, her unhappiness quite forgotten, Marguerite trotted ahead of the limping goatboy and his burden. The newborn kid was light in her arms, and she was happy for the first time in a year. She felt warm and content inside – almost as if she was loved. Perhaps friendship was what was meant by love. Perhaps her mother was indeed with the angels, and she had asked them to send a friend.

Above in the Hermitage the light of the candle flickered to welcome the two young people home.

Angels might be there, too. Perhaps there might be angels after all.

15

Life with Tonin

To outside observers the alliance between the goatboy and the girl from the Hermitage might have seemed odd, but to the two young people it was entirely natural. Both were lonely. Both were outsiders. Each needed the other like parched earth needs the rain.

'A goatboy is not a fit companion for *une jeune fille bien élevée*,' said Madame Blanchette every time she encountered Tonin – a not infrequent occurrence since *monsieur le curé* had made it quite clear that the goatboy was always welcome at the Hermitage.

'I won't hear a word of that nonsense, Madame Blanchette,' scolded Father Patrick. 'Tonin shall come and go as he pleases.'

Until Marguerite came into his life, Tonin had never had a proper friend, still less a friend as useful as Marguerite. She knew where and when to gather the herbs which could heal a lame-footed billy or strengthen a newborn kid, and she prepared a special ointment for him to rub on his withered leg when it ached in the winter cold.

At other times it was Marguerite who needed Tonin's help. Like the time soon after the night of the Réveillon when Abelard went missing. As the twilights lengthened into spring, the owl did not always return to the Hermitage from his night-time forays. One morning, after the owl had been absent for two days running, Marguerite found not one but two owls roosting in the dim recesses of the roof.

Abelard's female was wild and shy, and took flight immediately, blundering clumsily around the refectory until she found the arrow-slit which led her to freedom.

Abelard pined, refused to go out hunting, but frantically tried to balance a collection of bits and pieces of feather and straw in one corner of his roosting beam.

'We need a nesting box,' said Father Patrick firmly.

Tonin made the wooden box to Father Patrick's instructions, sawing and hammering until the old priest was satisfied that the entrance hole was the right size and there was plenty of room inside.

'We don't know how many babies,' said Tonin.

'Plenty,' said Marguerite.

The box was fixed conveniently near the arrow-slit. Meanwhile Tonin went searching for the female. He used lime on a branch and a little tethered tomtit to catch her – but he kept this to himself. In his experience, girls were silly about things like that. This was before he had realized that Marguerite was different.

The female was caught, installed and the entrance hole closed for three days, so that she could get used to her new home and new husband. Marguerite set up one of the olive-pruning ladders – the ones with the narrow top which did not damage the delicate growth at the top of the tree – so that she could monitor the romance.

Abelard did not particularly mind, but his wife got very angry indeed, so Marguerite was careful only to inspect when the parents were out hunting.

Sure enough, five eggs were laid, one at a time with two days between each, and soon there were five little owlets for the pair to keep supplied with furry prey. They hatched in sequence, so the eldest was much bigger and fatter than the youngest.

Tonin explained the mystery. If it was a bad year and

there were not many mice for the parents to catch, the firstborn owlet simply ate the youngest, and so on, each one disappearing inside the other like Russian dolls until there was only a big fat one left.

'Disgusting,' said Madame Blanchette, who did not approve of Tonin or Abelard, and still less of the mess the owlets made when they stuck their small backsides out of the nesting box and squirted their droppings all over the walls of the writing room.

Marguerite was delighted with the whole enterprise, and Father Patrick gave her a large Irish umbrella to put up when she was taking dictation in the ledger.

By midsummer the owlets were fledged and the female gone. When the leaves began to fall, it was time for Abelard to snooze all day on his perch and for Marguerite to go back to school.

Tonin had taken Marguerite's education seriously from the outset. He knew from Father Patrick that she had not been doing any work, so he started to coax her to return to her studies.

He carried her books to school in the morning, and was there waiting for her in the afternoon when the class came out for the day.

'I p-promised Father Patrick,' he said.

He did not seem to mind at all that Marguerite's schoolmates made fun of his stutter and the way in which he thought very carefully before he spoke on any subject he did not understand. Some of the ruder girls would make a show of clipping a clothes peg on their nose when they saw him coming. They soon tired of it, though, because Tonin would just grin and wave, and hobble off back to his flock.

Marguerite did not mind at all that Tonin smelled of goat. She knew that to Tonin his goats were his people, and he cared about them as much as people cared about their children.

For his part, Tonin was proud of Marguerite's education: of the beautiful copperplate writing and the English that Father Patrick had taught her, of the way she could do complicated sums in neat columns or even in her head, and could read history books, quote poetry and reel off the names of all the important philosophers.

'You must work hard and learn, Marguerite – not like me. You're clever. You're going to be someone in the world. You need an education.'

'I don't want to be someone in the world,' said Marguerite, narrowing her green eyes crossly. 'Why don't *you* want it if education's so important?'

'Goatboys don't need education.'

That was true enough, up to a point. Tonin did not need anything to make him better than he was at what he did. He was the most responsible goatherd in all the mountains of Provence.

'You know plenty of things, Tonin – things that are much more interesting than they teach you in school.'

This was also true. Book-learning was one thing – and that was all it was. Tonin understood matters far beyond her schoolmates' imagination. He could read the messages the wind brought, follow a pathway guided only by the stars, knew by the movements of birds when a forest fire might be expected, where the night herons roosted and how to track a fox to its lair.

These were part of what Marguerite called his wolf-tricks – Tonin's peculiar way of assessing what was happening in the world around him. Wolf-trickery applied to people just as much as to his flocks. He could tell by the smell on people's bodies if they were happy, sad, frightened or ill, or just liked the look of something they saw. And he knew from the little movements of people's faces and the way they arranged their bodies whether they were lying or telling the truth. This knowledge came partly because he was what the village called an *idiot savant* – a wise fool – and partly because he understood his flocks so well.

Tonin did not want anyone else to know about his wolf-tricks – although he did not mind obliging Father Patrick when the old man thought one of his visitors was not telling the whole truth.

'Why can't anyone else know?' asked Marguerite, who was all for spreading the news round her schoolmates that her new best friend was as good as a fairground fortune-teller.

Tonin considered the matter carefully. 'Because p-people are scared of wolves.'

'*I'm* not.'

Tonin grinned. 'You're not scared of anything, *ma belle*.'

That was true. She had had to learn not to be scared. Apart from Tonin, there was no-one to look out for her, now that her mother had died, and Father Patrick was a priest not her real father.

After her thirteenth birthday, the age at which most of her schoolmates began to go steady, Pierre the butcher's apprentice began to pay court to her. He was a stocky fifteen-year-old with a face as beefy as his trade. One day he asked her to go to the Saturday cinema with him in Valréas.

A few of the girls – Célandine, for instance, who looked like butter would not melt in her mouth – made the running. Girls like that were known as *bicyclettes*, a reference to saddles and pedals which needed no explanation.

Just the same, she had noticed that Célandine was very popular. The village boys were always after a bit of fun, especially if they could get away with it; which mostly, in such a small community, they could not. There were not many opportunities anyway, village life being what it was, except in the back of the special Saturday bus.

The bus went bumping down the road to the cinema at

154

six and came back at eleven, when the back seat was left for courting couples attempting to put into practice what they had just seen on the screen. There was always such a shrieking and a groaning that it sounded just like a farm-yard.

Célandine knew how to take care of herself even though she was a Catholic and the Pope disapproved.

'It's not the Pope I fancy,' she said with a saucy little pout.

She bought mysterious packets at the chemist's in Valréas, and on the way home there was much giggling and much snapping of rubber. Marguerite listened and watched. The whole thing sounded fraught with diffi-culties and dangers, and not a little absurd.

Nevertheless, for the 'good' girls, the ones who did not know how to take such precautions, there were conse-quences. There had already been two girls only a little older than she bundled up the aisle in the family way. 'Celebrating Easter before Palm Sunday' was the phrase for it.

To go to the pictures with a boy, rather than in a gaggle with the other girls, was a serious step, a declaration of intent. There was no point in asking Father Patrick's advice, and she never talked about such things to Madame Blanchette, so she consulted Tonin.

'Pierre wants to take me to the pictures, Tonin.'

Tonin watched her, saying nothing, but she could tell from the way his eyes glittered that he was paying close attention.

'He said he would pay for my ticket,' Marguerite added.

In the etiquette of the village, this meant that certain favours must be rendered in return. There was a scale for such things – and a ticket meant at least one good squeeze, and probably a bit of kissing as well.

Tonin's ears went red – a sign that something had embarrassed or annoyed him.

'D-did he? And what did you say?' Tonin was wearing his wolf-look by now, but as if he was rather an unhappy wolf.

Marguerite giggled.

'I said, "Thank you prettily, Pierre – but not this week".'

'That's *good*.'

Tonin's voice held such vehemence that he himself was confused. He had realized as soon as she spoke that he did not want her to accept the invitation. Marguerite was much too good for the butcher's boy. She was much too good for any of the village boys. Someone who was going to be someone did not let herself be courted by, still less marry, a butcher's boy. When she married it would be to someone very important, someone who could help her make her mark.

But Marguerite had not finished yet.

'Why don't *you* take me to the pictures, Tonin?'

Tonin was even more confused by this suggestion. 'What about my g-goats?'

'They won't miss you at all on a Saturday night,' said Marguerite. 'They'll be doing what everyone else is trying to do on a Saturday night. Making babies.'

Then Marguerite looked at him in that funny way she had, with her eyebrows making little wobbly question marks.

'Don't talk like that, Marguerite.' His voice was a warning growl – almost as if he really *was* a wolf.

Marguerite stopped instantly. You could only go so far with Tonin.

After this, and in spite of his reluctance, she appointed him her authority on all matters to do with human relationships. Most of the questions arose from what she heard when she was taking down dictation from the confessions.

One time it was: 'Tonin, what's a "termination"?'

Tonin was startled, and an expression of worry crossed his face.

'Why do you want to know, Marguerite?'

'No, it's not what you think,' she said hastily. She thought she had better explain, even though it was indiscreet, and Father Patrick had told her never to be indiscreet.

'One of the young ladies confessed that she had had one. Father Patrick seemed to think it a very bad sin. I want to know if I've guessed right.'

'What did you guess?'

'That she got rid of the baby on purpose. *Pop!* Just like that. You can do it with herbs, too, you know,' she added, just to reassure him. 'I know exactly how to do it. It's the same as bringing on the monthly bleeding.'

She recited in a sing-song, just as her mother had taught her: 'Take a wineglass of marigold petals, two pinches of sage, three heads of hops, four pinches of clover, as much absinthe as will sit on your thumbnail, seven sprigs of herb of the Virgin, crush in a pipkin with as much water as will cover. Drink it all up and there you are. *Whoosh!*'

'You know t-too much, Marguerite.'

'Bad, is it? Ten-decades-of-the-rosary bad?'

Tonin nodded.

'Do *you* believe it's a sin?'

'Of course.'

'And do *I* believe it's a sin? As a Cathar?'

'I don't know, but I think . . .' He hesitated. 'Perhaps you don't.'

This told Marguerite that Tonin and she might have different views of things. It was all quite confusing but very exciting. She felt different and special, different from everyone, from Father Patrick, from Madame Blanchette, and now she felt different from Tonin as well.

Another time, she had a new phrase which really pleased her. 'Tonin, what's "anal intercourse"?'

She watched Tonin slyly out of the corner of her eye, enjoying the way he shifted from one foot to the other.

'I'm certainly not going to explain *that* to you, young lady. Even if I could,' he added hastily.

'Why not? Madame Blanchette says you're a very rough person without any education, so you should know all about this sort of thing and not mind in the least telling me about it. Certainly Father Patrick wouldn't dream of telling me. He thinks I don't even listen when his visitors say all those things. And I can't ask anyone else or I would have to say where I'd heard it. Which would be what Father Patrick calls indiscreet.'

Marguerite put her head on one side, her green eyes mischievous. 'In fact', she added, 'you should consider it your duty to educate me. Otherwise I'll have to ask Pierre. I'm sure he'd be only too glad to *show* me.'

After that veiled threat, Tonin answered her questions as best he could, and he let it be known that any boy in the village who laid a finger on Marguerite Dieudonnée Leblanc would be answerable to him.

This arrangement worked perfectly well as long as Marguerite did not take matters into her own hands – which she did not choose to. Yet.

It was not ignorance which kept her without a sweetheart. It was true love. True love was Tonin. And, if he did not yet know it, there would come a time when he would.

Part Three

1962-1963

16

The Tribulations of Youth

'Behave yourself, Sarriette.'

Marguerite was milking the bell-wether, and Sarriette had decided not to co-operate. Goats were canny creatures; they could withhold half the milkings if they did not like the mood of the milker.

Tonin lifted his head from his own animal's flank and cast a wary eye at his best friend. Marguerite was in a funny mood this morning, just as she had been in a funny mood yesterday evening, and the bell-wether was a terrible one for knowing things like that.

'Now look what you've done!'

For answer, the nanny goat had given the bucket a sharp kick. Marguerite was not quick enough to save the milk, which spread out in creamy rivulets and vanished into the beaten earth of the borie's yard.

Spilt milk meant one less cheese for market. This small disaster reflected her feelings.

Six years had passed since that memorable Réveillon. From that time, in spite of Madame Blanchette's disapproval and the tongues which sometimes wagged in the village, Tonin and Marguerite had become inseparable.

It had been Marguerite's idea for Tonin to make the bories his summer quarters, convenient for pasturing his flocks in the high meadows which were under snow all through the winter.

Tonin thought he knew why his friend was irritable.

Marguerite was always a little bad-tempered when the monsignor paid his annual visit to the Hermitage. In order to keep out of his way, she had spent the night in the borie village, where she had chosen one of the dwellings for herself. Usually she enjoyed this, particularly when, as on the previous evening, Tonin had trapped and skinned a rabbit and they had cooked it with thyme and rosemary over a little brush fire.

He had done everything to please her because he knew that the monsignor's visit reminded her that she had no real right to be living at the Hermitage. Father Patrick had lied to keep her from being sent off to the orphanage, and the monsignor believed that her mother's family had taken her in.

If the warden had had his way, she would have been packed off long since to the Poor Clares to be educated in housework and the womanly virtues. Quite apart from the horror of this happening, housework and womanly virtues held very little appeal for Marguerite.

Milking the goats was another matter. Usually she was very good at this, quick and skilful, her light touch calming the first-year nannies and reassuring the crabby old ladies like Sarriette. Not so this morning.

Tonin called out cheerfully: 'Never mind, princess.'

Marguerite did not reply; she simply righted the upturned bucket and set to work on Sarriette again. When he called her princess, it usually made her smile. It was his private nickname for her – partly a joke and partly in earnest, since it underlined the difference between them. The princess and the goatherd had been one of Marguerite's favourite stories when she was little. Of course there was nothing high-born about Marguerite – except that she was born in the Hermitage and, thanks to her mother and Father Patrick, she had had a high education, which, in the village at least, made her special.

Even now that she was a grown woman by the

standards of the village, Tonin considered Marguerite his responsibility – although not in the same way that he considered his mother and his young sister Annie his responsibility.

His mother and sister might receive two-thirds of his wages every month, but Marguerite received something far more valuable: his unquestioning devotion. She was the sister he had chosen for himself – not one which had been allotted to him by the ties of blood. His real sister, on the few occasions when his mother visited, was all dressed up like a little duchess, with grand manners to match.

Marguerite was different from all the girls he had ever known. Unlike the girls of the village in their nylon stockings and tight skirts, she wore none of the badges of girlhood, no lipstick or false eyelashes or the black lines the others drew on their eyelids to give them the fashionable oriental slant.

Today, as always on the hill, she was wearing her *bleu de travail*, the workman's blue cotton overalls, and these accentuated the boyishness of her figure. She had rolled the trousers up above her knees and tied the bib round her narrow waist to reveal a white singlet. It showed off her strong square shoulders, sinewy well-muscled arms and the outline of small high breasts.

She wore her hair in a ponytail secured with a twist of twine. In winter and spring, Marguerite's hair was the tawny red-gold of autumn bracken – and in the summer, when the sun bleached it, it had brilliant highlights. Like all the unmarried girls of the village when they were no longer children, Marguerite grew her hair long. When it was pulled back it showed the neat shape of her head and the small ears with the gold studs shaped like tiny daisies, bought for her at this year's spring fair in Valréas by Tonin for a birthday present.

Whatever she wore or did not wear, anyone with half

an eye could see that Marguerite Dieudonnée Leblanc was a beauty. She was clever, too. Clever enough to have won a place at the *lycée* in Valréas to do her *baccalauréat*.

In fact, if it had not been for her quick temper and the teasing she sometimes subjected him to, Tonin would have considered her as perfect as anyone could possibly be.

'Never mind, princess,' he repeated.

The monsignor must certainly be the cause of the bad temper. His visits always reminded her of the loss of her mother. It was unsettling.

But Marguerite just shrugged. Contrary to what Tonin imagined, Marguerite was not thinking about her mother, unless to wonder what she would have done under the present circumstances. Tonin was right that she was cross, but for a very different reason.

She had been planning for the monsignor's visit for weeks because it provided her with the perfect excuse for spending the night alone with Tonin.

Marguerite was angry because she had been frustrated in love, and this was Tonin's doing.

She loved Tonin for many reasons: for his tousled brown hair, his patience and the strength in his lopsided body; for the way his ears went red when she said something which embarrassed him; for his stutter, particularly noticeable when his mind went faster than his tongue, and when she embarrassed him with her directness – her 'forward ways', as Madame Blanchette called it.

If she had been as forward with any of the village boys as she had been with Tonin the previous evening, she would certainly have got what she wanted. At her age, most of the girls were already spoken for or even married. All except the ones who were either plain or lacked prospects. Marguerite fell into the latter category naturally. But she had lately, as Madame Blanchette put it, filled out nicely.

A pretty girl with the right curves could always find a

suitor, whatever her prospects, particularly one like Marguerite, blessed with so refined an upbringing. Pierre was not the only interested party; there were others who would be only too willing.

All except Tonin, who was resolutely unwilling.

She had known that seducing her best friend would not be an easy task, but she was very determined – so much so that she had already taken the necessary 'precautions'. This in itself had been an exciting new experience.

She had worn a disguise and bought two packets of *préservatifs* at the chemist's in Valréas last market day. This was taking a considerable risk since if she was recognized the *pharmacien* was more than capable of getting word to Father Patrick. As the self-appointed keeper of the citizens' virtue, the chemist took a dim view of immoral behaviour. It was all very well if you were married – then you could do whatever you pleased.

Knowing this, Marguerite had tucked her bright hair into a matronly kerchief and borrowed a pair of dark glasses. A quick application of scarlet lipstick, a curtain-ring on the fourth finger of the left hand, and she was more than a match for the *pharmacien*.

Marguerite walked confidently through the door and straight over to the shelf where the baby requisites were stacked. With an air of what she hoped looked like long experience, she selected a box of rusks and a large tub of nappy cream.

'Baby's got a bit of a rash,' she explained to no-one in particular.

When it came to her turn, she casually placed both items down on the counter, willing the chemist to draw his own conclusions. Then she pointed to the top shelf behind him, where the *préservatifs* were kept.

'And a packet of those, please.'

Seeing his hesitation, she said, 'Two packets,' figuring that no-one would buy two if they were not married.

The chemist was unimpressed. 'Your age, mademoiselle?'

'Madame,' she corrected. 'Twenty-one. Why do you ask?' She twiddled the ring ostentatiously. For good measure she gave him one of Célandine's saucy winks. That did the trick. Miraculously the packets were hers.

After the milking was all done, Tonin would build a fire and cook her supper. And when they had eaten their meal and drunk some wine which Marguerite had been careful to bring with her, along with her night-things bundled up in a little bag over her shoulder, they would make love. Once they were all cosy and warm together in the borie, she meant to kiss him, just to get things going in the right direction.

All this happened just as she had planned, except for the last bit.

Tonin had no intention of letting her seduce him.

As soon as she said 'Tonin?' in a particular way, Tonin's wolf-senses howled a warning. Marguerite had that unpredictable look in her green eyes which meant trouble. He never knew with Marguerite from which direction trouble was coming.

'Yes, princess?'

'Just that, Tonin, don't you ever want to, you know, choose a sweetheart, that kind of thing? Marriage? Babies?' she finished lamely.

'What would I be doing with marriage and babies? I've got enough on my hands,' said Tonin, busying himself with stoking up the fire. But she could see that his ears were red.

At least this was a start. He was thinking along embarrassing lines.

She had come so far, she was not going to give up easily. She really did love Tonin – particularly now, with the firelight on his curly hair, that he was looking so adorably worried.

166

She stretched back on the hay bales he had set up as a bench. The hay smelled sweet and clean, like the first time they had met and she had believed the unkempt goatboy to be the devil himself.

She wished that there was a little more of the devil about him now.

They had come a long way together since that night of the Réveillon. And she fully intended that they should go a lot further.

The villagers might continue to consider him a *ravi* – a wild-eyed simpleton of a goatboy – but this was no longer strictly true. Marguerite was responsible for some, but by no means all, of the new Tonin. It had been at Father Patrick's prompting that he had changed his mind about learning his letters. Regular nagging by Madame Blanchette had persuaded him to keep his hair trimmed and take at least one bath every week, even if it was only in the cold water of the High Pool, the reservoir above the borie village. Encouraged by this, Marguerite mended his clothes for him, patching and darning so that he looked presentable when he went to sell his cheeses in the market.

In fact she was almost a wife already – except in one all-important respect.

This was not to say that she wanted to get married. Her mother had never needed to marry anyone, so there was no particular reason why she should, either. In a small community like Pernes-les-Rochers, coming and going as she did in and out of people's houses, first with her mother and now as a healer herself, it was clear that marriage did not solve anyone's problems.

Take Françoise, for instance. Ever since she had been going steady with Michel-Giles, Françoise regularly appeared with big blue-and-yellow bruises on various parts of her person – including some which involved rolling down her stockings to reveal quite intimate parts of herself. Only the other day she came in dark glasses, which she removed to disclose a black eye.

'See that? That was my Michel-Giles. He gave it me 'cos he's jealous,' said Françoise with evident satisfaction. 'Shows he loves me.'

Marguerite found this unnerving. She wondered what kind of love expressed itself with a black eye and blue-and-yellow bruises. Her mother had told her quite different stories about love. Her stories had been all about gallant knights, fair ladies and love forever true, and said nothing at all about the risk of broken bones.

'Love hurts,' said Françoise, fingering her black eye admiringly.

'Doesn't look much like love to *me*,' said Marguerite dubiously.

'That's 'cos you don't know *anything* yet – stuck up there with the priest and running around all day with that smelly goatboy.' Françoise sniffed. 'And him a hunchback with no education. My mother says a young lady like you could make a respectable marriage. In spite of everything and all. Find yourself a proper sweetheart, like my Michel-Giles.'

Marguerite opened her mouth to reply, but swallowed her tongue just in time; she had nearly told Françoise what she thought of a proper sweetheart who beat you black and blue, and her opinion of what married life was likely to hold in store for Françoise.

While it was certainly true that in the troubadours' tales the path of true love never ran smooth and there was never a rose without a thorn, none of them featured black eyes. She was quite certain that if anyone tried to give her a black eye, with or without love, she would give them a black eye right back.

Anyway, Françoise was quite wrong about Tonin. He might not always smell of rose petals, but he certainly was not stupid. Nor was he a hunchback; he had a beautiful, smooth muscular back. It was only his leg which was a bit odd. And he was as good-looking as any of the village boys – better-looking in fact.

And, whatever she said or did, Tonin would never give her a black eye. He might tease her, just as she teased him, but he would never hurt her.

Tonin had big hands which looked rough but, she knew, were very gentle. She wondered how they would feel when they were not calming a frightened beast but caressing her breasts.

These thoughts brought her to the moment of truth.

'Tonin?'

'What is it, p-princess?'

'Kiss me.'

Tonin looked very surprised, and then pecked at her cheek very quickly, as if he were picking a tick off one of his goats.

'Don't be silly. Do it properly.'

She puckered her mouth expectantly and closed her eyes.

She looked like a woman, she felt like a woman – and everyone but Tonin knew it. Pierre the butcher's boy certainly knew it – even though she had given him absolutely no encouragement.

Well, she was giving Tonin plenty of encouragement.

'Now. Do it now.'

Nothing happened.

'I'm waiting, Tonin.'

She opened her eyes. Tonin had his wolf-look all right, but it was a very scared wolf.

'What's the matter?'

Tonin took a gulp of air, a sign that his stutter was giving him trouble. 'N-no, Marguerite.'

'What do you mean?'

'Just *no*.' The emphasis was strong, and there was no stutter.

Marguerite felt her cheeks blaze.

'Why not?'

'Because I don't want to.'

'Why not? Don't you love me?'

'Of course I love you. You know that perfectly well.'

'Then, why?'

'It wouldn't – wouldn't be right.'

'Why wouldn't it be right?'

'Because – b-because you're special.'

'*Special?*' Marguerite was astonished. That was the stupidest reason she had ever heard for not kissing someone. She knew perfectly well that she was special. If you thought someone was special, you kissed them. And, once you had kissed them, one thing led to another.

They were not too young, either. Seventeen and twenty-two made it more than time one thing led to another. He was right about marriage and babies, though. Tonin and she would have lovely babies, but that would come all in good time, when she had passed her *baccalauréat* and mapped out her career. The law, perhaps, so that she could fight for the poor and needy.

Right now it was she who was poor and needy. And still Tonin would not relent. Try as she might, she could never seem to get him to see her as anything except a little girl, a child in need of care and protection.

Well, she had the protection. It was currently burning a hole in her pocket. Now all she needed was the care.

It was ridiculous. Everyone had a sweetheart except Marguerite. Everyone in all the world was in love. And that included beasts and birds and insects, too. The place was alive with it. Crickets were screaming about it, frogs were spawning all over it. Even Abelard was busy with his mate and a second clutch of eggs. You could not get away from it – it was like a disease to which everyone in the world succumbed. Everyone but Tonin.

It was this singular failure the previous evening to catch

what everyone else in the world had caught which had put Marguerite in such a bad temper this morning.

It was Marguerite's bad temper which had made Sarriette kick over the bucket. And Sarriette's hoof which had left Tonin one cheese short for the midsummer market.

'For goodness' sake, Tonin. What's one cheese between friends?'

And then Marguerite spun on her heel and flounced off down the mountainside – or with as a much of a flounce as someone with bare feet and wearing *bleu de travail* can manage.

17

Father Patrick Strikes a Deal

'The land is ours, just as the people are ours. We have a bounden duty!'

Father Patrick thumped his fist on the table. It was too bad that the warden's annual visit had concluded the previous afternoon, or he would have sent him up to see the damage for himself.

Tonin had arrived that morning with the news that a broad crack had appeared in the rampart of the High Pool where the water for summer irrigation was held.

'It's a disgrace to us all,' said Father Patrick.

Tonin had never seen the priest so angry. Father Patrick knew he had good cause to be angry. Worse than angry, he was ashamed. He fully intended to communicate that shame to his superior – appeal to *his* superiors, if that proved necessary.

It was not simply Tonin's report. He was not so blind that he did not see the evidence of decline for himself.

He would scarcely need to remind the monsignor that the fields had returned to fallow, the millwheels no longer turned, the ancient olive trees went untended and the orchard fruit lay ungathered.

Nor, indeed, was it necessary to underline that the village was rapidly emptying. The old people who died were not replaced by newborn infants, since the young people were obliged to move away for lack of work.

But it was worth pointing out that, although this decline

was not an unusual pattern in the uplands, the valley of the Hermitage had always been self-sufficient. And this, as the soldier-monks had intended, should have ensured the community's survival.

Sometimes Father Patrick thought that this subtle form of land-clearance was what the warden had in mind – that he thought the village unnecessary, welcomed the depletion of the population, was happy to divest the Church of responsibility for the flock. It was as if he was one of the English landlords whose absentee ownership had brought Paddy O'Donovan's native Ireland to her knees.

Even the vocabulary of refusal was familiar.

'The place must pay its way. We are not yet profitable enough to justify unnecessary expense. Promissory notes to be redeemed in heaven are no longer sufficient for the modern workman. Everything costs money.'

Money, it seemed, was the key.

Other communities had been able to restore their fortunes after the war years. The only reason that Pernes-les-Rochers had not been able to follow suit was because its landlord willed it otherwise.

The trouble had started right at the beginning, when the warden had first taken up his appointment. The two men had agreed that new investment would be financed by charging the visitors to the Hermitage – voluntary contributions into the collection box could no longer be considered sufficient.

'We are in business, Father, to provide a service. We must cater to our customers' needs. Flexibility is of the essence. We have to generate a regular income like any business. A profit has to be shown.'

Patrick O'Donovan had never had much of a head for business; but, then, he would not need one, explained Monsignor Melton. The warden would take care of the profit-and-loss account, collect all moneys due, invest profits wisely. The Hermitage might then look to the future with confidence. This, at any rate, was what the monsignor led him to believe.

Now, five years later, even essential repairs were still left undone.

'Next year,' said the monsignor this year, as he had said every year. 'When the Hermitage shows a profit.'

'Next year', said the old man crisply, 'will be too late.'

The ensuing clash of wills had determined that the warden's annual visit had not been a success. In fact, if Patrick O'Donovan had been younger and more vigorous, he would have thrown Charles Melton out on his ear, and the highest authority would have known the reason why. He might be only a humble priest, but he was not entirely without influence in the holy corridors of power. Longevity guaranteed that at least one or two of his old friends from Vatican days had achieved high office. The new Pope, John XXIII, had appointed Albino Luciani Bishop of Vittorio Veneto, and he had the ear and trust of the Pontiff himself.

Furthermore, Father Patrick wished to make known his objections to certain visitors. He was an old man, and he might be as good as blind, but he was by no means senile. Whatever the warden might suppose, he knew a bad penny when it dropped onto the collection plate – and there was no doubt that there had been a whole purseful of bad pennies at the Hermitage since the new warden had implemented his business plan.

Even Marguerite, scribbling away in her cubbyhole, noticed that these visitors were different. They were invariably middle-aged men, and their transgressions were always financial. The old priest did not give these particular visitors their quota of Hail Marys or their decades of the rosary as penance. In fact he did not give them any penances at all.

'That will do, my son,' he would say firmly, and snap

his Catechism shut. 'Ego te absolvo.' And he would make the sign of the cross.

When these special visitors first began to appear, the old priest had told Marguerite that they were the warden's 'personal clients', and she must be sure to keep well out of their way. These guests appeared to have some difficulty in grasping the rituals of Catholicism, which confirmed his suspicions that they were not bona fide penitents, but that there was some other, more practical reason for their need of sanctuary.

At first, Father Patrick was genuinely concerned for the spiritual health of these visitors, and would call on Tonin to use his wolf-skills in determining how to handle them.

'I need to know about this one, Tonin,' he would say. And Tonin would move quietly around in the vicinity of the visitor until he had got the measure of him. Mostly his verdict confirmed what Father Patrick had already concluded: that they were cheats, thieves, liars, or all three.

When the delicate matter of who was and was not eligible for sanctuary had first been broached, Father Patrick had agreed to tolerate the warden's choices on the understanding that these maverick refugees, 'imperfect seekers-after-truth' as Monsignor Melton called them, would pay for the essential repairs to the Hermitage's properties.

But still, in spite of what Father Patrick knew must have been a trebling or quadrupling of the Hermitage's annual income, annual expenditure remained at a standstill, and no investment in the future was possible until past neglect had been remedied.

'Beware of priests and bachelors,' Thérèse used to say. 'But most particularly bachelor priests. They have no stake in the future.'

Father Patrick, priest and bachelor, had his stake in the future; Thérèse had seen to that. The future was

Marguerite, just as the past had been Thérèse. He could not let either of them down.

The final straw which decided the resident to dig in his heels and demand the Hermitage's dues was the behaviour of one of these visitors, a smoothly tailored lawyer whose Catholicism, if he had ever been of the Faithful at all, was so far lapsed he could not even deliver a Hail Mary.

There was, it was abundantly clear, no point in even going through the motions of confession. The priest decided to bring the interview to a rapid conclusion.

'My son, do you earnestly repent—?'

'Don't preach at *me*, sonny boy. The price was unmarked bills. In advance. Just as your superior requested.'

Father Patrick was slow to anger, but this time it had gone too far. It was perfectly obvious that the man had no allegiance to the Church, no reason for claiming her protection. The warden must have known this perfectly well before he recommended him for sanctuary.

Money was a potent force for evil. Father Patrick's time in the anterooms of church power had taught him that men of the cloth, no less than ordinary mortals, were susceptible to temptation.

The warden had turned the Hermitage into a refuge for evil men, and the resident had no wish to be his involuntary henchman – not least because Charles Melton, the patrician Englishman, absentee landlord, represented all those things against which young Patrick O'Donovan had fought.

Father Patrick made it clear that he had not accepted the responsibilities of the Hermitage in order to serve the cupidity of others – whether they had taken holy orders or not.

For all that one was officially the superior of the other, they were finally obliged to call a truce. But not before Father Patrick had threatened to bring the matter to the attention of the well-placed Bishop of Vittorio Veneto.

'I don't think that will be necessary, Father. I'm sure we can reach an accommodation.'

The accommodation was that essential repairs would be put in hand immediately and plans for the future approved if, and only if, Father Patrick provided Monsignor Melton with detailed plans, timetables and costings.

'I shall hold you responsible, Father. Every sou.'

'To be sure you will, Monsignor.'

Melton looked sharply at the resident, but he knew that he had met his match.

As soon as the warden had safely departed and Marguerite had returned from her night in the bories, Father Patrick explained what had been agreed.

'If facts and figures are what's needed, facts and figures are what they'll get.'

Tonin had just delivered the news of the cracked wall which caused Father Patrick to lose his temper.

This confirmed the urgency. Something would be done, and done at once.

Father Patrick rocked in his chair, clicking his rosary through his fingers, while Marguerite rolled a clean sheet of paper into the secondhand typewriter she had purchased with the money she earned from her ministrations.

She had installed the rickety machine on her writing-shelf and taught herself to use it. The ledgers continued to be handwritten, but modern life required modern skills.

Marguerite waited, her hands poised over the keys.

'What's to be done, *mon père*?'

'Tonin?' Father Patrick turned his face to the goatboy. Quite apart from the usefulness of his wolf-tricks, Tonin served as Father Patrick's eyes and ears in the valley – and this had been so almost since that first night of the Réveillon. The two – the *ravi* and the old priest – had found common ground immediately. On that Christmas night, they had sat up long after Marguerite had curled up to sleep on the settle, discussing what might be done to restore the valley to its former prosperity.

Father Patrick, realizing the depth of the goatboy's practical knowledge, later encouraged him to learn his letters so that he might study the old planting plans and household books.

These manuscripts – and there were at least a dozen of them – provided a complete record of all those crops which had once been grown in the valley, and all were accompanied by maps of the ancient fields, detailing where the irrigation-channels ran and which slopes were suitable for which particular crops. Annual production, methods of harvesting and sowing, together with notes on their proper husbandry, were all written down by the old monks in the most careful and precise detail.

Although only a few terraces of vines and the olive groves still remained, there had once been cherry and apple orchards. In fact, everything from saffron crocuses to several varieties of wheat, barley and oats had once been produced in sufficiently large quantities to feed all the thousand or so inhabitants of the valley, with enough to send to market as well.

After five years, Tonin was as knowledgeable about rotation planting and catch crops, natural fertilizers and the benefits of strip-cultivation as any professional land agent.

Rapidly, without a trace of the stutter, Tonin began to outline his plans. As he began to speak, Marguerite forgot her quarrel with him of the previous day, and listened enthralled.

'Let me see the maps!' she said.

With careful hands, Tonin unrolled the ancient maps and spread them on the table.

'Look here – and here. These lines show where the old

walls run – they're all overgrown, but they're there. And over here – on the north-facing slopes where the spelt was grown – I've seen the threshing floor.'

Fired by her enthusiam, he pointed out the ancient terracing where new plantations of olive trees might go, which weed-choked meadows might once again be turned to orchard.

'It'll take time – centuries, if we had nothing but the tools these old fellows had. But now, with the machinery, it takes one man to do the work of a hundred. It can be done, and done well and quickly, if we have the means. I'm sure of that.'

Marguerite listened with passionate intensity. She had never thought to hear such things – never imagined such a thing might be possible. But now, as Tonin traced the ancient workings on the yellowed parchment, she was suddenly certain that the valley would live again. She could see it all. The village would once again be full of folk, there would be new crops to bring a new prosperity – asparagus and strawberries, early vegetables for the markets of Lyons and Paris. It would be a miracle, the triumph of hope, the rebirth of an ancient community, a shining beacon to light the way to a brilliant future.

Listening to the two young people as their excitement mounted, Father Patrick's spirits soared in response. He, too, could see it all in his mind's eye – even if he might never see it in the flesh.

'Not so fast, mavourneen!' he said finally. 'Get to your infernal word-machine. We have work to do.'

More soberly, there were Tonin's warnings to be heeded. Before plans for the future could have any meaning, there was the legacy of past neglect.

The most pressing problem was the restoration of the High Pool's wall. Originally the pool had been a work of nature, a deep fissure in the earth's crust fed by under-ground springs. These natural waters were contained by a man-made rampart. The monks had been too canny to content themselves with this alone. They had hacked out a series of shallow lakes which froze over in winter, thawing gradually to provide a supply of snow-water for the High Pool through the summer months. The lakes were edged with boulders, roughly hewn but closely packed, cemented together over the centuries by siftings of earth which offered a foothold to tufts of hardy vegetation.

This natural mortar had been weakened by the frosts of that fierce winter which had claimed Thérèse and destroyed many of the olive trees. Now, seven years later, the boulders were beginning to shift in their beds, releasing an unusual press of water to lap against the retaining rampart of the High Pool. It was this which had produced the crack.

'If the rampart goes, the High Pool will overflow and the valley will be drowned.'

All three contemplated this prospect in silent dismay. The bleak warning could only be accepted for what it was. Notice of a sword of Damocles suspended quite literally over their heads.

If the winter rains came early, or if there was a midsummer storm, more dangerous still because of the melted snow-water, the valley was already doomed.

Finally Father Patrick banged his stick and rose to his feet.

'It never rains in the valley at midsummer. When the rains come, we will be ready.'

In spite of Father Patrick's comforting words, that night Marguerite's dreams were troubled. There was fire and water, earth and air. Her mother, too, reaching arms towards her, warning of disaster which was yet to come. Something to do with the village, the borie village which had once sheltered her ancestors. When she awoke, the dream was no more than a faint memory, a shadow of disaster foretold, lacking substance.

18

The Feast of St Jean

It never rained in the valleys of Upper Provence on the night of the St Jean. Never in living memory.

This was as well for the village of Pernes-les-Rochers, for the festival of the Eve of the St Jean was celebrated with pagan rituals conducted on mountaintops, in city streets, in the squares of villages – in short, anywhere where the canopy of heaven gave uninterrupted access to the ancient gods. The dependants of the Hermitage might have been Christian for a thousand years, but the old gods still had their day.

Their day was the Eve of the St Jean, the feast-day of John the Baptist, that hairy saint who bore more than a passing resemblance to the goat-god Pan. With the green-crowned flute player in charge, a little courting was not only in order but positively demanded. Liberties were taken which could not be taken at any other time.

The village was no place for a priest on the Eve of the St Jean, even though when Father Patrick was younger he had left off his priestly clothes, donned the uniform black and white, and escorted Thérèse to the dance.

This year, for the first time, Father Patrick had given his blessing to Marguerite's attendance. Something told him that her mother would never have forgiven him if he had not.

His beloved Thérèse was much in his thoughts these days, perhaps because her daughter grew more like her every day. Above all, it was her spirit which showed her to be her mother's daughter. She had that confidence in the set of her head on her shoulders, that sureness of her own desirability which could be seen in the swing of her hips, the firmness of her walk, the set of her chin. She had Thérèse's directness, too, the belief that all things were possible.

He was glad of this, glad for the daughter of his heart, for Thérèse who bore her, for Tonin who cared for her, for himself, and for the villagers who would soon be looking to her for their prosperity. She would serve the valley well, he had no doubt of that. The belief that all things were possible was the strongest card anyone could hold.

With this in mind, the plans for the valley – both for redressing past neglect and anticipating future prosperity – had been typed and checked and typed again, finally being consigned to the post for London.

The monsignor's reply had not been long in coming. Fresh reminders of his resident's friendship with the Bishop of Vittorio Veneto had clinched the matter. Luciani was a moral man, some said a little too moral for a bishop, but it was undeniable that he had the ear and trust of the Pontiff, the kindly and relatively incorruptible John XXIII. In Melton's world, there was a time for attack and a time for retreat. This was indubitably the moment for the latter.

By return of post to prevent hasty action on his resident's part, the warden was pleased to be able to assure Father Patrick that funds – not as much as was hoped for, but enough for the present – would shortly be forthcoming.

Father Patrick made the joyous announcement to his parishioners the day the letter arrived, calling a meeting in the square and standing in front of the Mairie with the mayor at his right hand.

*   *   *

That was yesterday. Today, as it was the Eve of the St Jean, there would be much for the village to celebrate.

The morning of the festival, on the pretext of making sure his breeches were clean and mended and his shirt washed and hung to dry on a thorn bush, Marguerite went looking for Tonin.

It would be just like him to forget all about the party.

The tinkle of bells told her exactly where to find him. As she swung easily down the narrow path towards him, she thought that he did not look much like a young man in a flurry of preparations for a night out with his sweetheart.

In fact, he looked rather like a goatboy who has no intention of doing anything but herd his goats.

'Wait for me, Tonin!'

He waved to her, and sat down on a rock to wait for her to catch up.

As she reached him, she noticed that he was not looking at her directly, but sideways with his eyes narrowed and glittering. She recognized his wolf-look – never a good sign when she wanted him to do something he did not want to do, and something told her that this was certainly the case.

'What's on your mind, princess?'

A sudden unease came over her. 'You've not forgotten the Saint Jean, Tonin?'

'No.' Tonin was still not looking at her.

'You're coming, of course?'

After a moment's pause, he said: 'You know very well I can't.'

She frowned. 'Why not, for heaven's sake?'

'You know very well.'

'I *don't*.'

He sighed. He would have to spell it out.

'I c-can't dance, Marguerite.'

'Of course you can. Anyone can dance.'

'Not me. I look r-ridiculous, and p-people laugh at me. And they'd laugh at you, too, if you were my p-partner.'

He was beginning to feel miserable, so his stutter got worse.

'All you have to do is *escort* me,' coaxed Marguerite. 'I don't mind a bit if you don't dance . . .' Her voice trailed away uncertainly. Then she added, as if Tonin did not already know: 'I'm to be the queen this year. I can choose the king.'

'I know that p-perfectly well, princess.'

'I want to choose you.'

'No, you don't, princess.'

Marguerite stamped her foot – a gesture which might be expected from the likes of Célandine, but was quite un-characteristic for Marguerite, as was the next thing she said.

'I simply won't take no for answer.'

'You'll have to, *ma belle*.' He was grinning at her.

Marguerite was so cross she could have punched him in his slanty yellow eye, and it would be black just like Françoise's.

No. That was not the way. You catch more flies with honey than you ever do with vinegar, as Madame Blanchette was fond of saying.

She tried a quick fib. 'Father Patrick said I couldn't go unless you were my escort. He said you'd keep me out of trouble.'

'Father Patrick knows better than that.' Tonin shook his head, still grinning. 'I've never been able to keep you out of trouble.'

'That's not very polite.'

'What can you expect from the goatboy?'

Tonin reached out a broad fist and ruffled her hair cheerfully.

'Stop that.' She pushed his hand away. 'I'm not one of your smelly goats.'

''Course not. You're the queen of the Saint Jean.'

'I'm perfectly well aware of that.'

'Good. Then, you're perfectly well aware that you won't miss me at all. They'll all be queuing up.'

'But it's *you* I want,' she wailed.

'Too bad, princess.' He could be as stubborn as an old billy-goat when he put his mind to it.

A new idea struck her. 'Anyway, it's not just me. There's lots of girls looking forward to seeing you at the Saint Jean.'

'Don't be silly.' His voice was sharp.

'It's true. You don't know the power you have over women.'

This was another of Célandine's lines. Marguerite glanced slyly at Tonin. Surprisingly, it had had an effect. The wolf-look had vanished, to be replaced by what almost seemed like curiosity.

'Who, then?'

'Lots of them.' Marguerite waved her hand to indicate a wide choice.

'Name one,' Tonin persisted – not that he believed her for an instant, but still he was curious.

Marguerite cast around wildly for a credible candidate. Certainly not Françoise, who was already well and truly spoken for, and he would never believe Célandine. Inspiration struck.

'Marie-Pascale. She asked me all about you. Said how handsome you were and she did so hope you liked her. She was quite pink and excited.'

This last was transparently a lie. A capacity for pink-ness and excitement was not in Marie-Pascale's nature. A large raw-boned girl with a face and figure like a doughnut and a brain made of the same stuff, she lived in a big house with its own garden, and her family owned twenty acres of good arable land close to the village. This meant that, in spite of her plainness, as an only

185

child and an heiress she could be considered a catch.

It was as plain as the nose on Marie-Pascale's face that Tonin would not be allowed anywhere near her.

Tonin knew it, too. His face fell.

'Don't tell f-fibs, princess.'

'It's not a fib. I don't tell fibs about things like that.' Marguerite searched wildly for circumstantial evidence. 'Ask Françoise. Marie-Pascale tells her *everything*. She'll tell you it's true.'

Tonin looked at her. The wolf-look was back, but it did not seem to be picking up the right signals.

'Are you sure?'

'Absolutely.' Marguerite tipped up her chin, another gesture borrowed from Célandine, daring him to contradict her.

'Marie-Pascale', she added, lowering her voice conspiratorially, 'asked me to tell you to meet her under the mulberry tree at midnight.'

Tonin absorbed this information. He had not thought about Marie-Pascale in that kind of way. In fact, he had not thought about Marie-Pascale at all – let alone that she might be interested in a goatboy such as he. Now he thought he remembered small signs – a glance, maybe even a sigh, a brushing of fingers as they passed in the street, or met in the bakery, or stood at the bus stop waiting for the market bus.

'She really said that?'

'You heard. Goatbells deafened you?' Marguerite suddenly lost patience. She was already woman enough to know that the Marie-Pascale story was a mistake.

She tossed her head.

'Anyway,' she said.

But what she meant was what the devil was the matter with him? If he was willing to think about Marie-Pascale in that kind of way, why not her? She was much prettier than Marie-Pascale, and much cleverer, altogether a much more interesting and infinitely more desirable person. It could not possibly be Marie-Pascale's undeniable possession of a dowry. Tonin never worried about things like that.

'See if I don't,' she said.

What she meant was that she would show him. She would wear her new dress and leave the bodice's drawstrings loose, like the other girls did, to show off the swell of her breasts and the pretty curve of her neck. She would get out her needle and thread and raise the hem of the skirt to show off her legs. Marguerite thought of her legs with satisfaction. She had much more shapely legs than any of the other girls in the village. Ten times more shapely than Marie-Pascale's.

Tonight, tonight at the party, he would know that she was the only woman in the world for him. Except that he would not be there. He had already said so, and by the look of him the only thing which might make him change his mind was Marie-Pascale.

Marguerite chewed her lip. Then she said nastily: 'If you can't dance with me because you'd make me look stupid, you can't dance with Marie-Pascale, either. She'd look a lot more stupid.'

Getting no reaction, she added: 'Anyway, Pierre would be *delighted* to escort me.'

She stole a quick look at him. Tonin's eyes were all narrowed and glittery so that once again she could not tell what she was thinking. It could be anything – her or Pierre or even, perish the thought, Marie-Pascale. Nor could she tell if the look was disapproval, or disappointment, or something buried deeper than she could reach.

But all he said was: 'If that's what you want.'

'Just see if I don't!'

With this enigmatic threat, Marguerite spun on her heel and stormed off. She was soon making her way through the olive groves in towards the village, where the preparations for the festival were already well under way. The sound of laughter rose to greet her through the still summer air, and all at once her spirits fell even further. It might have been a sudden stab of loneliness triggered perhaps by Tonin's refusal, or the sweet scent of herbs crushed underfoot, or the laughter from the soon-to-be merrymakers. Or quite simply that, on this sunny midday of the Eve of the St Jean, Marguerite was reminded most poignantly of her mother.

'Maman,' she whispered to herself. 'I miss you, maman.'

A tiny spark of rage flickered into life. This small flame needed nothing special to feed on. It drew its sustenance from nothing and nowhere. It blazed suddenly into life, licked at whatever it was given, and finally died back, leaving the anger behind.

Anger had its uses. Like the application of a hot poultice to an infected wound – somehow the hurt drew the pain. A desire for revenge took the place of anger. She would seek her revenge against Tonin – not for what he had done, but for what he most decisively had no intention of doing. Revenge must have a vehicle. The butcher's boy would do very well for the purpose. She would have her revenge at the St Jean. She would dance with Pierre and let him hold her as tightly as he pleased, and squeeze her anywhere he wanted, and touch her. Even *there*, where the nice girls did not let anyone touch them before they were safely married. A brief moment of doubt at this notion was brushed aside. There were moments when sacrifices must be made.

Even if Tonin was not there to see, she would make sure he knew all of it, without sparing a single detail. She would let Pierre do anything he wanted with her. Well, almost. In spite of the fact that the thought of what Pierre wanted to do with her sent little shivers of disgust down her spine. In spite of the fact that letting Pierre do anything at all with her would be a more than considerable sacrifice.

But, under the circumstances, letting Pierre do what he wanted was a sacrifice she might just be prepared to make.

As the daylight faded, the bells rang out clear and loud from the dark bulk of the Hermitage – the signal that the celebrations might begin.

This acknowledgement of a pagan festivity was Father Patrick's annual gesture of disobedience to his church. And after Thérèse's passing he saw it as a memorial to her as well as a thanksgiving for the daughter she had left him.

This year Marguerite, beloved child that she was, was to be the queen, the most beautiful girl at the ball. With this in mind, Father Patrick rang the bells with redoubled vigour.

Marguerite bathed and dressed with care. She filled the hip-bath in her own little bathroom with hot water from the copper in the kitchen. While she was waiting for it to cool down a bit she decided that she had to reassure herself that Tonin had been quite wrong to reject her advances.

She had to climb on to a chair to get a proper view, and even so she could only see a bit of herself at a time, but it was enough. She was slender certainly, but she had all the necessary bits in all the right places, even if these were not as obvious as those boasted by Célandine or even Françoise, let alone Marie-Pascale.

No doubt her breasts were on the small side but they were nicely rounded, like little melons centred with pink nipples which rose into tiny cones when she tickled them. Her waist curved in and her hips curved out, and there was a soft reddish-gold fuzz on that secret place between her legs where she felt interesting and exciting things, sort of meltings and ticklings, when she went to the pictures and the film stars kissed each other on the screen. She felt these things, too, when she was with Tonin, but absolutely never when she was with Pierre.

Her mirror also told her something else. The strong limbs and broad shoulders, the flat stomach and taut flesh were those of a young huntress rather than of a voluptuous maiden. There was no doubt that she had a body which looked as if it would have no trouble looking after itself.

Perhaps that was the problem. Tonin did not see her as a woman. The village girls were proud of the softness of their flesh, the paleness of their faces, their helplessness and vulnerability. Helplessness and vulnerability were certainly powerful weapons in the armoury of woman-hood but they were not qualities she could carry with any conviction.

Tonight she would do her best to overcome this undoubted handicap in the battle of the sexes, and look the very picture of appetizing femininity. The clothes would help, of course – and she meant to make the best of these.

The traditional costume of the girls at the St Jean was a crimson petticoat worn beneath a full white skirt with a bodice laced and sashed with scarlet. Madame Blanchette had overseen the cutting and stitching, which meant that the neckline showed absolutely nothing at all and the skirt reached to mid-calf.

'Modesty in all things,' muttered Madame Blanchette as she pinned and tucked. 'Particularly in the *demoiselle* from the Hermitage.'

Marguerite had known better than to argue. She simply waited until Madame Blanchette had finished for the day and gone off home to the village, then she set to work with scissors and needle. A few snips here and a deep tuck there, and she was confident that hers would be the lowest décolletée and the shortest skirt at the gathering.

The dress was undoubtedly becoming. It was even more becoming when she wrapped the bright red sash round her narrow waist. Her hair, long enough now to reach to her shoulders, fell in a soft curtain of russet curls which framed her oval face. She was ready now for the finishing touch – the make-up.

For this, too, she had made secret provision, knowing quite well that Madame Blanchette would disapprove. She had cut out and saved from the *Cahier du cinéma* a photograph of Jeanne Moreau, which she propped up by the mirror for inspiration, along with the scarlet lipstick acquired for her visit to the chemist, a tiny jar of blue eyeshadow and another of rouge, and, most important of all, a little block of mascara with its own tiny brush. Françoise had already shown her how to use the mascara as an eyeliner as well as to darken her lashes, demonstrating how to draw two thick lines of black with an upward tilt at the corner to give the fashionable slant-eyed look.

With deep concentration, she set to work. After a few false starts, she was satisfied that she looked as much like the star of *Jules et Jim* as she was ever likely to. Considering that she could not get hold of her Jules and she did not relish the advances of Jim, it might all be a wasted effort.

Just the same, it was quite a transformation. She was certain she looked much older and more sophisticated than her years – at least twenty-one – and this no-one could fail to notice.

Encouraged and heartened, she splashed herself vigorously with lavender water, paying particular attention to the well-displayed bosom, and loosened the drawstring of the blouse so that her breasts curved more seductively over the lace-whipped edge. With one last glance in the mirror, she set off for the village.

The sun dipped to the horizon in an extravagant haze of gold and pink, giving way to the moon, a pale crescent trailing soft ribbons of violet cloud – a sign, at any other time of year, that there was rain to come. She dismissed the thought. No-one had such a thing as rain in their head on the midsummer's eve.

Marguerite, soon to be the belle of the ball, ran down the path to the village as music and laughter floated up through the olive groves to greet her.

There would be wine, and delicious things to eat, and then there would be the dance – not the sort you did at the Saturday-night hop in Valréas, but the *tarascon* and the *triputin*, the country dances whose rhythms her feet had tapped before she could walk.

As she entered the village, she forgot all about Pierre and Tonin and everything except the spectacle itself.

The narrow streets had been transformed into a fairyland of twinkling lights and scarlet bunting. Arched over the alleyways were leafy branches decked with ribbon. The balconies had been decorated with flowers and draped with bright hearthrugs. By the great stone fountain all covered with moss, a tall pole, twined with scarlet ropes and honeysuckle, awaited the dancers. From every courtyard rose the plaintive notes of the *galoubé* and the *tambourin*, the ancient instruments of the musicians of Provence.

'Marguerite – *à la bonne heure*!'

In an instant she was surrounded by the young people whose night this was, of whom she was the crowned queen. All in white, they eddied and swirled round the flames of the bonfire like so many pale moths. The uniform for the boys was newly laundered shirts, Sundaybest, tucked into baggy white cotton trousers bound round with long, fringed scarves of scarlet cotton.

'Françoise, Célandine, Marie-Pascale!' And 'Pierre!' Of course there was Pierre, and his sausage-fingered expectations – expectations which Marguerite was more than prepared to handle.

The market square was crowded, the numbers swollen

by those returned to the village for the festival from the towns of the plain. In the middle of the square, under the medieval canopy which normally housed the market-stalls, were set trestle-tables covered with white cloths, flanked by long wooden benches improvised from sawn logs and rough planks. Tall jugs of wine were ranged like soldiers along the boards, already set with dishes of glistening black olives, pickled cherries, white bloomed *saucisson* cut into thick pink slabs. The bread was specially baked to the ancient formula, crisp-crusted and rich with oil. The leaf-shaped *fougasse*, yellow-crumbed *pompe*, *gimblette*, *navette*, *oreillet*. There were no knives to cut the loaves. Feast-day bread could not be touched with steel, or bloodshed would surely follow.

On the ground stood a line of bubbling cauldrons filled with saffron-scented stews of tripe and cow's heel, the juices thickened with ground almonds and seasoned with verjuice, the bitter green sap of unripened grapes. From the steaming pots, wooden bowls were filled – and filled and filled again. Then came pastries stuffed with apple and plum, meringues and caramels and sugar tarts with strange names – nuns' sighs, fingers of the Virgin, navels of Venus.

In the narrow streets of the village, the midsummer heat boiled, encouraging the singers and inflaming the dancers. Courting couples took advantage of the busy throng to steal kisses and more, if the boys had their way and the girls would permit.

Above all, Marguerite loved the ribbon-weaving, maypole-circling, garland-throwing rituals whose rhythms are not learned but bred in the bone. Graceful and sure-footed, she led the gatherers in the ancient patterns through whose couplings and uncouplings are mirrored the pursuits and captures, betrothals and betrayals of the oldest story in the world.

Pierre had such things on his mind for Marguerite – and

it was clear from the wandering hands as he swung her in the dance that he saw her as soon to be his, and Marguerite made no attempt to discourage him.

As the night wore on towards morning, there was only one small cloud on Marguerite's horizon. She would dearly have loved that Tonin had been there to share her triumph. Even as the festival began, she had thought he might have changed his mind. She had imagined a dozen times that she had caught a glimpse of him among the throng, only to be disappointed once again.

Even so, the evening passed swiftly for the queen of the dance, slender, bright-haired, graceful as a willow among the revellers.

The final ritual was yet to come, but it was the most important of all.

The first light of the morning brought the gathering of the herbs sacred to the saint. The seven medicinal herbs – thyme, rosemary, sage, hyssop, marjoram, sarriette, fennel – are believed by the country people to have magical properties when they are gathered in the dawn dew on the longest day of the year.

It was customary that it was the young people – those who were of marriageable age – who did the gathering. The flirting which began at the dance was inevitably continued in the high meadows, which was where the sweetest and most scented herbs were to be found.

Soon it would be time for the gathering, and then surely Tonin would be there. Please God let him be there. She would be seen at her best in the soft dawn light, with her eyes sparkling and her cheeks flushed.

How could he not come, when he knew that she would be his princess and he her prince?

19

The Gathering

This year, as every year, it did not rain in the valleys of Upper Provence on the night of the St Jean. But high in the mountains where the headwaters gathered, fifty miles and more to the north, the rain had already fallen softly and steadily through three days and three nights.

The rain fell at first in great oily globules, like the droppings of some gigantic bird. The drops which fell on the dry hillside shattered into a thousand glittering shards under the racing moon. The red dust of summer formed a skin round the droplets, holding them for an instant, until like trapped sea-creatures they broke free.

By the end of the second day the rain had filled the underground caverns which provided a natural reservoir for the rivers which watered the valleys. Already the waters were searching for new outlets.

As the drops began to fall more rapidly, the water which at other times of the year would have been a welcome libation failed to find a purchase. Instead it formed itself into small streams which carved narrow channels through the iron-hard earth. Unimpeded, the streams gathered momentum until they found a natural destination in the High Pool which irrigated the valley of the Hermitage.

The snow-water had already filled this natural reservoir to the brim. The waters licked, fastidious as a cat, against the cracks and fissures which the passage of time had carved in the stone parapet. They were in no hurry to break free. They would always find a way.

The water from the streams which did not immediately find release formed an ever-widening pool which, whipped by a light breeze of its own making, rippled against the retaining rampart, sparkling as prettily as the lights which twinkled for the revellers in the valley below.

On the slope of the hill immediately below the High Pool the sun was already dipping below the ridge by the time Tonin finished the milking in the borie village.

The task had taken longer than usual. There was a sultriness in the air, an uncertainty which matched his own mood. The older nannies, more sensitive to such changes, were restless. He had to be more patient than usual, coaxing the heavy teats into yielding their burden.

'Bien, les dames.'

Finished at last, Tonin slapped the rump of the last nanny to send her skittering out into the enclosures. He counted his flock. The goatboy did not like to leave any unaccounted for at night. There were rumours of wolves in the high hills beyond the valley; and, if not wolves, packs of savage dogs which had gone wild during the war years. The old billy, bad-tempered over the loss of a horn, was missing. Tonin set the pails of thick creamy milk in one of the empty bories and went in search of him. The animal had wandered some distance into the ravines, and was unwilling to be corralled.

'Easy does it, *mon vieux*.'

Tonin rarely had to use force. He used his voice to calm his charges, and his hands. But the billy was angry and frightened, and it took all of Tonin's strength to bring him down to the safety of the stone enclosures.

By the time he had completed his tasks, the sounds of revelry were already rising from the valley, borne upwards on the evening thermals. Not only his hearing, but also his sense of smell was as acute as only that of a *ravi* can be.

The scent of cooking, of pot-simmered meats and caramel-dipped pastries reminded him that he was ravenous.

He fetched bread and cheese and, after a moment's thought, a skin of wine. He laid out this modest meal on the bench he had set for himself by the borie's entrance.

He paused for a moment, his wolf-senses troubling him. It was not Tonin's way to reason things through or take rational decisions – although he had learned to do this when required for Father Patrick. On the hill with his flocks, he did not need to think rationally. His five senses decoded the meaning in the ripple of grasses, the dampness of pebbles, the hum of insects, the scent of earth, the bitterness of sap, as naturally as breathing. In this respect, he was very much like his beasts, and he valued their opinion as much as his own.

It had been a troubling day, and there was a full moon hanging low on the horizon, which always made Tonin a little uneasy. In the distance, an owl hooted. Had he but listened to his senses, he would have realized that what disturbed him was not the usual noises of the evening – the rustlings of the newly emergent night creatures, the shift-ings of roosting birds – but the absence of noise. All nature was silent, waiting for what was to come.

Unconcerned, Tonin chewed hungrily, washing the food down with big draughts of wine. The air seemed oddly heavy, although perhaps this was an effect of the alcohol.

Afterwards he stretched wearily. His body as exhausted as his mind, he lay down on the bench under the stars and fell immediately into a deep slumber. His dreams were troubled, those strange dreams in which those who have wings cannot fly, those who have legs cannot run.

It was the soft light of the long summer dawn, an almost imperceptible lightening of the eastern sky, which finally roused him from his wooden bed. His body felt cold where the night air touched it. His muscles ached, his head throbbed.

197

The air was still heavy, and all at once he knew why. The smell of rain, metallic and sharp. His flocks knew it, too. He could hear the shiftings and snortings which told him that they, too, feared the storm which sometimes struck in high summer, although never on the Eve of the St Jean.

The dawn was rising. It was no longer the Eve, but the day itself.

He rose swiftly and took the path which led to the High Pool. At first he could see nothing amiss, except that small waves lapped the rampart and the waters which usually made a perfect mirror for the sky seemed unusually disturbed.

Reaching the stone parapet, he kicked off his boots, stripped off his breeches and plunged in, trusting that the icy snow-waters would clear his head.

The water was warm. This alone should have been enough to tell him that somewhere in the distant peaks the deep wells which fed the underground springs were already brimming. That the warmth of the water, so pleasant to the bather was, in its dilution of the snow-water, a signal of danger.

It was the eddying of the current against his naked skin which told him that the water was rising from beneath, rising steadily, its pressure forming the little eddies which broke the mirrored surface. All at once he understood.

More sinister still, every nerve in his body told him that there was rain on the way, even though the deep blueness of the sky, the brilliance of the sunrise gave his senses the lie.

'If the rains come, the ramparts cannot hold.' His own warning echoed in his head.

The ramparts. Cold with fear, Tonin began to push rocks into crevices, dam streams before they could turn into rivers, pile earth on earthworks and stones back into tumbling walls.

As the sun lifted over the horizon, his strength was spent, and still the water rose higher. Wherever it was coming from, it would need more than his solitary strength to stop the flow.

As this final realization came to him, the rain clouds from the mountains rolled out of the north.

At this instant, Tonin remembered Marguerite and the gatherers. If the walls of the High Pool gave way, they would be first in the path of the flood.

In the darkness which comes before dawn, while Tonin was still slumbering on his bench outside the borie, the young people assembled for the gathering. Each carried a basket.

Marguerite had collected hers when she returned to the Hermitage to fetch Abelard.

The girls brought enough provisions for two, while the young men carried empty baskets to be filled with the gatherings. The plainest of the girls took the most trouble with their provisions – good housekeeping counted for as much as a pretty face or even a modest dowry in the marriage market. There was almost as much competition over the best-provisioned basket as there was for the lowest-cut neckline, and many a betrothal could be laid at the door of the gathering-baskets.

Marguerite had packed her basket under Madame Blanchette's critical eye. She had made a lemon cake and baked a round loaf with hazelnuts and raisins. To go with it, thick slices of that same salty wind-dried ham which had once been her birthday treat, and fat tomatoes, scarlet and juicy. There were shiny black olives of her own pickling, and little pink radishes tied in a bunch like a wedding posy.

'The food must be plain, Marguerite. Nothing too spicy. Nothing to inflame the blood.'

Inflaming the blood, Tonin's blood, was exactly what Marguerite had in mind. After Madame Blanchette's inspection, she had remembered to slip in one of the little packets of *préservatifs*. She still hoped Tonin would join the gatherers. She could not imagine that anything would keep him away.

The procession set off in silence. There was no moon or stars to light their way, and the young people carried no lanterns to mark their passage through the olive groves. The mystery of this walk through the darkness was part of the ritual of the gathering. The young people walked in single file – the younger ones sleepily following the older. Led by Marguerite, with Abelard's soft feathers against her cheek, they mounted the steep path to the ridge.

The sky lightened slowly in streaks of violet and black which hung just above the skyline.

Had they but eyes to see or ears to hear, there was danger to be read in the silence of the olive groves, in the brilliance of the sunrise, in the stillness of the air, the absence of birdsong. Caught in the magic of their quest, none of the gatherers noticed these small signs. Abelard alone was restless, showing his nervousness by digging his sharp little talons into his mistress's shoulder and nickering softly in her ear – until, irritated, she set him by on a branch to wait for her to finish her picking.

The hills were blanketed with sage and rosemary; hyssop and the lilac-blossomed sarriette flowered among scented pincushions of thyme. For refreshment, as the gatherers made their way to the high ground, there were berries to be picked – blueberries and tiny fragrant wood strawberries.

But Marguerite filled her basket distractedly – she had been hoping to hear the goatbells which would tell her that Tonin was near. She was beginning heartily to regret her encouragement of Pierre. But with the sun already a pale glow in the east there was no sign of the goatboy and his flock.

The young people began to form couples as they moved

across the slopes, gathering armfuls of herbs and pausing to nibble at the berries.

Pierre was already red-faced and puffing before the climb began, and his mind was certainly not on the task. The young men had agreed among themselves in advance who they were to court, and Pierre had already staked his claim to Marguerite. As he dogged her footsteps, grinning at her in what she thought was a very idiotic fashion, she wished now that she had not dropped her neckline and raised her skirt so high.

'Leave me alone, Pierre,' she snapped as he tried to slip his arm round her waist or steal a kiss.

To Pierre, the herb-gathering was not be taken seriously; it was just an excuse for the courting. Herbs and wild leaves were no good for anything but goats. He did not see why anyone should wish to eat grass when they could eat meat, and he hoped that Marguerite had borne that in mind when she packed her basket. He was hungry already. Furthermore, he was feeling a little aggrieved. He felt he had earned a bit of civility, and he was not getting much from Marguerite.

He could not understand why. He had done everything to court her at the feast. He had piled her plate with sugary delicacies and refilled her wineglass. He had made sure that she was never short of a partner, even though there were many other girls more willing than she. In short, he had paid his dues, and now he was ready to claim his prize.

By the time the gathering was halfway through, he was bored and hungry. For the basket or the girl – he did not care in which order.

'Come on, dumpling, give us a taste.'

'Not yet, Pierre – there's plenty of picking still to be done.'

Undeterred, Pierre reached out to grab the basket – only to withdraw his hand hastily as Abelard hissed and clattered his beak.

'Why did you have to bring that evil creature?'

'He's not evil.' Marguerite grinned at Pierre. 'Just nervous. He doesn't like sudden movements.'

Pierre decided to sulk. He dropped behind to walk with Marie-Pascale.

For a while Marguerite thought that she had managed to shake him off, but there he was again just as soon as she had set her basket down and Abelard had withdrawn to a nearby branch.

'Caught you,' said Pierre, pushing his face close to hers. 'What's eating you, sweetie?'

'Nothing's eating me.' She glared at him. 'And you're not eating anything, either.'

Marguerite picked up her basket. She had changed her mind. She had no intention of sharing anything with Pierre – not her food, let alone her favours.

He puckered his lips at her. 'A little something for your Pierrot?'

'Greedy pig, Pierre.' She tossed her head. She was really irritated now, and not only with Pierre. 'And if you paid a little more attention to the picking we might be done sooner.'

It was entirely Tonin's fault that the butcher's boy felt free to behave as if he owned her.

She called Abelard to her shoulder and moved upwards towards the ridge, where she could get a view of the bories.

Meanwhile Pierre had got what he thought was the message. Some girls like a little of the rough stuff. It excited them. He waited till she had stopped by a particularly lush patch of marjoram and lunged at her, intending to bring her down on to the soft bed of herbs.

This unprompted assault was too much for Abelard, who stretched his wings threateningly and took a quick stab with his needle-sharp beak at the clasping fingers. Pierre let out a squeal of pain – he was better at dealing with dead meat than with live.

'Merde!'

Marguerite swung round just as Abelard drew blood. Pierre was lucky. The tawny could just as easily have picked out his eye. Father Patrick's bird books were full of warnings. Pierre would not know that, of course. He probably thought an owl was a harmless pet, a kind of oversized canary.

She decided that she had better show a little solicitousness. 'Are you all right, Pierre?'

The butcher's boy was snivelling and peering at his hand.

'Let me see.'

She checked the pudgy finger. Abelard had not really done much. Just a small scratch. She did not point out that he was lucky. Pierre was a bully, and like all bullies he was a coward. She could see it now, as he backed away from Abelard, now back on his mistress's shoulder, clicking and rocking irritably.

'That bloody bird's dangerous. One of these days somebody'll shoot it.'

'*He*,' said Marguerite shortly. 'It's not an *it*, it's a *him*.' Then she added, smiling sweetly: 'And if Abelard gets shot I'll shoot you.'

She picked up her basket again and increased her pace. Pierre puffed after her. He was confused. He was not used to rejection from anyone, let alone from a chit of a girl with no family, no land and no prospects. She would be lucky to get him. He had expectations. A respectable family. His father's business would one day be his. He drove his own van, and last summer he had even taught her to drive it in the hope of a little something in return. Not only that, but he had land from his mother's side of the family. Land and prospects and family mattered far more than a pretty face, and Marguerite should consider herself fortunate that he was interested in her at all.

Certain of the strength of his hand, he decided to forgive

her. Accordingly he trotted along behind, keeping her just in view, until she stopped and set down the basket again, bending down to gather the flowering tips from a thick bush of rosemary.

He darted forward, keeping a wary eye on the feathered monster on her shoulder, and grabbed the basket. He flicked open the lid and peered inside.

'Ham. My favourite.' He licked his lips. 'Be nice, Marguerite.'

'I'm perfectly nice.'

'I mean *really* nice.' His small eyes flickered between the basket and the small patch of bosom revealed by the loosened drawstrings of Marguerite's blouse.

'Fuck off, Pierre.'

Marguerite suddenly lost her temper – as much with herself as with Pierre. Her eyes flashed; the mascara had smudged a little by now, enhancing their extraordinary colour. It was all her own fault for encouraging him in the first place. But now she had had enough. She could not imagine how she had tolerated Pierre's attentions for an instant – let alone encouraged them, even if only to make Tonin jealous.

'*Foutez-moi le cou!*' she said.

This display of temper had the opposite effect on Pierre. She was spicy. He liked a bit of fire in a woman as much as he liked it in his food. She was really a very appetizing dumpling. A fiery little chilli might be more accurate.

These musings reminded him that it was past time for the picnic. He returned his attention to the basket. Keeping a wary eye on Marguerite and her feathered guardian, he rummaged around in its depths.

After a moment his fingers closed on a little packet. Maybe a sliver of nougat or a piece of chocolate, he thought greedily. Something to stave off the pangs of hunger. He opened it and peered down at the contents, scarcely able to believe his eyes.

A broad smile spread across Pierre's face at the sight of the contents of the packet. He had misjudged Marguerite – she had never had any intention of not playing the game.

'What have we here, my little pepper dumpling?'

Marguerite straightened up from her gatherings and swung round.

'Give me that!'

She covered the distance between them swiftly.

'Naughty Marguerite – what would Father Patrick say?' His voice was teasing, delighted.

Her cheeks flamed.

'None of your business!' She reached out, dislodging Abelard, who took off in a flurry of outraged feathers.

Pierre was too quick for her. He had one of the condoms out now – was dangling the packet out of her reach.

'Come on, sweetie. Give us a break.'

'Go to hell!'

'More like a little bit of heaven . . .' He shoved three fat fingers into the rubber disc and wiggled them around so that it expanded suggestively. 'What's this for, then?'

'I—' Marguerite stared at him, her stomach churning. 'I brought them for a friend,' she said wildly.

'Of course you did, dumpling. I'm your friend.' Pierre's currant-bun eyes popped at her. In one smooth movement, he had her firmly round the waist, his mouth searching for hers. He whispered: 'All for me.'

She struggled to throw him off, but he was very strong. The other arm had found her wrist, and in an instant it was pinned behind her back. The next moment she found herself forced down towards the grass.

Tears of rage and pain started into her eyes as he twisted her arm upwards, pushing her down and round until she found herself on her back, the heavy bulk of the butcher's boy pinning her to the ground.

His face came down towards her, his mouth open, the

saliva wet on her face. She struggled for a moment, wondering whether to scream for help. But the other gatherers were well out of earshot. She went limp, turning her face away from his.

'All right, Pierre – just let me breathe.'

He relaxed his grip. Grinned down at her.

'That's my girl.'

He could not tell whether she wanted him or not, but by now he did not care. She would, just as soon as she had learned her lesson. They all wanted it, sooner or later.

This assessment was confirmed by what Marguerite said next. 'Put the thing on. I don't want to get pregnant.'

Triumphant, Pierre pulled back, fumbling with his clothes. As soon as she felt his weight lift, Marguerite heaved with all her strength, bringing her knee up sharply till it hit the soft flesh of his now-exposed groin.

She heard him gasp in pain, and the hands released her.

As she scrambled from beneath him, he grabbed at her skirts. Madame Blanchette's stitching was strong, and for a moment the seams held – and then, mercifully, gave way. Marguerite pulled herself free, leaving most of the petticoat in Pierre's possession.

'Bitch! Damn you, bitch!'

She began to run, her heart pounding. When she thought she had put a reasonable distance between herself and her assailant, she stopped to get her bearings.

The rest of the gatherers were already out of earshot. Her best, her only hope was Tonin. At least being rescued by Tonin would not be so humiliating.

A few yards ahead of her was a steep chimney of rock which she knew came out just below the ridge on the far side of which was the High Pool and the borie village. Oblivious of the thorns and the sharpness of the rocks, she began to work her way upwards.

Pierre was not used to scrambling around the hillside. He would soon give up the pursuit. She paused for a moment, listening. Far beneath she could hear him blundering around the bushes.

He had clearly recovered and decided it was all part of the game.

'Come on, dumpling. Where are you, my little darling?' His voice was once again hopeful. 'A game of *cache-cache*, is it?'

All at once, the broad wings of Abelard shadowed the light. Pierre might not have seen her, but the owl had no trouble at all. The bird dipped towards her, once, twice, and then settled back on her shoulder.

She ducked back into the scrub, but too late.

'So that's where you are, my little spitfire! Wait for your Pierrot!'

Wearily – bitterly regretting the stupidity which had landed her in this situation – she scrambled upwards towards the ridge.

Where the devil was Tonin? She could not hold out much longer. The night's revelling had taken its toll of her strength. She could hear Pierre gaining on her now; his occupation might not have equipped him with speed, but he had plenty of stamina.

She heaved herself upwards, sheer willpower dragging her on.

The first flash of lightning which heralded the storm was a sheet of blazing whiteness which bathed the high tops in an eerie brilliance.

At that same moment the owl screamed, the noise deafening in her ear, filling her with a sudden wave of blind panic.

Abelard rose high on pale wings, circled once, twice, three times, almost as if he was ashamed to have first betrayed and then deserted her. He swooped low over the ravine, vanishing into the soft mist which clouded the valley beneath.

She was alone now. There was no-one to come to her

rescue. She had no witnesses – not even Abelard. No-one would believe that she had not led him on. That she had not meant to deliver what Pierre thought he had every right to expect.

The 'precautions' were ample proof of her intentions. No-one would believe her. Not even Father Patrick. Probably not even Tonin. But what was the use of that? He, too, had abandoned her. If he had not, he would already have come.

Despair washed over her. It would be so much easier just to let Pierre take what he wanted. Just lie back and be done with it.

These were the thoughts in her head as she raised her face to the ridge, willing herself to make one last effort. In that instant, a new plan came to her. Just over the top lay the High Pool. She knew that Pierre could not swim – in fact he was terrified even of crossing the shallow ford which led to the Hermitage.

If she could reach the High Pool, she could swim to safety. She had no-one to rely on but herself. No-one to blame but herself.

The first rain fell as she reached the top of the ridge.

It was then that she saw him, a lad, distant still but unmistakable, the limping figure outlined against the storm clouds rolling out of the north.

20

The Storm

Tonin reached the top of the ridge at the same moment as Marguerite scrambled out of the ravine.

Behind him the thunder rolled once more.

Out of the clouds came a three-pronged fire, as sharp as the devil's pitchfork, and slammed into the rampart of the High Pool. The great rocks fissured and crumbled, sending shards of rock soaring towards the sky. At that same moment the clouds emptied their burden. The second prong spent itself harmlessly in the waters. The third buried itself deep in the earth, where it found a purchase in the tinder-dry roots of the sage-brush. The fire did not take hold immediately, but smouldered greedily in the subterranean sap, waiting its turn.

'Tonin! Thank God, Tonin!'

Marguerite tumbled into the goatboy's arms. Just behind her came Pierre, scarlet-faced and dishevelled.

Tonin took in the situation at a glance. His wolf-senses were not required to decode that particular story. But for now there was not a second to be lost. As soon as he had realized that his efforts to contain the waters were useless, it had taken him only a matter of moments to reach the vantage-point which overlooked the slopes where the gatherers would already be setting out their picnic-baskets.

His breath coming in short gasps, he scanned the thick scrub beneath the ridge.

'The others – where are the others?'

Misunderstanding Tonin's concern, Marguerite glanced at Pierre, now defiantly clenching and un-clenching his fists.

Pierre said quickly: 'I – we – left them behind. Down below, in the ravine.'

'For C-Christ's s-sake!'

Tonin started downwards, but Marguerite caught his arm. 'What is it? What's happened?'

Tonin stared at her, his eyes wild, and then turned and waved frantically towards the High Pool. 'Listen!'

Marguerite could hear it now, a curious sound, a rumble from deep within the bowels of the mountainside, like an army of muffled drums which seemed to shake the earth beneath her feet. More ominous still was the thick brown slick now moving slowly but steadily over the lip of the rampart.

At that moment the thunder rolled once more.

All at once Marguerite remembered her dream. There would be fire. There had been fire in her dream. Fire and water, air and earth.

'The bories!'

Tonin swung round. She was right. The borie village was the only shelter which stood even a chance against the flood which would surely follow the landslide.

Once he knew, he did not hesitate.

'I'll warn the others. You go straight to the village – now.' There was something new in Tonin's voice – an authority, an expection that he would be obeyed. 'Take Pierre with you. Get the animals inside. Then set the door in place and wait for us.'

'But Tonin—'

Tonin was no longer there. His limp forgotten, he was already plunging deep into the thorn bushes which lined the dry bed of the ravine. His voice echoed and bounced off the tunnel of rock, calling the gatherers. Filling his lungs and cupping his hands over his mouth, Tonin willed his voice to rise above the mounting clamour of the storm.

Marguerite waited only long enough to make sure that the gatherers were already on their way.

Far down the ravine, Tonin reappeared – carrying the youngest of the girls over his shoulder, tugging another by the hand. She could see the rest of the gatherers now, a straggling procession falling in behind the goatboy. There was no doubt of his authority, for all that he was not someone from whom they would usually take orders.

At the same moment, the rest of the storm clouds rolled over the ridge.

Marguerite, with the red-faced Pierre panting in her wake, reached the bories a few minutes ahead of Tonin and the others. There was a huge boulder which would have to be rolled back into position to block the doorway.

'Help me, Pierre!'

Together they heaved the rock into position. Not a moment too soon, the little procession reached the bories.

At that moment, with a boom like a thousand cannon-balls, the waters of the High Pool broke free. A torrent of boiling mud leaped down the stone conduits, churning down the narrow ravines, hurtling towards the broad bed of the river below.

Receiving the waters, the river rose slowly and steadily, a monster released from its underground cavern. The waters which had once brought the valley prosperity were now to be the instrument of its destruction.

Meanwhile, down in the valley, the village, built as it was on a small hill around which the little river had carved its own deep channel, was all unaware of the danger. The inhabitants, exhausted by the night's exertions, had slept on into the morning.

Even if there had been a warning, it might have gone unheeded. It was not the first time the river had over-flowed its banks – such an emergency was commonplace in winter, although it was quite unknown at the time of the St Jean.

All the same, a flood was not so unusual an occurrence that there was great cause for alarm, or that the people did not know how to take the necessary steps to protect their homes – rising sleepily to barricade doorways and seal up windows, moving household goods into the upper floors, evacuating the young and the old and the vulnerable to the higher ground. And then, as had always been the way, they would wait for the waters to subside, for the river to pass on its way.

This time – although they did not yet know it – was different. The landslide of mud from the High Pool had already blocked the river's natural channels, swelling the slow-moving current until it, too, broke its banks, feeding little tributaries which snaked across the dry terraces and into the cracked earth of the fields which surrounded the village.

Here and there where the water was deepest, the twisted roots of uprooted trees trailed streamers of tangled grass. The tributaries searched for new paths. Finding their way to the Hermitage, they meandered across the heretics' graveyard, wandered through the cemetery, caressing the carved feet of winged angels, eddying round the obelisks, slipping liquid fingers into cracked tombstones, tugging at skulls and toying with bones.

Tired of amusement among the dead, the water flowed on to play with the living. Soon the waters were lapping around the lower streets of the village, spreading into the market-place in an ever-widening lake. A few of the inhabitants, those who had been abstemious at the feast, turned in their beds, drowsily murmuring to husbands or wives. The sound of water was curious, but not yet frightening. There had to be some simple reason why the river had burst its banks.

Just at the moment that the people were rising sleepily

from their beds, the sky darkened once more. All at once a single sheet of lightning lit up the bowl of the mountains. It was not unknown in the dry midsummer for fire to follow storm. Sometimes lightning struck bare earth and buried itself deep in the roots of trees. The embers might smoulder underground for weeks, even months. This subterranean touch-paper could travel a considerable distance from the point where the lightning had originally struck, so you never knew when or where it might suddenly find sustenance.

This was not the case with this particular bolt. The lightning found its target immediately in the twisted trunk of an ancient pine dwarfed by summer drought. The resin in the branches turned the twigs into miniature torches which exploded into life like small Catherine wheels, scattering spokes of flaming pine-needles. Within minutes the fire had taken its hold on the dry pastures of the ridge.

All might yet have been well. One of the purposes of the irrigation conduits, the reason why the Hermitage and its village had survived for so many centuries, had been to control these lightning-triggered fires which in other parts could wreak such terrible destruction. The waters of the irrigation channels could always be brought to bear on the flames. But now, with the High Pool emptied and the conduits blocked with mud, there was no chance at all.

Within moments the bowl of the hills was plumed with a terrible parody of the fires of the St Jean. Tall sheets of flame, white and gold, licked across the high tops, feeding hungrily on the dry pastures, sending showers of sparks to light more little fires which, searching, found more fuel.

Seconds after the lightning had struck, from the rampart of the High Pool came a rolling tattoo of thunder. The mighty wave of sound beat again and again against the walls of rock, rumbling round the valley, bouncing off the precipices – rousing at last even the heaviest of the sleepers in the village below.

Disaster might even then have been averted had there not been a playful breeze which caught up the sparks and whirled them skyward, until, tiring of the game, it tossed them carelessly into the dry sage-brush of the lower slopes.

From the upper floors of the houses, where the villagers had crowded to observe the floodwater, the fire could now clearly be seen. The wind was in the east, and the flames raced towards the valley floor, licking through the branches of the olive trees, crackling and chattering as the oily fruit bubbled and burst, setting light to half-dried leaves and spreading burning droplets among the thistles and abandoned vines beneath.

At that same moment the villagers remembered the gatherers. All but the youngest of the children of the village were still out on the hill, the way back now blocked by the ever-advancing wall of flame.

It was not until the whole mountainside began to blacken that the people panicked.

'Listen.'

Célandine's voice was loud in the silent darkness of the borie where the gatherers huddled.

Even though the domed roof of the borie protected them from the river of mud, they could hear the mighty rush of the water.

In the sanctuary afforded by the thick walls, the air was heavy with the odour of fear, mixed with a strong scent of goat. The old billy occasionally let out a frightened bleating which punctuated the whimpering of the younger girls.

The boys, too, were scared. All, it seemed, but Tonin. The goatboy had assumed the leadership of the group as naturally as if he had been born to it.

The girls were all ranged close to him. When Marie-Pascale said, 'You're so brave, Tonin. If it hadn't been for you, we'd all have been killed,' her voice held such adoration that Marguerite felt a sharp stab of jealousy.

'We're trapped. There's no hope.' It was Pierre's voice, cracked and fearful. 'Buried alive,' he snivelled. A typical bully, the butcher's boy had lost all his bravado.

'Shut up, Pierre,' snapped Célandine. But there was no doubt that the air was growing staler by the minute.

It was Marie-Pascale's turn next. 'What do we do now, Tonin?'

'We wait.' Tonin's voice was deep and soothing. 'For the moment, there's no danger. This place is built like a fortress.'

Marguerite moved closer to Tonin in the warm darkness. The goatboy was hers; she shared his heroism.

Silence descended again.

After a moment, Tonin began to move round the walls, feeling for the opening which served as the doorway. Marguerite joined him, her fingers searching for the gap and encountering only a sheer wall of rock embedded in mud.

'I think it's jammed.' Marguerite's voice was a whisper. She had been concerned to pull the stone door shut behind them, not to make sure it could be opened again. Now the moving wall of mud had sealed it tight.

Tonin squatted down with his back to the door. She could not see his face in the darkness. After a moment she said: 'What now?'

There was a flash of white teeth. 'We use our brains.'

Marguerite contemplated this suggestion in silence. Then she said: 'Smoke.'

'What do you mean?'

'The smoke from the fire always rose. It must have got out somewhere.'

Tonin stood up and began to probe gently at the smooth expanse of the roof. Marguerite was right. There was a narrow flue, a weak seam of small stones designed to allow smoke to escape without permitting the rain to enter.

Marguerite's fingers touched his, following the line of the seam.

'Can we widen it?'

'Maybe. It's a risk.'

There was no need to elaborate – it would only scare the others. They both knew that broadening the channel would certainly weaken the roof, risking the collapse of the entire structure, dependent as it was for its strength on the perfect cantilevering of the boulders.

In silence, Tonin set to work again. After a few moments some of the smaller stones came loose, and a thin breath of cold air filtered through the damp mortar, creating a little breeze.

'You're right.' The relief in his voice did little to reassure Marguerite, who knew the danger well enough.

'Now for the keystone.'

She just managed to avoid that sharp intake of breath which would tell the others what she feared. The keystone was the single plug of rock which the builders had pushed in last, and which held the whole dome in place.

With a grunt of satisfaction, Tonin found what he was looking for. 'Here. Feel.'

He guided Marguerite's fingers along the edge of a roughly shaped disc of rock set a few inches proud of the roof, its edge fashioned into a lip which acted as a seal.

'Now for the work.'

He made a mental inventory of the gatherers, sizing up their strength and suitability for the tasks.

'Pierre, Michel, Jean-Claude – over here.' His stutter had vanished. 'Henri, you're the tallest. Get your shoulder under the keystone and keep it there. If that goes, the whole roof'll collapse. If it shifts by so much as an inch, shout and then get the hell out of the way – and that goes for everyone. The rest of you, do as I say.'

He divided the young men into two groups – one group to loosen the stones, the others to remove them.

The girls were put under Marguerite's direction to build a shelter of the few sticks of rough furniture in case the roof collapsed.

Under Tonin's expert direction, they set to work. The roof was several feet thick, the boulders densely packed with small stones, and it was an hour at least before a fine crack of light appeared between the boulders.

They saw the red glow of the fire before they felt its heat. The cool stale air of the borie was suddenly replaced with the warm stench of burning. The warm red glow illuminated the darkness.

'Fire.' Tonin's voice was even, emotionless, concealing his feelings. His eyes glittered red in the glow. He said: 'Plug the hole. We'll have to find another way.'

'The fuck we will!'

It was Pierre's voice, thick with a mixture of rage and fear.

Marguerite straightened up, suddenly aware of the new threat. She knew that the butcher's boy was already at boiling point. She also knew he had a skinning knife, the treasured tool of his trade. It had been at the back of her mind that he might have used it earlier against her on the hill, and it had been one of the reasons for her fear of him.

She glanced down. Sure enough, the slender blade was held like a dagger in his fist. The curved steel, honed to a razor-sharpness, shone red in the light of the fire.

Marguerite was no longer frightened. She was frightened of no-one and nothing.

She stepped forward, blocking his path. 'Pierre . . .' Her voice was calm. She held out her hand. 'Give me the knife.'

The butcher's boy lifted his eyes to hers. She could see the madness in them, the naked fear which makes a man risk all to save his own skin.

At that moment Tonin turned, the yellow eyes alert,

217

narrowed, glittering, the lopsided body bent half-double to spring.

Pierre's breath was coming in quick gasps. His face was beaded with sweat as he danced towards the crouching figure he had identified as his enemy.

'Out of the way, goatboy.' Pierre's teeth were drawn back from his lips. He gestured towards the gap in the roof with the glittering point of the curved knife. 'You got us into this hell-hole. I'm getting the hell out.'

Out of the corner of her eye, Marguerite saw the others, a ring of white faces bathed in the red glow from the roof, frightened bodies pushed back against the now-steaming walls.

The heat was coming in steady waves, the flames of the fire clearly visible through the widening gap. Cracks were beginning to appear in the remaining mortar. Soon the roof would be open to the flaming sky.

Tonin spread his hands, moving aside.

'Do it, then.'

He made no move to prevent what happened next. Even if he had wanted to, he could not have stopped Pierre, maddened and crazed as he was.

The ring of white faces held a mixture of shock and terror as the butcher's boy forced his body into the impossibly narrow channel, pushing frantically forward until, trapped by his own bulk, he could neither continue nor retreat.

He began to scream then, a high wail which seem to come from the depths of hell itself.

'Help me, damn you!'

Tonin hesitated for a single instant, but he knew he had no choice. The keystone would have to go. Loosened now, it was easy to dislodge, coming away in his hand in a shower of stones. Pierre's thrashing limbs found a purchase at last, using the leverage to propel themselves outwards and upwards, only to fall back to earth.

The butcher's boy, the scream knocked from his throat by the shock of release, landed in a crumpled heap on the flagstones which lined the borie. Above him spread the fire-streaked heavens. When the thin air of the borie met the blazing oxygen of the sky, a scorching wave was sucked down into the vacuum which the borie's interior had become.

The hot breath of the inferno pushed the ring of frightened faces even further back against the walls. For a moment it seemed as if the roof would tumble and the borie would be turned into a blazing oven.

Later Tonin did not know from where he had found the strength to push the keystone back into its place before the whole dome of the roof caved in. All he knew was that he had done it – and that a few moments later the others regained enough of their wits to come to his assistance. After that it was a matter of minutes to repack the roof channel.

This time no sound broke the silence, unless it was the whimpering of Pierre, attempting to soothe his blistered skin.

The young people could neither escape nor trust to safety in their shelter. Shocked and bewildered – even Tonin, his arm now protectively around Marguerite – they huddled together in the darkness and waited for what was to come.

Below in the village, the inhabitants assembled in the Mairie, their faces drawn and white. A decision had to be taken. There was no chance of fighting the fire.

No-one knew if the road to Valréas was still passable – or if the mud-slide from the High Pool had carried it away. Help could not be expected from outside. The single telephone line was down.

No-one could decide what to do. There were those who were all for evacuating the village immediately, and those who wanted to hold the line, trust that the storm had soaked the ground sufficiently and that the river had risen high enough to keep the flames at bay. Some took one decision, some another. Confusion reigned.

Alone in the Hermitage, Father Patrick had passed the hours of darkness of the St Jean as he usually did, in prayer and meditation. In the way of the old, he slept very little at night – preferring instead to catnap in the heat of the day. Near-blind as he was, he found the night-time soothing.

It was the return of Abelard without his mistress which told the old priest that something was wrong.

The owl slipped through the arrow-slit on silent wings, and landed on his perch in the rafters. Here he rocked from foot to foot, uttering the high short screeches which were his way of warning that danger was near.

Father Patrick was bewildered. There was no reason why there should be anything wrong, but Abelard was sufficiently agitated to convince him that there was.

The scent of the fire was enough to warn him. The sound of the water confirmed that warning. The gatherers were still out on the hill, his precious Marguerite among them.

There was a way up to the ridge which needed neither sight nor agility, being no more than a long tunnel – a precaution taken by the monks in case of attack, or perhaps even an eventuality such as this, when the Hermitage was threatened by fire or flood, or both.

The old man grasped his staff in his hand and called the owl to his shoulder. His fingers found the iron handle which gave access to the stairway which ran downwards into Aphrodite's cave. The entrance to the tunnel was there. Although blocked up for many centuries, it had been unblocked during wartime, when it had been used by members of Thérèse's Resistance group, allowing them to come and go unobserved. It would be of use again.

Abelard swooped ahead of the old man, returning again and again to brush his shoulder with soft wings, leading him upwards, the blind man and the night-sighted bird in alliance. Holy alliance, as Father Patrick told himself, his stick tap-tapping along the subterranean alleyway. Sometimes he had to crouch, and every now and again his feet splashed through water. But the monks had known their business.

It was slow going. The tunnel was more than a mile long, and there was more than one false passage which ended in a blank wall of rock. But Abelard made no mistakes. Neither tame nor captive, he acknowledged no master. He was a hunting bird. He came and went as he pleased. Father Patrick was wise enough to follow where he was led.

21

The Aftermath

The fire raged above the borie village all through the day. Night fell, and still the flames flickered.

For those in the borie there was no question of escape until the fires died down, and there had been no alternative but to repair the roof as best they could, and wait and hope.

The lack of air made it hard to breathe, shutting down muscles and acting like a soporific on the brain. One by one the trapped young people fell into a fitful slumber. Marguerite alone kept watch, while even Tonin closed his eyes and dozed.

In the darkness of the borie, the past invaded her thoughts.

In her waking dream, her hands held a posy of meadow-daisies, their parchment petals as pale as an angel's wing. Her fingertips were dusted with pollen. Bright butterflies danced all around. On her lips was the taste of wild strawberries, blush-cheeked, as sweet as honey.

She drifted into wakefulness; and, when she did so, her body ached, there was the metallic taste of fear on her tongue. She shivered, listening to the terrible noise of the fire and the water.

The walls of the borie glistened in the faint red light which made its way through the boulders. Shadows danced on the hand-hewn rock and the bodies of the young people heaped in fitful sleep. Black and yellow, the crystals in the rock glittered like gold.

She dreamed again, preferring the strangeness of her dreamtime to the nightmare of the waking.

It was the soft hooting of the owl which roused her from her stupor. Faint but distinct, at first she thought she must still be dreaming.

When it came again, she laid her hand on Tonin's arm. 'Tonin . . .?'

Feeling his muscles tense, she whispered: 'You hear it, too?'

'Abelard. Call him.'

It was nearer now, and unmistakable. At first she could not trace the source of the sound. It seemed to rise from beneath the floor of the borie.

Tonin was on all fours now, eagerly searching the flagstones for the looseness, the slight movement, which would tell him there was a trapdoor.

This time the answering call was close enough to touch. This time there could be no doubt.

There must surely be a trapdoor.

There was a softness to the edge of one of the larger flagstones which told him that over the years it had been moved.

'Henri. Michel-Giles. A hand.'

Sleepily the two young men roused themselves.

Together, breath coming in short gasps from the lack of air, they struggled with the heavy flagstone. The owl's call was louder now, and they could feel a light answering pressure from below.

Under their combined strength, the stone began to yield and lift. As the cold subterranean air rushed upwards into the sealed chamber, the rest of the young people gathered round. Even Pierre, blistered but scared as he was.

The stone rocked, creaked, and rolled free. White faces peered anxiously down. A flight of steep steps led down into the earth. Beyond could be seen a narrow passageway. At the top of the steps stood the old priest, the owl's soft wings brushing his beaming face.

Great was the rejoicing in the village that night. In spite of the terrible toll the waters and the fires had taken, the children of the village were safe.

Much was made of Marguerite. After all, the blessed bird, the miraculous guide for the blind old man, was the girl's chosen companion. Or her familiar – if you believed in such things as witches. Or even – and on a such a night no-one but a fool would question their existence – her guardian angel.

The absence of that guardian angel went unnoticed until the following day, the day which also brought the reckoning.

In the village the waters had drawn back, leaving devastation in their wake. Those of the newer dwellings on the lower slopes whose foundations were not set deep in the rock had suffered most, but even of the most ancient buildings there was scarcely one which had escaped unscathed.

Up and down the valley, a thousand years of toil lay in ruins, the walls of the High Pool all gone, the scorched terraces buried under a muddy silt, the olive trees uprooted and burned, the irrigation channels crushed.

The Hermitage had suffered least damage, being more or less untouched by the river of mud, although the heat of the fire had blown out the glass in the tall window of the library where Father Patrick heard confessions.

It was here that Marguerite came to look for Abelard, vanished in the helter-skelter rush back down the subterranean passageway to safety.

There was no sign of the bird, but she did not at first consider this of any importance. Abelard was probably off hunting – the twilights were long at midsummer.

Instead her attention was caught by the leather-bound

record-books stacked on their shelves in Father Patrick's room. The tempest had rushed in through the gap left by the blown-out panes, covering everything in the fine mist it had gathered on its path. The leather was now streaked with damp. Within, the pages were limp, although the ink, being that curious substance squeezed from cuttlefish, had not dissolved, but lay lightly on the surface of the pale parchment.

Thinking to save Father Patrick from further anxiety, Marguerite carried the books one by one down to the kitchen to dry out in the warmth, then carefully replaced them on the shelves. This activity took several hours – long enough for Tonin to search the hillside and find the tiny corpse.

Tonin had returned to the bories as soon as the brush-fires had burned themselves out. His frightened flock was still safely sealed into the mud-silted dwellings, but he already feared that the owl might have shared the fate of the other wild creatures whose small corpses littered the blackened hillside.

The little corpse lay close to the cracked roof of the borie. He knew what must have happened. The rush of the air, the shock of the faces peering into the passageway, all these had sent the owl into a frenzy. The frantic bird had escaped upwards, squeezing his light-boned body through the roughly sealed gap in the roof, pushing himself though the mud cracked with the heat of the fire. His feathers must have shrivelled into blackened quills as soon as he reached the outer air. Death must have been immediate – nothing could have survived the flames.

Grim-faced, the goatboy brought the tiny body down to Marguerite. He found her finishing her work in the library. Without a word he laid the body in her hands. She gazed down, tears starting to her eyes.

'Abelard? It can't be Abelard?'

She lifted the little bundle of water-sodden feathers and

scorched bone, cradling it against her cheek, as if her own warmth could bring him back to life. She laid him gently in her lap, rocking the tiny body, crooning softly. He was so small, so thin, her beloved bird, in death the bones as light as thistledown, the talons sheathed, the huge eyes dull beneath the double veil of blue.

Tonin watched her, grieving for her. This time he had no words to comfort her.

To Marguerite the grief was too much to bear. She cared nothing now for the disaster which had befallen the valley, of what might become of her, of the homeless villagers, of Father Patrick.

Most particularly Father Patrick.

For the second time in her life, she had lost that which she loved most. Now, as once before, she hated the man who, in her anger, she held responsible for that loss.

Father Patrick – it was all the old man's fault. Everything she loved, he destroyed. If it had not been for his stupidity, Abelard would not have been lost, her mother would never had abandoned her. Even now, she did not really believe in her mother's death. No more than she did in Abelard's.

She stood up and walked silently from the room, the body held in her white skirt, streaked now with mud. She buried the little body in the heretics' graveyard, in a shoebox, beside her mother. She said no words of farewell. Abelard was not a sentimental creature, and nor was she.

Once again, as before, she escaped to roam the hills, nursing her anger, feeding it on the death all around, on the charred flesh, the empty carapaces, the roasted bones of the small creatures which, like Abelard, had not managed to escape the flames.

The day passed swiftly as the waters retreated. There were plenty of minor injuries but no deaths reported, except among the domestic animals.

There was work for the priest, more still for the villagers. The flood had at least meant that the flames were quickly burned out, and the salvaging of what was left could begin immediately. The landslide had carried away the road, so the village was still isolated from the outside world, and likely to remain so for several days.

Sanctuary was required. It was the Church's duty to provide it. Father Patrick flung open the doors of the Hermitage to house the homeless, which was most of the inhabitants of the valley.

'Soyez bien venues,' he beamed.

Madame Blanchette, the schoolmistress and all the able-bodied women set to work with the sweeping and cleaning and the making up of as many beds as might be found. The monks' cells lost their spider's webs, the cellar hospital was dusted and aired. The bustle of that first evening was so cheerful, so nearly festive that it reminded the older folk of the day of the Liberation. This triggered stories of the camaraderie of wartime, and tears were shed over what now seemed – in retrospect at least – the best moments of their lives.

Madame Blanchette's meagre stores were augmented by the contents of salvaged larders; and the vast copper pans, each containing enough to feed two dozen hungry monks, were hauled from attic storerooms and set to bubble on the stove. Small children were everywhere underfoot, babies played in corners under the watchful eyes of grand-mothers.

That evening, carried away by the excitement, Father Patrick emptied his cellar of its bottles of communion wine and fetched up his last treasured bottle of potsheen.

Fortified by this, he felt impelled to mark the moment with a speech.

'Paysans de notre vallée,' he began in his Irish-accented French, giving his flock what he knew they regarded as their proper dignity. The people of those valleys were proud to be called members of the peasantry. The designation was honourable, speaking of generations of good husbandry, reminding his audience that the careful guardianship of the land was not only a duty but a responsibility. Knowledge gained from a thousand years of toil was not lightly to be tossed aside.

He told of the things of his own childhood, the good times – this was no time for the bad. His voice rose and fell as he spoke of the green hills of Ireland, the softness of spring mist, the warmth of summer, the joy of harvest, the barrenness of earth in winter.

At the mention of winter, Father Patrick's republican eloquence, so long dormant, came unbidden to his lips.

'There will be those among us, my friends, who will counsel us to abandon our homes, to renounce our rights, to uproot our children. I tell you now, that's the devil's work! The charity of godless men is cold comfort. Far better to follow the banner of the Lord. By the sweat of thy brow, thou shalt eat bread!'

This last quotation owed rather more to the potsheen than to the Holy Book. Nevertheless, the image was popular enough to merit a rousing cheer, spurring Father Patrick to new heights.

'My friends, let us not be deceived! Listen to no man's weasel words! Take comfort from each other and trust in God's mercy! We shall rebuild our village, restore our valley. The walls will rise again, the land will live! The Lord will help us: for that we have the assurances of His church – our church. Have faith, my flock! We shall overcome!'

Pandemonium greeted this familiar war cry. The Resistance had drawn many of its recruits from those who had communist sympathies, and the priest's words reminded many of that heroic time.

Hearts swelled proudly in breasts and bosoms. One by one the elders stepped forward, telling stories of their youth. Far into the night the villagers shared their hopes, wove stories round what had once been and would be again.

Those who knew all this was no more than the ravings of a mad old priest, no more than the romantic nonsense of those who had reached their second childhood, held their peace. The few who had the most to gain, who could see that there were fortunes to be made from the debris of disaster, knew that their time would come.

The euphoria lasted three days, until the road was opened and the authorities arrived.

With them came the monsignor – bearing words of comfort, naturally. And, equally naturally, plans for the relocation of the flock.

These were already well advanced. As soon as news of the disaster had arrived, Monsignor Melton had sought an interview with the pro-notary apostolic.

'Eminence, we need to clarify our thinking.'

'Of course, Charles. Terrible business. His Holiness was most distressed. Insisted on drafting the message of sympathy himself.'

'Such a comfort, a message.'

'Sherry?'

'Most kind, Eminence.'

Cardinal Giuseppe Navarino rose with a swish of satin-lined soutane. Melton watched the small ritual of the decanter with pleasurable anticipation. Navarino served excellent sherry, a little luxury which always reminded Melton of his own time in Rome. The wine was a manzanilla from Sanlucar, straw-pale and well chilled.

Melton sipped appreciatively.

'Try these. They're delicious. I have them shipped over with the wine.' The cardinal pushed over a small dish of green olives stuffed with anchovies. Then he leaned back in his chair.

'I imagine you have examined the options, Charles. We have responsibilities. The villagers remain our dependants.'

'I think I may have anticipated that.' Melton reached for an olive and savoured it thoughtfully. 'The French seem willing to take them on. Political expediency. At a price naturally. But I think we can come to some mutually agreeable arrangement.'

'Really?' The cardinal leaned forward.

'The authorities are proving most co-operative. They seem keen on solving the question of sovereignty. No-one wants another Monte Carlo. I have suggested a compromise. We keep the Hermitage. They take on the valley and the village. Agreement dated the day before the disaster. Otherwise, as you observe, we can be held responsible. It could be very tricky. Not to mention expensive.'

'Quite. After all, we're not a charity.' The cardinal delivered this without a trace of irony. 'Isn't there some English expression about clouds and silver linings?'

Melton permitted himself a small smile. 'Absolutely.'

'Nevertheless,' the cardinal continued smoothly, 'you might set my mind at rest about a matter which has been troubling me a little. I am informed that it was a fault in the irrigation system which caused most of the damage.'

Melton glanced quickly at his superior. God only knew where he had collected that particular bit of information. His Eminence's face gave no hint.

Melton hesitated again, then decided that there was no point in denial. 'There might be a case.'

'Unfortunate. Negligence?'

'Unprovable.' Melton's voice was emphatic. 'In any event, we had just authorized a programme of extensive investment in the infrastructure.'

'Had we indeed? Which events have now conveniently rendered unnecessary.'

Melton hesitated. 'I assure your Eminence there was no

particular urgency. Father O'Donovan made suggestions over the years. Privately expressed naturally.'

'Quite so.' The pro-notary's voice was dry. 'Just make sure they stay private.'

'Naturally.'

'And naturally you'll do the diplomatic thing. Make the right noises. Be seen to be there.'

'Of course.'

'Wouldn't do to look as if we didn't care.'

'One small complication, Eminence. This morning I received a radio communication via the Quai d'Orsay. The old boy down there seems to have acted on the spur of the moment. Jumped the gun, one might say.'

He pushed over Father Patrick's request for official sanction on what was already a *fait accompli*: the accommodation of the homeless villagers in the Hermitage. The language had been extravagant enough to make the warden think that his resident might have found a stash of his native miracle-water.

The cardinal glanced down, taking in the contents swiftly. He frowned. 'Inconvenient. Damned inconvenient – as your countrymen say.'

In silence the two men contemplated quite how inconvenient. Neither needed to remind the other that, quite apart from the need for discretion over the embarrassing nature of the records kept at the Hermitage, there were political and financial reasons why Father Patrick's action was thoroughly undesirable. Under the medieval agreement under which the Hermitage was held, the Church enjoyed certain privileges. These privileges would be lost if the Hermitage was used for any other purpose but that for which it was built.

The pro-notary sighed. 'In the strictest confidence, Charles, I should tell you I have already spoken to my opposite number in Paris. The French feel just as we do. The Quai d'Orsay says it's all very touchy, diplomatically speaking. The last thing anyone wants is a Gibraltar situation. Wouldn't do to draw attention to ourselves, particularly until His Holiness has found his feet.'

This was a euphemism for the confusion which reigned after the election of a new pope. It had been only a month since Cardinal Montini of Milan had been elected to wear the papal crown as Paul VI. A certain amount of retrenchment was inevitable until everyone knew where they stood.

'I understand perfectly.'

'Perfect understanding was always your forte, Charles.' The pro-notary allowed himself this small dig at his junior's well-known flexibility of conscience. He leaned back in his chair.

'The French have no intention of rebuilding the village. Far too expensive. Much cheaper to relocate. Compensation and so forth will be generous, and we might make some small gesture ourselves.' He paused. 'I don't need to tell you that this suits us admirably. Makes our responsibilities so much clearer in the future.'

Melton shifted uncomfortably in his chair. 'Yes. Maintenance. There are always expenses. Then, again, there's the balance-sheet to consider. As you and I know, one is under constant pressure to maximize profits, Giuseppe.' The warden slipped into the familiar use of the Christian name which reminded the cardinal that the two men were friends when not under the constraints of official business.

The cardinal nodded. 'True, Charles. On that, your record cannot be faulted.'

There was an unspoken understanding between the two men that the demands on those who served the Holy See's financial interests sometimes involved cutting a few corners.

'Priorities.' Melton pushed the point home. 'So fortunate that there are no fatalities. The dead *do* complicate things. Official inquiries and so on.'

There was a short pause, broken by Melton. 'I was wondering. Perhaps an appeal might be appropriate.'

'Careful, Charles. Don't want to upset the French.'

Melton smiled. 'It came to me that I should do nothing too precipitate.'

'Always an excellent decision.' The pro-notary's face did not change, but Melton could tell by the slight relaxation of the shoulders that his superior was relieved. Although it was impossible to deny the existence of the Hermitage, its function had to be protected at all costs. In this the interests of the Church and those of the warden coincided exactly.

'The Oratory at Christmas,' Melton suggested. 'Carefully worded. Blankets, food, toys, clothes. The situation will have quietened down by then. We must be seen to be doing our duty.'

The two men looked at each other in silence.

'No-one could predict an act of God, which is what I believe the insurance companies call this kind of thing.' The cardinal's heavy eybrows lifted, and his handsome dark-skinned face broke into a smile. 'And who are we to argue with the Divinity?'

The cardinal rose, retrieving the sherry glasses – a signal that the interview had come to an end.

'I don't need to remind you, Charles, that the last thing we want is a scandal. Plays havoc with the system.'

'Rest assured, your Eminence, the system's safe.'

It was precisely in order to protect the system that the warden arrived hotfoot from London just as soon as the road to the valley had been reopened – although it was not so much a reopening as a military operation to float a road over a river of scorched mud.

It was to protect the system that Monsignor Melton was

first into the village with the official rescue services – for all that the villagers and their priest had been making a perfectly good fist of their own salvation.

In the cold light of day, the reality dawned that the dream was over.

Father Patrick's ravings were no match for the warden's authority and the reasonings of the official representatives of a secular state.

The heavy guns arrived soon after, with a mighty whir of helicopters and a mighty blast of microphones. The peasantry was once again addressed. Paysans de France, Mon Général claims your loyalty.

The mayor could see which way the wind blew as soon as the Minister for Internal Affairs arrived with a large suitcase full of money. He lifted the lid so that the mayor could see the bundles of notes inside, all done up neatly with rubber bands.

'Citoyens, soyez prudent,' the minister urged from the steps of the Mairie. Beside him stood *monsieur le maire*, turncoat ever, a man who knew when to hunt with the hounds and how to run with the hare, and who could recognize a wad of money when he saw it.

'Citoyens,' urged the mayor. 'Do not refuse the substance for the shadow.'

There were a few – the old and wise and the young and hopeful – who were all for sending the suitcase packing, but there were many more who could see now that Father Patrick's plans were no more than the ravings of a crazy old man who would bring ruin to them all.

Most, although not all, were sure that a bird in the hand was worth a thousand in the bush.

It was the goatboy who found Marguerite and gave her the news of the decision to evacuate the valley.

Until then, she knew nothing of the aftermath of the disaster, of Father Patrick's throwing open of the

Hermitage, of the arrival of the monsignor, the intervention of the minister and the frustration of all their plans.

He had found her brooding among the ruins of the High Pool, careless of all but her loss. Once again it was he who brought her back, who reminded her that she was loved and needed, that there were those weaker than she who could not be abandoned.

It was curious that it should be he, the simpleton *ravi*, who could find a way through the wall she had built around herself, could choose the right words to touch her; who – when the flame of her anger had burned itself out – could bring comfort.

This was because there was something in Marguerite's nature which he understood as well as his own. Something which was as untameable as the wolf whose senses he shared, and which was just as capable of engineering its own destruction.

It was a delicate thing, the love he gave her. A dangerous thing, now that she had grown to womanhood. He had the wisdom to know that she was not as other young women. For all her beauty and intelligence, for all her willingness to tease and flirt, he knew that she would never truly belong to any man. She was as wild as any woodland creature. To cage her would be to destroy her.

Then, back in the now-abandoned Hermitage, a cunning new plan began to take shape – and the two young people began to think that there might, after all, be a way out. They could not accept that the Church had the final say on the fate of the villagers.

The more Marguerite considered it, the more certain she was that she had to go to London. The proposal she was determined to put to the warden was the right approach. None knew better than Marguerite how useful the Hermitage had been – and to whom. It was impossible to disregard what she knew.

She had an excellent memory, and in many cases she

could clearly remember the stories which had brought the visitors there.

It was not blackmail that she had in mind – merely a suggestion that those who had benefited from the Hermitage's hospitality might be glad to contribute to the valley's future.

She had a ledger of her own – a practice ledger which Father Patrick had given to her when she first began to help him. This she now began to fill with the stories she remembered. Then she went to find Tonin at the bories.

'I've written down all I can remember – the stories of the people who've been at the Hermitage. There must be some way of finding out who they are, even without the warden's help. I'm sure that once I explain what we need we'll get what we want.'

Tonin was not so sure.

'Why should they help?'

'Gratitude. That's the whole point. Not to me of course, but to the Hermitage. And, if they don't, all I have to do is show them this.' Marguerite put her hand on the ledger. 'Anyway, there's no reason why anyone should know that the request doesn't come from the warden himself.'

'You'd t-tell them that?'

'Not in so many words – I just wouldn't explain all the details. Believe me, Tonin, none of those people would think it could possibly be me acting on my own. An ignorant peasant girl like me – *et bien*, what else could I possibly be after?'

'But that's blackmail, Marguerite.' Tonin protested, shocked.

'Not exactly. All I know is that the Hermitage serves the purpose it has always served – no mystery in that. But then there are the ones Father Patrick didn't approve of – the ones on which he wanted your opinion, my old grey wolf.' She considered this thoughtfully. 'That's what makes me so sure it'll work.'

Tonin stared at her for a long moment. Then he shook his head. 'What if the m-monsignor finds out?'

She shrugged. 'It's a risk worth taking.'

'How will you know how much to ask for?'

'I won't.' She paused, then said vaguely: 'But it's like communism – you give what you can, you take what you need. We can sell shares, so people know they're getting something back. It'll help us in the future – all those powerful people who want our project to work.'

'Are you sure?'

'Of course I am,' she said with a confidence she was far from feeling.

There was no point in consulting the villagers yet, divided as they were by the issues of compensation and relocation, forming factions and laying accusations. Nor was there any point in enlisting the help of Father Patrick. The old man had retreated into his own despair, rocking in his chair by the flame-blasted window, saying his rosary and praying for the intervention of the saints – St Anthony, patron of lost causes, the Holy Virgin herself.

The sight of the broken old man stiffened her resolve. All was not yet lost. The warden could be, *must* be made to see reason. He must change his mind, agree to the extension of sanctuary, giving them space and time to develop their plans. The Hermitage could still earn its living – there was plenty of space for all.

Among all this confusion, Tonin was the only one in whom she could trust, whose belief in the future was unshaken.

'You'll do it, Marguerite. There's no-one else who can. For the sake of us all, you have no choice.'

Part Four

London, 1963-1965

22

The Monsignor and Marguerite

'Miss Marguerite Leblanc, sir.'

Monsignor Melton nearly choked on the olive in his preprandial martini cocktail.

God alone knew why the porter had let her in. The most charitable interpretation was that Wilberforce had taken the young woman to be his godson's fiancée – although such a mistake was scarcely credible. Even in these all too modern times, only a cretin could mistake a female dressed in the working overalls of a French peasant – none too new, either – for the Honourable Charlotte Willoughby. Dear sweet Charlotte.

Dear sweet Charlotte this most emphatically was not.

'Monsieur?'

The young woman was holding out her hand expectantly. Clearly she was unaware of the unsuitability of her appearance. Workman's overalls in the hotel's discreetly furnished reception room – club-like, so that the residents could feel quite at home – caused quite an embarrassing stir among the other guests. Many of these were known to the monsignor, and he had no choice but to rise to greet his guest as if an appointment with a young woman dressed as a plumber was the most natural thing in the world.

'Mademoiselle.'

As he shook the proffered hand, the priest noticed that the young woman's palm was dry and her gaze was direct.

Clearly she was not intimidated by her surroundings.

'Please . . .' Melton gestured to the chair the club servant had set ready for her.

Marguerite accepted tranquilly. So far so good. As for her attire, the priest's assessment was perfectly correct. Her mind had been concentrated on her self-appointed task, and apart from practical considerations – pockets for papers, comfort on a long journey – she had given no thought to what she was wearing. Anyway, the overalls were her best pair, clean and neatly patched, and they were the ones in which she went to market in Valréas. She had reassured herself that London had markets – she had heard reports of the stock market on the wireless when she was learning her English with Father Patrick – so she had not thought she would look out of place.

Nor had she considered it wise to make an appointment with the monsignor, in case she was refused. Forewarned is forearmed. Nevertheless, she had been a little surprised to discover that the warden's place of residence was a hotel. She had imagined that such a very important prelate must live in some kind of palace.

She had had no trouble convincing the porter to take her straight to Monsignor Melton. He had seemed to think that she was expected.

'Mademoiselle?'

She realized that the monsignor was waiting for her to explain herself. Perhaps he had forgotten who she was. After all, it had been some years since they had met face-to-face.

'Excusez-moi, monsieur. Surely you may not remember me, but I am the daughter of the housekeeper – the late housekeeper – at the Hermitage.'

'Indeed, mademoiselle. I remember you perfectly.'

Melton was suddenly aware of the amused interest of the other guests. He would have at least to make some pretence of normality, or heaven only knew what might be thought. Conscious that he must at least go through the motions of hospitality, he said: 'Some refreshment? Fruit juice perhaps?'

'Thank you. I'm afraid I'm very thirsty.'

She would have liked to add that she was also very hungry, but she thought that might be rude. She had noticed a bowl of peanuts on the table. Following her gaze, her host pushed it towards her.

'Please. Help yourself.'

Without any hesitation, she scooped up a handful and tipped them into her mouth, chewing ravenously.

With a sigh of resignation, Melton signalled to one of the waiters and ordered the juice, adding another martini for himself.

While they were waiting for the drinks to arrive, he had time to examine her. She was no longer a child, that was clear enough. And, in spite of the inappropriateness of her attire, with her clear skin, green eyes and coppery hair she might be considered personable. Even the overalls were worn neatly belted in typically chic French style. Here the warden's physical inspection came to an abrupt halt. There was absolutely no excuse for inappropriateness of attire.

It was evident, too, that she should have known better. She was clearly no illiterate peasant girl. Her English, apart from the faint Irish accent, was excellent, no doubt because the besotted old priest had made sure it was. He had long suspected that Father Patrick had continued to harbour her, although he had not bothered to enquire if this was indeed the case.

'Now, young lady,' he said briskly as soon as the drinks arrived, glancing at his watch, 'I have ten minutes. Perhaps you will be so good as to enlighten me as to the purpose of your visit?'

For the first time, Marguerite looked nervous. 'I am hoping to persuade you to change your mind, monsieur, about the Hermitage. The accommodation situation, that is. I – that is, we – have thought the matter out most carefully. I can assure you we do not need financial assistance. Only your blessing.'

'Blessing? On what precisely?'

Marguerite was silent for a moment. Then, knowing that she had only a little time, she plunged straight into the speech she had prepared, an outline of the plans for the redevelopment of the valley and the request to be permitted to use the Hermitage as a community centre – although she did not immediately tell him how she meant to raise the money. That, she knew instinctively, must be approached with caution.

'A *community*? A co-operative community in the *Hermitage*? My dear girl, this is 1963, not the Middle Ages. We are running a business, not some ancient monastic charity.'

Charles Melton's voice rose as he contemplated the full horror of his visitor's request.

The look of disappointment on the girl's face would have wrung the heart of a lesser mortal than Charles Melton. Others might find her charming, with the Irish accent and the innocence of youth. Not Monsignor Melton. He disapproved of the Irish, innocence was another name for stupidity, and he could not stand youth.

And now here she was, repaying hospitality with threats of communes and co-operatives and other ungodly nonsense.

'There has clearly been a misunderstanding. Father O'Donovan made some brief mention of community effort, but we were in agreement that that would not be necessary under the circumstances. I confess surprise that he has not communicated this directly to those who might – rightly or wrongly – consider themselves concerned.'

'Father Patrick does not know of my visit, monsieur.'

She stopped for a moment, aware that what she was about to say was not entirely the whole truth. 'But surely you are wrong about who has a right to be concerned. The villagers claimed the right of sanctuary in the Hermitage. Father O'Donovan promised that the Church will honour that right.'

Melton frowned. 'Nonsense. Father O'Donovan had no authority to make such a promise. The matter has been resolved. There are rules governing these things.'

'It's because of the rules that I – I mean we – hoped you might be led to consider the matter more sympathetically.'

'Young lady, I am perfectly sympathetic, but I am rarely led – unless for the good of the flock. In this case I can assure you that all has been done for the best.'

But Marguerite had not finished yet.

'The villagers have already claimed the right of sanctuary, monsieur,' she said quietly. 'It is a matter of judgement as to how long that sanctuary should be extended.'

'Are you telling me my business, mademoiselle?'

'Oh, no, monsieur. Simply reminding you of the Church's obligations.'

The warden's jaw dropped.

'If I had not known that you yourself have had ample reason to be grateful for the Church's hospitality, I might misunderstand your intentions.'

The Irishness swept over her anew, the words tumbling forth.

'And for sure it's more than grateful I shall always be, for all that, and most particularly to Father Patrick. For all that it was yourself that wanted to have me put in an orphanage when my poor mother was taken from us, may the Lord have mercy on her soul, buried as she was in the heretics' graveyard. As yourself would know quite well. And it is most certainly because of that that I – that is, we – have reason to hope that you will reconsider.'

Melton drummed his fingers on the mahogany arm of his chair. So that was the way the wind blew. The girl held a grudge. He would have to tread carefully.

'We are under no obligation. None at all.'

'Monsieur, I will be honest with you.' Marguerite found the strength from somewhere, and her voice returned to its carefully modulated tones. 'None of this would have happened if the money for the essential maintenance had come through when it was supposed to.'

Melton nearly choked on his second martini. 'No blame can be apportioned.'

'With the greatest respect, monsieur, we both know the truth of the matter. Father Patrick wrote many times to warn what might happen. He is willing to make representations to the Holy Father himself.'

The warden swallowed. 'Most inadvisable. As one who is not of the Faith, you may not know that the Church has a million claims on its charity, and all of them quite as worthy as this – in many cases, even more so.'

The warden looked at the young woman bleakly.

'Even so, we cannot intervene in secular matters unless the proper authorities put in the proper request. And in this case the very reverse is true. The proper authorities are the French state, and they have expressed their willingness to take over our' – he paused to search for the right word – 'residual responsibilities. The decision has already been taken. As a matter of courtesy – no more – it has been communicated to the warden. Furthermore, Father O'Donovan will be replaced in his post just as soon as a suitable candidate can be found.'

He paused to let this information sink in, then added: 'I'm sorry you felt obliged to make so long a journey to so little purpose. Now, if you have no further business—'

'Oh, but I do.'

'You can do nothing to change my mind. You cannot imagine how much your proposals would cost.'

Marguerite leaned forward eagerly. Here, at least, was safer ground.

'Surely on that I can set your mind at rest, monsieur. We have made very detailed plans already. It was yourself that asked for them to be prepared.'

Eagerly Marguerite began to pull out a large envelope from her capacious pockets. But the warden put up his hand to stop her.

'Your concern may be admirable, but this is no business for amateurs. Everything is already being done that can be done. These are things which are beyond our power to change. Mine as well as yours.'

'I don't believe that, monsieur. I believe things *can* be made to change.' It was now or never. There had been one obstacle until now. But, since Father Patrick was to be relieved of his post anyway, it was no longer an issue. She took a deep breath.

'I should first explain, monsieur, that ever since Father Patrick began to lose his eyesight it is myself that has been entrusted with the keeping of the ledgers. That is,' she explained carefully, 'the confessions in the ledgers have been taken down in my own hand to the dictation of the visitors.'

The warden stared at her, the realization dawning at last that not only was this young woman a dangerous idealist, but that she also had a powerful weapon.

'For how long?'

'Eight years, monsieur. Since my tenth birthday.'

'*Eight years?*'

Mistaking the warden's sharp intake of breath for concern over the quality of her record-keeping, she added hurriedly: 'Sure and my handwriting is as good as Father Patrick's ever was, and we always went over it together at the end.'

Melton gazed at her in silence. For the first time he was struck dumb.

Marguerite rushed on, anxious that the warden should not misunderstand her intentions, which were entirely honourable. 'Surely to goodness all those who have been guests would be only too happy to help. Some of them were in terrible trouble, and must be most grateful for what we – that is, the Church – have done for them. I can remember everything perfectly well, so there's no need to unlock the ledgers or for Father Patrick to betray the secrets of the confessional. I know that's very important.'

The warden winced. 'Young lady, you have a very incomplete grasp of the meaning of the secrets of the confessional.'

After a moment a thought came to him. 'Does Father O'Donovan know of these . . . plans?'

'Of course not.' Marguerite shook her head. She added, somewhat disingenuously: 'I didn't want to worry him.'

Melton let out his breath in a small sigh. At least he had some room to manoeuvre.

Then he asked the only important question. 'And the names? You can remember the names?'

She shook her head. 'Father Patrick didn't tell me. Some, at the beginning. But later he wrote them in himself.'

Melton leaned back in his chair. 'Thank God.'

'I thought perhaps you could help me with those, monsieur. It was the main reason that I came – after I had persuaded you of the rightness of our cause.'

'Did you indeed?'

Marguerite studied the warden's face. She did not know what this man was thinking. She longed for Tonin and his wolf-senses – he would know exactly what was in the monsignor's head.

She decided that perhaps, for an important man with so many responsibilities, what she proposed might be too much work. So she added: 'Don't worry, monsieur, about the practicalities. Surely I'm perfectly willing to talk to everyone myself, most certainly I am. I'm a hard worker, and capable. It's just the names and addresses I'll be needing. You will not be having to trouble yourself at all.'

'Won't I indeed?'

Charles Melton's mind was spinning. The girl was an unexploded bomb. She was so young, so eager, so innocent, so entirely convinced of the rightness of her cause, and these things made her doubly dangerous. At the simplest level, a young peasant girl with no education was hardly a fit repository for the secrets of the rich and powerful, however young and unaware of the value of that knowledge she might be. At best it was extremely indiscreet; at worst, if the information fell into the wrong hands, the consequences would be disastrous. And, if Marguerite's hands themselves turned out to be the wrong ones, it was the warden himself who would be held responsible.

Melton could see no way out. Except one. He would have to buy her off. He would have to do this without letting her know the strength of the cards she held.

'My dear, you are young. All this will soon be behind you.' His voice was soothing. Melton had a fine voice, honey-smooth. 'A pretty girl like you has all her life ahead. You are of an age to think about your future. You will fall in love. Perhaps you have already done so. Your mind will turn to more important matters. A husband. With God's blessing, children.'

Marguerite's eyes widened. Mistaking this for cupidity, Melton played what he knew must be his master card. She was a peasant. She would have the ambitions of a peasant: a bit of land, money tucked under the mattress.

'A word in the right ear, my dear. A farm, a little nest egg. Soon all this will be behind you. Loyalty and discretion will always be rewarded.'

Marguerite stared at him, unable to believe that she was being so misunderstood. 'Monsieur. You know perfectly well that's not what I've come for.'

'I'm well aware of that, my dear. And it does you credit that you do not consider your own needs. And, believe me, I'm only too sorry we can't make your dream come true. But we can at least make life a little easier for those who deserve our – I hesitate to say it – charity. I have discretion.'

She could hear it loud and clear. What she was being offered was no more or less than a bribe.

'Discretion – to pay me off?' Marguerite's voice had risen in volume, and those close by had turned to listen.

'Calm yourself, my dear; no need for raised voices.'

'Would you be pleased to repeat that, monsieur?' Marguerite was angry now – angry and humiliated. 'These ladies and gentlemen might be interested to hear what you propose.'

Melton felt the beads of sweat break out on his brow. Worse was to follow. His tormentor stood up and then rocked back on her heels, putting her hand suggestively to her belly.

'And just how much would you be prepared to pay, monsieur?'

Her voice was very loud now, loud enough for everyone in the room to hear. He gazed wildly round at the all too familiar faces, seeing the nods of amusement, hearing the faint ripples of laughter.

Melton could feel his face turn as scarlet as a cardinal's hat. He rose to his feet.

'Young lady, I cannot imagine what you are implying. I only know that it is time to bring this discussion to an end. You have my last word on the matter.'

At that moment, Wilberforce came to his rescue. It was smoothly and discreetly done. Within seconds the porter's hand was under Marguerite's elbow and she found herself propelled towards the double doors through which she had entered.

'You'll regret it, monsieur,' she called over her shoulder. 'You know where you may find me. I shall await your answer.' She was so angry now that she could feel the tears start to her eyes.

It was probably the most undignified exit that anyone could ever have had to make, and had she not been so humiliated she would never have found the courage. And now she was on her way to being unceremoniously dumped in the street. All of a sudden a figure barred their way.

'Let me handle this, Wilberforce.'

The porter hesistated, uncertain if he should abandon responsibility for what was clearly a female of questionable virtue apprehended in the very act of importuning one of the hotel's most distinguished resident's.

'Your Lordship is acquainted with this . . . young person?'

'Indeed, I am.'

The hand on her elbow was replaced by that of a young man who had been leaning against the doorway, observing the scene with some amusement.

'That's quite all right, Wilberforce. I'll see mademoiselle to her taxi.'

'If you say so, sir.'

'Indeed, I do. Shall we go, my dear?'

'I'm sorry—'

'Naturally, I forgive you.'

Marguerite's rescuer took no notice of her bewilderment; he simply guided her firmly down the steps which led to Park Lane, chattering brightly as if they were indeed old friends.

A few moments later Marguerite found herself installed

in a taxi. The young man did not even introduce himself. He simply hailed the vehicle, opened the door and thrust her inside.

'But I've nowhere to go. I don't have any money for a taxi.'

'Think no more of it.'

It all happened so quickly she had no time to protest – not even when she found a bunch of keys pressed into her hand.

'My place. Make yourself at home. Eat. Take a bath. Borrow some decent clothes. In that order. I'll be back later for coffee.'

'But, monsieur, I don't even know who you are . . .'

Suddenly she relaxed. She did not care who he was or why he was so determined to rescue her.

She had already spent nearly all her and Tonin's savings. There had been so many things to pay for. A night's lodging in Avignon so that she could acquire the documents which allowed her to travel, rail tickets, boat tickets, tips. She had not even had enough money for a proper meal. Nor had she made plans for her return; she had simply expected that she would be able to persuade the monsignor, and everything would fall into place.

'Good girl,' said the stranger, and banged the door shut.

The cabbie had been following this exchange with professional interest. He could tell a toff when he saw one – and he knew this one's face from the society pages in the papers.

He looked down at the banknote the young man pressed into his hand. Good tippers, the nobs. You could always tell.

'Where to, guv'nor?'

'Old Church Street. Number eleven – the river end. You'll see a red sports-car pulled up at the door.'

The cabbie took a quick glance into the rear-view mirror. The girl was a looker all right. The toffs were good pickers – you could give 'em that. He waited, the engine ticking, while the young man leaned through the window for a final word with his passenger.

Even then it was not the amused grey eyes and the shock of blond hair which revealed the identity of Marguerite's rescuer, but the remark he threw at her as the cab drew away.

'Hope you enjoyed the chocolates.'

23

Pastures New

Now Marguerite knew exactly who her rescuer was. Young Master Benjamin had changed – but if she had not been in such confusion she would have recognized the shock of yellow hair and the strange grey eyes.

What she did not know was why he had made such a quixotic gesture. Even if it was spur-of-the-moment gallantry, surely his godfather would be furious with him for giving succour to what he must now regard as a very ill-mannered and troublesome young woman indeed.

Though she did not know it, the cabbie had already put his finger on at least part of the reason.

'His Nibs seemed to have taken a fancy to you, miss. Good friend, is he?'

'His Nibs?'

'His Lordship the Earl of Malvern. Took me a moment, but that's because he's a new one. Just been promoted. When his grandad kicked the bucket.'

'Kicked the bucket?'

'Passed on. Don't know much, do you, miss?'

'No. I most certainly don't know much.' At least with this Marguerite was in total agreement. 'And I don't understand why he's changed his name to . . . whatever it was you called him.'

'The Earl of Malvern. He inherited the title on the death of his grandfather. That's what it said in the papers. I take an interest, see. Like to know who's in the back of the cab.'

Marguerite digested this. Ben had not said anything about being earl of anything, and she had only the haziest grasp of what this might mean.

The taxi headed south towards the river. The river was important to London; Marguerite knew that because she had studied the maps and learned her geography. London was a port, with ocean-going liners, merchant ships, and docks with cranes as tall as several buildings. She had seen them on the newsreels in the cinema in Valréas. The East End was where they were.

The taxi now rounded a leafy square and turned down a broad avenue.

'King's Road,' said the man. 'You'll see some sights.'

Marguerite wound the window down, the better to appreciate the short-skirted girls and velvet-coated dandies of the most famous street in the world. Even in Pernes-les-Rochers, they knew all about Swinging London.

All too soon the taxi turned south again.

'We're here, miss.' The cabbie drew up beside a little red sports car in the forecourt of a pretty little house which was joined to a row of other pretty little houses.

'Take my advice, miss. Don't let His Nibs sweet-talk you into anything,' was the cabbie's parting advice.

And, although Marguerite had no idea what the phrase meant, it would have been better for her if she had.

The reason for Ben's change of plan was not what it might have seemed. It was not the demon drink or the pursuit of loose ladies which kept him from the pleasant task of renewing old acquaintance with a pretty young woman who had good cause to be grateful to him, but a sudden and uncharacteristic attack of philanthropy.

Lunch with his godfather and his fiancée had been a somewhat sticky affair. Not, as Marguerite had feared, because Monsignor Melton had noticed his godson's demonstration of gallantry towards her – he had been too preoccupied with the recovery of his own dignity to notice anything else. No. The primary cause of the stickiness was Ben's fiancée. Charlotte had unfortunately climbed out of her own taxi just in time to witness what she took to be a tender farewell between her betrothed and a young woman dressed as a plumber.

A female plumber was an unusual object for Ben's attentions, but Lottie knew her fiancé well enough to believe him capable of anything.

'It's not what you think, Lottie.'

'*Really?*' No-one could pack as much disapproval into two syllables as Lottie. Anything which smacked of open competition for Ben's attention was the one thing she would not tolerate.

Ten minutes later, as they joined Monsignor Melton for the walk to Wilton's, he was still reeling from the rough edge of his fiancée's tongue.

Ben had not really intended to contract matrimony with anyone – still less with someone as undeniably suitable as Lottie. Suitability was not a virtue which had ever recommended itself to Benjamin Catesby, tenth Earl of Malvern.

That he had acquired a fiancée at all was an indirect result of the decision of his trustees – principally his godfather – to cut down his allowance. The monsignor thought it necessary to underline that the modest trust fund which had been sensibly invested to produce an income was not enough to support the extravagance of his lifestyle.

What Ben needed, his godfather pointed out, was a second income.

'Time you settled down, Benjamin – found yourself a wife. A girl from a good Catholic background with the right qualifications. I shall make enquiries.'

'The right qualifications' was a euphemism for a sufficiency of fortune. The enquiries produced Charlotte

256

Willoughby. Lottie Willoughby had what was known as expectations. She was the only daughter of a successful industrialist from the Midlands, although this did not itself guarantee anything but a respectable dress allowance, with perhaps a little extra to pay the nanny when the children came along. Fortunately, however, Lottie's expectations were already safely in the bank. An American great-aunt had left her the controlling interest in a Texan oil well, making her a considerable heiress in her own right.

Her socially ambitious parents had thought it unwise to burden her with too much education, and she had left her private boarding school early in order to be finished in Switzerland and Paris. This had been followed by 'doing the season' – even though curtsying to a cake was not much of a replacement for presentation to the monarch. During the course of this social jamboree, she had achieved the title of Débutante of the Year, a dubious honour awarded by the gossip columnists for a combination of money, looks and breeding – with particular emphasis on the money.

Monsignor Melton, who kept a keen eye on the society columns, made a discreet approach to the Willoughby parents. With the connivance of those who had their best interests at heart, the two young people found themselves placed next to each other at the dinner parties which preceded the balls, and thrown into each other's company at weekend house parties.

By the end of the season, with Ben safely metamorphosed as the Earl of Malvern on the death of his grandfather, Monsignor Melton delivered an ultimatum to his godson.

'Time you popped the question, dear boy.'

Ben knew better than to cross his godfather. He had been brought up to believe that love did not play a large part in such arrangements. Suitability was all.

As far as Ben was concerned, there was a further reason for Charlotte's eminent suitability. She did not particularly want to have children.

This had been revealed quite casually by Charlotte herself, one evening when he was driving her home from a dinner with her parents during which the talk had turned to having progeny. Lottie's mother, not a woman noted for tact or sensitivity, had been waxing sentimental about her longing for grandchildren. Mentally at least, and before Ben and Lottie had even formalized their engagement, she was already dusting down the family pram.

'Stop that, Mother.' Charlotte's voice had been sharp. 'You know my feelings about infants. I have absolutely no maternal instinct and I have no intention of ruining my figure. Not for a long time. And possibly never.'

'Really, Lottie!' Her mother had looked shocked. Then she had laughed nervously and glanced at Ben. 'I'm sure Benjamin wouldn't agree with that. After all, he is the tenth Earl of Malvern . . .' Lottie's mother loved a title and was longing for Ben to propose to her daughter. A daughter who was the Countess of Malvern would be something to boast about to all her friends – and it was absolutely unthinkable that this might not lead to a little grandson to inherit the title.

Charlotte was shrewder than her mother. She had picked up a few remarks Ben had made which had led her to think that he might well not have the same dynastic priorities as her mother.

'Do *you*, Ben? Want children?'

Charlotte was always perfectly direct; it was one of the things he appreciated in her. Ben watched her for a moment, and then said something noncommittal about it being far too early to think about things like that. Later, on the way home, he tested the water again.

'Did you mean that, Lottie? About not wanting children?'

Charlotte snorted. 'Of course. What's the point? One has quite enough to do to look after oneself. And I'm told they're terribly expensive.' She looked at Ben. 'Of course, I can see Mother has a point. You might feel obliged to pass on the title – as Mother would no doubt put it.'

'I feel nothing of the kind.' The answer was so emphatic that even Charlotte was startled.

'Never? Not even your duty as a Catholic?'

'Never.'

'Excellent. That's settled, then.'

The engagement was duly announced in *The Times*. Shortly afterwards, a portrait photograph of Lottie – wearing a Hartnell evening dress, her mother's pearls and a suitably virginal expression – appeared in the front of *Country Life*. As was considered proper, the engagement was to be for a year, after which the happy couple would be expected to celebrate their nuptials.

As the first of 'her year' to be spoken for, Lottie was the object of some envy among her female contemporaries, who lost no time in making sure she was not left in ignorance of her fiancé's reputation. Lottie was unmoved by the warnings. An old-fashioned country girl, accustomed to mastering horses and whipping in hounds, she was confident that she could bring him to heel.

'All the dear boy needs is a firm hand.'

Nor was she at all disturbed by their suggestions that Ben's main interest in her was her fortune. She had never expected anything else. This attitude was born not of cynicism but of blind optimism. Her own parents' apparently perfectly satisfactory marriage had been contracted under similar circumstances – her father had married the boss's daughter – and she was simply following family tradition.

Benjamin could be made to change. She set to work immediately on the more obvious of his bad habits: his reputation for keeping loose company. She arranged to spend three days of the week in London where she took up shared residence in a flat in South Kensington with two schoolfriends, and lost no time in reorganizing Ben's social life.

'Tuesday, we've been invited to dinner at the Fortescues'. Wednesday, I told Bunty we'd be at Quaglino's by nine. Thursday, Mummy wants us for lunch at the Berkeley Grill.'

She softened these demands by exposing her perfect teeth in a sweet smile and by allowing him to take a few extra liberties with her person. Not all the way naturally. So far, as a reward for the sapphire-and-diamond ring she sported on the fourth finger of her left hand, she had permitted him to unhook her bra-strap and fondle her breasts, but that was the limit of her generosity. Nothing below the waist, it went without saying.

'Naughty boy,' she protested if his hands wandered, but without the slightest rancour. Heavy petting, as it was known, was for shop girls. The ground rules – how much and how far and when – were discussed tirelessly with her girlfriends over unlimited refills of china tea and chocolate éclairs in Fortnum & Mason's fashionable Soda Fountain. If there was one thing Charlotte Willoughby held in high esteem, it was her own virginity.

'Purity is a pearl without price,' her mother assured her – unusually poetically for so practical a woman. 'A man will never pay for what he has already had free.'

This gambit worked well enough. Ben was not used to girls who turned him down, and he found Charlotte's determined limitation of his advances unexpectedly stimulating. His godfather might hold the purse strings of his modest allowance, but Charlotte held the key to a more than comfortable future. With the announcement of the engagement, he was well and truly hooked.

On her first visit to Ben's bachelor quarters – suitably chaperoned by a girlfriend – Charlotte decided that

Chelsea, with its shifting population of layabouts, fashion photographers, glossy-magazine journalists and pop musicians, was no place to embark on matrimonial bliss.

She added house-hunting to her duties. She had in mind somewhere in the country within range of a decent hunt, the Belvoir for preference, and a small flat in reliable Eaton Square.

Lottie's remaining daylight hours were taken up with appointments at the beauty salon, weekly visits to the hairdresser, pedicures, manicures and shopping – an occupation at which she acknowledged no peer. She had a seemingly insatiable appetite for the acquisition of material goods. Her wedding lists – Givans, Irish Linen Stores, The White House, Thomas Goode – were works of art. Sufficient monogrammed linen to fill a dozen airing-cupboards, several pantryfuls of bone china and Waterford crystal, enough silver to fill a bank vault. On the rare occasions when Ben could think of no further excuses for not spending the weekend banging away at pheasants on her family's acres, he inspected the mounting piles of wedding presents with gloom.

Even window-shopping gave her a little *frisson*. From her limited experience she suspected that sex – even if you went all the way – was not nearly as exciting as the thrill of a well-dressed window. Fortunately a long engagement offered infinite opportunities for indulging the one without the necessity fully to accommodate the other.

Meanwhile Ben continued to play his usual games on the days when Charlotte was absent. He was careful to keep the two worlds in which he now moved as separate as possible. The rules were perfectly clear: never mix business with pleasure, and Lottie was business. There were plenty of girls, mini-skirted and liberated by the contraceptive pill, who were willing to deliver what Charlotte would not, and plenty of amusement to be had in the drinking dens of Soho.

After Ben's quixotic gesture towards Marguerite, the lunch was not destined to be a success. Charlotte sulked throughout the meal, cheering up only when she remembered a pressing appointment at her dressmaker's. She left before coffee. As soon as she had gone, Ben took the opportunity to question his godfather about Marguerite – having first made sure that he had not seen him rescue her. He had not dared to do so earlier for fear of irritating Charlotte even more.

'What did that young woman want, Godfather?'

At first, irritated by the realization that there had been yet another witness to his humiliation, the monsignor was not to be drawn. 'I don't wish to discuss the matter, Benjamin. And I find your interest indiscreet, considering that you will soon be a married man.'

Ben grinned. 'Come along, Godfather. I haven't seen the girl since we made that trip when I was a boy.'

Melton shook his head. 'Just as well, Benjamin. That young female has no notion of the proper order of things.'

This reminder of the extent to which Marguerite was not aware of the order of things plunged the monsignor into further gloom. However, an excellent bottle of port worked its soothing miracle, and he began to mellow. With a little prompting he grew expansive, even emotional, on the Church's generosity to the girl, the purity of his intentions in offering to provide for her.

'Of course, it's no surprise. After the mother died the girl ran wild.'

Ben set down his glass in surprise. 'She's an orphan?'

Melton nodded. 'I should have put my foot down immediately, made sure my wishes were obeyed. The orphanage was the only place for her. But one cannot see to every detail.' A thought suddenly struck him. Perhaps the girl was pregnant; after all, she had implied as much with that ridiculous demonstration.

He added thoughtfully: 'Young girls are so emotional. Under certain circumstances.'

'Circumstances?'

The monsignor waved a ringed hand. 'You are a man of the world, Benjamin. Those peasants breed like rabbits. Tried to blackmail me into turning the Hermitage into some kind of commune, no doubt for her own convenience. But there might have been someone else behind it, some man. Anyway, she was hysterical, making all sorts of wild accusations.'

'About what?'

The monsignor's face took on a guarded look. 'The Church had certain responsibilities. As landlord. She felt we had not discharged them adequately.'

'Any truth?' Ben was risking his godfather's ire, but he was intrigued enough to want to know the answer.

'Certainly not. Ridiculous notion.'

Melton considered his godson with a frown, wondering if Ben might after all be useful to him. After a moment he sighed and took another sip of port.

'These things, Benjamin, are never clear-cut.'

'I take it the answer is yes.'

Melton examined the glowing end of his cigar thoughtfully.

'I suppose you couldn't do anything, Benjamin? She might trust you. Does no-one any good to have things stirred up.'

'What have you in mind?' Ben's voice was deliberately casual.

Melton waved his hand. 'Make her see sense. Tell her to take the money and go home. I implied my offer would be quite sufficient to set her up for life. Marry the father – if the poor idiot will have her. Do the right thing, instead of running around making trouble for everyone.'

In a few short well-chosen words, Monsignor Melton explained to his godson exactly what Marguerite had been doing in the past, what she intended to do in the future, and how she intended to go about it.

Ben listened with a mixture of interest and amusement. The girl had guts – and courage.

He looked at his godfather gravely. 'So you think the money will do it?'

'Absolutely, dear boy. And you're the man to persuade her.'

'And if I do?'

'I'd consider it most . . .' Melton paused to give the word emphasis. '*Responsible*.'

The implication was clear, but Ben knew his godfather well enough to need open acknowledgement. 'Responsible enough to loosen up on the overdraft?'

'You have an inborn vulgarity, Benjamin, which you certainly haven't inherited from your estimable grand-parents. But, yes, I suppose so. I imagine it might go some way to convince me.'

'Good. It's a deal.'

Melton frowned. 'Discretion, Benjamin, is of the essence. I would not wish to be the cause of any mis-understanding between yourself and dear Charlotte.'

'Wouldn't dream of it, Godfather,' Ben said hastily. 'Not my sort.'

'I am relieved to hear it, Benjamin. Although there are moments when I think there are very few of what's ludicrously known as the weaker sex who are not your sort.'

Ben grinned. Nevertheless his godfather was perfectly right. Marguerite was certainly not a reason to get himself in trouble with Lottie – and most particularly not a girl who might or might not be in a spot of bother. Lottie was likely to jump to conclusions – and that would spoil every-thing.

'Consider it done, Godfather.'

'Good.'

His godfather pulled out his chequebook, filled in one of the cheques, folded it over discreetly and handed it across the table.

'Better take this. Speed things up.'

Ben nodded and slipped the cheque into his pocket.

Leaving the monsignor in contemplation of a final glass of port, he escaped into the bustle of Old Compton Street. It being a fine day, he decided to walk home. He was looking forward to hearing the girl's story from her own lips. It was not until he had reached the comparative tranquillity of Green Park and was well on his way home that he gave any thought to the cheque.

He removed it from his pocket and studied it with interest.

The first thing he noticed was that it was made out to bearer – a precaution his godfather always took when he did not wish a transaction to be traceable. The second was the size of the sum.

It was very tempting. And, if there was anything Ben found impossible to resist, it was temptation.

Temptation led him to change direction and make his way back across Piccadilly, down Berkeley Street and past the Connaught Hotel, until he reached the gilded portals of his favourite gambling haunt, the Clairville Club in Grosvenor Square.

24

A Jaunt in the Country

'Dear Sir, I have borrowed your car. I shall return it' – Marguerite chewed the end of the pencil thoughtfully – 'in due course.'

She hesitated over 'Sir' and 'in due course'. 'Dear Earl' did not sound quite right, and 'Dear Ben' was too forward now that he was ennobled, but 'in due course' sounded formal and very English – a guarantee that she was taking her responsibilities seriously.

Then she put in 'Please do not do anything to stop me,' and added as a PS 'I shall explain everything when I return'.

She signed her full name, gave her address as the Hermitage, and then propped the note against the telephone where it would be seen immediately.

Marguerite did not mean to steal the car, just borrow it for a while.

The cabbie's casual remark had put the idea into her head. 'That's His Nibs's vehicle,' the cabbie had said.

She remembered this just as soon as she woke up in Ben's house early in the morning, the day after her unfortunate interview with the warden.

The house was silent. Ben, for whatever reason, had not returned as he had promised – which was something of a relief, considering her own state of exhaustion. She had been so tired she had simply fallen asleep on the sofa, and not woken up again until the dawn light flooded through the uncurtained windows.

She had been very surprised by Benjamin Catesby's house. Almost as surprised as she had been to hear him called a lord – or an earl, or whatever was the right version of his title. She knew nothing of titles. It all sounded a little ridiculous to her egalitarian republican ears.

If she imagined anything at all about what the cabbie called a 'nib', it would be that he lived in a mansion with liveried servants. The place should be filled with velvet curtains, plush carpets and gilded furniture. Instead she found herself in what looked more like a barn than a house, with bare floorboards and no curtains, and huge paintings on the walls which did not look like people or landscapes but were composed of brightly coloured blobs and squiggles. In every corner were piles of magazines and records, and tapestry-covered cushions were scattered at random for seating.

He did not seem to have servants, either. The tables were piled with dirty mugs and empty wineglasses.

Although she felt a slight twinge of guilt at what she was about to do, she told herself that there were times, as Father Patrick sometimes said, when the end justified the means. Taking someone's possessions without permission – in this case a scarlet topless MGB – was not a very civil thing to do, considering that she should be rewarding the owner with gratitude, not pinching his movable goods; but at certain times gratitude got you nowhere. The Lord, Father Patrick had been fond of telling her, helps those who help themselves. That and a measure of luck.

It was luck that Ben had given her free run of his house. It was luck that the first object she laid eyes on when she entered the hall was the car keys. Just as it was lucky that Pierre had taught her to drive his elderly delivery van. The butcher's boy had thought that the chance to be alone with her might win him tangible rewards; but, as usual, Marguerite had been more than a match for him.

But the best bit of luck was that she had managed to remember the name of the first visitor whose confession she had taken down for Father Patrick, and recalled that Miss Belinda Fitzherbert lived not far from London, at a place called Daisyford Hall in the county of Suffolk. She remembered the house because of the name: Miss Fitzherbert explained about daisies and marguerites being the same, and she had thought Margueriteford sounded even prettier than Daisyford. She remembered the address because Father Patrick had told her about North Folk and South Folk being the counties just to the north of the capital.

She had been too tired to eat before she slept, and now she hurriedly bolted down the contents of a half-eaten tin of sardines which was all she could find in the fridge. Everything else had already grown a furry green hat. Then she rifled through a chest of drawers where she found a clean pair of jeans and a soft silk shirt. Both were a size or two on the large side, but she hoped that her leather belt, well cinched, made the look fashionably casual.

Hurrying just in case Benjamin Catesby suddenly reappeared, she looked up Daisyford in a motoring atlas she found among the stacks of books on the floor. The Hall was marked clearly with a little picture of a castle, which indicated that it must be an important place. Surely Miss Belinda Fitzherbert must be rich if she lived there, and there must be at least a chance she would be willing to contribute to such a good cause.

Even a small contribution would make a start. She could not possibly go limping back home – if indeed the Hermitage could now be called home, with Father Patrick soon to be relieved of his post. Nor could she possibly return to face Tonin empty-handed – by now he would be rallying the villagers, explaining that all would yet be well.

The argument with the warden, his attempt first to intimidate and then to bribe her, had left her even more determined to succeed. For an instant she even regretted that she had not accepted the money; she could have turned it to good account as the first of her donations. That would indeed have been a nice twist to fortune.

Perhaps not. You could not build a dream on a lie; and stolen treasure, as everyone knew, did no-one any good.

Borrowing was different.

With this in mind, she carefully pencilled in her route on the atlas, tucked it under her arm, and left the house, locking the door behind her. Then she posted the keys through the letter box in a used envelope on which she had written: 'Thank you. Sorry. Marguerite.' She added a line of small X's at the end, just to show that she was truly grateful.

It was a sunny day, and the sports-car's top had been left down, so it took only a matter of seconds to slip behind the wheel. The engine turned over sweetly at the first twist of the key.

She found the right gear and reversed carefully out of the parking space. Reflecting that at least Pierre had given her something for which she might be truly grateful, she moved forward as smoothly as she could to join the stream of traffic flowing down the King's Road.

Her progress was thoroughly uncertain at first. The traffic was on the wrong side of the road, and there were a great many parked cars which had to be avoided. Nevertheless, with care, compared to handling a heavy delivery vehicle on the rough roads of the valleys, or holding her own on market day in Valréas, manoeuvring the little car in the smooth streets of London was not so fearsome a task.

As she grew more confident, she began to take note of her surroundings. Many of the places and names were already familiar from her evenings listening to the wireless with Father Patrick. The reports of traffic jams in central London suddenly had a reality in pavements swarming with shoppers, streets choked with gleaming new vehicles.

As she had already observed through the windows of the taxi, it was the sheer size and quantity of everything which was most astonishing. The closest she had ever come to a big city was her visit to Avignon, but London far exceeded her wildest dreams. She had never seen such towering buildings, such massed ranks of shops with vast windows packed with heaps of glittering goods, such a press of brightly clad people, old and young. Businessmen in bowler hats, women in bright summer dresses, parks full of babies and children. To Marguerite the scene was like something out of a fairy story, seductive and thrilling.

She spun the dial on the radio, picking up the tinny resonances of a popular song. With 'Love, love me, do' pounding over the airwaves, the summer breeze whipping her hair, and the powerful little car responding to her touch, for the first time since the disaster in the valley she felt her heart lift.

In the gaming club in Grosvenor Square, Lady Luck had been as fickle as always, and Benjamin Catesby was risking all on one last throw.

'Numéro sept. Rouge et impaire.'

The little white ball bounced once, twice, and came to rest in the number seven slot.

A dozen pairs of eyes swung from the silver whirlpool to the impassive face of the croupier, and then across the squared and numbered green baize to check the disposition of the bets.

It was rare that a punter came up *en plein* – that is, put his entire stake on a single winning number – and when it happened you could be sure the player was an amateur. No-one so careless of the odds could ever belong to the élite pack of professional gamblers who were capable of breaking the bank, but were equally capable of losing enormous sums.

Such men – and a handful of women – were worth their weight in gold to the gaming houses. Their reputation drew the lesser fry – the ones who provided the bank with its bread and butter. Wilful as Hollywood stars, they were fêted and greeted by name – or by pseudonym, if that was their fancy. Hotel rooms were booked for them, limousines dispatched for them, companionship arranged for them. Those who had fallen on hard times were provided for – they might be offered a position as a house player, tame steers whose function was to render the bull more tractable.

Ben was neither a gambler nor a house player. He belonged to a small band of personable young men of good family but limited means who were encouraged to use the club's excellent restaurant to entertain their friends at the management's expense. Possibly the evening might end with one or two of the friends having a little flutter at the tables, although this was by no means essential. Ben and his like provided what the interior decorators could not supply: youth and glamour. The punters liked to see beautiful people, just as they liked to drink the best champagne and eat real caviar. They found these things reassuring.

It was pure theatre – the players the actors, the gaming tables their stage. The croupier pushed out a slender wooden rake, deftly gathering in the losers and picking delicately around the winners – those who had bet on the uneven numbers, or the red, or the single chip which lay on the number itself.

The spectators – those taking a brief respite from the blackjack table, or who had been knocked out of the backgammon tournament being played in the smoking room – leaned forward eagerly, calculating the spoils. Each time such a thing happened, the word went round and the players gathered. A winning streak could be shadowed – and there was a chance that the player might play on.

The magic of the game lay in the suspension of the ordinary. In this enclosed world none of the usual rules of daily life applied. The tokens themselves were no more than cowrie shells bartered for beads, valueless to the uninitiated, representing neither a day's labour, nor a month's salary, nor even a year's revenues from the great estates many of the players had inherited from their ancestors.

It was of little significance to any of them that the Clairville Club was the most glamorous gaming house in the world, unless it were that such surroundings were where they felt at home. They scarcely noticed that the magnificent rooms were furnished with Chippendale and Hepplewhite, that the exquisite arrangements of flowers were daily replaced, that the window draperies were of Venetian velvet, that the ceilings were hung with magnificent crystal chandeliers and the portraits on the walls were genuine Gainsboroughs. As in any soldiers' barracks, any one of them would have bet on raindrops racing down a grimy window, bluebottles blundering into a spider's web.

The roulette wheel was a frivolity in this place, a concession to the amateurs – the wives and girlfriends of the high rollers. Sometimes even for the serious players it offered a brief respite – limited risk, no more than might change hands as a tip to a croupier. But the professionals' energies were saved for those contests in which skill counted as much as luck. In the hands of a master, the stacking of a deck, the roll of the dice could always – or nearly always – be turned to advantage.

'Yours, my Lord?'

This was a statement rather than a question. Everyone round the table knew who had placed the winning token, who was due to collect the reward. Ben hesitated. He could take his winnings or let them lie.

'My Lord?' The croupier was still waiting for a decision.

'Leave it, Henry.'

'Suivez.'

For the second time, he left the stake to roll up, or vanish, according to the spin of the wheel.

The original bet he had placed on the single number had been the last of his borrowed stake. The monsignor's cheque had nearly gone – all except one small chip, the minimum the club permitted. He had never intended to place the whole of the proceeds of the cheque at risk. It was simply that the tokens which represented the money had been in his pocket and he had been gripped by a sudden attack of altruism.

The cashier had not questioned the size of the sum he had been asked to encash. He had simply pushed over the chips to the full value of the bearer cheque. This was merely a matter of form. By the end of the evening's play, when the float had been swollen with the evening's takings, the cashier was well used to his Lordship returning with the full total to be turned into currency. To Ben the arrangement was simply a convenience – so much easier to keep his affairs private by paying his bills in cash.

This evening had been different. He was, as Lottie would confirm, in a peculiar mood.

It was the peculiarity of mood which led him to the Clairville, the same peculiarity which prompted him to put the money on the spin of the wheel. It was the peculiarity of the wheel that for once it delivered – in duplicate.

They were already serving kedgeree and salmon fish cakes in the private dining room when Ben cashed in his winnings, slipped the wad of notes into the breast pocket of his dinner jacket, and walked home whistling through the bright summer morning.

It might have taken all night, but doubling the money was a most convenient result.

He saw himself persuading the young woman to do what his godfather wanted – for her own good naturally.

She would have had a good night's sleep and time to think it over. Particularly if she was, as his godfather had implied, in the family way. He hoped that she did not intend to ruin her life by taking the wrong decision. Or by failing to take the right one. Let alone marrying the father: whoever he might be, it could only be one of the locals. It would be a terrible shame to waste a thoroughbred on a country donkey.

The sum was more than generous. Anyone who would turn down that kind of money must either be mad or have absolutely no idea of the practicalities of life. Had he been in a similar position, Ben had no doubt that he would have accepted without a moment's hesitation. After all, he had been prepared to take on Charlotte – and, heaven only knew, the price of that decision was far higher than simply agreeing to keep his mouth shut.

If Marguerite accepted, well and good. He would keep his own winnings; he had doubled the stake and earned his share.

If she refused, he could return the stake to his godfather with suitable expressions of regret. Marguerite would still have her cash, direct from him, with no strings attached. Then she could make up her own mind on what to do with it – and incidentally, if she did indeed require a little visit to a sympathetic doctor not unadjacent to Harley Street, it would make the right decision all the easier if she had the money to pay for it.

He would not begrudge her the windfall. Gamblers' winnings are not real money. There were many things lacking in Benjamin Catesby, but generosity was not one of them.

25

Miss Elsie Potter Receives a Visitor

'Come quickly, Bassett!'

The young second footman moved swiftly. Miss Elsie Potter, chatelaine of Daisyford Hall, indulgent great-aunt to many nephews and nieces, including Miss Belinda Fitzherbert, did not tolerate delay in the servants. And Bassett, it being his first week at the Hall, was doubly nervous because he was aware that his shoes squeaked.

'Madam?'

'The orchids, Bassett. My precious cymbidiums are parched.'

Elsie pushed a ring-laden finger into the rich loam which surrounded her favourite blooms. She extracted the finger and held it up to her nose, and then examined the evidence disapprovingly through gold pince-nez.

'Every week without fail, Bassett, they must be thoroughly soaked. One hour, up to their necks. Didn't Mr Wilkins explain?'

'Yes, madam,' murmured Bassett. The butler had indeed explained. Just as he had explained that he had been in the family's service since he was a boy, just as most of Miss Potter's servants had been there since they were little more than children. And, although there were three full-time gardeners employed to see to the exterior horticulture, the potted plants were the responsibility of the indoor servants.

'Heavens, they're practically gasping.'

'Right away, madam,' said Bassett, his shoes squeaking like demented mice on the polished tiles as he transferred the earthenware pots to the porcelain sink. Bassett's shoes squeaked because they were new. They were new because all new employees at Daisyford were issued by the house-keeper with two complete uniforms. Miss Potter liked everything properly presented, including her staff.

In spite of her eighty years and the early hour at which she had chosen to inspect her conservatory, Miss Potter was a supremely elegant figure. She was not yet dressed for the day, but wore an impeccably pressed tea-gown, a full-length garment which dropped in a smooth line from neck to ankle. The tea-gown was her favourite garment, and she had a dozen similar hanging in her wardrobes, neatly tailored in pastel nun's-veiling, a fabric made of woven wool as fine and soft as silk.

Although she had never married, Elsie Potter had been – still was – a beauty. As with racehorses, many gener-ations of breeding had produced a thoroughbred. In her girlhood she had been considered quite wild – a daredevil on the hunting field and a good sport in company.

Miss Potter took care of herself. She would no more be seen in public without her make-up than be found in town on a Sunday. Although it was not yet eight o'clock of a fine September morning, her eyebrows were already neatly drawn in, the heavy eyelids brushed with mauve shadow to accent the still-brilliant blue eyes, the lashes carefully mascara'd, the cheeks powdered and – a wise concession to her age – the lips painted not the vampish scarlet of her youth, but a becoming pink.

In the daytime she wore her hair, once gold, now silver, swept back in a plain chignon. She had never approved of short hair in women, not even in the Twenties when absolutely everyone bobbed their hair. For the evening she had it dressed by Hilda Humphreys, her personal maid, in an upswept Edwardian bun reminiscent, but not slavishly copying, the style of her girlhood.

On weekdays there was little to justify this careful toilette. From Monday to Friday – at least on Miss Potter's side of the green baize door – Daisyford was a lonely place. Elsie had never chosen to marry – from choice or from circumstances, no-one knew which. In her later years she always explained that she preferred friendship to the complications of matrimony.

But at the weekends the place sprang to life. House-guests were expected to arrive no later than cocktail time on Friday evening. They always left immediately after Sunday luncheon, having tipped the butler and the house-keeper; and woe betide the guest who overstayed his welcome or failed in his duty to augment the servants' wages.

Friday dinner was informal by Miss Potter's lofty stan-dards, with only three courses instead of the customary five. Elsie's hospitality was at its most splendid on Saturday evenings, when the local gentry, along with those of her relatives who lived on the estate, were bidden to swell the London guests. The guest list was never known in advance. The locals could never be sure before they arrived if the plain-clothes policemen so discreetly in evidence were there for the protection of a minister of the Crown, or some foreign dignitary, or even a member of the royal family.

Monsignor Melton was also among those regularly privileged to enjoy the hospitality of Daisyford, even though, as a member of the Church of England, Miss Potter did not entirely approve of the Catholic clergy and only invited him when she needed to make up the numbers.

'Such a useful spare man, Charles. So dependable.'

So, when her great-niece Belinda Fitzherbert got into a little trouble over a young man and had to be spirited away to think the matter over, he had been happy to recommend the girl, being a left-footer on her father's side, as his first 'client' on his appointment to the wardenship of the Hermitage.

For this, Miss Potter had been financially grateful. As the head of the family – all the men, including her brother and his son, the girl's father, having been killed in one or other of the world wars – she controlled the purse strings.

Although Elsie Potter's hospitality was not to be sniffed at, and she frequently entertained important politicians and financiers of the kind most likely to need Monsignor Melton's services, it was the house and its magnificent setting which gave the monsignor the most acute sensation of satisfaction.

Daisyford Hall was surely one of the most beautiful houses in England. It had been designed by John Nash in the Palladian style to the order of Elsie's great-great-grandfather, Ebenezer Potter. The founding father of the dynasty which had come to a halt at the childless Elsie had made a fortune from Australian goldmines – and knew enough to employ the best.

Landscaped gardens by Lancelot 'Capability' Brown provided a glittering setting for Nash's architectural gem. A lake had been excavated, islands equipped with ruined temples, a ha-ha dug so that cows and sheep might be pastured to add interest to the view. The splendid façade looked over a sweep of lawn whose velvet perfection was enhanced by ornamental fish ponds centred with classical statuary – nymphs and shepherds and the like. At a suitable distance – far enough to provide a brief stroll for the lady of the house and her guests, but not so far as to inconvenience the less nimble – a walled garden was laid out with pebbled paths and low hedges of box arches of espaliered apple-trees. The neat rectangles of vegetables and fruits were cultivated as much to delight the senses as to supply the busy kitchens.

Those who had followed had seen no reason to make

changes to the main fabric, although a conservatory and orangery had been added in Victorian times. As was customary when the house was built, the furnishings were designed for the rooms. Sofas, chairs, tables, curtains, carpets – all had been made to order. Even the paintings – several fine Van Dycks, a series of Turners (Venice from the sea) and a matching pair of Constables – had been chosen to blend with the décor. Subsequent cosmetic additions included murals by Rex Whistler in the dining room (a view of Lake Como in the Italian style featuring members of the family and their pets), an all-white sitting room designed by Syrie Maugham, and a library recently redecorated by David Hicks in green and crimson, with gilding.

The Potter fortune had descended to Elsie virtually intact. Ebenezer Potter had made prudent investments, and the establishment of trusts had ensured that his descendants continued to prosper among the material goods he had provided. All this prosperity required the attention of servants – a great many of them. Each of these servants had his or her allotted place in the hierarchy and a particular time of day in which certain services were required.

Bassett, as the lastest addition to the servants' hall, was doing mornings. This was because the morning was not a socially exacting time at Daisyford, which gave Miss Trotter ample opportunity to train him up.

'Then, do it, young man. Do it.'

In Elsie's view, the modern world had come adrift in various ways, one of which was the scarcity of junior footmen. And even when you had trained up a new one, as she knew to her cost, they repaid you by giving notice in favour of employment at any of the other grand country houses where footmen were at a premium. It was too bad. Daisyford was one of the best-run households in England, so anyone who could claim to have been trained by Miss

Potter could be sure of a well-paid position in any other establishment.

Mr Wilkins the butler was to all intents and purposes the male head of the household. As such he was not required to appear in his employer's presence until luncheon at weekends – weekdays were far less formal – when he served the meal with consummate skill and in white gloves, assisted, if there was company, by a lace-capped parlourmaid and the senior and second footmen.

Normally the senior footman's duties continued into the afternoon, which was when the second footman was set to polish the silver. The afternoon was when Miss Potter received her visitors, so more finesse was called for than was necessary in the morning. Not that in these modern times it was the custom to pay formal visits. Gone were the days when it was customary to turn down the corner of the visiting card if the visitor had paid the call in person. No – what might have been so since Jane Austen's day no longer applied. But Miss Potter did, nevertheless, keep up standards.

As the years went by, Elsie found that she had plenty of acquaintances but no close friends.

'Not another one,' she would sigh as she found the obituary notice of one of her contemporaries in *The Times* at breakfast. 'Sometimes I think I shall be the last one left.'

She was not of a generation which would normally consider it proper to seek new friends among those younger than herself, and her childlessness gave her little access to them anyway.

Elsie's existence had not always been so solitary. Two separate tragedies had altered the course of her life. The first had been the death of her twin brother in the trenches of the Somme. He had nevertheless left his young wife – scarcely more than a child herself – and his baby son to the care of his sister. Within a year or two, the young widow had remarried, leaving her small son in the care of his adoring aunt. It seemed perfectly appropriate that, since her nephew would one day inherit Daisyford and all its responsibilities, Elsie should raise him as her own.

Twenty years later a new war was declared, and once again the young men were called to pay the price. Tom Potter volunteered for service in his father's old regiment and left his penniless young fiancée Rosie to the care of his aunt. Victory had already been declared when the telegram arrived bearing the news of the sniper's bullet. Until that moment it had seemed to the two women who loved him that Tom was to be one of the lucky ones. After a suitable period of mourning, Elsie declared that Rosie was too young to spend the rest of her life an old maid, made ample provision for her, and sent her off to a new life in America.

Elsie had occasional news of her doings – three husbands at the last count – but did not keep up the intimacy they had enjoyed during the wartime years.

At Daisyford, Elsie's daily routine varied little. Mornings were given over to paperwork and the running of her household and the estate. Her afternoon visitors were almost always those with whom Elsie had business to discuss. She took an active interest in her investments and liked to brief her stockbroker in person. Or her visitor might be a lawyer – Miss Potter did not like to be bested in an argument. She involved herself in local politics, taking the side of farmworkers when they came up against authority, quarrelling vigorously over the desirability of a new road, or whether right of way should continue to be granted through her extensive apple orchards.

Today, with no visitors to amuse her and a morning spent rearranging her beloved cymbidiums and trimming their leaves – she liked to move the flowering plants into her boudoir – Miss Potter was bored.

She was also, with the inexperienced Bassett still

learning his trade, relatively unprotected from the common herd.

Both these things were shortly to work to Marguerite's advantage. The hand of Providence – or luck, or whatever name you cared to call that mysterious benefactor who sometimes assists the innocent – had been busy on her behalf.

First of all, Marguerite had had a glorious drive. She had enjoyed the feel of the powerful little car; she was rested and fed, since a diversion through the backstreets of the East End had revealed a small French-owned café which served croissants and coffee to the market traders of Petticoat Lane.

Once she left the crowded streets of the city and reached the open roads which threaded the green countryside, the journey had been relatively easy. The pastures beyond the flowering hedgerows were lush and full of plump, contented cows.

To Marguerite's eyes, accustomed to the rough uplands of Provence, the countryside of England was astonishingly beautiful. At this time of year, her native valleys were dusty and barren. Here, in this unfamiliar land, were apple orchards and tall stands of hops, and all seemed a vast carpet of emerald prosperity.

As she approached her destination her progress was slowed by the need to draw in and consult the map, which meant it was nearly lunchtime before she slowed down in the village of Daisyford.

In the middle of a tiny hamlet with no more than a dozen houses, a post-office-cum-shop and a handpainted sign proclaiming the Potter's Arms open for 'Fine Ales and Beers from the Keg', she spotted the turning to the Hall. This led her down a narrow lane which brought her to a set of handsome double gates which led in their turn to a wide avenue of chestnut trees.

Once through the gates, the landscape changed dramatically, and she found herself driving through a vast parkland. Here were no wild hillsides where the goats might browse, but on either side stretched rolling lawns, scattered here and there with ruined temples and sculpted pools reflecting graceful clumps of trees with multi-coloured leaves. A herd of deer, their russet backs flashing in the sun, raised their heads briefly, and immediately returned to their leisurely cropping. Clearly in this manicured landscape even the wild creatures were tame.

Marguerite slowed to a halt as she turned into the gravelled courtyard. The house itself, half-hidden by waves of topiaried box clipped into fantastic shapes – crowing cockerels and strutting peacocks – was quite simply the most beautiful thing she had ever seen.

Its lines were as pure and innocent as a child's drawing, a triple row of veined marble pillars surmounted by a triangular pediment carved from a single slab of snow-white stone. Between the pillars were triple tiers of tall windows, the shimmering glass reflecting sky and trees. A perfectly symmetrical sweep of exterior staircase led up to brass-studded doors flanked by carved marble lions.

Marguerite caught her breath in amazement. If this was indeed Miss Belinda Fitzherbert's home, she must be not only very wealthy indeed but some kind of princess.

After a minute to compose her story for what must have been the fiftieth time that morning, she made her way up the staircase to ring the bell which summoned the squeaky-shoed Bassett.

She was a little nervous when she saw that the servant was in uniform, but she felt much more confident now that she had raided Ben's wardrobe and replaced her *bleu de travail* with something at least a little more *soignée*.

'Excuse me. Is the mistress at home, please?'

It was fortunate for Marguerite that Father Patrick had encouraged her to read the novels of Jane Austen, in which this form of impersonal enquiry was commonplace. She worried for a moment that she did not have a calling card to present, but was reassured when the uniformed servant replied in the affirmative.

It was also fortunate that it was the inexperienced Bassett who opened the door to her. Had it not been that the footman was still wet behind the ears, he might have thought her a little young for one of the weekend visitors his mistress had told him to expect.

Had he questioned her more closely, he would have certainly directed her back to the village, where the former Miss Belinda Fitzherbert had embarked on married life in one of the estate's tied cottages with the Honourable Ferdie Forsyth, a more suitable suitor than the one with whom she had done such naughty things in her youth.

Or, if Marguerite's reply had been more circumspect, she would certainly have been sent round to the servants' entrance to state her business to the housekeeper, the formidable Mrs Ena Spittleswell. Mrs Spittleswell came from a family of Kentish fishermen who had ample reason to loathe both the French and the Irish. This might well have ensured that Marguerite would never have been conducted into Miss Potter's presence at all.

As it was, the young footman led the visitor straight to his mistress's boudoir.

26

Miss Elsie Potter at Home

'Miss Marguerite Leblanc, madam. Driven up from London.'

The uniformed footman held open the door for Marguerite to enter, and immediately withdrew, closing the door firmly behind him.

The vast room appeared at first to be empty, its corners shadowed by the fine mist of organdie curtaining which drifted across the windows and gave teasing little glimpses of the view. Outside was bright summer sunlight, but inside was cool and shadowy.

'Astonishing. Absolutely astonishing.'

The voice emerged from the shadows, nearly startling Marguerite out of her wits.

'Miss Fitzherbert?'

'Absolutely not. A silly girl, Belinda, even if she is my own niece.'

Marguerite could just make out a figure perched in a high-backed chair at the end of the long polished oak table behind a bank of orchids. Tiny and bird-like, with upswept white hair and a full-length gown of pale grey velvet trimmed with a jabot of creamy lace, she looked as if she had stepped out of one of the magnificent pictures which covered the walls.

'Name?' The question was startlingly abrupt, almost rude. Marguerite hesitated, thinking she should offer some explanation for her presence, and immediately decided it might be wise simply to give the answers required and withdraw as soon as possible.

'Marguerite Dieudonnée Leblanc . . . madame.'

Marguerite wondered for a moment if she should drop a quick curtsy, then thought better of it, remembering her republican roots.

'Not *your* name, young woman. Bassett has already made that clear. No. *This* . . .'

The heavily ringed hands cupped a tangle of fleshy leaves and silvery tentacles from whose heart sprang a spray of magnificent tawny-lipped flowers.

'Exquisite, don't you think?'

'Indeed, they are.'

'Come closer, child. Admire the detail. We share a rare privilege. The lady flowers only once in seven years. It was my grandfather who discovered her in the jungles of Guatemala. He was on his way to subdue the natives, but found himself captivated instead.'

Marguerite approached and put out her hand to the blossoms. They were indeed extraordinary, their speckled beauty almost predatory. 'Like tigers,' she breathed.

There was a pause while the bird-like old lady inspected her visitor through pince-nez. The blue eyes were quite pale but very bright. The glass gave them an odd magnification, curiously owl-like.

'Very good, child.' The old lady nodded, pleased by the reaction. 'Some of her sisters *are* carnivorous.'

After a moment, Miss Potter set the pot of tangled greenery tenderly back in its porcelain dish. The gnarled fingers moved on.

'And this – this marvellous creature. The Aztecs used the tubers as an aphrodisiac. There are only a dozen specimens in captivity. My grandfather named her *Cymbidium vaginatum* – either because he had a particularly vivid imagination or because my grandmother was anatomically somewhat unusual. Or do I need to translate?'

'No, indeed. Father Patrick taught me a little Latin.'

Marguerite added the last bit hurriedly, not wishing to be thought ignorant or without connections by this bewildering old woman.

'Father Patrick? A Catholic priest? And was it he who gave you your charming name?'

'I believe so.'

'Dieudonnée. Gift of God. A distinction traditionally accorded to bastards. Are you a bastard, child?'

Marguerite was startled by the old woman's directness. 'I'm sorry?'

'One should never be sorry. Particularly not if one is a bastard. Please answer my question.'

'Then, yes, madame. In a manner of speaking.'

This time Marguerite's clear green eyes did not flinch from the blue stare.

'Good. That's settled, then. And your father – he is the priest? Or is that also "in a manner of speaking"?'

Marguerite felt the blush rising to her cheeks.

'No. I mean, my mother never told me. Except that my father was a young English officer, very handsome and blond and fair-skinned, like all the English. It was a wartime romance, I suppose.' She hesitated and held out her hand. 'He gave her this ring. I promised my mother I would always wear it.'

Elsie Potter glanced down. Then her eyes widened – but for a fraction of a second. Only someone who knew her very well indeed would have read anything at all into the small flicker of the eyebrow and the darkening of the irises which betrayed the shock of understanding.

When she spoke again, her voice did not show any emotional change.

'And your mother? I assume by your use of the past tense that she is dead?'

'That, too.'

The old woman nodded calmly.

'Even better. A bastard and an orphan, with a priest in-a-manner-of-speaking for a father. I, too, am an orphan and a bastard, although I cannot claim God's anointed as a father. We share two distinctions, you and I.'

'You, madame?'

'Certainly. No need to look so shocked, child. My mother was a famous flirt. She died when I was eight – but not before she had presented my father with four children. Only the first was his. The heir naturally. Killed in the trenches of course. The girls – my two younger sisters and myself – were sired by the Prince of Wales. Everybody knew it, and nobody turned a hair – least of all my father. A couple of acres of central New York saw to that, and he had a perfectly good mistress himself. Try getting away with that these days.'

The old woman let out a bark of laughter. She then applied the gold pince-nez to her nose and began a detailed head-to-toe examination of her flustered visitor. When she had finished, she nodded, apparently satisfied.

'How old are you, child?'

'Eighteen, madame.'

'Good. French, I hear – but with a touch of the Irish.' Elsie Potter smiled to herself. 'And the right age, about eighteen, just as I thought.'

'I am well old enough to take care of myself, madame.'

'I'm sure you are, child. After all, you are here to prove it. And, since you have the good manners not to enquire, I am Elsie Potter – young Belinda's aged great-aunt. *Miss* Potter. I never married. You, on the other hand, are far too young to concern yourself with such things. Already we have found something else in common.'

Marguerite was beginning to feel a little out of her depth. She felt that she should reveal her business: that she had been admitted under false pretences.

'Miss Potter, I think I should explain—'

'Never explain, my dear. A cardinal rule of life.

Most particularly when luncheon is on the table.'

'But—'

Marguerite's hostess held up her hand to forestall any protest. 'No argument, child. You are already under my roof. There's nowhere else in the neighbourhood where you could possibly take refreshment worthy of the name. As a Frenchwoman, I suppose you can appreciate good food. That I can offer you. In return, your company will give pleasure to a lonely old woman. In short, I expect you to amuse me by telling me all about yourself.'

The self-confessed lonely old woman sailed out of the room without a backward glance.

Luncheon, served in a small dining room with tall windows giving out on to a broad panorama of the park, was a buffet arrangement. A variety of covered dishes had been set on silver warming-plates, with prettily arranged platters of salads on a long table covered with a gleaming white cloth. Several places had already been laid, presumably in anticipation of unexpected guests such as herself.

The whole effect was welcoming, generous – reminding Marguerite of the place set for the stranger at the Christmas feast. At this memory of her home, or what had once been her home, a strange feeling came over her – a warm feeling, almost as if she had at last reached the sanctuary the Hermitage had never really offered her.

The bird-like old woman patted the chair beside her, lifting the lid from the nearest dish. A scent of rich stew rose in a puff of fragrant steam.

'Please, child, help yourself. I shall expect you to do justice to Mrs Crabtree's cooking. The poor dear thing constantly despairs of my appetite.'

Marguerite was happy to obey Miss Potter's instruction. The croissants and coffee had been consumed several hours ago, and she was famished.

The food was strange but absolutely delicious: little pots

of tiny peeled shrimps embedded in peppery butter, crisp curls of paper-thin toast, heaps of finely slivered cucumber dressed with some unfamiliar herb.

Afterwards a creamy gratin of sliced potatoes went with the deliciously fragrant stew. From the first mouthful, she realized that Mrs Crabtree could rival her own mother in the preparation of what seemed to be a *daube*, but was somehow richer, more exotic, spiced as it was with cloves and cinnamon rather than with the herbs of the Provençal *maquis*.

'Venison, my dear, from our own herd. I hope you like it.'

Marguerite nodded, her mouth already full.

There was wine, too, pale and delicately sparkling.

Elsie Potter sipped her wine and pecked at her plate. Seeing her young visitor was ravenous, she would allow no conversation.

'I have changed my mind. Eat first. Talk afterwards.'

When Marguerite had finished – the raspberries and thick yellow cream could not possibly be resisted – she laid her napkin down with a sigh.

'Good. I can see you enjoyed your meal.'

'It was wonderful.'

The old lady nodded. 'A clean plate will adequately express your feelings to Mrs Crabtree.'

Miss Potter leaned back in her chair and picked up her pince-nez. 'Since the inner man is satisfied, we shall turn to the outer. You may now tell me what brings you here.'

Marguerite hesitated, scarcely knowing where to begin.

'I – I really have no idea . . .'

'Take your time, child. I'm not nearly as frightening as I look.'

'I don't think you look frightening at all, to be sure I don't and really I don't—' Marguerite blurted out with a passion which caught her all unawares. As her own words echoed in her head, she realized that this was perfectly true. There was something about the old lady – her direct-ness, the quick intelligence in the blue eyes – which made her feel not only that her bark was probably considerably worse than her bite, but also that she could be trusted.

The whole thing – the beauty of the place, the deliciousness of the meal and the memories the flavours had evoked, the exhaustion of the last few days – was suddenly too much for Marguerite.

For the first time since she had left the Hermitage, she felt the tears welling up in her eyes and a lump rising in her throat.

She fumbled for a handkerchief, failed, and found instead a scrap of lace-trimmed lawn thrust into her hand.

'Here, child. Use this.'

This small kindness, the touch of the hand, the over-whelming peace of the place after the bustle and noise of the city, opened the floodgates. She found herself being led over to an armchair by the window, settled gently into it, and allowed to sob till she could sob no more.

When she finally stopped, she found the old lady watching her quietly.

'I think you'd better tell me all about it, child.'

The whole story came tumbling forth. The death of her mother, Father Patrick, Tonin, the fire and the flood, the terrible fate which had befallen Abelard. The plans for the Hermitage and the valley, and her frustration at Monsignor Melton's refusal to listen to her. She had not known that she had felt such loneliness, that she had lost so much – could have been so crazy as to hope for so much.

Elsie Potter watched and listened with mounting aston-ishment. Even so, she was only listening with her ears. It was the watching which occupied her mind and heart. The girl was a true beauty, and Elsie valued beauty above all. In objects certainly, in her possessions both inherited and acquired, and in the natural world. But above all in her own kind. The girl obviously needed her, and she was ready to be needed.

When Marguerite finally came to the real purpose of her visit, Elsie had already made up her mind to do what she could to help the girl. But the old woman was wise. She would have to be circumspect about it. The girl was young, her plans were ambitious, but she needed a purpose in life far more than she needed a solution to her immediate problems.

And beneath it all was the responsibility laid on her by that ring.

'Child, all of this sounds most intriguing and very admirable. But – forgive me – you might perhaps lack experience. Do you have someone to help you?'

'I – no – that is, there's Tonin—'

'The goatboy, I think you said? My dear, it's a little ambitious to expect a young man without any experience of such things to be able to cope with all the problems which will surely arise. You may be asking too much of him, however willing he may be to learn.'

'Tonin's wonderful,' Marguerite said defensively. 'He knows more about the whole thing than anyone. Everything which has ever happened in the valley. He's read all the books. And he's lived there all his life.'

Miss Potter nodded. 'I'm sure he has. But he may need professional qualifications if he is to convince others.' Her face was thoughtful. 'You have to approach it more gently, my dear. Rein in your passions and harness them. When you are as old as I am, you will understand the value of patience.'

Marguerite bounced up and began to pace the room. 'But there's no time – don't you see? It's already too late—'

'Child, it's never too late.' Elsie's voice was quiet. 'Not even for me – and I shall never see my eightieth year again.'

She walked over to the window, her small head carried high on the lace-draped shoulders, and waved her hand towards the view of the park, sparkling now in the early-afternoon sunshine. 'I have all this beauty – and yet I am not content.'

Marguerite waited. When the old lady spoke again, her voice was thoughtful.

'I've lived a selfish life by most people's standards. But, then, I'm not as most people, and I have more to be selfish with than most.' At that moment, as if to confirm the truth of her words, a herd of deer moved gracefully across the vista, to vanish behind a decoratively ruined pavilion.

'I'm sure—' Marguerite began hesitantly, wishing to offer reassurance, but the old woman cut her off in mid-sentence.

'You are sure of nothing, child. You are far too young to be sure of anything.' She paused to give her words emphasis. 'But you are right in what you were going to say. I am generous – even to strangers such as yourself. I have been scrupulous in the care of my inheritance – and by that I mean the working men and women who depend on me. I give employment to many, and take care of my people when they are no longer able to work. And I have been more than generous to my family, by normal standards and even beyond. I have housed the less provident of my siblings, looked after their descendants, made sure their children's school fees are paid. If you were me, you might take pride in the discharge of what was not only a privilege but a duty.'

'If I were you—' Marguerite began eagerly, only to be interrupted once more.

'But you are not me, child. You know nothing of what has formed me – or that I, too, may need redemption.' She stood up. 'Come. I have something to show you.'

Marguerite followed Miss Potter through the long gallery towards a glass door through which could be seen a high wall which must surely enclose a garden.

*   *   *

The walled garden was not a single enclosure, but a series of huge rooms open to the sky, leading off one another through an arched wooden door, each enclosed in a cocoon of warm red brick.

Elsie did not speak or look for Marguerite to reply; she simply walked slowly through the series of rooms, occasionally pausing to examine a flower or pick a dead leaf from a shrub.

Every now and again she would stop, waiting for Marguerite to catch up with her. Marguerite for her part could scarcely believe the evidence of her own senses. Sight, smell, touch – even the birdsong to bring pleasure to the ears – all were engaged to the full.

Each of the rooms seemed more beautiful, more magnificent, more intriguing than the one before. Each had its own character and colour. The first was devoted to scarlet flowers – deep red roses and paler peonies, poppies and many others that Marguerite could not even recognize. The next was a billow of white – lilies and drifts of snowy daisies and unfamiliar plants with silvery leaves. Then there was blue, and yellow and purple – each more marvellous than the one before. Some, too, were crammed with neatly hoed lines of vegetables – lettuces and onions and marrows, tall stands of climbing beans. Another was given to the cultivation of herbs with multicoloured leaves and a thousand scents – these above all she recognized.

'Your thoughts, child.'

They had come to the last garden, and Marguerite was silent. Her heart was too full to speak. She could think of nothing to say, nothing which could possibly reflect the delight she felt, the peace that the place brought her.

'No need. I can see you feel as I do.'

The old woman's voice was gentle – gentler even than when she brought her comfort when she wept. After a moment the voice came again.

'Your eyes, child. Tell me what you see.'

Marguerite was still silent. Then she said hesitantly, looking for the words which might express what she felt, knowing this was impossible: 'I see . . . the most beautiful place I have ever seen filled with the most beautiful living things I have ever seen—'

'You're wrong, child.'

The old woman turned away from the younger. She walked slowly, as if reluctant to yield the final secret, towards a single tree which occupied the very centre.

This last of the rooms was planted with fruiting trees – peaches and apricots espaliered against the red walls, plum-trees and cherries carefully tended and neatly pruned. Greenhouses, as tall as the walls, lined the sides, within which were vines twisted and heavy with grapes.

Some of the trees were known to Marguerite only from the old books Father Patrick had encouraged her and Tonin to study. All were named and tagged. Fruits so ancient they were still close cousins to the wild, their flavours now forgotten – citron and bird-cherry, bullace and medlar. Some were familiar to her from the gatherings of her childhood – mirabelle and pomegranate, the sunny little fruits of the strawberry tree, bright as buttons.

Through the centre ran a double arch of apple trees, the scarlet fruit hanging like lanterns among the thicket of green, but this was interrupted to permit the single tree to spread its vast canopy of green, beneath which the old lady now stood.

This central tree was an ancient fig, its trunk polished by time to a pearly smoothness, its leaves like glossy green fists cradling the ripe purple fruits, its branches spread over a wide circle of meadow grass starred with daisies.

'Beauty, you say? What you see is not beauty, but patience. The patience to be born, to grow, to flourish and to die, only to be born again. This tree has been here for as long as the earth which nourishes her. Her seeds are no bigger than a speck of dust, but from them spring new trees as broad and generous as she. Birds nest in her, bees sip nectar from her blossoms, squirrels breed in her branches, beneath her roots small creatures flourish. She gives two crops. The first of the spring, the last of the autumn, one black, one white. She was here when I was born, and she will be here when I die. If I have my wish, I shall be buried here, beneath her shelter. She is the first fruit of the earth and she will surely be the last. She is our past, our present and our future.'

The old woman's voice held neither sorrow nor joy, but something far beyond those simple emotions – something which came from the very depths of her soul. With the clear vision of youth, Marguerite knew that this was something the old woman had never told anyone else in all her life.

'You, child, may be wise enough to learn the lesson she teaches. I have struggled to learn it all my life, and I fear I have failed.'

A smile of incandescent happiness now lit up the wrinkled face, the blue eyes as bright as the summer sky.

'Now do you see why I shall help you?'

She paused again, reached up into the branches and plucked one of the ripe fruits. She took Marguerite's hand and placed the fruit in her palm.

'Look again, child, and learn. Even beauty such as yours will wither and die. But this – this is immortality.'

Marguerite looked down. The blue-blushed cheek was slashed with scarlet through which a golden slick seeped tiny seeds.

'I shall help you, child, but it may not necessarily be in the way that you have planned. What you propose is the labour of a lifetime, but I no longer have a lifetime left. Your greatest enemy will be loneliness. I recognize myself in you, and I fear you would not take kindly to the yoke of matrimony. For a while yet I shall keep you company.

Make the best of it, my dear. You won't have me for long.'

The old woman smiled again – this time lightly, almost girlishly.

'Enough of that. I shall expect you to return next Friday evening. You will spend the weekend. By then I shall have laid my own plans for your future. No doubt you now have other matters to attend to. I shall keep my promise. I have no doubt that you will keep yours.'

A week until she could return. A week in which she knew she would long to return. It was not until she had left the beautiful place and its strange owner far behind, and was once again manoeuvring the little car through the busy streets of the city, that Marguerite remembered she had not told Miss Potter where she might be reached. And then she remembered. She had nowhere to live, no place to lay her head, no home. She belonged nowhere, to no-one.

Ben waited until as late as he dared to allow Marguerite time to return his car. Its absence did not bother *him*, but it might well bother his fiancée, whom he was due to drive down to her parents for a long-overdue weekend.

By the time Marguerite was gaining admittance to Miss Potter's presence, he was beginning to suspect that she must have taken the vehicle in order to drive back to the Hermitage in which case there was no knowing when he could expect her to return it. But return it he was certain she would.

By tea time, when she still had not returned, he could no longer delay telephoning Charlotte to explain exactly why he could not pick her up. When she heard what he had to say, and the reason, he heard no more than the click of the receiver being replaced.

The silence lasted for half an hour – just long enough for Lottie to arrive on his doorstep.

'I don't know who to blame for this . . . this *monstrous behaviour*. You or that . . . *trollop*.'

'Her name's Marguerite. And she's not a trollop.'

'She's a common thief. You must inform the police.'

'Nonsense. She's only *borrowed* the thing.'

'In my book, that's stealing. None of my friends would dream of such a thing.'

'None of your friends would actually have to.'

Charlotte's mouth pursed. 'What's that supposed to mean?'

'Nothing. Just that she must have been pretty desperate.'

'That's no reason for letting her get away with it.'

'She *did* get away with it.' He grinned. 'Showed me a clean pair of heels. Probably at the Channel ports by now. And she's been through enough, poor girl. I'm certainly not going to spoil her fun by having her arrested.'

'You think it's fun? Stealing a car is fun? You have a curious sense of humour, Benjamin. And why you let her into your house I'll never understand. I hope Daddy doesn't get to hear of it.'

'I didn't mean for her to stay. And, anyway,' he added swiftly, suddenly seeing a new line of attack opening, 'I wasn't even here.'

'I should hope not!' The outrage in her voice was as genuine as the Hermès scarf, the pearl necklace and the Gucci loafers she must have donned in unusual haste – considering the length of time it usually took his fiancée to dress for the street.

She considered Ben suspiciously.

'So where were you?'

Ben sighed theatrically and pushed his hand through his hair. 'Gambling. Drinking. Clairville Club. Check if you like.'

'I've no intention of doing any such thing. Just so long as you weren't doing anything naughty.'

'I don't do anything naughty, Lottie. Not any more. You asked me not to, remember? Drinking and gambling, yes. Naughty things, no.'

'I should hope *not*.'

'She left a rather sweet note.' Ben held out the paper. 'Here – read it. It's touching, in a simple sort of way.'

'Touching! Simple!' Charlotte sniffed loudly. She did not even bother to glance down. 'I'm surprised she can even sign her own name.'

She narrowed her eyes. 'Don't think it'll get you out of the weekend, Benjamin. The Barings are coming; I told Daddy you were looking for something in the City, and Tommy knows all the right people. There's dinner on Saturday with the Lord Lieutenant. And, on Sunday, Mummy's organized a hand of bridge with the Smith-Ponsonbys.'

'The Smith-Ponsonbys, is it? And it would be very inconsiderate of me to back out now?'

'Absolutely.'

'Plays havoc with the *placement*? Upsets the Lord Lieutenant?'

'Honestly, Benjamin, sometimes I think you take nothing seriously.'

To Ben's relief, Charlotte's attention was suddenly diverted by the mess in the room, and she began to plump up cushions and neaten piles of papers.

'This place is a pigsty. No wonder people walk in and take things.'

Crockery clattered into the sink.

'Please stop that, Lottie.' Ben folded up his long legs and sank into one of the cushions, watching his fiancée through dramatically lowered lids. 'You're giving me a headache.'

'No wonder. You drink too much.'

She began to pile the abandoned glasses and empty bottles on to a tray.

'Of course I do. I always have. I shall continue to do so. I enjoy it.'

'Then, clear it up afterwards. A tidy room, a tidy mind. Discipline.'

'None, as you know.'

Charlotte stopped abruptly. 'I've been discussing your prospects with Daddy.'

Ben held up his hand. 'Don't. You know perfectly well it's no good. I freely admit I lack ambition. I can see that money is useful, but I see not the slightest reason for making any more if one already has enough. I admit I sometimes can't pay my own bills – temporarily embarrassed, as I have to explain to my esteemed godfather. But you, my sweet, as we both well know, have more than enough for both of us.'

'That's not how Daddy sees it.'

'Of course not. Your father believes in the law of the jungle. He wants to be able to boast to his friends about how much his son-in-law earns.'

'You're in a very peculiar mood today, Benjamin.'

'If you say so, Lottie.'

In a conciliatory voice she continued: 'I'll get Mummy to lend us the Volvo – we can drive down early tomorrow.'

'Marvellous.' At the news that the agony was to be delayed if only for a night, Ben cheered up immediately. 'I'll see you home, Lottie.'

At that moment a small red sports-car drew up outside the window.

It was all a little unfortunate. A little later and there would have been no-one there to answer the doorbell at all. The place would have been deserted, Marguerite would have popped the keys through the door and gone elsewhere about her business, Ben and Lottie would have driven off into the sunset, and the future would have been very different for all three.

As it was, the doorbell rang, and Marguerite stood

smiling on the doorstep, the car keys dangling from her outstretched finger.

'Sorry about that,' said Marguerite. 'I didn't think it'd take so long.'

Her green eyes sparkling, her cheeks flushed from the drive, her russet hair tousled from the wind, she looked like a young woman who has just received some thoroughly good news.

She gazed from one face to the other.

'Oh dear,' said Marguerite. 'I can see I shall have to explain.'

'Not to me, you won't,' snapped Charlotte, and pushed her way past the unwelcome visitor. 'I'll see you at Mummy's, Benjamin. Or else.'

With that, and a flick of the blond hair, Charlotte was gone.

27

Benjamin Catesby at Home

'Miss Potter? Elsie Potter? Not *the* Miss Elsie Potter of Daisyford Hall?'

'I think so. Surely so.'

Marguerite smiled and nodded. She was enjoying herself. She had not thought herself capable of astonishing anyone as sophisticated and important as Benjamin Catesby in his new incarnation as the Earl of Malvern, and it was rather a pleasant notion. The cross young woman who had been there when she returned with the car had vanished down the street, and she had just finished giving Ben a thumbnail sketch of her day.

'You lunched with old Elsie?'

'Yes. She's an acquaintance of yours?'

Marguerite liked the sound of 'acquaintance'. It sounded exactly what a lord would have. Except that Benjamin Catesby did not seem to behave much like a lord. Nor did he seem to live like a lord. Miss Elsie Potter was much closer to what she had imagined a lord would be.

Ben grinned. 'Not an acquaintance exactly. But she was a friend of my grandparents. I met her a few times when I was a child. A formidable old dragon, as I remember. How on earth did you find your way to her lair?'

'She's not a dragon. She's . . .' Marguerite searched for the right word, only succeeding in coming up with 'marvellous'.

Ben felt a small twinge of jealousy. This was his damsel

in distress. He had rescued her from one dragon, and he felt irritated that she had thrown herself so quickly into the arms of another. Even if that other was an old battleaxe like Elsie Potter.

'Marvellous? Why marvellous?'

'Because she's explained exactly what I have to do and why I have to do it in the way that she says. And she's told me she'll help me. More than that—'

Marguerite stopped abruptly, suddenly thinking that she must be careful. Miss Potter might not like her discussing her business with others. Something also told her that Miss Potter might particularly not approve of her confiding in Benjamin Catesby. Ben would not be considered a serious person by Miss Potter.

'More than what?' Ben prompted.

Marguerite shrugged. 'She says she'll— I don't really know. She seems to know how to make things work.'

'You astound me, child.'

Ben sank back into his cushions in theatrical amazement. This was only half an act. He was indeed amazed. All the more because he had been so concerned over her, so eager to do battle with Charlotte over his right to befriend her. To think that he had pictured himself handing over his winnings from the gaming table and explaining magnanimously that all the money was hers for the spending.

The most irritating thing was that he had thought that she might relieve the tedium of his existence. Fear of tedium was what made Benjamin Catesby tick. He had imagined taking her in hand, introducing her to the pleasures – perhaps not of the flesh, which would be stretching Lottie's tolerance a little too far, but certainly of society. His own particular society, the sort of which his fiancée disapproved but from which she had not yet managed to wean him. Surely that would amuse him – and with Lottie on the warpath he would need a little amusement.

And now here was the girl back on his doorstep, with her eyes shining and this extraordinary tale of gaining instant access to one of the most fortified citadels in Britain. Not any old Miss Potter. But the famous, the notoriously tyrannical Miss Elsie Potter of Daisyford Hall. What on earth had the girl said or done which could possibly have caused Elsie to take the girl in?

It could not have been the story the girl had spun. From what his godfather had told him, her plans amounted to blackmail, and this he himself had found highly entertaining. Miss Potter was hardly likely to share Ben's sense of humour. Elsie Potter was famous for her business acumen, not for her susceptibility to scams. Scams were Ben's area of amusement, and he had been looking forward to encouraging Marguerite's endeavours.

'I don't believe it. The old trout must have thought you were someone else.'

'Nonsense. And she's not a trout.' Marguerite's voice was calm. She had never been so certain of anything in her life than that the old woman could never in a million years have mistaken her for anyone else.

To prove it, she decided to confide in Ben after all, and gave him a brief outline of her conversation. Ben was not very interested in tales of fig trees and immortality, but he *was* interested in Marguerite. As he listened to her excited chatter, a new thought struck him.

'So you're not in a spot of bother at all? In the club?'

Marguerite stopped, startled.

'In the club?'

'Dear child, I'm asking if you're pregnant.'

'Pregnant!' Marguerite gave a shout of glee. She bounced up and pushed a cushion under the voluminous shirt, giggling helplessly.

She could see that Ben was getting irritated, but she could not help herself. The notion of pregnancy was not only wonderfully poignant, but also marvellously absurd.

Considering the trouble she had gone to on that particular score – for all that it seemed that the events of the St Jean had taken place in some other incarnation – it was a truly hilarious suggestion.

'Well, are you or not?' Ben demanded.

'Guess!' She danced around the room, pushing the artificial belly in front of her.

'Stop that at once.' She had somehow managed to turn the tables on him, get the upper hand. Whatever she was – penniless stray, car thief, helpless damsel in need of rescue – she was certainly more than a handful.

'No, your Lordship,' she managed to splutter, 'most surely I'm not pregnant. Not in the least bit pregnant. Not even *that* much.' She pinched an inch of air between her fingers.

'So what about the boyfriend?'

Marguerite froze. 'How did you know about Tonin?'

'I didn't. My godfather seemed to think you had a boyfriend and a baby, or a baby and no boyfriend, and that that was what was making you so – as he put it – *unmanageable*. Put you up to it all.'

'Put me up to it? Don't be silly. I'm the one who puts Tonin up to things. And if you really want to know, Benjamin Catesby, I'm most absolutely and undeniably a virgin. *Virgo intacta*, as Father Patrick might say. No fault of mine, either. You've no idea how hard I tried.' Another shout of laughter punctuated this admission.

Ben studied her gloomily. 'That settles it, then.'

'Settles what?'

'Your social life. Finished. I can't possibly be seen around with a virgin. Too humiliating.'

Marguerite considered this. 'No-one could tell.'

'Most certainly they could. Don't you know that every virgin looks in her mirror the morning after she's lost it?' He grinned at her. 'It shows.'

'I have no experience of that, your Nibs.'

'*Your Nibs*, is it? You have a fine grasp of cockney slang – for a frog.'

'I *do* know what that means.'

'Good. I shall take you out to dinner tomorrow and you may eat them. I know just the place.'

'What about the young lady? The one you're supposed to be with or else?'

'Charlotte can do without me this weekend. She's too used to getting her own way. She takes me for granted.'

'Perhaps you take her for granted.'

'What would you know about that?'

'More than you think,' said Marguerite. 'Anyway, I thought you said it was too humiliating to be seen out with a virgin.'

'Not if you behave yourself.'

'I thought behaving oneself was not what a gentleman had in mind when he offered a lady his company.'

'You're not a lady, and I am rarely a gentleman. Besides, I make it a rule never to touch virgins. My fiancée doesn't like it.'

Marguerite considered him, her face serious. 'The lady is your fiancée?'

'Indeed. Charlotte Willoughby. My fiancée. The woman I love.' There was a note of mockery – as if the words might apply to others, but not to him. 'The girl I shall marry.'

'She doesn't mind if you touch people who *aren't* virgins?'

'Indeed, she does. But she especially objects to virgins.'

'Where I come from,' said Marguerite, 'a fiancée is a fiancée.'

'I don't live in your country, child. Where's your luggage? I assume you *do* have luggage?'

Marguerite picked up the neatly rolled *bleu de travail* which had somehow escaped Charlotte's attentions. She began to rummage around in the pockets, laying out the contents one by one.

'The plans for the Hermitage, rejected by your god-father. *Le passeport, la brosse à dents, le lipstick* – I *do* have *le lipstick*. And *le billet de cent francs*, which is' – she brandished the note in triumph – 'all I have in the world. Ah, I nearly forgot.' She pulled out a small but inter-nationally recognizable packet. '*Les préservatifs*.'

Ben looked at her, startled. 'What on earth are you doing with those?'

'Optimism. Like I said before, I did *try*. But it's a long story.'

'Tomorrow, then. Tonight you'll need to tuck up early. You've had a long day, child. I imagine you have not arranged your own accommodation?'

This was indeed a problem Marguerite had not yet tackled. She replied with a confidence she was far from feeling: 'I'm sure I can manage.'

'Don't be so *tiring*, Marguerite. You can't manage anything at all.'

He uncoiled his body – he had a curious snake-like way of doing this – and went over to the door which, she had already ascertained, led to his own bedroom and bath-room.

The house, she knew from her investigations during Ben's absence the previous day, occupied three floors of which only one was furnished. It had only one bedroom and only one bed, although this appeared far too large for a single person, even one who was a lordship or an earl-ship.

But she was definitely sure that whatever Ben Catesby proposed would be dangerous.

'I don't think—'

'What don't you think?'

Ben had stopped at the door, and was looking at her

307

with the lowered lids which she was beginning to learn veiled his amusement, or his anger, or boredom. Sometimes he reminded her a little of Abelard. The owl, too, had had a quick flick of the eyelids which was just as difficult to read.

If it was amusement, that almost certainly meant an improper suggestion.

'I really don't think—'

But Ben had already guessed her thoughts.

'No such good fortune, my child. I have something else in mind than offering a share of my lonely bed. Accommodation. Independent. Bearing in mind that you no longer – if my godfather is to be believed – have a hook on which to hang your hat.'

'Hang my hat?'

'Try not repeat everything, child. Somewhere to live. To eat, dress and sleep. To take a bath and go to the lavatory. I assume you do all those things?'

Marguerite looked at him, her eyes steady. 'Of course.'

'And you need somewhere to do them?'

'Naturally.'

'And you lack the wherewithal to pay for them?'

'Not yet – but surely I will very shortly.'

'Then for the time being, you're obliged to accept my charity, since I don't deal in credit. I am pleased to be able to offer you my bolthole. I am glad to be able to do so, so don't thank me. I was beginning to think you needed nothing from me at all. And that would have been a pity.'

'Why would that be?' Sometimes Marguerite could not entirely keep up with what he was saying – and it was easier just to take notice of the last thing he said.

Ben shrugged. 'I'm bored. You amuse me.'

'And if I stop amusing you?'

'Then, you will bore me, and we will part company.'

Marguerite considered this, and then nodded. 'D'accord!'

'Good. We're agreed. Then follow me.'

Ben led Marguerite through the hallway and out of a door which opened into a small garden. There did not seem to be another house in the garden, just a lawn surrounded by flowerbeds – an untidy jumble of rambling yellow roses and purple poppies. Ben made his way towards a wooden door set flush into the brick wall at the far end.

'Your quarters, mademoiselle.' He flung open the door and stood aside for Marguerite to enter. 'The previous owner was a painter – he used this place as a studio. Naked models no doubt.' Ben grinned at her.

The bolthole was a single large room with a little bathroom tacked on the rear. The place was sparsely furnished with another of the large beds which Ben seemed to favour, a square table round which were placed four chairs, all the furnishings being simple but functional. There was even a telephone on a desk in a corner.

'You don't know how privileged you are, child. No-one knows about it – not even Lottie. It's my bolthole. Where I go when I need to hide.'

'Hide? From whom?'

'Jealous husbands, women who think a one-night stand's a commitment for life – you know the kind of thing.' He glanced at her, his eyes mischievous. 'No. Perhaps you don't.'

Marguerite bristled. 'I have been taking down confessions for Father Patrick ever since my tenth birthday. I know everything about such things.'

'Do you indeed? Everything? No wonder my sainted godfather was in such a state.' The hooded eyes were full of laughter. 'But I don't imagine you've ever been caught red-handed in the ancestral broom cupboard with your host's wife? No? Well, I can heartily recommend it as a reason for avoiding your fellow man.'

Marguerite looked round. She was tired. The bed looked very inviting. Ben was very confusing.

'Well?' Ben was leaning against the door, waiting.

She had no choice – not yet at least, not until she found her feet and could earn her own keep by her own exertions or whatever means Miss Potter advised.

'It's . . . it looks very comfortable.'

'That's settled, then.'

She said cautiously: 'What will you be wanting in the way of rent?'

'There's only one currency I accept from any woman. And in your case we've already ruled that out.'

She relaxed suddenly, laughter bubbling. 'Sure and I brought that on myself.'

'Sure and you did,' he mimicked, and suddenly his face broke into a glorious smile. For an instant her heart missed a beat, and she could see what women might see in him.

'Thank you kindly, then. I shall pay you. Just as soon as I can.' Then she added, conscious that she might be being rude: 'Don't be thinking I'm not grateful for the offer.'

'And I am grateful for your gratitude, child, since I see it is not an emotion which comes easily to you.'

Marguerite was stung by this. 'Sure and I'm grateful. And I'll thank you for not calling me *child*. I have had eighteen years to claim my womanhood – and, where I come from, that's sufficient earnest of maturity.'

'Then, as a mature woman, you will see you must accept.'

Again the glorious smile, followed by: 'The rent is simply that you continue to amuse me. Boredom terminates the tenancy.'

'Done!' There was laughter between them then, laughter and a shared complicity.

Ben could feel the money in his pocket. Later. Right now he was enjoying her dependence.

* * *

Relieved of responsibility for her own welfare, she ran a bath, throwing in a handful of scented crystals from a jar on the shelf, slipping happily into the warm suds.

There was a large soft towelling bathrobe hanging on the back of the door. When she had finished her bath, she put the bathrobe on. Somewhat disconcertingly, although it was perfectly clean, it smelled faintly of Ben. Sandalwood perhaps; but something else, too – something which Tonin would have recognized as being that peculiar individual perfume which distinguishes one human being from another. The power of smell is potent – and all the more so because it is the one sense which is not subject to the intellect. The subtlest of the senses, it is the most subversive.

None of these things occurred to Marguerite as she wrapped herself in the bathrobe and began to search through a cupboard which held a sink and a little hob to see if there might be a tin of something edible. It had been eight hours since Miss Elsie Potter's luncheon, and she was once again famished.

Just as she was trying to decipher the label on a tin which had no picture of anything on it, but seemed to promise tomato soup, there came a tap on the French windows which gave on to the garden.

She went over and slid open the double doors. Ben stood there with bag in his hand and the same lazy smile on his lips.

'Not chocolates this time. But I thought you might like some supper.'

He thrust the bag into her hand and was gone.

She opened the bag, finding two packets inside. One was a little paper tub with a wooden fork taped to the top, labelled 'Best Quality Jellied Eels'. The other was a bundle of newspaper which contained fish in some kind of crisp batter and a huge helping of hot chips heavily doused in vinegar. She prodded these strange foodstuffs with the caution of a cat which has just been presented with a dubious rat. She was hungry. She tasted.

Finding both of them good, she ate.

It had been a strange day. Strange food. Strange habits. But strangest of all were the people.

28

Breakfast for Two

'House guests make coffee. House rules.'

The voice was very close in her ear.

Marguerite opened her eyes, and then shut them again tightly. For an instant she had to struggle to remember where she was and who the voice might belong to.

The events of the previous day came flooding back.

Ben was looking down at her.

'House rules. Coffee.'

She pushed her hand through her hair, rubbed the sleep from her eyes, and blinked up at him. Even in the bright light of day, he was astonishingly handsome – dangerously so, even if a night's sleep had clearly not improved his manners.

'What's the time?'

'Coffee time.'

'Is that an offer or a request?'

'A request. I'm no good at doing things for myself.'

She struggled out of the tangle of blankets, conscious of his amused scrutiny, taking care to keep herself well covered. It seemed only seconds since she had closed her eyes. Now the curtains were drawn, and light was flooding in through the double windows, the green of the garden brilliant in the leaf-filtered sunshine.

Ben was wearing some kind of robe, a loose garment in very fine white wool embroidered at the seams with silk braid. This dress – or robe – did not look at all feminine, but hung from the broad shoulders and fell to the ankles in soft folds. Marguerite thought she had never seen such a beautiful garment in her life.

She noticed that he held another in his hand, rolled carelessly into a ball. He lobbed it over to her.

'Wear that. Then make the coffee. You'll find the makings in the kitchen in the main house. There's nothing much in here. I suppose you *do* know how to make coffee?'

'Surely I do.'

'Good. Then, do it.'

He vanished.

Thoughtfully Marguerite pulled on the garment. It felt soft and luxurious against her skin. She brushed her teeth, combed her hair, and followed Ben over to his house.

There was no-one in the main living room. The kitchen looked as if a bomb had hit it, the sink piled high with dirty crockery. She had to wash out two mugs and empty the grounds out of the cafetière before she could begin, but she was relieved to find a packet of good coffee – not the horrible powdered stuff the English who visited the Hermitage liked to drink.

When the coffee had brewed, she brought the mugs through to the main room and called: 'Ready!'

Ben appeared immediately.

She handed him the mug. 'Do you always have coffee in the morning?' she asked curiously. 'Everyone knows the English drink only tea.'

'I don't do what everyone knows.'

He smelled the coffee cautiously, then sipped.

'Good. What did you put in it?'

'Sugar and a little anise brandy – or I think that was what it was. It's called a Viva Maria. My mother used to make it for me if I was poorly.'

He raised the mug to her.

'Here's to Mother. And to you never being poorly again.'

She smiled and drank. The coffee was indeed good. Rich, dark and aromatic, with the kick of the alcohol hitting the back of the throat. It went a long way towards reviving her.

She glanced round the room, wondering how to enquire discreetly if Ben's fiancée was in residence.

'Your fiancée? She does not make coffee for you in the morning?'

'Good heavens, no. What an improper suggestion.'

'I didn't mean—'

'Of course you did. And I consider the implication thoroughly indiscreet.' The hooded eyes were on her, and there was a faint smile on Ben's lips. 'Since you enquire, Lottie doesn't cook – not even coffee. Other people cook for Lottie. Anyway, when you turned up, she went running home to mother. This relieves me of the duty of spending a boring weekend with her parents.'

'Her parents are boring?'

'Their house is boring, their friends are boring, their lives are one long yawn.'

'But you're going to marry her?'

'Indeed, I am.'

Marguerite wondered what Tonin would have made of this. The thought of his disapproval made her giggle.

'You find that amusing?'

'No. It's just that I thought—'

'Don't think. Make more coffee.'

When Marguerite returned with the fresh cup, she said: 'This fiancée of yours, she's jealous?'

He shook his head. 'Lottie's acquisitive. She likes to own things. I'm one of the things she owns.'

Marguerite frowned, struggling to understand this new view of matrimony.

'And you? You like to be bought?'

'Another impertinent question. But, yes, I'm quite happy with the arrangement, as long it's on my own terms. Besides, Lottie's rich. She can afford me.'

Marguerite shook her head. 'Not a nice thing to say about the colleen you are to wed.'

Ben laughed. 'That's where you're wrong, my dear. It's the nicest thing anyone can possibly say about the woman with whom one is to spend the rest of one's life. It's like racehorses. Or good motor cars. Expensive toys cost money. We need constant maintenance.'

Marguerite drew herself up proudly. '*I* don't. To be sure I can look after myself.'

'I might dispute that.' Ben looked at her quizzically, the lazy eyelids drooping.

Marguerite disregarded this. 'And she leaves you by yourself? With so many pretty girls, such short skirts. Short skirts all over the place,' she finished lamely, conscious that this did not sound very convincing.

'I'm rather old to be seduced by a short skirt.'

'How old?'

'Since you enquire with such grace, twenty-six next birthday.'

Marguerite considered this. Twenty-six was quite old by the standards of Pernes-les-Rochers. 'It's no wonder you're in a hurry to be wed.'

She was still curious about the young woman who clearly left Ben so much latitude. 'If she knew you'd lent me your' – she looked for the new word – 'bolthole?'

'Charlotte hasn't bought me yet. She's only put down the deposit. Besides, she's not always around.'

'*I* would be. If I truly loved someone.'

'And do you truly love someone?'

'Of course. I love Tonin.'

'Ah, yes. The goatboy.'

Marguerite's cheeks flamed. 'Sure and what my fiancé

316

does for his living is none of your business.'

'So you do have a fiancé?'

'Well . . . friend. *Best* friend,' she added hurriedly, just in case he got the wrong idea.

'I gather from that that you are not entirely convinced of the permanence of your choice?'

'It's not that at all—'

'Then, what? Surely not fear of being an old maid? My dear girl, you've a great deal of living to do. I'd prefer to think you hope to do better for yourself than a goatboy.'

'Tonin's the kindest, sweetest man a woman could ever hope to marry,' Marguerite protested vigorously. A little too vigorously, perhaps, since Ben was still looking at her quizzically.

'You haven't said you love him.'

'Well, I do.'

'Good. And he can provide for you?'

'We can provide for ourselves. We have plans. Neither of us is affeared of hard work.'

'I see. You would choose a life of honest toil over one of idle luxury. Very laudable. Let me see your hands.'

Before she could protest, he had reached out and turned them over.

'Not the hands of a labourer, my sweet child. You are made for prettier things.'

'I don't want prettier things. I want Tonin. And being a goatherd is a very respectable trade. And he's to be sent off to get his qualifications. Miss Potter explained all about that.'

But Ben was no longer listening. He had folded his long body on to one of the cushions and was sitting cross-legged, examining her intently.

Apprehension washed over her, but not because she feared – as she had certainly done with Pierre – that he would take advantage of her. It was a new feeling to her – a tingling all over her body, a kind of suppressed excitement which made her almost gasp for breath. A sudden wild notion that if she did not fight the feeling, if she let herself be swept up in it, there was no knowing where she might come down to earth – if she ever did.

To her relief, Ben was apparently unaware of this tempest which threatened to engulf her. His mind had moved on.

'It won't do, you know.'

Conscious of his scrutiny, Marguerite felt herself blushing again.

'What won't do?'

'Everything. You need a complete wardrobe. Shoes, hairdo, make-up. Everything.'

Marguerite tossed her head indignantly. 'And you engaged to be married! You, *mon vieux*, should certainly not be taking an interest in such things.'

'Don't be such a little peasant. Charlotte doesn't mind what I do – as long as she's not obliged to find out. Anyway, child, we've already established you're a virgin. And I certainly don't intend to change *that*.'

He held up his hand to forestall her torrent of irritation.

'No. My interest is purely aesthetic. You could be quite a beauty, properly handled.'

'What do you mean by that?'

'Simply that I loathe waste. Especially of beauty. You need money to be beautiful. London is terribly expensive.'

He frowned at her. 'Right now, by your own admission, you're a penniless peasant, a country bumpkin without land or prospects. You own nothing but the clothes you stand up in – not even those, as it happens. It's perfectly obvious you can't tie your own shoelaces without falling over them.'

He set down his coffee and stood up.

'Fortunately I am eminently qualified to play Professor Higgins to your Eliza Doolittle – if Father Patrick saw to your education in English morals and manners. But don't expect my assistance with your hare-brained schemes.'

'I'll not be expecting anything at all, surely I won't.' In her agitation the Irishness came flooding back. 'And it's not a hare-brained scheme it is. 'Tis a carefully considered business proposition which I am to discuss with Miss Elsie Potter and her business advisers next Friday.'

He yawned. 'I must warn you, my sweet, I spend my life trying to avoid business advisers. My interest lies elsewhere. I am to be the potter, and you shall be my clay. Of raw earth I shall fashion something which is not only beautiful but also useful, even if not to me. Now, that is an enterprise worthy of my talents.'

'What if I don't want to be anyone's clay?' Marguerite was beginning to feel that Ben's interest might be something of a mixed blessing.

'Then, we'll just have to feed you to the lions, won't we?'

'Lions?'

'Big cats with teeth.' He bared his own, making him look alarmingly predatory. 'But just to stop you from thinking I might take advantage of you – here . . .'

Ben pulled the winnings from his gambling out of his pocket and laid them on the table. He separated them into two equal piles, and pushed one of the piles towards her.

'What's that?'

'Our first business deal. One for you and one for my sainted godfather, who thoughtfully – if involuntarily – supplied the wherewithal. That's your cut.'

'My cut?'

'Yours, child. If you must, consider it as the first contribution to the commune – although I'd much rather you took the whole lot over to Paris and blew it all on a new wardrobe. Courtesy of my not-entirely-courteous godfather. Indirectly. After you gave him that memorable flea in his ear, he thought I might be able to talk you round. The sainted monsignor, as I've learned over many years,

319

believes money is the *only* thing which talks. Fortunately it talked to me. I put the money on a number. The number came up.'

Marguerite stared at him in astonishment. 'Monsignor Melton's money? How did you get hold of it? That was the money you gambled with?'

'The very same.' Ben grinned. 'Don't look so shocked. Everyone's happy. You have yours, and the monsignor gets his back. No strings. Don't worry.' Ben tapped the two piles cheerfully. 'I'll simply tell him you turned me down.'

'And a terrible risk you took!' Marguerite protested. 'What in the name of all that's blessed would have happened if you'd lost?'

Ben grinned. 'In the name of all that's blessed, I'd have thought of something else.'

Marguerite looked at him through narrowed green eyes. 'And what might that have been?'

Ben shrugged. The hooded lids were lowered, and the full mouth was amused. Oh, the *Irishness* of her. 'What would you imagine, my dear? White slave trade? Put you out on the streets to earn your keep?'

He smiled at her suddenly – and the brilliance of it, the sheer communicable pleasure in what had pleased him, once again made her heart miss a beat.

Whatever else he had, however dangerous he might be, the charm was undeniable.

'We'd better make the best of your week of freedom. The old don't understand that the young are not simply there to pay the bills they failed to pay in their own lifetime. A cardinal misunderstanding. I shall consider it my duty to subvert you before Elsie gets her hands on you.'

That evening brought the first of many such subversions.

'Time for a bath and a change. I imagine you do usually bathe and change your clothes before dining?'

'Not necessarily,' Marguerite replied carefully. She did not wish to give his Lordship further ammunition for teasing her about what he called her peasant habits, although Ben would not have considered it teasing but the discharge of his self-appointed duties. These included numerous outings. Charlotte, it appeared, was sulking.

Over the next few days, the meals in Ben's company proved a minefield for Marguerite – particularly as they were always in public, at one of the noisy restaurants down the King's Road. These always seemed to be crammed with people he knew and were very social occasions.

It seemed she knew nothing about how to behave in these places, that Father Patrick's careful minding of her manners had been all in vain. This glass was for white wine and the other for red. Don't hold your knife and fork like a pair of pistols, Marguerite. And don't drink the water in the little glass bowls, they're for washing your fingers – this in a restaurant where Ben had insisted on ordering oysters, which were raw and shrank a little when you squeezed lemon on them, but tasted quite wonderful in a seaweedy sexy kind of way. She knew they were sexy because Ben told her they were a famous aphrodisiac, taking care that she understood the meaning of the word. However, she had had no chance of putting this to the test, since Ben kept as beady an eye on her as Abelard ever had.

This confused Marguerite. Something in her – she was not quite sure what, since it was certainly not the same as her feelings for Tonin – found Ben very attractive indeed, and yet he most definitely belonged to someone else. Even more confusing was his encouragement of the advances made by other young men who admired her. Up to a point, but no further. Ben set limits on the young men's advances. This, too, was confusing as he had no reason at all to lay claim on her. Confusing but also thrilling.

'Come along, Marguerite,' he would say firmly as he

appeared from nowhere and interrupted yet another attempt to discover her telephone number at one of the parties he took her to.

Ben seemed curiously anxious that no-one learned where she lived, and she could only put this down to his not wishing to upset Charlotte.

Ben took care to explain to Marguerite that his fiancée was staying in the country for the whole week, which was convenient as it gave him time to spend on what he described as her education in the social graces.

The social graces included plenty of flirtation. None of the rules which applied to courtship in Pernes-les-Rochers seemed to apply in London. She had never seen such good-looking young men and women, and all of them flirting with each other in the most open way imaginable.

In addition, her new life seemed to involve a lot of eating and drinking. Until that week of her education, she had never been out to dinner in her life. *Le diner* was what you had at midday. *Le souper* was what you had in the evening – and, unless it was a special occasion, it was always a bowl of soup. Going out to eat in the evening was a whole new experience.

The first time he took her out to dinner, Ben looked her up and down with a frown.

'For heaven's sake wear something which makes you look a little more like a female. My reputation doesn't include boys – however pretty.'

Marguerite was intrigued by this notion. She had heard mention of such things, but so far she had no direct experience. As far as she was aware, in Pernes-les-Rochers girls were girls and boys were boys. There were jokes about goats, of course, but Tonin seemed to take these in good part. In Valréas, there had been rumours of unnatural goings-on among the few tourists who came through the place, but it was not an area of human behaviour in which she had any personal experience.

'A dress. As short as possible. Your legs are perfectly acceptable.'

'Yes, your Lordship.'

Marguerite bobbed a mocking curtsy, and went off obediently to change. It was true that, in spite of her new wardrobe, she preferred to wear jeans, and had managed to beg several pairs of them from his stock, along with a few more of the beautiful shirts.

Ben himself seemed to have a bottomless well of clothing, each item designed for some different activity. Shooting-clothes of thick tweed, and clothes in which to play tennis; suits, the jacket and the trousers both matching, made of dark stuff with a fine stripe running through it, which Ben explained were for visiting bankers, although in Marguerite's experience the bank was where you went to put in your takings after market and everyone queued up in their *bleu de travail*.

There was also a velvet coat called a smoking-jacket, and another which was known as a dinner jacket, this last mysteriously including trousers with ribbon stitched down the seams, and a white shirt with a beautifully pleated front and cuffs which needed to be fastened with little gold links, and a black velvet bow-tie. Also – and most intriguing of all for Marguerite – white woollen garments which Ben explained were the correct attire for playing cricket.

Marguerite knew all about cricket. It was one of the things she had listened to with Father Patrick on the World Service, and Ben was amused by her knowledge of such luminaries of the pitch as Len Hutton and the Bedser twins. There was a wireless in the studio, and she would tune in to it just to remind her of the Hermitage, and Father Patrick, and even her mother who would always be sewing something or seeing to her herbs while they were listening to the score.

She soon got used to the gatherings at mealtimes. Under

323

Ben's tuition, it would have been impossible not to. It was not that he made any effort to make her comfortable in any of the unfamiliar places to which he took her, or among the strange people who formed his circle, it was more that he simply thrust her into the middle of it and expected that she would cope.

In between these experiences, came Ben's choosing of her wardrobe – funded by the money from the gambling.

'Perfect. Absolutely perfect.'

The sales assistant at Quorum, a fashionable boutique in the King's Road with a darkened interior and a changing room where everybody crammed into the same mirror-lined space, stepped back so that Marguerite could admire herself.

Ben had given the salesgirl strict instructions not to let her leave until she was, as he put it, *presentable*.

'I'll be back soon,' he said.

Marguerite twirled in front of the mirror, scarcely able to contain her delight. The elegant gown – a slither of indigo crêpe cut high at the front and dipping to a deep décolletée at the back – swirled around her hips and fell in a smooth line to her feet.

It was indeed perfect. The narrow cut displayed to advantage not only the narrow waist and small but shapely bosom, but the breadth of her shoulders and the smoothly muscular back; and the colour – so dark it was almost black – suited her tawny hair and green eyes wonderfully well.

'Here you are, child. Just a few more of the little essentials.'

Ben had returned, this time with a carrier bag containing half a dozen little boxes. The bag was navy blue and embossed with a gold crest which proclaimed that the supplier was the purveyor of fine perfumes and toiletries to several royal ladies.

He tossed the bag on to the buttoned-leather sofa which was provided for the benefit of those who accompanied the clients and threw himself down beside it.

Marguerite stood waiting for his approval, feeling half embarrassed, half delighted at this curious relationship which Ben had established.

'Cousin,' he called her, when he remembered to call her anything but 'child'. Turn this way or that, cousin. Move the buttons. Take up the hem.

Heaven only knew what the saleswomen thought. Perhaps that she was his mistress – certainly not that she was his 'cousin'. Perhaps he went shopping with Charlotte. Perhaps he examined her with the same appraising eye.

Considering that, she did not think so. She had a feeling that it was the fact that Ben saw her as an ignorant young peasant who amused him – she presented a challenge, and there were not many of those in Ben's life.

What was it he had said about his fiancée? That shopping was far more than a casual necessity for Charlotte. 'She's a professional – it's what she does in life.'

Over the dress went a coat – exquisitely tailored in slate-grey Harris tweed, full-length, full-skirted, with a nipped-in waist marked by a delicious little peplum. The whole effect was old-fashioned in its grace and elegance, but somehow completely modern.

It was also absurdly expensive – at least two months of Tonin's wages. Marguerite found thoughts of Tonin quite confusing enough without this added complication of guilt.

Ben nodded. 'It'll do, cuz.'

At first she had protested vigorously. 'I can't possibly afford it, Ben.'

'It's vulgar to discuss money in public. In private, it's boring – and we have already established the consequences of *that*.'

Marguerite giggled and gave in. It was too late for regrets. They had already spent what seemed like an enormous sum of money.

The first stop had been an appointment with a hairdresser in Sloane Street for the fashionable geometric cut.

'We can't have you the country cousin.'

'I can't see how it can be helped by a haircut.'

Just the same, in spite of her scepticism, there was no doubt that the smooth cap of shining russet which replaced her naturally wild curls gave her a sophisticated look.

The transformation continued with several hours spent at Elizabeth Arden in Bond Street. The beautifully painted lady into whose hands she was delivered cosseted and creamed her into sleepy acceptance of her fate. For the first time, she learned how to apply make-up to enhance her own fresh beauty, shading her cheeks to give them the fashionable hollow beneath the cheekbones, learning to define her lips with the merest slick of bronze pencil and the palest of lipgloss, to shade her eyelids so that her eyes were of the deepest and most brilliant green.

'An improvement,' was all that Ben had to offer by way of admiration.

They visited Delisse in Beauchamp Place for the most exquisite handmade boots to wear with a maroon velvet trouser suit Ben chose for her in a startlingly expensive shop one door down from the beauty salon.

'Perfectly suitable,' was Ben's laconic comment.

'Perhaps a little . . . *frivole*?' she enquired anxiously. 'For the businesswoman I mean to be?'

The lids drooped lazily. 'Of course it's frivolous, my little peasant. It is also, as you lose no opportunity to point out, visibly expensive. In business as well as in pleasure, first impressions are all that matter. We're struggling to make you socially acceptable.'

Finally they went to Annello & David in Covent Garden

for fashionable flat-heeled pumps to wear with the mini-dress – very figure-hugging and short-skirted – Ben insisted on buying for her in Mary Quant.

'A present. Party-time.'

'I'm supposed to wear this in public? Where?'

'You'll see.'

29

High Society, Low Dives

As soon as she walked into the room, Marguerite did indeed see what Ben had meant by insisting that she accept the tiny dress.

Anything other than the smallest of skirts would have been as out of place here as wearing the full-length ballgown to the market in Valréas.

'Don't you take your fiancée to parties?'

'Not this one. The hostess isn't Lottie's sort. Caro and Lottie don't exactly see eye to eye.'

She soon discovered what Ben meant. Charlotte Willoughby and Caroline Radcliffe, Ben explained, had been to the same expensive boarding school; but, while Lottie had followed the path prescribed for young ladies of her class, Caro was a member of what was identified as the Chelsea set. Open to all or clique-ridden (according to whether or not you were accepted amongst its number), libertarian or amoral (according to how you viewed morality), the only qualification for membership was glamour. Whether the behaviour of the set was stylish and brilliant, or degenerate and self-obsessed, was a matter of opinion. This was the matter on which Lottie and Caro did not see eye to eye.

If the Chelsea set was a court, Caro was its queen. And Ben appeared to be its crown prince.

'Darling – such a relief!'

Caro swooped on Ben as soon as he set foot over the threshold.

'What joy! Kiss.'

'New bird?' This comment appeared to apply to Marguerite. 'Delicious. Make yourself at home, sweetie.'

Ben seemed to know everyone, and the sprawling house in Notting Hill was already packed with bodies. Half a dozen rooms led out of one another, all with low ceilings and all tented with what looked like some kind of eastern embroidery in which were embedded tiny scraps of mirror. The walls had been painted midnight blue on which had been stuck tiny silver stars.

'Spliff, anyone?'

The hostess had just finished hand-rolling what appeared to be a very fat cigarette, waving it enquiringly at the smoke-wreathed throng.

'Acapulco gold?'

'What else?'

One of the dancers lifted the cigarette from her hand, lit it, and continued his solitary gyrations before passing it to his neighbour.

Dance music shook the floorboards, and those guests who were not dancing had to shout to make themselves heard. This made very little difference to Marguerite since she understood almost nothing of what was said.

The strangely scented smoke curled everywhere, mingling with a heavy perfume which rose from the tall beeswax candles, thick as a fist, which were the only source of light.

'Who's the dolly?' This was the most frequent remark addressed to Ben, and also seemed to refer to herself.

Marguerite needed to know. 'Dolly? Bird?'

'Means you're groovy,' Ben offered. 'One cool chick.'

This was still somewhat mystifying. There was clearly a

329

great deal more to learn, but Ben soon tired of her questions.

'Do your own thing,' he advised her, and disappeared into a dark corner with a blonde girl whose skirt was certainly the tightest and shortest in the room – and there was plenty of competition. Marguerite glanced down at her own attire. She would pass muster, but only just. Her skirt, although very short indeed, looked positively virginal in this company. She thought a little ruefully about the white dress with the scarlet sash whose petticoat she so daringly raised an inch for the St Jean. Chelsea and its set was a world away from Pernes-les-Rochers.

Failing any possibility of verbal communication, she danced. That at least was a language she understood. It seemed no partner was needed, which must be what Ben meant by doing your own thing.

No introductions were offered, or indeed required. You just joined the mêlée and moved with the mass. The rhythms were exciting, the movements easy to follow. Couples formed and parted without any apparent need for formalizing their partnership. The only difficulty came in the slow bits, when doing your own thing gave way to attempting to do someone else's. Sausage-fingered Pierre would have had a ball.

There was plenty of wine if you wanted it, but most of the guests seemed to favour a selection of unidentified substances, ingested through various orifices, which everyone but Marguerite seemed to find essential to their evening's enjoyment.

By two o'clock in the morning, she had had far too much to drink and more than enough of doing her own or anyone else's thing.

'Having fun, child?'

Ben was looking down at her. The grey eyes were hooded as usual, the smile mocking. In one hand was one of the hand-rolled cigarettes; the other was draped over the blonde girl's shoulders, his fingers slipped casually inside her shirt.

'Amanda, this is Marguerite. Say hello Marguerite, Mandy.'

'Mmm . . .' said Amanda, and lost interest immediately, preoccupied as she was by Ben's attentions. And, judging by the little bumps of nipple rising under the play of his fingers and the way she was rubbing herself against him – like a cat on heat, Marguerite thought to herself – she had plans for the rest of the evening.

Ben removed his hand from the accommodating breast. 'Now, now, Mandy. Not in front of the children.'

Amanda responded with a high-pitched giggle.

'Splitsville,' said Ben to Marguerite. 'On your feet, child. Amanda wants to go home.'

'To be sure she does,' Marguerite observed drily, following the pair through the door. It seemed that this behaviour was entirely normal. None of the girls seemed to mind very much who they went home with, as long as they went home with someone. There seemed to be no rules, no pretence of courtship, no promises of enduring love, and this was a most surprising experience for Marguerite.

Clearly she would have to work out how to deal with all these new things she had learned.

All the way back in the little red sports-car, with Marguerite perched uncomfortably in what Ben referred to as the dicky – a boot with a little seat in it which also doubled as a luggage-rack – Amanda stuck to Ben like glue. Not that Ben seemed at all anxious to unstick her.

This was Marguerite's first experience of Ben's partying. It was all very strange, this world of Ben's. Strange but dangerous. And to Marguerite, wide-eyed and innocent as she was, exciting and intriguing.

But most intriguing of all, because he was the most dangerous of all, was Ben.

The morning after the party, Ben had need of two mugs of anise-spiked coffee before he would even wish Marguerite good morning.

It had clearly been a busy night. All that remained of Amanda's presence was a pair of jet-black false eyelashes, curled up like two dead spiders beside the debris of a bottle of champagne.

That week passed all too swiftly in a round of similar parties, and Marguerite saw that for Ben each evening followed the same pattern.

On the Thursday evening before she was due back at Daisyford, Ben had a new plan.

'Queenie's, I think.'

'Queenie's?'

'Freda's place. Done the high life, time for the low.'

'Please explain, Ben,' Marguerite said plaintively.

'Dear child, Freda's place is in Soho. Where the tarts come from.'

'Tarts?'

'Crumpet. Hookers. Ladies of the night. Soho's where the bad girls are.'

'I've heard of Soho,' said Marguerite carefully. And indeed she had – on the World Service news, when there had been a clear-out of the brothels and trouble between gangsters and policemen. Soho was a very dangerous place indeed, according to Father Patrick.

'Of course you have, my sweet. And I can see by your face the good Father warned you against the sins of the flesh. No need to looked shocked – Freda runs a drinking club, not a cathouse. The Queen's Own Empire and Colonial Club, otherwise known as Queenie's. Sleaziest dive in Soho, but strictly for boozers. No drugs, no hookers unless off-duty. Freda's old-fashioned that way, although you wouldn't know it to hear her talk.'

Seeing the alarm on Marguerite's face, he grinned.

'Don't worry, child; she'll love you. She'll think you're good for me.'

'Good for you?'

'Freda's my surrogate mother. The only one who knew my parents. I love her. She's an old ratbag, but she's all I've got. She knows everyone. If anyone can help you marry your confessions to the names, she's the one.'

He glanced at his watch. 'We'll catch her after last night's hangover but before she's well on her way to tomorrow's.'

No-one knew exactly what Freda's origins were – except, curiously enough, Benjamin Catesby. Freda had been a presence in Ben's life for as long as he could remember. She was the only friend his dead parents had bequeathed him – and as a little boy the story of how their friendship came about never ceased to thrill him.

'Tell it to me again, Aunty Freda. The bit about when the Russian soldiers came and were going to shoot you, and my mummy and daddy rescuing you, and how you ran and ran . . .'

And Freda would tell it all again. Adding a bit more barbed wire here, and few more soldiers there, and the little boy drinking it all in. He could never get enough of her tales of his father's bravery and his mother's beauty. Her kindness, too, and her cleverness. And how she had given Freda the chance she would never have had, a Russian peasant girl, a kulak, with nowhere to run to, no friends, no family, no hope.

'And then?'

'And then . . .' Freda's face would darken, and she would fall silent. They never spoke of how or why his parents died, neither when he was a child, nor in youth, nor even now he was a man. It was as if that part of the story was locked away in a box, never to be opened. That, too, was part of it: the knowledge. The knowledge that there was an agreement between them not to speak of it. That the boy and the woman both had their reasons for this.

Freda always kept an eye on him throughout his school-days, putting in sporadic appearances at sports days wearing feathered hats, tippling champagne with the monks and flirting outrageously with the other boys' fathers.

In adolescence, once he had found his way to Queenie's, any serious girlfriend was always subjected to a visit of inspection. Friends, too – Freda was ruthless in her judgements.

Even though she could in no sense of the word be described as a girlfriend, it was inevitable that Ben should take Marguerite to visit Freda.

'Come right up, cocky!'

The proprietress of Queenie's was, as always, perched on a bar stool at the top of the stairs which led down to the street. This allowed her both to screen new arrivals and keep an eye on the customers.

'And up you come, too, my little sweetheart; poor old Freda won't bite.'

The voice was raucous, the accent indefinable. A more sophisticated ear than Marguerite's would have identified it as a combination of east of the Urals and the East End of London, combined with the genteel vowels of a seaside landlady and the vocabulary of a navvy.

'What's my pretty boy brought for his mummy today?'

Ben squeezed Marguerite's arm encouragingly and pushed her gently upwards.

'A new one, is it, cocky? Don't mind Freda. She won't bite.'

This announcement delivered at full volume did little to reassure Marguerite. In all her life she had never seen a more fearsome-looking creature than the proprietress of Queenie's.

A hooked nose and high forehead crowned by sparse handfuls of dyed black hair lacquered into a peak gave her the look of a scavenging bird of prey. The eyes were like black shoe-buttons, the cheeks and lips painted fiery red, and the wrinkled skin had been thickly powdered to an even whiteness. The skinny body was enveloped in a man's voluminous tailored suit of brown tweed, worn with a black feather boa round the thin neck. The whole outfit was finished off incongruously with a pair of tartan carpet slippers.

The apparition reached towards her.

'Come to Freda, darlin'. Don't be shy.'

Marguerite found herself grabbed by two surprisingly strong hands and brought bodily within inches of the old woman's face. Crème de menthe and black tobacco washed over her in waves as the old woman peered at her. After a moment she rocked back, satisfied.

'My, but she's a beauty! A natural redhead – and the eyes to go with it. Where did you find her, you bad young man?'

'Be gentle, Freda. She's very young.'

'I can see that for myself, cocky. Does the pretty creature have a name?'

Marguerite was suddenly irritated by being treated like a child. It was all very well for Ben to tease her, but this was absurd.

'My name is Marguerite Dieudonnée Leblanc, Miss Freda. And I'm surely not too young to speak up for myself.'

'*Miss Freda*, is it? Well said, dearie darlin'. Give the bastards hell.' The claw-like fingers caressed Marguerite's cheek approvingly. Looking at Ben, she said: 'What have you done with the other one, cunty?'

'Charlotte's in the country. And you're a wicked old

ratbag,' Ben replied without rancour.

'*Ratbag*, is it?' The old woman let out a delighted cackle. 'Hoity-toity! The cat's away, the mice can play.' The black eyes switched back to Marguerite. 'I hope the bastard hasn't been playing with *you*, dearie?'

Marguerite hesitated for an instant, then she said perfectly evenly: 'Sure and the bastard assures me he never plays with virgins.'

The old woman slapped her thigh in delight. 'Fuck me with a feather but the girl's got balls! You heard that, cunts?' She swung round to address the crowded room.

Silence fell; a dozen male heads, somewhat the worse for the drink, swivelled towards Marguerite. There was a scattering of applause, to which Marguerite had the presence of mind to drop a curtsy – a small piece of bravado which raised a ragged cheer.

Freda thumped the bar. 'A round for the virgin! A round on the house!' The wicked old face was wreathed in laughter. 'Keep it that way, dearie. Take a tip from your Aunty Freda – don't let the bastards get so much as a sniff. Lock it up and throw away the key.'

She turned back to Ben. 'And as for you, young man – she looks to me a damn sight better than that toffee-nosed fiancée of yours, for all her money. Mealy-mouthed madam, if you'll pardon my French.'

'None of your business, you old witch.'

'*Witch*, is it now? Where's the respect?' She smiled fondly. 'But I still love him – don't I, Benjie?'

'So you tell me.' Ben leaned over and kissed the thickly powdered cheek with genuine affection. 'Which is why I've brought you such a pretty one.'

Freda inspected Marguerite with renewed interest, her head on one side – no longer vulture-like, but with a genuine kindliness in the bright eyes.

Then she reached out a slippered foot and prodded the

nearest drinker off the neighbouring bar stool. 'Off you go, cuntie.'

She patted the vacant place beside her. 'Sit here, darlin' duck, next to old Freda. You can tell me all about it without his Lordship interruptin'.'

The glittering eyes fixed Ben with a disapproving look. 'Run along now, cocky. Girl talk.'

Ben grinned. 'Don't believe anything she says, Marguerite.'

'Off you go, cunty. Go play with the boys.'

Once she had made sure that Ben was safely out of earshot, Freda leaned towards her. 'By the way, darlin', you on the Pill?'

'Pill?'

Freda bellowed with laughter, hugging Marguerite and swinging round to share the joke with her clientele.

'Listen to her, cunties! Little darlin' never heard of the Pill!'

Embarrassing though this was, there was nothing malevolent about Freda – and Marguerite found in the raucous old woman an antidote to Ben's cool detachment. While Ben made her feel like an alien species, a laboratory specimen to be experimented with at will, Freda simply opened her arms and welcomed her in.

Keeping one beady eye on the bar-takings and the other on the arrivals and departures of the raffish clientele, Freda fell immediately to telling raucous stories of Soho life – the painters, musicians and writers who moved between Queenie's and the French Pub and the seedy dives for which Soho was as famous as it was for its strip-joints and brothels. Marguerite listened entranced to her tales of young men who took money for their favours, girls who made love with other girls, men who dressed as women, women who dressed as men, the working lives of the working girls. These, Marguerite soon decided, could only be what Madame Blanchette would most certainly have described as girls who did not have to work at all.

All these and more could be found propping up the bar at Queenie's throughout the day and long after midnight. But then, in the small hours of the morning, when the drunks had all gone home, the place turned into a refuge for anyone who lacked a home to go to, the tramps and strays who wandered the streets of the city.

'A cup of tea and a chat, strictly no business,' said Freda.

Mostly, in Freda's Soho, it was the women who were the heroines. The men were either johns, which Freda explained meant the working-girls' clients, which made them fools and hypocrites; or they were villains – pimps or thieves or bent coppers. This last, Marguerite learned, meant dishonest policemen, members of the *gendarmerie* who took bribes or tipped off thieves, or even, as Freda explained with relish, accepted payment in kind from the working girls.

Then there were the villains who demanded protection from the shopkeepers and bar-owners of what Freda called the 'manor'.

'Didn't try it more than once on old Freda. Know too much about their girls, their nasty little habits. All scared of their mummies. Told 'em to spin on it, ducky,' said Freda, extending the middle finger of her left hand upwards in a graphic gesture familiar to Marguerite from the school playground in Pernes-les-Rochers.

'Anyone thinks old Freda's going to be warned off by a bunch of nancy boys with gold rings on their pinkies has another think coming.'

The old woman rocked on her stool, cackling with satisfaction.

And then, with a faraway look, Freda told Marguerite about her girlhood in a little village on the border between Russia and Poland, the poverty, the hunger and the terror

338

which had led her family to flee the land of their birth.

'We're mongrels, you and I, darlin'. You don't need to tell me, I can see it on your face. We don't belong – we never will. Not like cocky there, my Benjie, your young man.'

Marguerite laughed. 'He's not my young man, Freda – and surely he never will be, seeing that he's already engaged to be married to Miss Charlotte Willoughby.'

'We don't even speak of her, darlin'.' Freda shook her head vigorously, the helmet of hair dancing as if it had a life of its own. 'Myself, I was never the marrying kind. Seen too much of it for that. But, then, his young Lordship was never one to take Freda's advice. No more than his father was, God rest his soul.' Freda crossed herself quickly. 'His mother, she was the one – worth a hundred of the rest of them. The women always are, my darlin'.'

Marguerite leaned forward. 'Ben's parents? You knew them?'

''Course I did. The best friends I ever had, my darlin' duck. Loved them, too, each in their own way.' Freda looked into the distance, her eyes misty. 'I was there, you know. When he was born. And then – that terrible business . . .'

'Terrible business?'

'Freda looked at Marguerite, the black eyes wary. 'He didn't tell you?'

'Tell me what?'

But Freda only shook her head. 'What's done is done.'

She swung herself round on the bar stool.

'Cocky! Look after your woman. The pretty one's had enough of old Freda. And don't you go messing with her, either – hear that, cunty? Tie a knot in it. She's much too good for you.'

And, with a broad wink to Marguerite, Freda turned her attention back to her other customers.

As she joined Ben, Freda's words buzzed in Marguerite's head. Until that moment she had not made the connection.

The box of chocolates had been payment for a service rendered. So Ben had got what he wanted. He must have seen the entry in the ledger.

She resolved to look for the right moment to ask him about it, or perhaps he might even confide in her. Benjamin Catesby did not discuss those things he did not wish to discuss, but Marguerite felt that she had a right to know. She had a vested interest after all.

The noise in the bar and a long evening spent drinking champagne in the company of yet more of Ben's acquaintances – this time of a rather different sort from those who gathered at Caro's – meant that there was no opportunity for private talk that evening.

Nor was there to be an opportunity the following day, which was Friday. On Friday she was due to return to Daisyford to learn what Miss Elsie Potter had in store.

30

Miss Potter's Plans

'Bring things for the weekend,' had been Miss Potter's final instruction to Marguerite.

This time she would take the train to Daisyford's little station, a branch line from the main line, and in itself something of an adventure for Marguerite. There would be the chauffeur to collect her, Miss Potter had said, so she must be sure not to miss the connection.

She packed her borrowed suitcase with care, mindful of Ben's instructions that presentation was all. Certainly Ben had been very sure of what was a proper wardrobe for a young lady about to embark on the most important weekend of her career. And her career, she most devoutly hoped, was what Elsie Potter had in mind.

One thing the week had taught her – and her head was spinning from all the new things she had learned – was that Benjamin Catesby lived not only a very exotic life, but also a thoroughly indolent one.

He did not seem to care about the same things that she did, and she was bewildered by this. She did not know which of them was right – he with his conviction that the world was his playground and boredom the only enemy, or she with her certainties that there were things to be done and people to be saved.

She felt like one of Abelard's fledglings, flapping on the edge of the branch, uncertain if its wings would carry it aloft or if it would tumble to earth. She knew she could fly, but she needed someone to show her how.

Miss Elsie Potter also knew that Marguerite would need all the help she could get.

To guarantee this, Elsie had summoned George Flowers.

On the day she telephoned, Gypsy George, as he was known, as much for his dark good looks as for his quick-silver brilliance in turning unpromising deals into a huge fortune, had been just on his way out of his office, leaving for the airport. He was due to attend a meeting with the Soviet Minister of Finance in the Kremlin.

'Cancel it, George. You won't regret it.'

George obeyed. He knew better than to refuse. Elsie very rarely made such a request, and never for a frivolous reason.

Elsie felt perfectly justified in making her demand. Certain things were more important than the pursuit of fortune – and, apart from his friendship with her, nothing else ever engaged George's attention.

George, Elsie was certain, was the answer to the ravishing young girl's prayers. And she was just as certain that, given time – and as yet her wings were scarcely spread – Marguerite Dieudonnée Leblanc would be the answer to his.

If she had been fifty years younger, she would have claimed George for herself. At thirty-eight years old, George was darkly handsome, with the physique – the broad shoulders, strong neck and well-balanced body – of a prizefighter. Elsie had always liked muscular men, although such thoughts were not considered dignified in old women such as she. Nevertheless, such thoughts meant that what she was about to do was an act of supreme generosity.

Some would say she was a scheming old woman, but

no-one would ever know how hard it would be to let him go – open her hand and let the butterfly float free. Nevertheless what she planned was precisely that.

Today he would meet the woman, as yet no more than a child, she had chosen for him. The age difference was perfect. Twenty years was by no means too great a separation of years between a man and a woman, although the suitability is reversed when women are old. Men are at their best in their middle years, after they have passed the age of making love and war with equal carelessness, and have the courage to be men. And women, their time is in the years of child-bearing and, again, when they are old and achieve wisdom. The middle years are dangerous for women, whether or not they have bred.

The girl was very young, but she was quite old enough for Elsie to know what she would one day become. She was already a beauty, and she would grow more beautiful as the years passed. But, far more than that, she had the makings of a true matriarch, one of those women who change the world.

Putting these thoughts aside, she rang for the butler. George deserved a little cosseting. She had a case of port which was just coming into its prime, and the cigars had to be put into the humidifier if they were to be smokable on Saturday.

'Mr George will here this weekend, Mr Wilkins. The Warr's '63, I think. And be sure not to forget the Havanas.'

Elsie Potter smiled. George would earn his cigars and all the comforts which Daisyford could offer. She had instructed him to arrive no later than teatime on Saturday. His office was in Threadneedle Street, convenient for the Bank with which he did much business, and perfect for the Home Counties to the north of London.

Elsie liked him to take the head of the table at dinner. It made the *placement* so much easier. This wish she now conveyed to the butler.

'Yes, madam.'

Newspaper profiles might describe George as a self-made man, but the truth was that it was Elsie Potter who had made him what he was.

On the most superficial level, George had all the social graces. Most of these had been acquired under Elsie's instruction, since George's upbringing – if such a word could be applied to a childhood spent as a Romany, a Hungarian gypsy, in Hitler's Europe – had left him with the survival instincts of a hunting cat, but little in the way of formal education.

In return he provided her with a window on the world she no longer had the energy or inclination to experience for herself, and for this she felt not only affection but gratitude.

'Dear George – amuse me, George.'

George was happy to oblige.

He reported back to her on what was happening in the sale-rooms of London and New York, brought her the latest gossip from the salons of Paris, Madrid and Rome. The social skills included making up a four at bridge and tennis, sharing her taste for opera and bringing her the latest recordings. But, more important, he kept her in touch with the world of international finance, and her investments had prospered under his guidance.

Elsie Potter was, although he took care not to treat her as such, the mother he had never had a chance to love. But she was far more than that. She gave him access to a world of inherited privilege he would otherwise have had great difficulty in penetrating. She taught him how to meet on their own ground the English aristocrats, public-school-boys and graduates of Oxford and Cambridge he encountered in the boardrooms and ancient banking institutions of the City of London. He loved listening to her stories of pre-war balls and shooting parties, of the season and the presentations at Court.

George was a bachelor and lived simply when he was not enjoying Elsie's hospitality, which he did whenever possible. He was a ladies' man of course, and she never minded when he brought a pretty young woman down for the weekend. This weekend she had made it perfectly clear that he should do no such thing.

'Alone, George, please.'

None of the other guests had been bidden until Saturday, to allow Elsie plenty of time to go over the plans for the Hermitage with Marguerite.

Marguerite had taken care to pack them – they had been the only thing she had brought with her from the Hermitage in the headlong rush to convince the warden.

Now, looking down at them spread out on the long table where the pots of orchids had been set aside to make room for them, she was worried that Miss Potter might find them not sufficiently professional.

Elsie waved her hand. 'The details are of no importance, my dear. We pay people for that. The idea is all that matters.'

The maps were unrolled, the plans examined.

Elsie Potter had been running a vast estate all her life, and she understood perfectly what might and might not be done, how much time and money was needed. Better still, she had the wisdom which comes with age, the sureness of touch which can only be learned from experience.

Soon after Saturday's lunch, which was another of the exquisite buffets, the butler announced George's arrival.

The old woman waved. 'Sit down, George, and don't interrupt.'

George had no intention of interrupting – he was far too interested in Elsie's visitor for that. Elsie had told him all about the girl – that she was possessed of a remarkable intelligence and had a most unusual firmness of purpose – but what she had not even hinted at was the girl's extraordinary beauty. Marguerite Dieudonnée Leblanc was the most exquisite young woman George Flowers had ever seen. She was also, young as she was, the most desirable woman he had ever seen. But she was more than that, he knew in the very depths of his being that she was the only woman he would ever – could ever – want. He had had more than his fair share of beautiful women, but he had never felt so powerful an attraction in his life. Just the same, he was not so foolish as to think that this beautiful young girl might be struck by the same bolt of lightning. George knew enough about women to know that the hard-won heart is the truest. He would have to be patient – and Gypsy George found patience hard. He would have to lay siege gently, to wait and woo her – she was so heart-breakingly young. He wanted to scoop her up into his arms and carry her away, like some wild medieval knight.

'Come live with me and be my love,' sang his heart. His head told him to be on his guard, not reveal his feelings. Not for now – not until the wooing was complete.

But, oh, those eyes, that sweetness which lay within, the delicacy of the features, the curve of the body – the raw untamed honesty of her as she and her hostess discussed their plans.

Dusk had already fallen when Elsie Potter rang for the squeaky-shoed Bassett to show Marguerite to her room in time to change for dinner.

Marguerite had listened intently as Miss Potter outlined what should be done to realize her dream. She had not realized until then how hard it had been to have no-one to advise her, and how, in her discovery of this wise old woman, she knew how much she had lacked, how long a shadow had been cast by the loss of her mother and the lack of a father – or at least one who might acknowledge her.

While Bassett was on his way, Elsie Potter beckoned over the new visitor.

'George – meet Miss Leblanc. Marguerite – this is George Flowers. Gypsy George – but I shall leave you to work out the reason for yourself. George, I intend to hold you responsible for Miss Leblanc's happiness while she is under my roof.'

The dark-haired man crossed the room, and Marguerite found her hand held lightly in strong fingers.

'Enchanted, Miss Leblanc.'

The accent was noticeable, but Marguerite could not place it. The dark head dipped quickly, the lips scarcely brushed her hand – yet the gesture was curiously possessive.

'George Flowers, at your feet.'

He raised his head and looked directly into her eyes, and for the first time she saw him. Truly saw him – not that she had not been aware of his presence before. George Flowers had too powerful a presence for that. Thickset, physically powerful, dark – almost saturnine, but with an undeniable magnetism. A ladies' man, as Freda would say, and Marguerite was pleased with herself for observing that the formal pinstripe tailoring was lined with scarlet silk and in the buttonhole a rosebud which exactly matched the colour. She was learning fast.

Gypsy George was what Elsie had called him. And certainly there was a flamboyance about him, the way the black hair curled on the collar, the brilliance in the dark eyes. Perhaps he really did have gypsy blood. She knew something of the Romanies. The gypsies came through Pernes-les-Rochers at the end of winter, on their way to the Whitsun pilgrimage in the Camargue, and when she was little her mother had often taken her to join them round their camp-fires. The gypsies shared her knowledge of the healing properties of plants, and Thérèse had always sought them out.

She studied him more closely. He was older than she had thought at first. This pleased her – she was not quite sure

347

why, unless it was that she felt in need of a fatherly presence in her life. She glanced down at the hands, which in the way of the gypsies bore several rings, none of which was worn on the marriage finger.

What was she thinking of? She had no life as yet. She had work to do. Unfinished business – twenty years of struggle before her plans would bear real fruit.

Elsie Potter's voice cut through her thoughts. The hostess was turning her attention to her guest's welfare.

'Bassett will show you to your room, Marguerite.'

The old woman paused, and then added: 'And, Bassett, you may tell Humphreys she is free to attend to Miss Leblanc. Perhaps there might be something found for her to wear for dinner.'

'But I do assure you, Miss Potter, I have brought plenty of clothes, and I am told they're quite suitable . . .'

Marguerite was flustered. She did not want her hostess to think that she had come unprepared, or that she did not know what dressing for dinner might mean.

Ben had coached her very carefully. Tennis clothes, croquet clothes, riding clothes, a black dress for wearing at a cocktail party – whatever that might be. And a three-quarter-length full-skirted frock to be worn at dinnertime – or suppertime, as Marguerite knew it – if the gentlemen were in black tie, which was, it appeared, another way of describing the costume otherwise known as a dinner jacket.

'Daisyford's bound to dress for dinner,' Ben had said as he supervised her packing, bursting into laughter as he saw Marguerite's bewilderment. 'That means formal evening clothes, my little peasant. The ladies wear long frocks and all their jewels.'

'But I don't have any jewels.'

'*You* will be the jewel.' It was a pretty compliment, but it did little to assuage Marguerite's anxiety.

And now Miss Potter seemed to think that she would

not know how to dress herself, or even have anything suitable to wear.

'To be sure, Miss Potter—'

But the old woman held up her hand, smiling. 'Forgive me, my dear, for my lack of courtesy. I don't for a moment imagine that your wardrobe is not entirely adequate, or that you are not entirely capable of completing your own toilette.'

She paused, still smiling. 'No. I ask only that you humour me – just for this evening. Humphreys is my personal maid – but I'm not such an infant I cannot dress myself for once. You may trust her to look out something to suit you. We have cupboards full of things – none of them in the current fashion, of course, but some pretty dinner frocks from Paris. Good frocks never really date, and I'm afraid I have always been a little self-indulgent.'

She glanced at George. 'Anyway, I'm too old for such vanities, aren't I, George? And I want none of your gallantries, young man. Nothing wrong with the brain, but I am well aware of the wrinkles.'

George smiled back at her, his teeth very white against the tanned skin. 'Elsie my dear, I shall tell you that you are still as beautiful as the day I first met you, and your heart will melt.'

'Nonsense, George. That was twenty years ago. And even then I was what one might politely call a faded rose.'

Marguerite, on her feet now, glanced between them, wondering what had joined two such unlikely people as the aristocratic old lady and this flamboyant financier – and surely that was what he must be – in what was clearly an old and comfortable friendship.

The blue eyes were on her again; this time there was a shrewd look in them. 'Run along now. Drinks in the library at seven.'

'I really don't know how to thank you, Miss Potter—'

'Then, don't.' The old woman's voice was brisk. 'I am

selfish enough to enjoy getting my own way. As George knows only too well.'

There was a note in the voice which told Marguerite that once again Miss Potter meant exactly what she said.

'Well? What do you think?'

Elsie put out a ringed hand and laid it conspiratorially on George's arm. Seeing the expression on his face, she smiled. 'None of that yet, George. She's too young for you – for the moment. And, besides, she's been through enough. Heaven knows, even from me.'

George was surprised. Had his interest been so obvious? Could the old woman read his mind? He said casually: 'I have no intention of putting her through anything, Elsie.'

'Good. I'm glad to hear it. Because I've taken a very strong liking to her. Very strong indeed. And I mean to see she gets what she wants. She will be my swansong, George. The best thing I have ever done.'

George waited. Elsie always got what she wanted, and if this young woman's success was what she wanted he was sure she would find a way to get it.

'There's one small problem,' Elsie continued with a frown. 'She's made a powerful enemy. Monsignor Charles Melton.'

'Melton? How's she managed that?'

'Use your head, George.'

Elsie knew perfectly well what George thought of the warden of the Hermitage. She never invited Monsignor Melton when George was there. George made no secret of the fact that he did not approve of Charles Melton. There was something about the man which did not smell right. George had a gypsy's nose for such things.

And when Elsie had told him how helpful the monsignor had been in assisting one of her great-nieces out of a little problem he had made discreet enquiries. The enquiries revealed what looked suspiciously like spiritual insider trading, and although George's Catholicism was certainly lapsed he did not approve of dishonesty in business. Particularly not when those practising it claimed the odour of sanctity to disguise the stench of corruption. George knew all about Charles Melton's little sideline; but, although he disapproved of it, it was not his business to put a stop to it, even if he could. This he had explained to Elsie.

Thinking of this now, he could see what Elsie had meant when she said: 'I imagine that must be the problem.'

'The young woman's ambitions directly threaten the Church's – Melton's – interests. Not to mention the Vatican's bankers,' George added thoughtfully.

It was well known in his world that the Vatican Bank sailed close to the wind, and he had been startled by how many shady deals seemed to have holy money behind it.

Elsie sighed. 'Powerful enemies, George. And if the good monsignor gets wind of my involvement he'll know that young Mademoiselle Leblanc is not without powerful friends of her own.'

'Powerful friends?' George leaned back. 'What have you in mind, Elsie? A donation to her crazy enterprise?'

The old woman smiled. 'It's not so crazy. Not by the time I've finished with it.' She shook her head. 'Not a donation – far too impermanent. Much more than that, dear George. I mean to give her *you*.'

George stood up, walked over to his old friend, and took her hands in his. 'Do you know what you're saying? What makes you think I'll be willing?'

'I know you too well, George old friend. I have watched you for too long to be fooled by that mask you put on for others. You are willing. You are more than willing.'

Then her eyes clouded over briefly, as if seeing a past she could not have, a future she had always longed for.

351

She stood up, picked up her skirt in her hand, and swept gracefully towards the door.

'We'll discuss the details tomorrow. In the drawing room in an hour, George – with Miss Leblanc. And I shall expect you to be attentive, charming – and thoroughly discreet.'

31

Elsie Potter Entertains

If an angel had walked in and announced that this was heaven, Marguerite would not have been in the least bit surprised.

Daisyford was quite simply the most beautiful place she had ever seen – let alone been allowed to enjoy as a guest. If the public rooms were magnificent in their grandeur – the oak panelling and marble fireplaces, the frescoed ceilings and sumptuous embroidered silks which framed the tall windows, the towering arrangements of beautiful flowers, the Aubusson carpets with their polished parquet surrounds, the glittering displays of china in polished cabinets and the massed ranks of gold-tooled books – the private apartments were intimate masterpieces of comfort.

Marguerite's bedroom was furnished in white and green, with furniture painted to look like bamboo, and a bed shaped like a grown-up child's cradle, with deep wooden sides lacquered in Chinese red, painted with birds of paradise. The whole effect was sophisticated and simple at the same time, and deliciously feminine. Posies of miniature yellow roses stood on every surface, so that the air was delicately scented with their perfume.

The bathroom was also decorated in white and green. In the middle of the room was an enormous bath, standing on claw legs, with gleaming brass taps. It had already been filled with water, and the ladies' maid, a pink-cheeked, grandmotherly woman in a neat black dress, was testing the temperature with her hand.

'Miss Potter's instructions, I'm to spoil you, miss.' The motherly woman had a cheerful face, now wreathed in smiles.

Marguerite smiled back. 'I wouldn't want to disobey Miss Potter.'

'I've unpacked your things, miss. I'll leave you in peace to have your bath. Be back in ten minutes.'

'Thank you—' Marguerite hesitated. 'I can't just call you "Humphreys". You must have a name?'

'It's always the way with ladies' maids, to be called by their surname,' the smiling woman explained comfortably. 'Young girls in service answer to their given names, but once you reach the top of the profession that's how it is. But if you prefer, miss, my name is Hilda.'

'Oh, I do prefer,' said Marguerite.

She slipped into the scented water. She was looking forward to being spoiled by Hilda Humphreys.

The promised ten minutes later, Hilda was back holding out an armful of shimmering silks which glistened through fine lawn clothes bags which smelled faintly of lavender and fresh ironing.

'Miss Potter thought these might suit you, miss. You're to choose whatever you want.'

Marguerite noticed the crest immediately. Each of the clothes bags had one, small and beautifully stitched, and she put her hand out to admire the perfection of the workmanship. As she examined the crest more closely, she saw that it was a mailed fist holding a rose, the design identical to that on the signet ring she had promised her mother she would always wear.

Father Patrick had told her about coats of arms and crests, and how to recognize the different designs of the fleur-de-lys and the English lion rampant which could be found on the tombstones in the cemetery of the

Hermitage. No two families, said Father Patrick, had the same crest. But, if that was so, did that mean that she and Elsie Potter were somehow related? And, if so, why had Miss Potter not said anything to her when Marguerite had shown her the ring that day of her first visit?

A terrible thought struck her. Perhaps Miss Potter thought she might try to claim kinship – establish a claim on her fortune? Marguerite frowned. How terrible if she had imagined for an instant that Marguerite might be a fortune-hunter. There were plenty of those in all the stories about titled people and those who had large estates like Daisyford. If that was the case, why had she invited her back, offered to help her? If Miss Potter thought she had any desire to claim anything from anyone, she did not know Marguerite at all. Marguerite needed no-one and nothing she had not earned for herself. She never had. She was certainly not going to start now.

'Miss? Is anything the matter?'

Hilda Humphreys was watching her anxiously.

Marguerite shook her head. 'No. Not at all. It's just – is that the family crest?'

'Indeed, it is, miss. It's romantic, isn't it? Miss Potter once told me that the motto means that beauty must be protected by strength.'

'Does it indeed?' said Marguerite thoughtfully.

The ladies' maid waited for a moment, and then began to take the clothes out of their bags.

'Miss Potter is most anxious you should choose something to suit you. She says she won't take no for an answer. That you're not to worry about anything.'

Marguerite decided to relax. Perhaps Miss Potter had not noticed anything after all. Marguerite surely hoped that she had not, and she was certainly not going to be the one to tell her. Surreptitiously she slipped the ring off her finger and slipped it into the pocket of her jeans.

In spite of her confused thoughts, Marguerite was captivated by the beautiful things being laid out for her inspection. She watched as one exquisite garment after another was laid tenderly on the Chinese silk bedspread, beguiled by the notion that it was not just Benjamin Catesby who felt the urge to reorganize her wardrobe and dress her in finery.

But Miss Potter's finery was of a different order altogether. These were the work of artists, not of ordinary craftsmen. Bias-cut, hand-stitched, lined and interlined with the softest crêpe de Chine, each had its own feather-edged stole or fur-trimmed cape or little sculpted jacket. There were shoes, too, and tiny evening bags, each one exactly matching its dress.

'I'm sure we can alter anything if need be.'

The beautiful garments were more than clothes – they were a whole philosophy. The women for whom they were designed did not need to shock or even to conform. They were pampered birds of paradise, their duty to give pleasure, their calling to be adored. In spite of herself – of her feeling that such impractical garments were not for her – Marguerite was completely captivated by the riches laid out for her inspection.

'Miss Potter was most anxious you should find something to please you,' said Hilda, watching the young woman's reaction to the beautiful garments. 'Is there anything you'd like to try on?'

'Oh, yes,' Marguerite breathed.

She held up a column of lilac silk jersey, bias-cut, draped low at the back, perfect in its simplicity, adorned with a single silk rose, its petals hand-tinted, shading from the deepest purple to the softest violet, delicately beaded with crystal dewdrops.

Hilda beamed. 'An excellent first choice, if I may say so, miss.' She reached out and touched the silk – a tender gesture, as to a child. 'From the house of Vionnet, the greatest of them all. It looks so little in the hand, but on the body a masterpiece.'

'Can I really try it on?'

'Of course, miss.'

Marguerite stepped out of the towel she had draped round herself after the bath, and held her arms over her head so that Hilda could drop first the underslip and then the garment itself over her naked body.

Hilda nodded approvingly. 'That's how it should be worn, miss. Madame Vionnet cut to the body. See for yourself.'

She tilted the cheval mirror so that Marguerite could understand the effect, then tut-tutted, stepped forward and tugged quickly at the folds. The skirt flipped into handkerchief points. 'Good. Now it is exactly as Madame Vionnet would have wished. As I should know well enough, miss. When I first came to madam, she sent me to Maison Vionnet to be trained. "Hilda," she said – and I was only a slip of a laundrymaid then – "you have neat fingers, Hilda. You shall go to Paris. To the House of Madame Vionnet. To be trained."'

'It must have been wonderful!'

'Indeed it was, miss. We lived all together, the sempstresses, at the top of her *atelier*. And it was hard work. She was a perfectionist, Madame Vionnet, and not just with us. She would not dress plain women, or women who were too plump or whose proportions were wrong for the clothes.'

Hilda had been flitting around Marguerite all the while, making small adjustments. She frowned, searched her lapel for a pin, and made a minute tuck.

After a moment she continued. 'Naturally Miss Potter was one of her favourites. She would say that the English understood her clothes; they knew that fashion didn't matter, but that workmanship did.'

In went another pin.

'Madame Vionnet said she wasn't interested in fashion, because she was a dressmaker, not a designer of clothes. A *couturier* is not a *costumier*. Today there are no couturiers any more. People no longer have the time for workmanship.' Hilda sighed and shook her head. Then she produced a needle and thread from the lapel which had yielded the pins, and began to convert the pin-tucks into minute seams.

'Madam always scolds me for chattering on. But perhaps miss understands what I mean?'

Marguerite nodded. 'I think perhaps I do. It's a bit like the place I've lived all my life – it had all been cut and stitched and made to fit. And now . . .' She hesitated. 'Now it's all destroyed, and I don't know what will become of it.'

'Perhaps you'll make it come alive again, miss. Just as you do when you wear these dresses.'

Marguerite smiled. 'Perhaps.'

'The Molyneux now?' A waterfall of crystal-beaded chiffon, its bodice held in place with a spider's web of tiny glittering straps, replaced the Vionnet.

Marguerite held up her arms obediently so that the dress could be slipped over her head.

'Maybe.' Hilda considered the slender figure reflected in the mirror. 'And, then, maybe not.'

She darted over to the bed and selected a ravishing full-skirted frock in midnight-blue taffeta, its bodice a sunburst of tiny pleats. 'The Balenciaga. I nearly forgot.'

The silk rustled as it fell round Marguerite in rippling waves. A tight petersham ribbon clasped her waist, and the gleaming taffeta fell into place.

'Madame Vionnet thought highly of Cristóbal Balenciaga, even though he was a man and a Spaniard. He, too, was a dressmaker.'

She smoothed the crisp silk. 'The workmanship, you see.'

Marguerite turned this way and that while Hilda made her little tucks and dartings.

'Magnificent certainly. But there's no question of the correct choice.'

'The Vionnet?'

'Of course.'

Chattering on happily, Hilda selected the shoes, the bag, the fur-trimmed cape.

'The barest of make-up, miss – just a little rouge. Like so. And perhaps a little darkening of the eyelashes. And the merest hint of shadow on the eyelids. And the hair – I think upswept would be most becoming. And an aigret – Madame was always very particular that the look should be perfect in every detail.'

By the time Hilda had finished, Marguerite scarcely recognized the sophisticated beauty who looked back at her from the mirror.

She was, Elsie Potter decided as Marguerite made her entrance, all that she had hoped.

Now it remained to be seen if she passed muster in the gathering. A lack of formal social education was unimportant. It was the spirit which counted.

Here, too, she shone – and most surprisingly brightly, considering her youth. She promised well. A little polish, a little maturing, and she would be formidable. The beautiful dress gave her a sparkling radiance and an assurance far beyond her years – and this was no more or less than Elsie had planned.

In addition, as if she needed further encouragement, there had been the attentiveness of George Flowers and the flattery of the maharaja. The young prince wished to whisk her off to his palace.

He had pressed his suit with ardour. 'Oh, but I insist. There will be much rejoicing and many parties. It will be the most wonderful experience of my life.'

Marguerite had handled the excitable young man with skill and tact. Clearly, thought Elsie with satisfaction, her protégée could add diplomacy to her other attributes. She was a most unusual young woman.

That she was a most unusual young woman had also been the opinion of the man placed on Elsie Potter's right hand. Cardinal Giuseppe Navarino was a house-guest of one of her neighbours, Lady Celia Markwell; and Lady Celia had rung her up only that morning to ask if she could bring the cardinal along.

'Sure you don't mind, Elsie? Giuseppe rang up out of the blue. Last-minute decision. Otherwise I'd be a bit stuck.'

'Of course, Celia dear. By all means bring him. I shall be delighted.'

Elsie was not at all delighted. She wondered if there was some reason for the cardinal's last-minute decision – if somehow he had got wind of the presence of her young house-guest.

She dismissed this thought – it must surely be a coincidence. And, if it was not, she would rather have the slippery cardinal in her sights than out of them. She was a poker player, used to reading the inscrutable faces of her opponents; but, even so, the cardinal was not giving anything away. He was equally charming to everyone, and seemed to pay no more attention to the young woman than to anyone else.

After dinner they played charades, and Elsie insisted that Marguerite entertain the guests by modelling some of the beautiful clothes she had tried on earlier. Of all the guests, none applauded louder or paid more attention to the beautiful garments and their graceful model than Cardinal Navarino.

While she watched her, Elsie had been intrigued to notice that her young guest was no longer wearing the signet ring she had told her mother she would always wear. This could only mean one thing: that her young guest had become aware of its meaning, and had no desire to draw attention to any family connection.

Elsie felt her heart lift. If she was right, the young woman was as honourable as she had thought her.

After the party had broken up, the guests had gone, and Marguerite had been delivered back into the capable hands of her maid, Elsie motioned to George to follow her to her boudoir.

'Well. Wasn't I right?' The old woman settled herself in her favourite chair, set close by her precious cymbidiums.

'You're always right, Elsie.'

'Not true. I am the first to admit my mistakes. Not this time.'

'You're a wicked old woman.'

'Not at all wicked. Simply selfish. I have my reasons to want. I have a right to take.'

'She may not want to be taken.'

'She's a sensible young woman. I shall offer no more than she will be able to accept.'

George persisted. 'But if not?'

'Do you need an excuse, George?'

'A reason perhaps.'

'Reason? You want reason?' The voice was mocking, the blue eyes sparkled with laughter. 'Since when has Gypsy George been a man of reason? Instinct perhaps; foolhardiness, some say. But never reason.'

His eyes, so dark that the pupil was almost indistinguishable from the iris, returned her gaze steadily. Then, as if to hide what was written there, turned aside. Too late. What she had seen had told her what she needed to know. Gypsy George was hooked. The girl was too young, but time would see to that. For Marguerite at least, time was on her side. For her, but not for Elsie.

Elsie sighed. She had been born too soon – or George

Flowers had been born too late. Time passed so swiftly; and, although she had long since accepted that her body was old, her face wrinkled, her limbs creaking, her mind was as swift and keen as ever, and she could so easily forget the truth to be read in the mirror. She knew exactly what she was about. She meant to see that George's woman was of her choosing. Better still, blood of her own blood.

'You're right of course, George,' she said quietly. 'At my age, games are all we have left. Anyway, you're already involved.'

George looked at his old friend sharply. Of course she was right. There was nothing else in the world he would rather do than involve himself with Marguerite Dieudonnée Leblanc in whatever capacity she would have him.

He would have to keep a careful eye on her. The girl was in trouble already. By her impetuous visit to the warden, she had already shown her hand to the enemy. Elsie Potter's backing would confirm that she could reach the rich and powerful, and steps would immediately be taken to stop her.

Charles Melton had allies in high places. Men with allies made dangerous enemies.

George stood up. One other question, direct as always when dealing with Elsie Potter. Elsie was not a woman to beat about the bush. 'Because I need to know these things, do you intend to make her your heir?'

Elsie looked at him for a long moment. 'A most indiscreet question. But I'll tell you that there is a reason for my interest in this young woman. A reason I am not yet ready to reveal, even to you, George, and certainly not to her. It's far too soon. I mean to keep her at arm's length for the moment, let her find her own feet. I gather she's made some arrangement with old man Malvern's grandson. An unsuitable young man, if I remember, but I am sure that

that will present no problem, dear George. You will enjoy the challenge.'

'Challenge?'

'Did you think I would make it so easy for you?' The blue eyes danced. 'Furthermore, I thoroughly enjoyed this evening. I was most interested to see how our young guest coped with the maharaja; his Imperial Highness was as captivated as you. Perhaps he, too, will want to carry her off on his white charger. Perhaps you will even be jealous. I think I should enjoy that, George.'

'As you say, Elsie, we must take our pleasures where we can.'

She laughed at that, a mischievous laugh – girlish and light. 'We do, George. We do.'

She stood up, smoothed the silk of her skirts, looked at him directly. With something of a shock, George realized what an extraordinarily beautiful woman she must have been, how much she must regret the passing of that beauty.

It was too late now for that beauty to bring its proper reward. There was no direct heir to follow her, no son or daughter to carry her ancient name. She was the last of her line. After her, the estate would be broken up, its treasures dispersed. In spite of her possessions, of the power that money gave her, she had no stake in immortality.

George, with his gypsy's instinct, knew the pain that this must surely cause her. Deep inside this formidable old woman was a loneliness so profound he could not even guess at the depth of its wellspring. It was a loneliness which he understood only too well.

'Elsie?'

'None of that, George.' As always, Elsie dismissed him. She always knew exactly what he was thinking. 'You know perfectly well I cannot abide sentimentality.'

With her head held high, the old woman was gone.

*　　*　　*

At lunch on Sunday, which proved itself an almost equally entertaining meal with a new cast of characters to swell the number of the house guests, George was delighted to discover that Marguerite had arrived by train.

'Perfect. Then, I claim the privilege of seeing you safely back to your door.' And with that he ushered her to the open-topped Bentley waiting outside.

The dark-haired banker – although he seemed to do so many things that it was hard to say exactly what he was – took the opportunity of the drive to question her about her plans.

'Elsie persuaded me that I could be of service to you, although in this case little persuasion was needed. The upshot is that I have agreed to keep an eye on you. Offer advice and support when required. That is, if you're agreeable?'

Marguerite smiled at him. 'Surely I am absolutely and completely agreeable. I shall need plenty of guidance, and surely there's no-one I'd rather have to guide me. I promise I'll be a good and hardworking pupil.'

'Excellent. We will make a fine partnership.' He paused. 'We must tread carefully at first. An offshore company, a charitable foundation perhaps – something which won't immediately attract the attention of those whose interests might not coincide with yours.'

'Do you mean the monsignor?'

George nodded. 'Charles Melton, yes.'

Marguerite grinned. 'He offered me a bribe. Enough to buy myself a husband.'

'Did he indeed? How very old-fashioned. And what do you feel about that?'

Marguerite giggled, making him aware once more of how young she was. 'I said, "Thank you most sincerely for the offer, but I have no intention of doing any such thing". Except I didn't say it quite so politely.'

'Then, the man's already your enemy. We must tread

carefully indeed. So far, from what Elsie has told me, your fund-raising notions are a little on the – shall we call it? – raffish side. That must change immediately.'

Marguerite flushed. 'I have no choice.'

'Of course. But there are ways to remind people of their obligations – delicately. We must be purer than the driven snow. Not a whiff of scandal. Your monsignor knows exactly how to spread a rumour. Melton's not a fool. He'll be out to stop you at the first sign of trouble. He's clever and he's subtle. You will not be able to defend yourself. Trust me, I know.'

'Is he so powerful?'

'He has powerful friends. Vested interests to protect his endeavours. In simple language, my dear, he makes a lot of money for his masters.'

'His masters?'

'A certain faction in the higher reaches of the Church. To put it crudely, the Vatican's very own version of the Mafia. You met one of them yesterday – Pro-Notary Apostolic Giuseppe Navarino. Cardinal Navarino doesn't like anyone interfering in the Church's business. He takes it personally.'

'You make it all sound very dangerous.'

'It is. It always has been. The first million's the hardest. Believe me, I have some experience in these matters.'

She glanced over at him, smiling. 'Surely and my ambitions don't run to millions.'

'Then, change your ambitions.' The reply was swift almost rude. Then George turned his head to smile at her, and she saw the charm of him again in the sweetness of that smile. 'My dear, don't think I disapprove of raffishness. There has never been a fledgling enterprise which did not need some manure. But now, if you'll forgive my frankness, it's time to take the shovel out of the shit.'

Marguerite threw back her head and laughed.

'I didn't know I had a shovel – let alone the shit.'

'Believe me, you have both. More dangerous still, you have a vision. And, as any politician knows, a man with a vision is a dangerous thing, but a woman with a vision is lethal.'

'But if all I want is for the good—'

George cut her off. 'It's of little matter if what you want is good or bad. Hitler and Christ both had a vision. And look at the trouble they caused.'

At this moment Marguerite noticed that they were nearly home. The scarlet sports car was missing from its parking space. Ben must have gone to the country with Lottie.

'Number thirty,' she said. 'Just on the right.'

After he had pulled into the kerb, George continued: 'Good ideas are not enough in themselves, and nor is money. But you have youth – and, as the estimable Elsie had no need to point out to me, you are blessed with your fair share of beauty. But, above all, you know exactly what you want. With the right advice, there's nothing you can't do.'

'And will you give me that advice?'

The look he gave her was long and searching. 'Rest assured of that, Miss Marguerite Dieudonnée Leblanc. You can count on my support in all things.'

There was a long pause. Then he said: 'I shall be away for a couple of weeks – pressing business in Russia which Miss Elsie made me delay in order to meet you. I suspect she thought that of more importance than a deal with the Kremlin. Elsie is never in any doubt of her priorities.'

He nodded, flashing the brilliant smile again as if to confirm that Elsie had been right. 'But when I return we shall get started immediately. Meanwhile I have no doubt you will find plenty to do. I suggest looking for premises, the appointment of bankers, the setting up of a nominee company which can be ready to trade. My secretary will make the necessary appointments in my absence.'

After he had left her, pressing his card with his private number on her, she found herself missing his comforting presence already.

She was confused by this – confused enough not to notice that they were being watched.

He, too, was confused – or he would have noticed the man with the camera who stepped out of the shadows and photographed Marguerite going into Ben's house as the car pulled smoothly away from the kerb.

32

Marguerite Takes Action

'Come right on up, my dearie duck.'

Monday at Queenie's was usually a quiet day; but, even so, the room was filled with the usual fug of cigarette smoke and the quarrelsome chatter of those who had not yet had enough to drink to make them morose, but had had more than enough to make them talkative.

'How's my pretty virgin? Come without the boyfriend, then? Quite right, too.'

The parrot-squawk was comforting; at least Freda hadn't forgotten her. And, considering what she was about to ask, that was just as well.

The Monday after her return from Daisyford, with Ben still absent – clearly he was paying for his week's diversions with a long weekend at Charlotte's parents' – Marguerite made up her mind to put her plans into action immediately, without waiting for George or Elsie's help. She needed to prove that she could do it on her own. Although George's promise of support had given her confidence in her own abilities, she wanted to show him – and the mysteriously generous Elsie Potter – that she could make things happen without anyone's help. George had said that he would be away for two weeks. By the time he returned, she would have enough in the bank to convince him that his faith in her was not misplaced.

The first thing was to make a list of possible donors. She had the stories in her head; all she lacked was the names.

She made up her mind to tackle Freda immediately. Surely she would help her. Freda was a refugee herself, so how could she not be sympathetic to the valley-dwellers' plight?

Satisfied with her reasoning, she spent the morning making notes from memory of the confessions she had taken down at the Hermitage, and by lunchtime she was ready with the first half-dozen. She hoped that Ben was right, and Freda did indeed know all the gossip. Nothing ventured, nothing gained, as Father Patrick was fond of saying.

She knew her way around Chelsea well enough by now to catch the bus to Piccadilly Circus, from where she could walk into Soho and retrace her steps to the drinking club. She loved travelling on the top of London's double-deckers, and would always choose a window seat so that she had a good view of the shops and the passers-by. She could see into the offices from her vantage-point. People seemed very busy. George said that his office was in the City of London. She knew that that was where the main financial institutions were housed. She wondered what George's office was like. Did he have a big picture window and a huge desk, and ranks of pretty secretaries to take dictation and keep unwelcome visitors away?

There were so many things to learn, so many experiences to savour. Even if she had not had Ben to guide her through the maze of London's social life, she would still have found London the most exciting place in the world. Nothing – not the summer fair in Valréas, not even the St Jean in Pernes-les-Rochers – could possibly hold a candle to everyday life in London. To Marguerite it seemed that there was a party in progress on every street corner, in every one of the little gardens where people grew flowering shrubs rather than vegetables, under every tree in the green-pastured public parks. That it should be necessary to have open spaces for people to walk in was in itself astonishing to a girl who had had a wilderness for a playground.

The best of it was that all these thrills could be experienced, albeit at second hand, by observation. Tonin would have loved it. It was like going to the movies, sitting on the top of the bus as it stopped and started in the West End traffic, watching the city's inhabitants going about their daily business of bustling and hustling, parading and primping.

What was most amazing of all was the money they must be spending. In the city everything cost money, there was nothing which was not a commercial exchange, and to Marguerite this – perhaps because a country girl never put her purse in her pocket unless she was going to market – was the most exotic notion of all. She had noticed, too, that people threw things out as soon as there was something which needed a little mending. The dustbins were full of perfectly good possessions just waiting for the dustman. You could furnish a whole house from people's dustbins. And there were perfectly able-bodied beggars, too, and people who had to sleep in doorways. This never happened in Pernes-les-Rochers, or even in Valréas. There were gypsies and travellers of course, and the *mutillés de guerre* who sold matches in the market, but you did not see beggars who had no reason to beg.

'Shaftesbury Avenue. All change.'

The conductor's voice floated up the stairs, and Marguerite woke from her reverie with a start. Shaftesbury Avenue was the street with all the theatres which marked the southern edge of Soho, her destination. She had walked along it on the first day she had visited Freda with Ben, and been astonished by all the famous names written in lights outside the theatres. She recognized many of them from the Arts programme on the World Service – she had enjoyed the theatre reviews when they let you hear snippets of the plays themselves, and she could imagine herself acting the romantic lead.

The events of the past few days had seemed as unreal as anything on the stage, and sometimes she had had to pinch herself to make sure that she was awake. Her enjoyment of all these new things seemed a little disloyal, even frivolous, considering the terrible events which had brought her here.

Father Patrick would certainly not approve of Elsie Potter, heiress to those very colonists who had made their fortune out of the poor of Ireland. But perhaps Marguerite was different – her mother's choice of father had made her different. Perhaps a love of luxury ran in the blood.

She would have to fight it. She resolved that, from now on, she would do her duty and only her duty. But, still, she did enjoy all the pretty things, and the delicious food which you neither had to gather nor to cook – and no washing-up afterwards.

She made her way through the throng of tourists heading for Carnaby Street. Carnaby Street, she knew, was Beatle territory, offering a chance of a glimpse of George or Ringo or John trying on a Mao jacket in John Michael, or a Rolling Stone picking up set of leathers, or even an eyeful of Marianne Faithfull hanging out with Mick.

Firmly denying herself these promising diversions, she made her way past the displays of exotic fruits and vegetables hawked by the barrow-boys of Rupert Street and turned along Old Compton Street, politely refusing an offer or two from the furtive customers loitering at the entrances of the strip clubs and massage parlours. She was a woman on a mission.

'So how's my pretty one today?' Freda's squawk caused several of the customers' heads to turn. 'Lost it yet?'

Marguerite hesitated, for a moment not understanding

what the old woman meant. Then she grinned and shook her head.

'Not yet. But I promise you'll be the first to know.'

'That's my duck. Make 'em wait. Make 'em pay.'

The fearsome old woman was peering at her speculatively from beneath her sparse helmet of reddish hair – garnished, this being a Monday, with a fine hairnet to keep her newly rollered curls in position.

'What's troubling my little precious?'

Marguerite hesitated. 'I need your advice, Miss Freda.'

'Of course you do, my darling duck. And, by the look of you, there's no stopping you getting it.' And with a cackle of laughter, as she had done that first time, she prodded the occupant of the neighbouring bar stool off his perch with an amiable 'Off you go, cunty. Important business.'

Patting the vacant stool, she poured a glass of champagne from the bottle which sat permanently by her elbow and seemed to be charged to whichever of her clients she knew had just had a financial coup at the race track.

She pushed the glass towards Marguerite and waited until she had taken the first sip.

'Now, then, my dearie duck, tell Freda what's on your mind.'

Telling Freda what was on her mind had produced all and more than even Marguerite had dared hope. Freda had listened intently to Marguerite's story of the evacuation of the village and the destruction of the valley. Then Marguerite told her about the difficulties she had experienced at the hands of the monsignor, and Ben's gallant rescue of her from the clutches of the doorman. At the end of Marguerite's spirited account of the interview, Freda threw her head back and laughed uproariously, threatening to dislodge the hairnet and drawing the attention of the drinkers towards the source of the merriment.

'I think we'll adjourn to the kitchen, my pretty.'

Here, among the debris of hangover cures and fish-and-chip suppers, Freda cleared a space for Marguerite's notes. Ben had been right. There was nothing and no-one Freda did not know. She seemed to have no difficulty in identifying the Hermitage's visitors as soon as she glanced down the pages. They were all gossip-column stories, all connected with some scandal or troubles of which the old woman seemed to have an encyclopaedic knowledge.

Each story had a different twist to it. Miss Belinda Fitzherbert's problems were relatively simple compared to the manoeuvrings required to extricate a certain powerful politician from allegations of homosexuality, or a multimillionaire financier from the consequences of his wife's penchant for stealing Fabergé boxes from her dinner-hostess's table-scapes.

'Wonderful, my darling duck. Won't we have fun?'

Marguerite swallowed hard. *Fun* did not seem a good description of what was under consideration. In fact, the more Freda told her about the powerful people she was supposed to approach, the more she was beginning to regret that she had taken the decision to embark on the enterprise at all.

'Nonsense, girl,' admonished Freda firmly. 'It's just a matter of getting your pretty little foot in the door. We'll concentrate on the men – any woman gets herself into trouble, there's always a man behind it. When the prick is hard, the brain is soft. You'll have 'em eating out of your hand.'

Marguerite shook her head doubtfully. 'Couldn't I start with something easy? Like robbing a bank?'

'The next-best thing, darlin'. A movie producer. Sir James Jarman. Outside Hollywood, the most famous of the lot.' Freda's bony finger stabbed at the second name on Marguerite's list. 'That's his mistress – ex-mistress.'

Marguerite glanced down. The story was about one of

373

the Hermitage's most recent visitors who had spent nearly six weeks in residence and given Madame Blanchette an unusual amount of trouble. Marguerite had been sure that she must be an actress because she arrived with three trunks full of clothes and teetered around on high-heeled mules even when she walked down to the village to buy another pack of Gauloises. Since she was never glimpsed without dark glasses and her hair bundled up in a scarf, it was almost impossible to tell what she really looked like.

From her brief but histrionic confession, Marguerite had gathered that it was her involvement in a messy divorce which had obliged her to seek shelter at the Hermitage. After the first week, a ferocious duenna who shouted at Madame Blanchette in Italian-accented French arrived to keep her company. Soon after this a movie-projector was installed in her private sitting room, and orders were issued that meals were to be served there.

'Gloria Gabriel – the Italian sex-bomb,' Freda explained. 'Jimmy fell hook, line and sinker, poor bastard. Forgot he had a wife and kids. When she wouldn't fuck him, he went down on one knee and proposed marriage, the lot. Apparently Gloria came over all Catholic, wanted a white wedding with all the trimmings, so Sir Jimmy had to buy himself a papal annulment. Cost him a packet. He had the devil of a time tucking Gloria away until the dust had settled. If you're after an annulment, a mistress isn't on.'

'Has he married her now?'

'Gloria? Not on your sweet *labia minora*, my duck. Took him down to Cartier for the ring – not to mention the matching necklace – made him bankroll her new movie, and *then* told him she preferred the ladies. Well, *I* could have told him that. Her girlfriend was the minder. Jimmy couldn't handle it at all. Sat on that same chair with his elbows in the fish-and-chip paper, sobbing like a baby. Silly bugger. Scared shitless it'd all get out and he'd be made to look like a total arsehole. Not that he isn't an arsehole anyway.' A bark of laughter concluded the assessment.

Marguerite absorbed this news. None of these strange sexual complications had come out in the confession – and, even though her mind had always been inclined to wander in the details, she would surely have paid attention to something so unusual. But, then, Gloria was an actress, so perhaps she could make anyone believe anything. Father Patrick had given up digging into the affairs of the monsignor's special-category visitors, so perhaps this was not surprising.

His wife refused to have him back, his children wouldn't speak to him, so the poor bastard had to talk to *someone*. Hairdresser, tailor, the barman – anyone, as long as they're outside the compound.'

She picked thoughtfully at a piece of cold fish. 'I get a lot of 'em. Everyone knows old Freda doesn't dish the dirt when it matters. Silent as the grave when it comes to the hacks. No journo will rat on Freda – or he'll find himself out on the street with a boot up his arse. I've a reputation to keep – my own. And don't you forget it, girlie.'

Freda looked at her sharply. The small eyes glittered, reminding Marguerite once more of a predatory bird. 'Not that I think you will, or I wouldn't be trusting you. And I *do* trust you, my duck. I've a nose for it. Freda's never wrong.'

She paused, nibbling thoughtfully.

'Anyway, old Freda's not been a good woman, but she's kept faith with her own kind. Call me a foolish old cow, but I've a mind to even up the score. I know what it's like out there – and so do you, my darlin' duck. There's not many of us with the spunk to carry it off. Strike a blow for the rest of us.' She stopped again; her eyes narrowed. 'He'll see you, make no mistake about it. Jim'll be your first hit.'

'But, Freda, I can't just march in there—'

''Course you can. Get them by the balls, and their hearts and minds wlll follow – as I tell my politicians. Don't worry, we'll dress it up nicely.'

Marguerite's head was spinning. Dressing it up nicely was perhaps not what George Flowers had had in mind. But, then, how else was she to prove herself? For a moment she wondered whether to tell Freda about George's warnings about shit and shovels, and immediately decided against it.

She had embarked on a course of action. She had Freda to guide her, as Ben had said she would. She was not going to give up before she had even started.

Marguerite took a deep breath and made up her mind. 'I'll do it.'

''Course you will. Never expected anything else. And not a word, mind – not even to young Benjie – that it's Freda that marked your card.'

Freda hooked a pair of spectacles over her nose and peered down at Marguerite's notes once more. She snorted. 'Discreet little fucker, for an actress. But, then, Jim won't know that. Your business is to keep him guessing.'

'How do I do that?'

'Listen carefully to your Aunty Freda, and do exactly as she says.'

Marguerite listened carefully. It was no fault of Freda's that she did not do exactly as she said.

33

Marguerite Follows Through

'Miss Leblanc? Sir James will see you now.'

In the first instance, Marguerite did exactly what Freda said. This secured her an appointment with the great man for the Wednesday after her Monday visit to Queenie's.

She had been surprised by how easy it had been. The telephone number Freda gave her was answered by a brisk male voice.

'Sir James Jarman's secretary.'

'Sir James Jarman, please.'

'May I enquire who's calling?'

'My name is Marguerite Leblanc. I'm a friend of Miss Gloria Gabriel. From the Hermitage. I have a business proposition to put to Sir James.'

'Hold on a moment, mademoiselle.' The young man had picked up on her French accent.

She waited. Clicks and whirrings were followed by a brief burst of music Marguerite recognized as from *Irma la Douce*, the latest hit in London's West End. Sir James was clearly a diligent publicist of his own successes.

The music stopped, and the voice returned.

'Sir James is busy now, but he can make space for you in person on Wednesday. Would eleven o'clock be suitable?'

She agreed that the time would indeed be suitable, made a note of the address, and set down the phone thoughtfully. So far so good.

This promising beginning led her to spend some of Ben's

winnings on a neat black suit and a businesslike briefcase. Well, she had a business proposition. Sir James Jarman had agreed to discuss it with her. She was a woman with a purpose.

At five minutes to eleven, just right for the eleven o'clock appointment, she found herself walking up the steps of an imposing double-fronted house in Belgrave Square. The brass-studded door was opened immediately by a smooth young man in a pinstriped suit who looked more like a banker than a secretary, and she was shown into a splendid drawing room to await the summons to the inner sanctum.

The young man had given her an admiring look as he admitted her, and she wondered for a moment how many other young women had trodden this path. Maybe he might even have thought she was a film star or at least a starlet, in her new clothes with her elegant new haircut, although the briefcase would surely tell him that she was here on business.

The paintings on the walls and the statuary in the marbled niches in the magnificent room were strangely familiar. She had not realized until she glanced at a copy of the *Connoisseur* laid out on the central table that James Jarman was also the owner of the largest private collection of Renaissance art in the world.

'Please be good enough to follow me.'

Marguerite rose to her feet, straightened the slim skirt of her severely tailored black suit, and followed the secretary up the wide stairway to the first-floor offices of the theatrical empire of which Sir James Jarman was the founder and chief executive.

Five minutes in the elegant room among the trappings of wealth and privilege had been enough to sap her confidence once more. But as she ascended the staircase only the slight trembling of her hands betrayed that she was at all nervous, let alone that she was once more regretting that she had ever embarked on the enterprise at all.

Her guide stopped outside a heavy door, knocked once, and entered.

'Miss Marguerite Leblanc, sir.'

'Thank you, Henry. Be right with you, Miss Leblanc.'

A silvery-haired middle-aged man, the sole occupant of the room, was seated at a vast desk at the far end. A telephone conversation was apparently in progress, and the man – recognizable from the portrait photograph in the *Connoisseur* as Sir James Jarman – had to put his hand over the mouthpiece in order to address her.

He returned to the conversation immediately.

The room was flooded with sunlight, temporarily blinding her after the gloom of the stairwell. Marguerite stood still for a moment, adjusting her eyes to the light. The telephone conversation allowed her to take note of her surroundings.

There was very little furniture in the room. One wall was stacked with books – not upright on shelves, but piled in pyramids on the floor, as if they had been thumbed through and then set aside. In contrast to the drawing room where she had waited, there was only one picture on the walls. This, a vast canvas, was a dreamy oil painting of water lilies shimmering in sunlight. For a moment she forgot everything in the beauty and tranquillity of the image, so familiar in reproduction, so overwhelming in the reality.

All at once she noticed that, although the conversation was still in progress, her host was watching her intently. He waved his hand apologetically, but did not replace the receiver on its cradle. This small charade was well known to his secretary, who knew perfectly well that there was no-one on the other end of the line; it was simply a ploy to allow Sir James to take stock of a visitor without being seen to do so.

The secretary found this intriguing because it indicated

that his employer was nervous of his visitor. In this assessment he was perfectly correct. Sir James was indeed nervous. It was this nervousness which had decided that he must meet Marguerite Leblanc in person, in private, as soon as possible.

Like all powerful men, Sir James's strength was also his weakness. He was prepared to acknowledge no failures in his professional life – still less in his private affairs. It was a matter of pride. In a lifetime of winning battles, Gloria Gabriel had been his single defeat. Worse, far worse, she had made a fool of him, had even persuaded him to bankroll her new movie which, to add injury to insult, was shaping up to be a real turkey.

It was not the money. The business could weather the storm. It was not even that this was the first enterprise in which the infallible Jim Jarman had come unstuck.

The trouble was not the threat of the public failure of a single enterprise. It was the private failure of judgement – *his* judgement, the judgement on which he had based his success. Sir James Jarman – the knighthood had been a reward for services to the British film industry – had been led by the nose, and by a woman. A man in middle age does not like to be made to look foolish in business – still less in the bedroom.

All these things were going through his head as he awaited his visitor, and were still in his head as he replaced the telephone on its cradle and walked round the desk to greet her.

All these things had also been put into Marguerite's mind by Freda. In this at least the protagonists were equal.

'Forgive me. Delighted, Miss Leblanc.'

Without taking his eyes off his visitor, he said: 'That will be all for the moment, Henry.'

The proffered handshake was dry and firm, the smile as warm as the eyes were wary.

'Good. Excellent. Please, sit down.'

A wave of a manicured hand indicated a leather-upholstered armchair, one of four round a low table on which was set a tray with a silver coffee pot and two tiny cups and saucers.

Marguerite settled herself in the chair while her host busied himself with the coffee pot. He was fastidious, neat, clearly a perfectionist.

While Sir James attended to filling the cups, she had a chance to study him at closer quarters. Her host was a very handsome man indeed, with a trim figure well displayed by the perfectly tailored grey suit with a pink rosebud in the buttonhole. The shirt was button-down blue silk completed with a formal navy-blue silk tie tied into a loose knot. The silvery hair was emphasized by the light suntan and the brilliant blue eyes.

This, she thought, was a man who was well aware of his effect on women – and on men, too – and used it for his own ends.

Freda had warned her of this. 'The old bastard can charm the hind legs off a donkey, but he's ruthless. Got a hide like a rhinoceros; Gloria was the only one who ever got under his skin. So don't kid yourself, my duck.'

He handed her the cup.

'Thank you, Sir James.'

It sounded oddly intimate, the use of the given name, but that was how Freda had said he should be addressed. She stirred the coffee, set it down, and leaned back. She would need all her wits about her.

There was a smile on the lips, and the face was tranquil, but the eyes were wary – almost steely.

'Now, what have you to say to me, Miss Leblanc?'

He glanced at his watch – a subtle, almost casual gesture, but nevertheless an indication to her that her time was limited. She took a sip of coffee. She would need all her wits about her, and the coffee was deliciously strong.

'Sir James, I am well aware that you are a busy man,

so I will come straight to the point.'

She crossed her legs in their new nylon stockings so that they were prettily displayed, just as she had seen in the movies, and leaned forward so that he had a glimpse of cleavage. That at least was a card that any young woman could play.

The steely blue eyes did not waver. It was a card all young women played when confronted with Sir James Jarman. A card of which he was only too well aware, and which, in all but Gloria, never had the slightest effect on him.

She reached down and set the briefcase on the table, forgetting that there was nothing in it but an old copy of *Vogue* she had found in Ben's kitchen.

'I have a proposition to put to you, Sir James. Gloria—' She hesitated for a second at the outrageousness of what she was about to do, and then ploughed on. 'Gloria suggested you might be . . . sympathetic,' she finished lamely. This was not the hard-hitting young woman of business that Freda had told her to be.

'Did she indeed? Sympathetic to what? And it was at the Hermitage that you discussed this proposition?'

'Sure and it was. That is to say—'

But the face had hardened now. 'Miss Leblanc, are you attempting to blackmail me? If that is the case, I suggest that you name your price. But I warn you not to be greedy. And, if we should come to an' – the eyes were un-fathomable – 'arrangement, be assured I shall not forget your name, your face, or your actions.'

Marguerite found a scarlet blush engulfing her. 'That's not the case at all. Not at all.' This was all going terribly wrong.

'Not the case? You astonish me. Then, what is it you want from me? I do not normally bankroll young women unless they have something to sell. Do you have something to sell, Miss Leblanc?'

'No. I mean, yes.' Marguerite was beginning to panic.

'Miss Leblanc, I am beginning to lose patience.'

'Please don't do that, Sir James. Please hear me out. I have not the slightest intention of blackmailing anyone – only to raise money in a good cause from those who might have reason to be grateful to the Hermitage. I was born there, you see, and it's my home – which is more than can be said for the villagers, turned out of their homes as they will surely be because of the fire and the flood—'

'This is all very biblical, Miss Leblanc, but I don't see how it could possibly concern me.'

'To be sure it does, sir. Because of Mademoiselle Gabriel—'

'Mademoiselle, is it, now? Young lady, I'm beginning to think you're not even on first-name terms with dear Gloria. Let alone that she suggested you should approach me in her name. Are you some kind of domestic servant? Have you perhaps been reading private correspondence?'

Marguerite's temper suddenly flared. The arrogance of this man was intolerable. Here was a perfect example of what Father Patrick had been fighting all those years of the Troubles in Ireland. He had made sure that she had Yeats's poetry by heart and could recite 'Easter 1916' almost from her cradle.

Her eyes blazed, and she rose to her feet. 'Sir James, it is ashamed of you and your kind that I am. Sure and all I ask is a future for the people of my valley, shelter for the homeless until they can rebuild their lives, enough hope for the young people to sow what they may expect to reap. If you are not prepared to listen to what I have to say, then you will be the poorer in your soul.'

'Indeed?'

The blue eyes were watching her now with new interest. This was a remarkable young woman. Far more remarkable than a friendship with Gloria would warrant. He, too, rose to his feet.

'Young lady, if you wish to attract funds to your enterprise, I suggest you control your temper. Your passion does you credit, but your methods of gaining admittance to your audience are – how shall I put it? – somewhat primitive.'

Marguerite's green eyes blazed. 'Am I to believe I would have gained admittance if I had not suggested that I knew something it might be in your interest not to have made public?'

The impresario looked at her in silence for a long minute. Then he sighed. 'No, young lady, I don't imagine you would. Perhaps you had better explain exactly what you *do* know. And then we can discuss how much.'

''Tis not for myself—'

Sir James held up his hand to halt the tirade. 'I understand that perfectly well. But you must be aware that so far you have offered me no other reason to – how shall I put it? – be of assistance.'

She shook her head fiercely. 'Not yet, to be sure. But there will come a time when you will have cause to be proud of helping us.'

'In that case, mademoiselle, I await your prospectus with interest. But I must warn you: my financial advisers are not easy to convince.'

Marguerite stared at him, the blood pounding her head. 'Then, let's go back to the blackmail, Sir James. It's safer ground.'

'Good.' His voice was still expressionless. 'At least you are a woman who knows her own mind. Now, what have you to sell?'

Marguerite was still angry, but this time her anger was cold, all-embracing, the kind of anger she had felt when her mother died. When the crow-black thing perched at the edge of her mind. She had no idea if she was right or wrong; she just knew that she had to do it.

She said quietly: 'The visitors to the Hermitage have to

confess their sins to Father Patrick so that he can keep a record in the ledgers. The ledgers are locked and stored. It's the price of sanctuary. It always has been. I know what's in the ledgers because for the past eight years it has not been Father Patrick but I who have made all the entries.'

She did not look at him after she had said the thing she had promised Freda she would not say. Which George had warned her against. She could feel the rage pounding in her head. She could feel this silver-haired man's eyes boring into her.

'I see.' The soft voice betrayed nothing. After a moment she heard the sound of a pen scratching on paper. 'I have made it out to bearer. This ensures that you may cash it without the embarrassment of putting it through a bank account. I trust that will be sufficient to conclude our business.'

The cheque was laid on the table in front of her. She looked down.

'Pay to bearer the sum of one thousand pounds only.' She made a quick calculation. In Pernes-les-Rochers it represented a small fortune. Two years' wages for a farm labourer at least. But at what price? She knew that this was not what she had planned.

The anger came to her rescue. It was no more than justice.

She took the cheque, slipped it into her briefcase, and left the room without a backward glance.

Marguerite was young and innocent and full of hope. Youth and innocence were no match for the powers ranged against her.

After a moment's consideration, Sir James picked up his telephone again. He did not mean his pretty visitor any harm. In all truth, he did indeed admire a woman who knew her own mind. And a thousand pounds was scarcely more than petty cash. Nevertheless, he was curious enough to wish to check that Mademoiselle Marguerite Leblanc was indeed who she said she was. And once he had established her credentials he might consider making a more substantial donation through the proper channels. He had read about the disaster in the newspapers.

When he wanted to know something, he went straight to the top. He flicked through his private address book and dialled a number.

The number connected him directly to the personal telephone which sat on the desk of His Eminence Cardinal Giuseppe Navarino. Sir James Jarman, with a much-admired documentary on His Holiness under his belt, was one of the few who had it.

'Giuseppe? Jimmy here. A word in your ear . . .'

34

The Perils of a Good Lunch

'I really don't think that will be necessary, your Eminence.'

Melton held the telephone receiver gingerly away from his ear, as if to set Cardinal Navarino's suggestion at arm's length. 'We do things a little differently over here.'

The telephone exploded again.

'I understand your feelings perfectly, Eminence. And I'm very grateful that your people are so efficient. Now I know what the girl's up to, I'll take the necessary steps.'

The receiver rattled with renewed vigour. Melton listened patiently, reflecting that His Eminence's ideas of how the young woman might be taught a lesson were, to say the least, melodramatic. Next he would suggest bundling her up in a bag and dropping her in the Thames.

'I know. You don't need to remind me of that, Giuseppe. Rest assured.'

Another short burst of verbal gunfire brought the conversation to a pyrotechnical conclusion.

'Leave it to me, Eminence.'

Melton sighed, and replaced the receiver. It was Ascot week, and he had been invited to Lord Mander's box. Luncheon in the Jockey Club tent would have to be replaced by luncheon at Claridges with his godson. It was really too inconvenient.

But, then, Marguerite Dieudonnée Leblanc was a most inconvenient female. This drawback applied to all the women he had ever known. All of them presented a problem of one kind or another. Cut the problem off at the roots, deprive it of sustenance, and it withers and dies. So far she would go, but no further. And if the price of stopping her was to put Ben through a little pain, then that was a sacrifice which he, like Abraham with Isaac, was prepared to make.

Benjamin never could resist temptation; but, even so, Melton had scarcely imagined that an ignorant young peasant girl would be to his godson's taste. But the modern world was so careless of its conventions; there was a terrible disregard for the social boundaries. The sacred institution of marriage was everywhere under attack. Men left their wives to marry their mistresses. Only the other day he had met a divorced woman in the Royal Enclosure. Divorce was not something which would ever be permitted to Benjamin Catesby. Nor, if the monsignor had anything to do with it, would a mistress – before or after marriage. Casual entanglements were one thing, but a mistress could upset the balance of wedlock.

Thank God for celibacy, thought the monsignor, as he waited for his godson to join him at the table.

'Ah, Benjamin.'

The note of surprise was just his little piece of theatre. He had already observed the young Earl of Malvern's arrival, but discreetly, from behind his copy of the *Financial Times*.

In spite of his irritation with his godson, he enjoyed the ripple of admiration as the young Earl of Malvern followed the maitre d'hôtel through the crowded dining room to the monsignor's usual table.

All the regulars had a 'usual' table, carefully selected according to whether the preference was for visibility or discretion. Each of the pink-clothed tables was placed a sufficient distance apart to permit the politicians and civil servants who made up the clientele to discuss their business in privacy.

Everyone knew where the Foreign Secretary would be seated, which corner was reserved for the wife of the multimillionaire owner of a famous department store, which table had been allotted to the American ambassador to the Court of St James. Those in the know on that particular day could have picked out the head of MI12 – twice as secret as MI6 – sharing a luncheon table with the man from Moscow with special responsibilities for outer space; a Greek shipping tycoon ordering caviar for his long-time mistress, a famous (and famously temperamental) opera singer; the heiress to a shoe fortune arguing with a Bond Street dealer over the price of a Renoir nude.

The circular *smorgasbord* table occupied the centre of the room, a casual arrangement which allowed the guests to make their own selection from some thirty different dishes. The Causerie's *smorgasbord* was justly famous.

Most of the interest Ben aroused was among the fairer sex. 'So good-looking, don't you think?' And Melton reflected that this was indeed true. But there was more to it than that – an easy charm which meant that both men and women fell easily under his spell.

Melton appreciated Ben's taste in clothes – in sartorial matters, his godson was as fastidious as he, although naturally the boy was permitted to be far more adventurous. Today he was dressed with his usual flamboyance, almost but not quite outside the rules, informal by the great hotel's standards. A corduroy suit in forest green which the monsignor knew could only have been scissored by Dougie Hayward at Blades, the *dernier cri* in tailoring. The newly fashionable polo-necked shirt in silk twill, its cut unmistakably Turnbull & Asser.

'Morning, Godfather.'

Melton glanced at his watch. 'Noon angelus long past, Benjamin. You're ten minutes late.'

He folded his copy of the *Financial Times* neatly into its original creases and set it beside his plate.

The two men lunched together infrequently, usually when Ben had landed himself in some scrape or other and needed either advice, intercession or help from his trust fund to extricate himself. So when his godfather summoned him for lunch at Claridges in the middle of Ascot week he knew that he was in trouble of some kind or another.

He hoped his godfather had not got wind of Marguerite's presence in the studio. He had returned the money, assuring the monsignor that he had done his level best to persuade her to accept his terms, but that she had refused.

He had told a similar story to his fiancée, although he did not tell Lottie about the money. She would have been irritated by the thought of Marguerite the car thief being offered a bribe, even more so if she had refused it.

If either of them discovered that Marguerite, far from being safely out of harm's way, was at that very moment in his back garden plotting insurrection – or whatever it was she was doing which got his godfather in such a lather – there would be hell to pay. Lottie was tolerant, but she did not like to be made to look a fool. But his godfather would be furious – might even cut off his allowance altogether.

None of these thoughts showed on Ben's face or in his manner.

The Causerie was Ben's favourite lunchtime venue, particularly when his godfather was paying. Deferential waiters, well-upholstered chairs, the deep pile of the midnight-blue carpet, the starched pink linen, all made for physical contentment. Had it not been that he knew his godfather would wait until the meal was over before broaching something disagreeable, he would have been perfectly happy.

His memories of the place went back to his childhood, to school exeats when his godfather had met him at King's Cross Station and taken him first to lunch here, and later, after a West End matinée of some well-reviewed and suitable play, to tea at Gunter's. Walnut cake. He remembered walnut cake with soft white icing. The thought made him a little nostalgic. His godfather had done the best he could by him. Whatever the old buzzard demanded of his future, he had taken care of the past.

The waiter placed the napkin deftly on his lap, and Ben made up his mind to enjoy himself while he could. 'Eat, drink and be merry, for tomorrow we die' had always been his motto.

Ben leaned over and tapped the newspaper. No sense in anticipating trouble.

'Counting the profits, Godfather? The Almighty's investments piling up?'

'Both on earth and in heaven, I'm glad to say.'

Melton smiled, thin-lipped and without mirth. He rose, nodding at the central display.

'Shall we help ourselves?'

They always chose from the *smorgasbord* table, even though there was an *à la carte* menu. Regulars knew that there was a ritual to be followed. The smoked and salted fish dishes had to be chosen first, then a selection among the salads, and afterwards there was a hot dish-of-the-day.

'What's it today, James?'

'Steak and kidney, your Reverence.'

Melton nodded. It was always a stew of some kind – nursery food, simple and comforting. Afterwards came the desserts. The Causerie was justly proud of its desserts. The Floating Island was particularly popular at this time of year, in high summer.

The priest and his godson moved round the central

391

table, loading their plates with smoked salmon, salt herrings, soused mackerel, pickled cucumbers. Melton had ordered a bottle of dry Moselle which was waiting for them in an ice bucket when they returned with the loaded plates.

He sipped the wine and nodded approval. Then, with a grunt of pleasure, he tucked the napkin under his chin. The walk across Berkeley Square had given him an appetite, and one should never ignore an appetite. He ate quickly, forking in the fish in large pieces and scarcely pausing to chew.

Ben had noticed this curious trait in his godfather ever since he had been a small boy. It was as if there had been a time when Charles Melton had not had enough food to fill his belly, so eager was he to satisfy the initial pangs of hunger. After he had finished, he blotted his mouth delicately, as carefully as a woman anxious not to disturb her lipstick, the fastidiousness of the gesture quite at odds with the greed.

He took another sip of the iced wine and leaned back in his chair.

'Good.'

This was an epitaph on the meal rather than a comment on his godson. *Good* was not an adjective which could be applied to the young Earl of Malvern. Even at his best he was an uncertain quantity. Money was the only thing which brought him to heel. Melton controlled his money.

It was time for business. The first thing was the girl's physical removal from London. He had been astonished to hear from Navarino that she had been a weekend guest of the formidable Elsie Potter. God only knew how Navarino had got wind of it in the first place. He had spies everywhere – mostly discontented servants, the kind that stole the silver. Sometimes he thought not a mouse moved in any of the great houses of England but the cardinal knew it.

Her presence at Daisyford showed a more formidable

adversary than he had first supposed. In this at least he was in agreement with the cardinal; it was only over the method to be employed to discourage her that they differed.

He was certain that, once deprived of his godson's protection, and the photograph taken by the cardinal's men was ample proof of that, she would be stranded. She had no money, no prospects, no option but to return to wherever it was she considered home. Certainly that could no longer be the Hermitage.

Failing that, if the worst came to the worst, she could be made a ward of court. The Hermitage itself remained sovereign territory and subject to English law, and this was a card he could always play.

And, if she was indeed pregnant, she could be taken into a home. The Little Sisters of Charity made a speciality of under-age mothers whose babies might be offered for adoption. He smiled to himself at this thought. What he should have done in the first place might come to pass through the girl's carelessness.

The easiest solution was to persuade Ben to withdraw his support of her without alerting him to exactly how supremely inconvenient she could prove, and this was the reason for his cautious introduction of the subject.

'What have you been up to, my boy?'

'Nothing much, Godfather. The usual.'

'Seen that young woman again?'

'Which young woman, Godfather?'

Melton's patience snapped immediately. 'I'm not a fool. Nor am I in my dotage. You know exactly which young woman.'

'Ah. *That* young woman.'

'It has come to my ears that the girl has taken up residence in your – I believe one calls it a *studio*, although in my day such places were reserved for artists. Since there are no longer any artists, I am told that their workplaces are now used for residential purposes. I await an explanation of her presence in yours.'

'How did you know about that?' Ben was not surprised, just curious. His godfather had an uncanny way of always knowing things. He could always, however, be counted on to be discreet, at least as far as Lottie was concerned.

'How I know is of no importance. What is important is that you know perfectly well you have defied my wishes.'

'I assure you, Godfather—'

'You can assure me of nothing. I had no idea you had any interest in her at all. Certainly not that you might take it into your head to harbour her, particularly in her condition.'

Ben grinned. *Virgo intacta* came into his mind. 'At least I can set your mind at rest about that. She's certainly not pregnant.'

'How do you know?' Melton stared at Ben. If that was the case, it weakened his own hand.

'She told me so and I believe her.' Ben shrugged and grinned – the engaging grin which usually won his godfather round. 'She's got a temper. I'm afraid when she gave you that impression it was probably to irritate you.'

'Irritating people seems to be her speciality. Did you know that she spent the weekend at Elsie Potter's?'

Ben hesitated, then admitted: 'I did know about that. She's rather a charming young woman. I think she sort of fell on her feet.'

'As you know, Benjamin, it was my intention that she should fall on her feet as far as possible from my affairs.'

'Yes, Godfather. And I'm sorry. I didn't think there was any urgency in shipping her off. I was just giving her a little time to get over her troubles.'

'Your tender heart does you credit, but I advise you to save it for a more worthy subject. The arrangement, even if impermanent, is unwise. Put an end to it. Now. Or I cannot be responsible for the consequences.'

'Consequences?'

'Others have noticed what I can only hope is no more than foolish generosity. I have been obliged to make excuses. I have no wish to have to explain myself further.'

Ben relaxed. So it was not his godfather who was behind this. It was the cardinal. Ben knew all about the pro-notary – the cause of many a fit of irritability in his godfather.

'Trouble at headquarters, Uncle Charles? His Eminence been on your back?'

'Not at all,' Melton lied. 'But questions have been asked.'

'Sorry about that, Godfather. Something came up – an old debt, you could call it.' The eyelids drooped over the grey eyes, so that Melton could no longer tell what going on in his godson's head.

'Debt?'

'There was a moment when Marguerite was rather helpful to me. I felt obliged to return the favour.'

'Favour?'

Ben nodded. 'That time when we went down to the Hermitage.'

'What kind of favour?'

He had rehearsed many times in his mind the questions he wanted to put to his godfather. He had not done so before for fear of getting Marguerite into trouble. And then, when she had taken matters into her own hands, there was no reason to protect her any more.

But now something in his godfather's voice made him draw back from the brink. He had meant to tell his godfather that he had seen the account of his mother's death in the ledger at the Hermitage, and that this was the favour – if favour it might be called – Marguerite had done him.

Instead he said, with a casualness he was far from feeling: 'I've been meaning to ask you, Godfather. My mother – where was she buried?'

'I don't see what that has to do with the matter under discussion.'

The reply was sharp, but Melton was picking up danger signals. The best policy was always denial. Deny everything, then sort it out later.

'However, since you ask,' he said carefully, 'I have to admit I never enquired. There was a rift between the two families – but you know that, too, since it was the reason I became your guardian. I always supposed it was in the graveyard at your paternal grandparents'. The family plot.'

'You imagine, but you aren't certain?'

'As you know, Benjamin, I was chaplain to your mother's family, but those were troubled times. I myself was in Rome when it happened.'

'I see. Well, I looked for her grave, but there was nothing there,' said Ben quietly. 'And no-one seemed to be able to tell me anything about it.'

Melton's eyes were watchful.

'My dear boy, the country was preparing for war. We had other things on our mind.'

'The Hermitage – was there any reason why she might have been buried there?'

'None that I know of. Why?' Melton's voice was as smooth as cream.

Ben's grey eyes held his. 'There was a stone in the heretics' graveyard. It had an inscription – initials in one corner. My mother's initials. A date. I saw it.'

Melton's blood ran cold. A date.

'Coincidence. Must have been someone else. You always did have a vivid imagination, Benjamin.'

Ben was perfectly still. For the first time in his life he had caught his godfather out in a lie. The ledger had confirmed what the stone had indicated. The knowledge of his mother's suicide had haunted him ever since.

His godfather, mistaking the silence for belief, relaxed.

'On that other matter. I think we – you – should reassure Charlotte. She was on the telephone to me only the other day. Some story about a stolen car. I did not at the time make the connection. Young women are so emotional – particularly when they are in love. But in the light of what I can only see as misplaced generosity to a misguided female who can only bring further trouble on your head – yours, as well as mine, Benjamin – I expect you to see sense. Get rid of the girl. Put her on the next train home.'

'And if she doesn't want to go?'

Melton looked sharply at his godson. This was hardly reassuring. God only knew what the silly girl had done to the boy. Inwardly he heaved a sigh. He would have to throw Charlotte into the equation. Not directly; just make sure she knew the form. Lottie was a woman; she would know how to make him see reason. Women like Lottie always got what they wanted in the end.

Navarino had mentioned that he had had a photographer following Marguerite. His Eminence was nothing if not thorough. Nevertheless, Melton could not help reflecting that even after twenty years the cardinal had still not fully grasped that democracy and the rule of law had their little drawbacks – not the least of these being the difficulty of manipulating the free press.

On the other hand, the gossips were always willing to slip in something on a tip-off.

He returned his attention to his godson.

'It may be convenient to be a little more discreet in future.'

'I may not find it so.'

'You will, Benjamin. When you've had time to think it over, I have absolute confidence you will.'

The threat was there, veiled, but there none the less. Ben was careless enough, but not careless enough to risk his future.

*   *   *

In her bedroom in her parents' house in Wiltshire, Charlotte Willoughby sat up in bed with a shriek.

The story occupied no more than a column inch, and could easily be denied. But the photograph was evidence – very public evidence. Ben at his own front door with his arm round what she was too much of a lady to describe as a tart.

Tiggy Trumpington had been first with the news – and the telephone shrilled its warning even before the maid had come in with her breakfast tray.

'Darling sweetie. Seen Hickey?'

'Of course not. This is the country, Tiggs. Nothing happens before nine.'

'Oops. Sorry.'

Three other similar calls followed before she had managed to down her first cup of coffee.

All of this had put Charlotte Willoughby in a very bad humour indeed.

What had the caption said? 'The Earl of Malvern and the French au-pair.' And then there had been the sniggering little paragraph about how understanding his fiancée must surely be.

Understanding? That was rich. After the row over the borrowing of the car, he had told her that the girl had dropped the keys off and disappeared into the night. He had sworn that he had not set eyes on her again.

'Fucking liar,' she said through tightly clenched teeth.

Lottie never swore. But she had had about as much as she could take. She added, by way of explanation: 'Where is she, you bastard?'

Charlotte had arrived at Old Church Street on the morning after Ben's lunch with his godfather with a newspaper under her arm. Uncharacteristically early, since she never normally rose before midday. She had immediately set about searching the house from attic to cellar.

· Ben did nothing to stop her. He had simply settled

himself calmly into his favourite chair, propped his feet up on the table, and waited for the storm to wear itself out.

When she failed to discover the evidence of occupation she was convinced must be there, she confronted Ben directly.

'Bastard.'

'Possibly. But that doesn't explain your behaviour.'

'*My* behaviour? Don't tell me you haven't seen it. Everyone else has.'

Ben shrugged. 'I don't know you're talking about.'

'Explain *this*, then.'

With an air of mingled triumph and rage, Charlotte opened the newspaper and spread it under his nose. He did not even bother to look down.

'You know perfectly well I never read the gossips. I *make* the gossip. I don't need to read it.'

'Bollocks. So where the hell have you put her?'

'Put who?'

'Her. This female impersonator you have apparently permitted to move in with you. What's she going to do? The plumbing? Don't lie to me, Ben. Your fancy woman.'

They might be betrothed, and this formal declaration of intent might suit them both well enough, but he did not like this new encroachment on his territory. She had never done this to him before – turning his house upside down and demanding explanations of what the newspapers saw fit to print about him. A lord was fair game. Everyone knew that. It was part of the price. As far as he was concerned, he had done nothing to deserve her wrath – at least, not with the object of Lottie's jealousy.

Ben was silent for a moment. Then he said: 'I presume you mean Marguerite. She's not my fancy woman. Far from it. I have never laid so much as a finger on her. She is simply my lodger; I allowed her the use of the studio. And, since you ask, I have absolutely no idea where she is.'

This was true enough. Marguerite had not been in to make the coffee that morning. He presumed she was sleeping late after the excitement of her weekend.

'Out. I want her out.' Charlotte stared at him, her eyes glittering. 'She's a troublemaker. I know all about her.

'Really. How?'

'Your precious godfather.'

'Ah. But I thought you read the story in the newspaper.'

'That's how I knew she was here. You can imagine what Mummy said. She telephoned Charles immediately. Mummy said this . . . this *person* is his responsibility. But I don't agree. She's *your* responsibility. And I want her out. Immediately.'

'Do stop saying that, Lottie. It's so tiring.'

This enraged Charlotte beyond all endurance. She had thought that all she had to do was to warn Ben off. That was what Charles Melton had suggested. 'Just a little hint, Charlotte. It'll come better from you.'

It had *not* come better from her.

She tugged angrily at the sparkling circle of sapphires which Ben had given her on their engagement.

'You have just lied to me for the last time, Benjamin.'

The ring glittered as she threw it in a wide arc. It clattered against a decanter on the sideboard, bounced twice, and rolled away into a corner.

'Don't be silly, Lottie. Nothing's changed. I've kept my side of the bargain – really I have.'

Charlotte's face reddened. 'The bargain didn't include holding me up to public ridicule.'

'But I haven't *done* anything. . . .'

This reference to what Ben might or might not have done was the last straw. Charlotte was a *good* girl. She did not go running around after plausible fraudsters. She should have insisted on having the girl arrested as soon as the car had been stolen. Ben was at best a gullible fool who must be taught a lesson. At worst a charlatan, unworthy of her hand.

But far outweighing any of this was the effect on her pride of the morning's telephone calls. The note of triumph in Tiggy's voice had been unbearable. They were all laughing at her now. Benjamin and the 'au-pair' – that was a good one. It had made her a laughing stock. And he was not even going to deny it.

'I've had enough of you, Ben!' she screamed. 'More than enough!'

Tears of rage and humiliation blinded her. There could not possibly be any explanation for what all the world already knew. No escape from what she had been the last to know.

In that moment the doors to the garden – the garden that divided the house from the studio – opened; and there, as if the visitor was well used to this casual mode of entry, stood Marguerite herself.

35

Marguerite and Ben

Marguerite hesitated on the threshold.

It was not the first time she had found herself in this situation.

'Just the person.' Charlotte's voice was low with anger. 'How convenient.'

'Steady on, Lottie.'

'Her or me, Benjamin.'

'Don't be silly. Marguerite will confirm what I've already told you.'

'You have the choice. Get rid of her. Now.'

'She's my lodger. And that's all. Isn't that so, Marguerite?'

The grey eyes were once more hooded – although Marguerite could not tell if it was amusement, or if he was preparing to throw her out.

Marguerite nodded helplessly.

'Surely it's true. Indeed, it is. And out of the kindness of his heart.'

'I see. A pathetic stray. A cat left out in the rain. A charity case.'

'Surely not. I fully intend to pay my rent.'

'And how will you do that? Standing under a red light in the street?'

'Stop that, Lottie.'

But Charlotte had had enough. With a swish of her skirts and a flick of her heels she was gone.

In spite of the risk of incurring Charlotte's further displeasure, Ben had insisted that Marguerite accompany him to one of his parties that evening.

'No, Ben. Better not. I'll have an early night.'

'Don't be so boring.'

Marguerite looked at him, but the grey eyes were full of laughter.

'Lottie? She'll get over it.'

So Marguerite agreed – in truth it was a party she had been looking forward to. A famous pop musician who was a favourite of hers, and a pair of film stars familiar from the screen in Valréas. She was growing more used to Ben's circle by now, and she had her own small group of admirers – more so now that she had been the little item in the gossips. An item in the gossips was a kind of baptism; it showed that you had arrived.

They returned late, this time without Ben's usual unidentified girl in tow.

Ben had been silent on the way home. Now he pushed the key in the lock and opened the front door, waiting for her to enter.

'Come in. Please. I want you to.'

Marguerite hesitated. This was breaking the rules. Always she would go straight to the side door which gave into the garden and led to the studio.

Something, perhaps Charlotte's accusations, made her agree.

Inside, he poured wine into glasses, handed her one, raised his own to his lips, drinking deeply as if the wine were water.

His eyes met hers again, and she could see that his mood had changed. The pupils were dark and full, so that the soft grey of the irises had almost vanished.

'Tell me, Ben.' She prompted him gently, not knowing what was troubling him.

She waited for him to speak. Receiving no answer, she said: 'Tell me about yourself. I know so little.'

He waited for a long time to answer, and then said quietly: 'What is there to tell? My childhood was nothing much to remember – a series of nannies and governesses. School.' He shivered. 'I hated that. Hated it more than anything – the loneliness. They sent me to the monks when I was six.'

'They?'

'Whoever decided what was to be done with me. My grandparents. My godfather. He was the one who seemed to take the decisions. I suppose I was brought up by my grandparents – at least it was with one or the other that I spent the holidays. When I was little, all I knew then was that my mother had died when I was born, and that my father had been killed soon after – during the Spanish Civil War. And that Monsignor Melton was my guardian – the grandparents couldn't agree on anything, so I suppose it was convenient.'

'That's all?'

He shrugged. 'Freda used to tell me things sometimes. She was the only one of my parents' friends who took an interest. Most of the others were dead anyway. She used to tell me that my parents were wonderful, my mother was beautiful and wonderful, and my father was brave, and that there were family difficulties over the consent to the marriage. But I knew that anyway – my maternal and paternal grandparents were not exactly warm towards each other. I seemed to remind them all of things they would rather forget.'

Marguerite frowned. 'Didn't you ask why? I've always wondered about mine; but maybe that's a different thing, and I think my mother never wanted anyone to know the truth. But yours is different. You being the heir to the earldom and all that, it must have been very important.'

Ben nodded. 'Of course. But what was important was

that I was legitimate. Bastards can't inherit titles, even if the parents marry afterwards. We never discussed it anyway – either of the grandparents. It wasn't considered proper. There were several of us at school who were what they called *problems* – death, divorce, whatever. You weren't supposed to talk about it, not even when you went to confession. No whining, no crying. Crying was for cissies – and cissies were beaten. I loathed being beaten. Never got used to it. I never whined and I never cried.'

'Poor little boy.'

He shrugged. 'It was normal. We all wanted to be normal.'

She watched him in silence for a while. Then she said: 'What about your mother?'

His reply was casual – too casual, she thought, for such a terrible thing. 'I was curious of course. I looked for her grave in the churchyard at home. And when I asked my grandparents why I couldn't find anything I was told not to ask impossible questions.'

'Odd,' said Marguerite.

'Not particularly. There were plenty of questions they considered impossible. Anything to do with sex. Love. That was nasty . . .'

He stopped, and then continued: 'I tried to run away from school once. I was about seven, and one of the other boys said that if I didn't have a father I must be a bastard. I asked the monks if it was true. That was when they told me about Spain and my father being killed. I didn't believe them, so I decided to run away and find out for myself. The place was out on the moors with a high fence all round it, like a prison camp. We all knew it was impossible to escape.'

'And did you?'

He nodded. 'I had to do it at night. I waited for a full moon and climbed down a drainpipe. I had a map, and I knew that if I reached the railway line I could get clean away without anyone knowing where I'd gone. There was a halt for the train where they took on the post. It was pitch-dark and very scary, but I got there just when the train arrived. I hid among the mailbags till we got to London. The police picked me up in Piccadilly Circus. I'd got it into my head that everybody in the world went to Piccadilly Circus, and sooner or later I'd find my father. My godfather came down to the police station to collect me. He took me straight back to the monks. Ten strokes of the cane and no more said about it.'

'What a terrible thing.'

Ben shook his head. 'Best thing I ever did. The bullying stopped, and I became a hero. Better than letting yourself be buggered by the fag-masters, which was the only other way of keeping out of trouble. Never one for buggery myself.' The grey eyes gleamed. 'You do know what buggery is, don't you, child? After that I had a reputation to keep up. Tearaway and hellraiser – keep your distance. The monks didn't know the half of it.'

'Didn't you have any friends?' Marguerite thought about Tonin and how he had protected her from the worst of her schoolmates.

'Indeed I did. Another boy in the same boat as me, but with an even worse reputation. He'd been thrown out of Downside – their rejects always came to us. Our monks had a reputation for toughness. His name was Alexander Cameron. His father had been killed in the Battle of Britain, and his mother was a bolter.'

'A bolter?'

'A runner. She ran away from people and places. Including Sandy and the ancestral frozen baronial. He showed me an article about her in some magazine – she'd just divorced her fifth husband and was renovating a dilapidated plantation-house in Jamaica. There were photographs of her and the new fiancé. She was still attractive, in an overblown kind of way. The boyfriend was half her age and as black as a liquorice allsort. We were all very impressed. She must have been a beauty – all Celtic blues and golds. Sandy had inherited her looks and was always being propositioned by the buggers behind the bicycle shed.'

Ben paused and poured himself another glass of wine.

'Sandy was a good deal more streetwise than me. He had had some unusual stepfathers and he knew how to work the system. He had the knowledge, and I had my own allowance – enough for both of us, if we spun it out. We smuggled in booze, dope – even girls. We found a field where magic mushrooms grew – we dried them in Matron's airing-cupboard in among the knee-length knickers and whalebone corsets.'

Remembering the curious tobacco at the parties, Marguerite asked: 'Did you smoke them?'

'Of course not. You made a kind of tea – milk and sugar optional, but less likely to get you caught. We flogged them by the ounce to the juniors. It was the first and only profit-making enterprise in which I've ever been involved. The monks never did work out why all these little boys looked so starry-eyed over their bedtime Horlicks, but they guessed it must have something to do with Sandy. They sacked him, but not me. A bad influence, un-specified. I imagine it was my assiduous godfather who persuaded them to let me stay.'

'Was that the year you came down to the Hermitage?'

'It was. My godfather insisted. I'm afraid I was not at my best. You were the nicest, funniest thing that happened all that summer.'

He grinned at her. Confused, she could feel the scarlet blush rising to her cheeks. Hurriedly she said: 'What about Sandy Cameron? What happened to him?'

Ben shrugged, his eyes once again hooded. 'Blew his brains out with a twelve-bore on his twenty-first birthday. Firewater and the chemical substances don't mix. Still,

407

Sandy always said he'd die young. We both did. Made a schoolboy pact. You know the kind of thing – all for one and one for all. I suppose I felt betrayed when he went before I did. But, then, he always had to be the first.'

'Ben – I'm so sorry.'

'Why? It was a terrific funeral. Sporrans a-flaunt and the rain pouring down by the bucketload. Nothing like the skirl of pipes and the wailing of the women to give a man a rousing send-off. The graveyard was a couple of miles over the hill in a peat bog – the hole kept filling up with water, and we kept trying to bail it out. We gave up after a bit and floated him off. Very romantic really.'

'Romantic?'

'Of course.' He looked at her, his face inscrutable. 'Don't you think?'

'No.' Marguerite shivered. 'Not romantic at all. Death is the ugliest thing in the world.'

The hooded eyes flicked over her. 'An excellent reason for finding it romantic. It makes the whole thing bearable. Let it all float away and be done with it. No point in holding on to things. After the grandparents died, my godfather suggested that the houses be sold – all but this one – and the money put in trust. And then somehow it didn't matter any more.'

'Didn't you miss it – the place you'd grown up in?'

'Why should I? There was nothing there for me. Charles Melton's all I have. He's a cold fish; there's always a reckoning and a price.'

She felt protective, motherly. She had not known that he was so vulnerable, as vulnerable as she.

Trying to comfort him, to reassure him of her interest, she added: 'But now, when you are to be married, and have children of your own—'

She stopped herself, puzzled at her own confused feelings about this acknowledgement that Ben Catesby had already been claimed.

408

Lamely, conscious that she might be intruding, she added: 'Your fiancée. She might want to hold on to things – even if you don't.'

'Lottie isn't interested.' The reply was swift, almost triumphant. 'She doesn't see the point of all that. Why hang on to secondhand stuff when there's plenty more in Harrods?'

Ben stirred, rose to his feet, wandered around the room, absentmindedly picking up objects and setting them down, replacing them in the little shiny pools revealed by their removal from the dusty surfaces.

Family photographs in silver frames: sepia-tinted images of Victorian shooting parties, christenings, weddings. Enamelled boxes with inscriptions inside the lids. A tortoishell snuff-box with silver initials. Portrait miniatures of curly-haired children. A leather case with military medals.

She saw the contradiction in the gesture. 'What about those – all those things?'

He stopped abruptly. He stood for a moment above her, shielding the light so that his face was in shadow. Even so, she could see that there was an anguish to the shuttering of the eyelids, the closing down of the mouth. Then he turned his back to her, and she had to strain her ears to hear his words.

Softly, as if to himself, he said: 'If that is all I am, I want none of it.' Louder, he said, 'The reason I'll marry Lottie – and she'll come round, she always does – isn't just because she can afford me. There are a lot of girls out there who can afford me. She doesn't want heirlooms and she doesn't want heirs. And nor do I.'

Anger flamed in her – anger against him, for the carelessness, the blindness, the arrogance which counted such things of so little account. Her brow furrowed, the green eyes blazed.

'If I were you, I'd find someone who'd be honest with

409

me. I'd want to know the truth. I'd want to face up to reality.'

Ben sighed. He would make one last effort to make her understand.

'You're right. I'm a coward. I've had enough of the search for truth. Truth is putting a gun to your head and pulling the trigger. Honesty is spattering your brains all over your best friend's boots. Reality is six feet of sodden peat.'

It was almost four in the morning when Ben came to find her in her own bed.

'I need company. Come over.'

When she came, Ben had his head in his hands. By the slight slur in his voice, he had been drinking. He looked sorry for himself. Bedraggled and spike-boned, she thought, like a bird which has been too long in the rain.

He rose, moving quietly around the room. He lit candles, put a record on the player – one of her favourites, an instrumental with an insistent West Indian beat. He opened a bottle of wine. The label was peeling, and the bottle was dusty.

'Here – share my vice. Croz Hermitage, 1945 – the year you were born. You should always drink your own vintage.'

'And yours?'

He shrugged. 'A bad year for burgundy.'

She sipped the wine. It was delicious, dark, rich and spicy. Cinnamon and oranges, the colour of blood. She took another sip, and then another.

She felt happy, trusting, content to be with him. Her mind was a little blurred, surely because of the wine. She put out a hand to him, touched him gently on the cheek. She was truly sorry for him now. She said: 'Never mind.'

'Oh, but I do mind, child. And I did look for the truth. On that day in the Hermitage when you told me about the confessions in the ledgers. You showed me where they were kept. You even told me where to find the key.'

Marguerite looked at him, her eyes troubled. 'That was the meaning of the scratches on the stone? I didn't know.'

Ben shrugged. 'I didn't, either. Not really – although I thought there was some kind of connection with the Hermitage from hints Freda dropped over the years. I felt I had to find out for myself. So when my godfather insisted I make the trip with him I jumped at the opportunity. God knows, I wish I hadn't.'

'Why?' Her voice was gentle, anxious. 'What did you find out?'

'What I had already known – just as soon as I saw the marks on the stone in the heretics' graveyard. There's only one reason a Catholic gets chucked out of the club.'

'What's that?'

Ben was silent for a long moment. When he spoke again, his voice was harsh. 'Suicide, my young innocent. My mother killed herself. It's all written there, in the ledger. Listen while I tell you the truth. My mother was a murderer. That she was her own murderer makes not the slightest difference to her intent. She left her child in its cradle. She made her way up that same narrow staircase. She reached the top. She opened the door. The wind was cold on her face. Behind her the newborn infant cried in someone's arms – probably Freda's, although she's never told me for sure. My mother listened, and then she walked to the edge.' Ben's hands were spread, protective. 'She knew what she was doing. She knew she wouldn't be the one to pay the price.'

The face was in shadow, the voice as dark. 'The walls of rock, sloped, uneven. The body bouncing from ledge to ledge. Flesh tearing itself on stone. The redness of blood and the whiteness of bone. Blood and brains. Death's a messy business. We have no business to meddle with it. Not suitable for the living. We're the ones who have to look it in the face.'

Marguerite said quietly: 'People die, children are born. There's no blame.'

'You're wrong, child. Whatever happened that day, I blame my father. He abandoned my mother. He killed my mother just as surely as if he had taken a gun and blown out her brains. I am the child of death. Now do you see?' The voice was bitter. 'Bad blood runs in my veins. I'll have no part of it.'

He was silent for a long moment. 'Sometimes I hate my mother, God help me. Whatever drove her to do what she did, I hate her for what she did to me. Not to herself. But to me.'

'You must forgive her, Ben. Forgive yourself. Above all, yourself.'

Wearily Ben raised his head. 'I forgive nothing and no-one. I live for myself alone. For now and only now. Not for yesterday, and most certainly not for tomorrow.'

'The ledgers don't always tell the truth.'

'What do you mean?'

Marguerite was silent for a long moment. Then she said: 'When I take down the confessions, I put down the words. I don't put down the little things which matter. The lies or truths we read when we look and smell and feel. So where's the truth in that?'

'No truth. Half-truth. Lies. But there's truth in the burial place of my mother. That at least is truth.'

Ben looked at her. The grey eyes were lighter now; there was a sparkle to them. 'It's not your fault. It's not anyone's fault. We can't help who we are. We are not responsible for what we do.'

A silence fell between them.

'Aren't we?'

Her voice was very quiet. The wine coursed through

her. She waited, scarcely daring to breathe. She felt help-less, her limbs turned to water.

He put out his hand to her. It was something he had promised himself he would never do; but with her there, so close, so soft and sweet – like a sleepy baby, he thought – he was not able to help himself.

'This is the truth. The here and now is our only reality. Not the past or the future. We both know it. You as well as I.'

She shivered at his touch. She said softly: 'Why now? Why do you say this to me now?'

'Because I love you.'

She held back, did not tell him what he needed to hear. Everyone she had ever loved had been taken from her. It was like a curse, as if some malevolent force could hear her and take what she loved from her.

Nevertheless, at that moment, she believed him. He almost believed himself. If there was a reason to love her, it was that the feeling he had for her was unlike anything else he had ever felt. He knew it now, just as he had always known it. Those things about her which made it inevitable that he should want her were the same things that had made him run from her.

Now he was ready, if only she would say the words. Not just her beauty, not even her bravery and her innocence – but the certainty, the strength she had in her, the vigour and energy she brought to everything she did. All these things bewildered him. Bewildered and fascinated. They had always done so, from the first moment he had seen her – then, indeed, no more than a child.

If there was a reason not to love her, it lay long before he had had the power to reason. He did not know how to tell her this, or how to explain that it was because of this that he was afraid. He had tried to explain it to her when he had told her about the death of his friend, what he knew of his mother and his father.

Everything, everyone he had ever loved had betrayed him. She, too, would betray him. Only the things he did not love could ever be trusted. The indolence, the frivolity, even his betrothal – all were a game.

Wildly he told himself it was too late. It had always been too late. That first betrayal had seen to that. It was not simply that he had had no mother to love him, no father to guide him, but that somewhere in that moment of his own birth lay the first betrayal.

'I love you, Marguerite,' he said. And waited. He knew that this was his moment of reality. Nothing on earth would matter if she said the words. For her he would abandon everything, cross the wilderness which divided them, and accept what was to be.

If she would only say the words, only say 'I love you, too'.

Not understanding – how could she understand? – Marguerite smiled then, and was silent, but hers was the sweet uncomprehending silence of contentment. She knew nothing. She had no truth but her own certainties – of who she was, and what she meant to do. She had no language to express what her heart felt.

'Sweetheart, my darling, come into my arms,' was what she said.

The words soothed him as much as the absence of those other words. To her there were no words – just as there are no words for the sound of the breeze which ruffles the first leaves in spring, the warmth of the earth in the first sunshine, the music in the first song of the lark.

'What now?'

Even as she spoke, she knew the answer. She was a woman now; she knew all there was to be known, understood the secrets of all creation. The earth might crack in a thousand pieces, the sun dance with the moon and the stars fall from the heavens, and this knowledge would still be hers. What she felt was without words – the warmth of skin against skin, the way that limbs entangle, that bodies curve together, the mingling of the secret juices, the touch of lips, the scent and softness of hair and cheek, the tenderness in fingertips, the curve of an ear, the rosiness, the sweetness of the lovemaking that was to come.

He undressed her slowly, with infinite care.

'My beauty, my darling,' he whispered, his voice in her ear.

His hands were gentle on her, his fingertips learning her secrets, exploring the smoothness and softness of her, sharing what he had learned.

Her body was helpless in his arms. She unfolded to him like a flower, welcoming him, sighing his name, shivering at his touch.

He placed soft kisses on her temples, her rosy nipples, her mouth, the soft flesh of her palms. His mouth searched for the pulse points at her throat. He cupped her breasts. And then, and then – the fingertips dancing downwards, to those dewy places where the heart's blood gathers.

She felt the strength of him against her, the rising of him, the urgency of his wanting her.

'Now,' she whispered. 'Come to me now.'

And so he did. Eagerly, with a delight, an innocence to match her own. Tears came to her eyes as he entered her. Tears neither of fear, nor of joy, nor even of the pain of that first moment – but like rain falling on dry earth, the blessing which comes to a desert after drought.

She turned and twisted in his arms, her breasts against his chest, her hands on his back, down the length of his thighs, her nails tearing at his skin. Her limbs twined round him, her back arched and she called his name; she screamed and fought as her body tossed in the waves of this unknown ocean.

She was a creature of foam and sea-spray, a being without substance, pure spirit, without the reality of flesh or bone, drawn downwards to the sea or upwards to the sky, spiralling weightless through eternity. Her body was no longer her own to give, dissolved like mountain mist in the warmth of the sun. This at last was the truth of it, a single moment which held all truth for all time, the gift without which she was incomplete. It was as if her limbs themselves were melting, as if she was floating weightless in his arms.

As he looked down at her, before his passion carried him to the final certainty, his grey eyes held such tenderness, such sweetness that she knew that this could only be for ever.

Her body melted around him, blood and sinew lost in that moment of completion. She was no longer sure which limb belonged to whom, which fold of flesh or angle of bone or twist of muscle might be claimed for either.

'Tell me, speak my name, hold me, never leave me.'

Soft words, sweet words which have no meaning except to the ear which hears, no form except to the mouth which speaks them.

There were no words in any language for the things that she now knew, that her body and her heart experienced at last.

The future, the past, the present – all came together in this moment of exultation. She, too, felt that fear, the fear of losing what she had found – a fear so great that for a moment longer she clung to him, using her body to give form and shape to those things which, shapeless, have none of it.

36

Trouble at the Hermitage

In the tall room in the Hermitage which had once been the crusaders' refectory, Father Patrick shuffled slowly across the worn stones till he reached the stacked shelves which held the ledgers. With bony fingers, wrinkled and spotted with age, he caressed the worn leather. A thousand years of secrets buried within. A millennium of Catholic guilt.

Taking the key from his desk, he unlocked each in turn. With infinite care the old man's fingers touched each page. The thick vellum felt smooth to his touch. It was his last duty, that final blind caress of what had been a lifetime's care.

Chinese ink applied to vellum which is then dampened by whatever agency – rain, or storm, or some accident of storage – and then set to dry in the quick warmth of a fire has a certain property. The ink lies lightly on the surface, lifts easily, leaving no trace.

As his fingers brushed and brushed, tiny glittering specks, blue-black as soot, broke free. For an instant they clung to the soft pads of his fingertips, then dropped on to the dusty boards and were lost. One by one he caressed the pages, leaving no book unopened, loving each one equally.

When he had finished his task, he turned the little key in the locks, and replaced each ledger carefully in its place, the blind fingers deciphering the volume number, the year, the date of commencement and completion. Embossed in the leather, that at least remained. For the rest, under his fingers, a thousand years of sin bleached white as snow.

Content at last, Father Patrick O'Donovan raised himself from his chair by the tall window through which fell, as always, the rays of the midday sun.

Sometimes he thought it would have been as well if the writings – the fair round hand of those thousand years of holy scribes – had been destroyed in the storm. Conscience was a terrible thing to bear. Far better that such things remain in the heart and do not make the transition to this cold-blooded record of wrongdoing.

For thirty years now, the Hermitage had been his life. He had always believed that under his stewardship the place would thrive. The people would prosper, the children would multiply, and some day that it was God's will that the valley would be restored to its former glory.

God's will was not his. The years stretched behind him. The future was for others. The old man had listened to the silence after the last of the children had gone. There might be hope for them in the plans which Tonin brought to him, in his assurances that the news from Marguerite was good – but it was not a hope which the old man could share.

The year turned slowly, and still he listened in vain for the sound of children's laughter.

These days, he had only Madame Blanchette to bustle around for an hour or two each day and set his midday meal on the table, or see to the few visitors the warden sent.

There was a new young priest to lift his daily burdens, to take confession and write the record in the ledger. A young Englishman, a convert to the faith, with the zeal and humourlessness of all converts.

Father Patrick did not care for excessive zeal, still less for young Englishmen with accents as rounded as those he remembered from his angry youth.

The Hermitage, the young priest told Father Patrick,

was no longer to concern itself with the troubles of the villagers – even those few who were left. Specialization was the way forward, and the Hermitage was to concentrate on its primary duty: the provision of sanctuary for the warden's guests.

His mind was wandering now. There were times when he thought himself a boy back in his native land, still others a young scribe in Rome, and at other times, the best of times, keeping company with his dear Thérèse. His blindness troubled him no more. It was a blessing that he could no longer see what he did not wish to see.

Taking his leave of that which had been his lifetime's care, he took his walking stick in his hand and went down to the place which was most in his heart.

Strange to hear the call of an owl in daylight. Some say that the owl is ill-omened, a harbinger of death. Father Patrick knew better.

The grass in the heretics' graveyard was soft and sweet-scented under his sandalled feet. The bird was closer now, so close he could hear the whisper of wings, feel the touch of velvet against his cheek.

A woman was there. Familiar. Smiling.

'You've been a long time coming, Paddy.'

There was laughter in his ears, full-blooded, joyous.

'Hail Mary, full of grace,' muttered Father Patrick, clicking his rosary through trembling fingers.

He shook his head. It was madness, all in the mind.

In answer more laughter, such familiar laughter.

'Paddy, oh, Paddy, when will you learn?'

He knew it must be a dream, more than a dream. Whether God-given or devil-spawned, he did not care. It was enough that she was there. His rosary beads were moving through his fingers. 'Holy Mary, Mother of God, pray for us sinners.'

And, indeed, he was a wanderer come home.

'Is it you?'

'Of course.' Her laughter in his head and in his heart.

'Flesh and blood? Or spirit?'

'Whatever you want me to be, I am.'

She was reality to him now. No longer in his mind's eye, not as she had been at the terrible moment of her death, but herself, in all her dark beauty, young and strong, with the laughter in her eyes and on her lips.

'Thérèse. My sweet Thérèse.'

For answer she reached out her arms to him. His longing for her was more than he could bear. And, oh, the sweetness of her; his body ached for her.

'I, too,' she said. She could read his thoughts; nothing was hidden. 'I'm waiting for you, Patrick.' The voice was clear and strong.

'Not yet, Thérèse. Not yet.' His fingers clicked the beads. 'Lord have mercy, Christ have mercy, Lord have mercy.'

'Come.'

And still he refused her, his fingers busy with his prayers.

'You are weary, my love. It's time to rest.'

His limbs felt like lead.

'I am here, waiting for you. No need to fear.'

He went to her then, and took her hand in his, feeling as he did so a terrible joy. All that he had been as a man was here, in the arms of this woman.

She said: 'Come. All will be well.'

She had reality now, a softness, a paleness on the edge of his sight. He walked into the silence, unafraid of the dark, knowing she was there.

'Come.'

He was trusting, his eyes on her, his blind eyes which could now see.

'Is it far?'

'Not far. Not far at all.'

There was a power in her which drew him to her. His

body was no longer weary, but light and strong as the boy he had once been.

Gladly he followed Thérèse, sweet Thérèse, his lost Thérèse now found. He followed her through the long halls of memory. Between the living and the dead he found a pathway.

Hand in hand, they came into the green hills of his childhood. He walked with her and talked with her, telling her all the things which were in his heart, those things he had told no man or woman or child. Not even the child they shared, forgotten now, abandoned once more in the joy they had together. The forbidden things, the hidden things, the secrets from the deepest places of his soul.

His body was nothing now, an empty shell. He reached out towards her, felt her warmth as she came into his arms. He held her close, her sweet voice in his ear.

'Paddy, sweet Patrick, my love.'

His eyes saw clearly again, his body was young and strong, his face was lifted to the light. He felt again the warmth of sun and the softness of rain.

It was Tonin who found the old man, the body stretched on the earth, the arms clasped to the breast as if holding something so precious it could not be let go, even in death.

How the old priest came there, blind and halt as he was, was held to be a miracle, in the way the country people have of confusing what was no more than the old man's madness with the fulfilment of some divine purpose.

As if a further miracle was needed, the old man's coffin, buried as was proper in consecrated ground, was found to have mysteriously removed itself in the night and re-interred itself in the meadow in the exact spot in which the body had been discovered.

Three times the gravediggers did their work, and on the fourth they went to tell the new young priest and his master the warden, come over from London for the burial, that it was perfectly clear that Father Patrick wished to lie beside his beloved Thérèse – whether it was the devil or the Lord who had decided the matter.

'Do it and be done with it,' the warden said. Melton had been glad of the excuse to come down to the Hermitage and tidy up a certain loose end.

After the business was over, Melton looked for that earlier gravestone.

Ben had alerted him to what could only be an unfortunate oversight. The rules were perfectly clear. The stones in the heretics' graveyard were always unmarked. Not in this case; he could see that now. The initials and the date. Careless.

He noticed that one of the pallbearers was lingering as if hoping to speak to him but not wishing to interrupt what might be private thoughts.

The monsignor's thoughts were indeed private.

'You! Young man!'

'Oui, monsieur.'

The youth came hurrying over. Melton noticed now that he had a limp. That there was no-one but the village idiot to do his bidding reduced the whole business to absurdity. In his halting French, he explained what he wanted. Then he told him to be quick about it.

'A l'instant, vous comprenez? Do you understand?'

'Mais oui, monsieur.'

Tonin was surprised by the monsignor's request.

The removal and destruction of a headstone seemed a strange thing for the warden to occupy himself with when, presumably, with Father Patrick gone and the new young priest to be briefed, there were many other and more important matters to be addressed.

Feeling the depth of the warden's anger, his wolf-senses told him to tread warily, not to ask questions about Marguerite's whereabouts. It had been clear enough that she had failed to change the warden's mind just as soon as the new young priest arrived to take up his duties. But Tonin had faith in Marguerite, and he was absolutely certain that if the path had been closed she would be searching out another.

Something told him that it would not be wise to ask the monsignor, as he had intended, to convey the news of Father Patrick's death to Marguerite. He suspected that the warden might not even know that she was still in London. With everything still at sixes and sevens, the warden could easily put a stop to all their plans. But where was she? It would soon be a month since she had gone, and he had been most anxiously awaiting news ever since.

But because he trusted his wolf-senses he held his peace and hurried off to do the warden's bidding.

When he returned with a barrow and tools, the monsignor was waiting for him in the heretics' graveyard to make sure that he made no mistake.

As Tonin levered the lichened stone out with a crowbar, he noticed that there were markings in one corner. The markings seemed to be a monogram, intertwined initials, carefully carved by a professional hand. A date.

The stone resisted the pickaxe, and he had to search carefully for a fault. He found it. With a sharp crack, the stone parted in two. The carved fragment split off as it fell. Tonin pushed the fragment aside with his boot, tucking it under a willow root. Whoever it was who had been buried beneath, their secret would one day be revealed.

'Again. Break it again.'

Obediently he swung the pick, and then again and again, breaking the stone until it was no more than a heap of rubble. Without the need for further instruction, Tonin shovelled the rubble into his barrow. Then he paused and looked enquiringly at the monsignor.

'Good. Now we take it down and tip it in the river.'

The monsignor watched the shards of stone vanish among the pebbles.

Nothing must be left to chance. Loose ends led to endless problems.

Until the lunch at Claridges, Ben had shown little or no curiosity about the manner of his mother's death, and for this Melton had thanked a merciful Providence. He had put the boy's lack of interest down to some infant memory of abandonment. No questions had been asked, so there was no necessity to provide answers, and Melton had been content to leave it that way. Suicide was unsettling, and Ben was a romantic. It was always possible that the boy would take it into his head to think that such things ran in the family.

Charles Melton made his way towards the room where the ledgers were kept. He used the hidden staircase Marguerite had discovered – as warden, the Hermitage held no secrets for the monsignor.

Halfway up the secret stairway, he stopped and listened.

The sigh of a breeze was like a rushing of wind in that silent place.

He made his way to the very top.

The door had had its uses over the centuries. It had once given directly on to a wooden platform which led on to the roof. Over the centuries the boards had rotted away, leaving nothing on which a human hand could get a purchase, nothing to break a fall – although to those who knew where to look the few cracked and battered spars bore witness to a tragedy.

The monsignor unlocked the door, looked into the void, and nodded to himself. No trace of struggle remained. No-one would ever know for sure what had happened that night.

This done, he made his way back to the lower doorway which led into the writing room.

He needed to refresh his memory on the exact content of Catherine Cuthbert's confession.

This entry was effectively a suicide note – convenient, as it happened, since none other had been left. Melton knew this because he had supervised the transcription himself, but in the light of Ben's new interest in dates and locations he wished to make sure that there were no loose ends. Today, having got rid of one piece of incriminating evidence he had overlooked, Melton wished to make sure that no further trace remained in the entry in the confessional ledger. Memory plays tricks.

'In the name of all that's holy . . .'

He stared down in disbelief at the pages of the ledger lying open in front of him on the table in the refectory. It was not what was written there, but what was most clearly *not* written there.

Frantically, his heart pounding with fear of what he knew he must find, he unlocked each one of the ledgers in turn. With trembling fingers he spread the pages. The sins of men and women forgiven, the slate wiped clean.

Practically speaking, how this had happened was a mystery he could not afford to unravel, since the unravelling would lead to discovery. Discovery would lead to explanations. And explanations would lead to the apportioning of blame. Charles Melton would be blamed. He would lose everything he had schemed and fought to win: his position, his value to his masters, the considerable income which somehow managed to make its way into his private coffers. Most certainly he would never be permitted to wear the scarlet robes he craved.

Disaster stared him in the face. All that was certain was that the thing had happened, and that it had happened under his wardenship. The best that he could hope for was that by the time the loss of the records came to light he would have gone to his own eternal judgement and could no longer be called to earthly account.

Shivering in spite of the warmth of the day, Melton locked the ledgers and replaced them on the shelves. As long as Charles Melton had charge of the Hermitage, the ledgers would be locked away and the key would remain in his possession.

The new young priest had been concerned by this, thinking it was his duty to take up the responsibilities of his residency in full.

'Would it not be wise to have a copy made, monsignor? I might need to open the ledgers, or remove them from the shelves. There might be a fire or a flood.'

Reminded of the previous fire and flood, one of the consequences of which had been that the library had been left open to the elements for several days, Monsignor Melton frowned and shook his head.

'Your duty is to the future, Father. You may safely leave the past to me.'

Tonin whistled cheerfully as he watched the monsignor's taxi chug away over the hill.

With Father Patrick laid to rest, he had no further business at the Hermitage. There was something about the place, with Marguerite gone and the village lying in ruins, which spoke of death and decay.

It was with a light heart that he made his way back up to the bories where his domed dwelling had been restored to its former modest glory.

Up there, all was new growth and hope. The flood and the fire had changed the upland landscape. The plateau was no longer a barren land littered with boulders, its meagre vegetation fit only for his goats. The river of primeval mud which had threatened to drown the domed dwellings was already misted with green. By next spring, what had once been a stony plateau would be well on the way to lush pasture.

Something new had happened – or perhaps it was simply that something very old had been reclaimed. It had always been a mystery why the original inhabitants had chosen to site their village in such seemingly inhospitable terrain. Now, with each passing day, new vegetation was springing up, and much of it from seeds which must have lain dormant for centuries.

It was clear that there had once been a time when the domed dwellings had been lapped by gardens and fertile fields, when there had been orchards and woods and pasturing for beasts on what was now no more than the bleak windswept uplands.

Seeing this, Tonin reconsidered the plans for restoring the High Pool, the irrigation channels, the terracing. It seemed to him that the monks might well have been the cause of the trouble in the first place. It might be that it was their labours which accounted for the vanishing of the valley's fertility, for the wilderness the uplands had become. It might have taken a thousand years to do it, but a thousand years was not so long when eternity was on offer.

He could see that nature had a way of knowing what was best for herself, of healing herself of the injuries of the past, of finding her own solutions to the present, of making her own plans for the future.

All that was needed, it seemed to Tonin now, was not the moving of mountains by machinery, or even the knowledge which could be gleaned from books, but simply those things which came naturally to a *ravi* such as he.

Miracles – that was all that was needed. A star in the sky to lead the way. If you believe in such things as miracles, you know that the Lord's intentions cannot be frustrated. He has infinite patience, and all eternity in which to exercise it.

Tonin, however, was human, and impatient for Marguerite's return.

427

37

Keeping Bad Company

'Fuck me with a feather, cunties,' announced Marguerite to herself.

It was going to be a Freda kind of evening.

She was fed up with being a victim. A victim was one thing Marguerite Dieudonnée Leblanc had never been. A victim was what Ben had turned her into almost overnight.

She examined herself in the mirror. She looked terrific. Tarty but terrific. She checked that the seams of her stockings were straight. Black stockings with seams meant sexy – one cool dolly bird. Marguerite was one sexy dolly bird, whether Benjamin Catesby knew it or not.

Things seemed somehow not to be going the way they had promised. Although, looking back on it, she was not at all sure what promises had been made. She had simply assumed that true love, once recognized and acknowledged in the usual way in which people showed each other that they loved one another, led to happiness ever after.

Instead, the week which had begun so wonderfully in Ben's arms, had ended in tears. Her tears – the tears of a woman who has loved and cannot understand that she has lost. And there could be no doubt that she had lost.

It had not been anything Ben had done. It had simply been what he had not done. The night following their love-making, he had made no move to invite her back to share his bed. He had simply stayed out all night and returned long after breakfast with Charlotte giggling on his arm.

She had somehow expected that when Charlotte flounced off, ending their engagement, that Ben was free. She had imagined that now they had found each other it would be happy-ever-after.

Instead of this romantic scenario, it seemed to be a case of 'see you later'. Much later.

The next evening it was she who arranged to be out. Thinking to teach him a lesson, she went out to a late-night movie on her own.

Things just drifted for the rest of the week. They did not even drift; they simply returned to normal. Ben treated her with casual indifference, as if nothing had happened between them.

Worse – Charlotte was being perfectly civil to her. She seemed to have changed her mind about Marguerite's presence in the studio. Ironically, since Lottie now had ample reason to insist that Ben show Marguerite the door, she now referred to her as 'the lodger', as if she had dismissed the notion that Marguerite might conceivably be a rival.

Ben, Marguerite reflected with mounting frustration, must have told her a pack of lies. Or was it lies? Was it simply the truth: that he had no intention of repeating what he clearly saw as a one-night stand?

And yet he had told her that he loved her. He had proved it, too, in the passion of his lovemaking.

It must be her fault. Something she had done. The only thing of which she could be sure was that Ben kept out of her way, giving her no opportunity to be alone with him. Perhaps he was bored with her – but how could it have happened so soon?

Marguerite was hurt and confused. There was no-one she could turn to for advice, for some kind of insight into the strange turn things had taken.

Freda had already warned her not to get involved with Ben. Elsie Potter, she instinctively knew, would be even more disapproving – and she was ashamed enough of her entanglement to avoid the old woman's telephone calls. George Flowers would scarcely be an appropriate shoulder to cry on; and, anyway, he was still abroad.

The final straw had come that very morning, when she had been made painfully aware of just how much Charlotte had to offer Ben.

'Darling Benjie-poo,' Marguerite heard her cooing, 'Lottie's bought him a present, just to show how much she loves him.'

Charlotte's token of affection, a gleaming new Aston Martin in what Marguerite considered a particularly vulgar shade of lavender, was clearly visible, replacing the scarlet sports car in the parking space outside.

Charlotte's voice floated through the open window. 'Benjie drive Lottie down to her mummy's? Lottie would love it so.'

Marguerite made a great deal of noise as she marched through the house. She had no intention of surprising anyone; that would be even more humiliating.

She popped her head round the door of Ben's living room. Charlotte was on the sofa as usual, looking like a cat with a bowl of cream.

'I'm off now,' Marguerite announced – unnecessarily, since she was clearly in her business-woman outfit. 'Got an appointment with George's accountant.'

'Have fun, child.'

The casual wave of Ben's hand and the reminder that he considered her a child plunged Marguerite into an unaccustomed state of anxious confusion.

When she returned from her meeting – George's accountant had been surprised by the thousand-pound cheque from Sir James Jarman – there had been a note stuck to her door to tell her that Ben had gone away for the weekend. Certainly with Lottie-poo.

The state of anxious confusion was replaced by something more positive: a state of angry determination.

She made a call to a young man she had met on one of her earlier forays with Ben. A not-quite-famous young actor who had just played second lead in a Fellini movie, he had the kind of good looks which could get him any girl he wanted – quite enough to make anyone jealous. Better still, he had pressed his telephone number on Marguerite. '*Call* me, kiddo. We'll have fun.'

'Having fun' was a polite phrase for all manner of illegal behaviour. Even Ben had warned her off. 'Bad news, child. Bad habits – even too bad for me.'

Bad habits suited her just fine. Bad habits were available that very evening, just down the road.

'I'll show the bastard,' she told herself as she slipped into the smallest of mini-skirts, the highest of heels and the skimpiest of tops. The black stockings were the finishing touch. She hoped they struck just the right note.

She made her way unsteadily on the unaccustomed high heels down to the Pheasantry – a tenement of artists' garrets and huge studio rooms populated by a shifting circus of photographers, actors, drug pushers, and young men with more money than sense. In other words, absolutely perfect.

By the time she arrived the dance music was already pounding out over the speaker system, the drink was flowing freely and the air was thick with the customary fug of exotic smoke.

'Let's twist again,' squealed Chubby Checker over the thrash of bodies.

'Where you *been*, sugar plum!'

All heads swivelled towards her as her host pushed his way through the crowd to greet her. He was as good-looking as she remembered. More so, in the frilled shirt and the tight leather trousers. Excellent.

She kissed him back. She would show Benjamin Catesby. She would show them all.

The dance floor was her natural territory. She loved dancing, she had always loved it, it came to her as easily as breathing, but this new music was different – she had felt it in her bones ever since the first moment she had listened to it on the radio in Ben's car.

Until tonight the music had been enough. She had needed no other stimulant, had always refused what was on offer – and there was always plenty on offer, just there for the asking.

She was already the envy of half the young women there – those who were not mooning around Mick, or staring resentfully at Marianne, or gawping at Sandie.

But tonight would be different. Tonight she would accept anything and everything. Anyone as well as everything. Anyone and anything at all, just so long as she could use it to hurt Benjamin Catesby. And, judging by the attention she was attracting with the way they were dancing, he would certainly hear all about it.

The studio was warm under the lights, and the dancing made her thirsty. Each time someone brought her a full glass, she drank it.

The actor was looking at her with a funny smile on his face.

'You wanna drop some acid, babe?'

'What's acid?' asked Marguerite.

'This.' He opened his hand. In it was a tiny scrap of what looked like wet blotting paper. 'A tab. Put out your tongue.'

She did what he asked. The paper tasted of nothing much, so she swallowed it.

She was dancing cheek-to-cheek now, and he was holding her so close that she knew exactly what he had in mind. Lumps and bumps in all the right places, if that was what you were after. She knew all about lumps and bumps now that she had lost her virginity. She giggled. She felt on top of the world. She was the world authority on lumps and bumps.

Those who were still dancing and not grappling on the sofas in the gloom were doing little more than holding each other up and swaying to the beat.

'Save the last dance for me,' swooned the Drifters.

'Feeling good, babe?'

She agreed wholeheartedly. Babe was feeling good. Something was happening, and it was good. Better than good, it was fantastic. It was all going on in her head, and it was fantastic. Beautiful colours washed over her, a rainbow of colour.

She was a flower opening to the sun. Her body was full of nectar. She was a blossom waiting for the bees. Buzzing bees around her, sweet as honeysuckle, rainbow-brilliant. She was floating on a rainbow, wild and free.

She loved everything and everyone, and they all loved her. She had an astonishing love for all things, all people, and most particularly the actor, who was no longer an actor but an angel.

She knew he was an angel because there was a halo round his head and wings on his shoulders, and because she had never seen anyone or anything so beautiful in all her life.

The angel said: 'Come here, babe.'

Marguerite did what he asked. He pulled her towards him and put his hands on her breasts. She liked that. She felt good about that, too.

'Wow, babe,' said the angel.

The angel kissed her, pushing his tongue into her mouth and grinding his teeth against hers so that they made clicking noises.

'Loosen up, babe,' said the angel.

Marguerite loosened up. She went so loose she found herself on the floor. The angel kissed her again. This time

433

she let him push his tongue right down her throat, all the way down until she began to giggle and had to come up for air.

'You all right, darlin'?' asked the angel.

'Wonderful,' said Marguerite, which was true. She did not even stop him when he nuzzled her breasts with his mouth, except that it tickled. She did not even mind when he undressed her. That was funny, too. Clothes were a bore. She felt much better without them.

The angel smiled at her. When he smiled there were little glittering stars all round his head.

'Some gorgeous chick,' said the angel.

Marguerite giggled again.

The angel said: 'Wow, man.'

Then he rolled on top of her. She parted her legs expectantly. She waited. Nothing much seemed to be happening, certainly not what had happened with Ben.

'Sorry, kiddo,' said the angel. 'Must be the booze.'

She was puzzled by this, but it did not matter. There were far more interesting things to look at and think about now. There were moons and stars and the shining tails of comets. Butterflies with enormous wings and huge round eyes which glittered and swayed. Birds, too – everywhere birds were singing.

She could fly, she knew that perfectly well, if only she could get the chance. If the angel had not been on top of her, she would have been able to fly.

Suddenly she was frightened. A dragon rolled towards her, belching fire. She was scared now, so scared that tears came to her eyes, rolled down her cheeks, trickled across her lips. The tears tasted salty on her tongue. She felt sorry for herself, sorry for all these people, the butterflies, the birds, the bees, the babies. Even the moon and stars were weeping.

Bitter bile rose in her throat. She struggled against it, tasting the harshness, the rawness, the poison in it. Holes for mouths and sockets for eyes, the black thing sitting on the fence.

'No!' she heard her own voice in her ears. And then 'No!' and 'No!' She screamed the screamings that were there, just waiting to be screamed.

She had to get away from the monster, but there were people all around her, pulling at her, dragging her back into the jaws of the monster. Silent screams vanished into the black darkness.

A hand slapped her face. A voice said: 'It's all right. Come back. You're safe now. It's safe to come back.'

Voices echoed around her. 'Bad trip. Wake up. Coffee, someone.'

'What the fuck?' said someone. 'The cops.'

A storm broke over her head. Lightning flashed and thunder rolled. There was light and voices, and banging and shouting. She was frightened. She searched frantically for somewhere to hide. She found a shadow, dark and comforting as a cave. She crawled beneath it. She felt like a little child, curled up in the darkness.

She opened her mouth to call for help, but no words came out.

Darkness fell.

'Miss! Open up, miss!'

Someone or something was banging on the door.

Marguerite lifted her head, and then thought better of it.

She was surprised to find herself in a bed at all, considering that the last thing she remembered was being very scared and hiding in a dark place to escape the monsters. She struggled to remember, and found nothing but a thick fog where her brain ought to be.

The banging was louder now. She pushed her head back under the covers. If she did not answer, maybe it would go away.

435

She must have been at a party last night. That much was clear. It must have been something in the drink. Nothing else could possibly explain the soggy watermelon which had replaced her head. Pink and black and rattling was the way it felt, as if someone had been using it for a football. Nor did she have the slightest recollection of how she had managed to drag herself back to her own bed.

If it *was* her own bed, which was by no means certain.

The banging reached a climax, then stopped abruptly. After a few minutes, she felt brave enough to pop her head out. She was not herself this morning. Whoever that might be.

There was a face at the window, framed by shrubbery. A female face popped up beside it. The two heads side-by-side looked absurd. The twin images reminded her of the Grand Guignol – the Punch and Judy show which entertained the children at the Valréas fair.

She saw nothing inappropriate in this. If Mr Punch and Mrs Judy wanted to come in and play, they were welcome.

The windows rattled. She waved back cheerfully, so that they knew she was going to let them in.

She suddenly realized that she was not wearing any clothes under the bedcovers. Naughty girl. She felt under the pillow for her *bleu de travail*. She remembered that she always kept it there, neatly rolled up with her valuables in the pockets, which was the sensible thing to do when you were travelling away from home.

She knew that she was not at the Hermitage, but she could not remember where she was. There was a great empty space in her memory where such things should have been.

Mr Punch and Mrs Judy might be able to tell her. Quickly she wriggled into her overalls under the covers, and then unlocked the French windows which led to the garden.

'Hello and good morning,' she said cheerfully.

Mr Punch and Mrs Judy were wearing navy-blue police uniforms.

'Miss Marguerite Leblanc?'

'Quite right.' She was pleased they knew her name. At least *they* knew exactly who she was.

'Detective-Sergeant Blunt, miss. And this is my colleague, Officer Mary Burgess.'

'How do you do?' Marguerite wondered if she should shake hands.

'Just a little look around, if you'd be so good, miss,' said Mr Punch. 'If you'd just step aside, miss. This won't take a moment.'

'We don't want to hang around on the doorstep upsetting the neighbours do we, miss?' said Mrs Judy.

'No,' agreed Marguerite, wondering who the neighbours might be in this place she could not quite remember but was beginning to think was perfectly familiar after all.

'We have a search warrant, miss.' Mrs Judy showed her a piece of paper. It looked very official and it had an address on it. 'So much easier if you co-operate, miss.'

She nodded. Of course she would co-operate. She was a co-operative kind of person. She just wanted to check the address.

'Are you looking for anything in particular?' she asked, playing for time.

'Just a little look around, miss.'

Mr Punch and Mrs Judy did not take long to find what they were looking for. In the foggy recesses of her mind, Marguerite wondered how it could be that they seemed to know exactly what to look for and where.

'This yours, miss?'

'This' was a small tin with 'Peppermint Humbugs' printed on it. Mrs Judy opened it to show her. Inside was a collection of strange items. A little packet of cigarette papers, a box of matches, a small knife and a large lump of what looked like brown sugar.

'I don't think so,' she said doubtfully.

She was not entirely sure of anything any more. Her memory was very foggy indeed. She was sure of one thing, though: she was hungry. A bit of sugar would be nice. She reached out, broke a piece off and popped it in her mouth.

'What did you do that for, miss?' Mrs Judy snatched the tin away quickly.

Marguerite chewed thoughtfully. The stuff tasted like ground-up goat dung, but she was not going to tell *them* that. She was not going to show her ignorance. She remembered the jellied eels. She remembered now that she was in London. They ate funny things in London. Maybe this was one of them.

'Try some.' She waved at the tin encouragingly.

'Certainly not, miss.' Mr Punch looked shocked – at least, she thought that was what he looked. It was hard to tell because he was busy writing things down in a note-book.

Meanwhile Mrs Judy was fussing around with the brown stuff. She tipped it carefully into an envelope.

Marguerite watched this in surprise. 'If it's yours, why did you ask me if it was mine?'

'No need to come the innocent with us, miss.'

Mrs Judy sounded annoyed. Marguerite did not want her to be annoyed. She wanted everyone to love her. She swallowed the chewed-up goat dung and fetched herself a glass of water to wash it down.

'Quite a little evening, was it, miss?' said Mr Punch.

She nodded. She could remember a bit about it now. She had been angry with someone, but she still could not remember who, except that it had something to do with where she was now.

It was being quite a little morning, too. Come to think of it, she could not remember how evening had become morning at all.

Someone must have brought her back here, to this place

which was becoming more familiar by the minute. But who? She found a name. Ben. Ben and Marguerite. Ben and Lottie. Certainly not Benjamin, the bastard. She knew all about him now. He was away all weekend in the country with Lottie. Cunt-ry was more like it. She giggled to herself. Much better. Her memory was improving all the time. It was a Freda-joke.

She tapped her head to make her brain work properly. Slowly does it. She started with the party. She had been having a lovely time until things began to go wrong and the monsters came and she had been scared.

She shivered. That bit had been horrible.

Then there were men in uniforms everywhere, and a great to-do and banging of doors, so Marguerite hid under something – maybe a table with a cloth over it – and when she came out again everyone had gone.

Not quite everyone.

There had been a kind man who had looked after her. She had needed someone to look after her because the floor was where the ceiling ought to be, which made it very difficult for her to keep her balance. The kind man had offered to drive her home in his car. It was not very far, but she had been very grateful, what with things being so topsy-turvy and it being easier to fly than to walk.

Fortunately the man seemed to know exactly where she lived, which was just as well since *she* certainly did not. She had had a little trouble getting the key into the lock of the door, and he had had to do it for her. She remembered now that he had come right in behind her, just to make sure she was all right.

This was not entirely necessary, since once she had remembered where the bed was she was fine. For some reason she was wearing nothing but a cotton bedspread – an Indian print in a becoming pink which might have been over the table under which she had sought refuge. This had made it very easy for her to undress. She could see a bit of the bedspread still sticking out from under the covers.

And then . . . For the life of her, she could not remember what happened then. Unless perhaps the nice man had left the brown stuff for her to cure her hangover. Yes. That must surely be what it was meant for. She was feeling much better now. A little light-headed, but certainly much better.

Perhaps Mr Punch would like to know this.

'I feel fine now,' she said. 'That stuff's probably a kind of medicine.'

'If you say so, miss.' Mr Punch stopped writing to look at her. He had a funny little smile on his face.

She added: 'The kind man must have left it for me.'

'Kind man, miss?' Mr Punch stopped writing.

'The nice man who brought me home after the party.'

Mr Punch wetted his pencil and began to write in the notebook again. 'Friend of yours, miss?'

'Never met him before in my life.' Marguerite blushed because she knew that this made it sound as if she would go home with just anyone. So she added: 'I was feeling very peculiar, you know. Come to think of it, I still am.'

'Don't you bother your head about it, miss,' said Mrs Judy. She was busy packing the cigarette papers and the matches into another envelope.

The effort of trying to unravel the meaning of all this made Marguerite dizzy again. Once again the room tipped over so the ceiling was where the floor was supposed to be.

'Miss? Are you all right, miss?'

'Perfectly all right, thank you,' said Marguerite from the safety of the floor. She did not point out that Mrs Judy was the one who was upside down.

'Come along now, miss.'

Mysteriously the room righted itself.

'Come along where?' asked Marguerite.

Mr Punch put his notebook away. The envelopes had

vanished into Mrs Judy's breast pocket. Mrs Judy had an ample breast and a large pocket with a button.

'All in good time, miss,' said Mrs Judy. 'They'll explain everything down at the station.'

'Station?'

'The police station, miss.'

'Why should I want to go to there?'

'They'll want to ask you some questions, miss. Now, if you'll be good enough to accompany us. Just bring your papers. Passport. Proof of means of support.'

'Support?'

Mrs Judy sighed, as if Marguerite had asked something very half-witted indeed. 'Do you have any money, miss?'

'Of course.'

Marguerite was indignant at this. Did they take her for a fool? She knew perfectly well that you needed money all the time in London, probably even in places like a police station. She patted her pockets. Her money and her passport bulged reassuringly.

'You can make a telephone call, miss,' suggested Mrs Judy. 'Is there someone who can vouch for you? Speak up for your good character?'

'Good character?'

'Someone who knows who you are, miss.'

Marguerite nodded sagely. Mrs Judy was certainly doing her best to be helpful, although Marguerite could not for the life of her imagine why anyone else should be called in to tell them who she was. They already knew that. Perhaps they had forgotten. Even she had managed to remember it now.

'My name is Marguerite Dieudonnée Leblanc.'

'We know that, miss. What we're after is a respectable member of the community who can vouch for your good character.'

Marguerite considered this. She was quite sure she must know respectable members of the community, but right now she could not remember any. Apart from Ben, who could not be relied on for anything at all and, anyway, was not a bit respectable in spite of being an earl.

In fact Freda was the only person she could call to mind, and that was only because of the Freda-type jokes which kept popping into her head.

Freda. She must ring Freda. Freda would know exactly what to do.

38

The Wages of Sin

As the owner of a Soho drinking club, Freda Winogradsky could scarcely be called a respectable member of the community. But she did consider it entirely normal to be summoned on a Sunday to vouch for a young woman in trouble with the law.

'Be right down, my darling duck.'

The surprise was that the young woman in trouble was Marguerite. And, by the sound of her, she was not in any state to look after herself.

'Keep your head down, girly. Don't tell the fuckers anything,' Freda advised her grimly.

Too late. Marguerite had already given the fuckers quite enough to be getting on with. The duty officer (female) and the desk sergeant (male, with a daughter of Marguerite's own age who was also a bit of a handful) had had a terrible time with her. Her inability to remember how to spell her own name, let alone come up with a convincing explanation of how she came by the illegal substances undeniably found in her possession, had left them with no option but lock her up in a cell to sleep it off.

Here she lost all track of time until the click of iron-tipped boots in the passageway heralded the unlocking of the door.

'Visitor for you, miss.'

The desk sergeant had brought her what he described

as a nice cup of tea. 'Two sugars, miss. Thought you might need 'em.'

She drank the brew gratefully. Her throat was parched, and she still felt light-headed. At that moment, another little nibble of the brown stuff would have done no harm at all.

When she had finished the tea, the sergeant led her to a little room with a table and two chairs. One of these was occupied by a woman in a brown tweed suit and a green felt hat garnished with a purple egret plume.

It was a few seconds before she even recognized Freda. And then she had never been more relieved to see anyone in her whole life. The parrot-shock of dyed red hair pushed into the hat, Freda looked astonishingly respectable – as respectable as Madame Blanchette on market day in Valréas. She flung herself into Freda's arms.

'Freda! I'm so glad you're here!'

''Course I'm here, my duck.' Freda waited until the storm subsided. 'Now, then, girly. What's it about?'

'For the life of me, I can't make head nor tail . . .'

'Slowly, my duck. From the beginning.'

Freda's presence calmed her. Marguerite did the best she could – given that her brain was still fogged up like a fish tank after you had fed the fish. She started with the party and finished with the discovery of what had been confirmed as a four-ounce block of high-quality Moroccan hashish, now reduced to three.

Freda allowed herself a snort of laughter at the sugar-lump story, then frowned. 'Just as I thought, my duck. You've been framed.'

'Framed?' It was not an expression Marguerite had heard before.

'Someone dropped the stuff and then tipped off the fuzz. Happens all the time down the manor.'

Marguerite struggled to decode this information, and then shook her head. 'Who'd do a thing like that?'

'If I'm not mistaken, the bugger who brought you home.'

'But I don't even know him,' Marguerite offered reasonably.

''Course you don't, cunty. What's the matter with you, girl? It's as plain as the nose on your face. You got fitted up.'

'But *why*?'

Freda looked at her pityingly and tapped her beaky nose. 'They're on to you. Out to get you. Just like I warned you. Something happened to warm 'em up. Could have been Jimmy. Who knows?'

The words sobered her up. Marguerite's brain was beginning to work again. Freda was right.

'Of course. Sir James – it must have been him. He wrote out a cheque – but only because I told him exactly how it was that I knew about his girlfriend.' She shook her head miserably. 'I lost my temper. I'm sorry, Freda. Didn't tell him you'd given me his name, though. Just the same, I made a mess of it.'

Freda's button eyes examined her speculatively. For two pins she would have torn a strip off her. But, then, the silly little cunt was in quite enough trouble without *her* adding to it. So all she said was: 'We live and learn.'

Marguerite was perfectly sober now. She said quietly: 'What happens next?'

Freda shrugged. 'They stitched you up good and proper, girly. They call the shots. Possession of an illegal substance. Possession with intent to supply. Possession with intent to supply with links to known criminals. Depends what they're after.'

'So what do I do now, Freda?'

Freda cocked her head on one side. 'You plead guilty, my duck.'

'Even if I'm not?'

Freda frowned at her impatiently. 'Especially because

445

you're not. They went to the trouble to plant it – they'll make it stick. My guess is it's a warning, or they'd have planted the hard stuff.'

'Hard stuff?'

'Coke. Heroin. Acid.'

Marguerite's head came up sharply. 'That's it. I recognize that.' She shivered. That was where the monsters came from.

'That explains it, my duck. Nasty stuff, acid. Wouldn't touch it myself. Stick to the old-fashioned vices – drink and fags.'

Marguerite nodded miserably. 'Sure and it was all my own fault.'

'Rule number one.'

'What'll it mean if I plead guilty?'

The button-black eyes narrowed. 'That depends.'

'On what?'

'The magistrate. In the morning, my duck.'

Marguerite's eyes widened. 'You mean I have to spend the night here?'

Freda reached out and patted her hand. 'Be all right, my duck. A night's lodging at Her Majesty's expense. Rest and relaxation, as they say in the business.'

'Are you sure, Freda?'

'Trust Freda. Guilty with mitigating circumstances – I'll do that, my duck. Pull out all the stops. Impressionable young girl. First offence, fined a tenner, bound over to keep the peace.' Freda patted her hand reassuringly. 'That's the way, my duck.'

The door opened to reveal the desk sergeant. 'Time's up, girls.'

Freda glared at him. 'Just a minute, cocky.'

She turned back to Marguerite. Fuck me, but the girl looked terrible, she thought. 'Keep your chin up. Here.' Freda rummaged in her bag and produced a toothbrush,

446

soap, a flannel and a hairbrush. 'Sleep it off and smarten yourself up. Freda'll be there in the morning. Don't you bother your pretty little head.'

This was the second time that day that someone had told her not to bother her head, but since her head was only loosely connected to the rest of the body the instruction seemed somewhat irrelevant.

As she followed the sergeant back to the cells, she hoped to heaven that Freda was right.

The crack of day brought a mug of tepid tea, a slab of bread smeared with something yellow and tasteless, and the news that she was due in court at ten o'clock.

She followed Freda's instructions to smarten herself up as best she could. At least her head had stopped spinning.

The courtroom was cold and grey. A few people, several in police uniform including Mr Punch and Mrs Judy, were sitting around on benches. To Marguerite's relief, Freda was already there at the back of the court, as she had promised.

A door opened at the far end, and everyone stood up. The magistrate – an elderly man in a grey pinstripe suit and what Marguerite had learned was an old-school tie – took his place at a long table at the far end.

'Is the defendant in court?'

'Yes, your Honour.' Mrs Judy indicated to Marguerite to move forward.

The presentation of the evidence began. Notebooks were produced and read from. Times were noted. Mrs Judy's two envelopes made their appearance and were duly entered in the record.

To Marguerite the whole business had a dreamlike unreality, and her mind drifted.

Had she but known it, she might have taken comfort from the fact that she was not the only one in court to whom the proceedings were unreal. The magistrate was also well aware of the Alice-in-Wonderland nature of what was unfolding.

He been quietly enjoying a restful Sunday afternoon in the garden when the minister came on the line.

'Bill old boy. Sorry to disturb you – day of rest and all that. Gather you're on the bench in Chelsea tomorrow. Something's going to come up. A young female. Name of Leblanc. A foreigner. Be grateful if you could handle it with your customary discretion.'

'Meaning what, Henry?'

'Get her out of the country. Pronto.'

'What's she done?'

'My dear man, I assure you you'll have all the ammunition. You know the ropes. We count on you.'

'We' meant the private club known as the Establishment. Politicians, judiciary, the great and the good. He did indeed know the ropes – a knowledge which had earned him more than one well-paid non-executive directorship of a public company. The Establishment looked after its own.

So they wanted the girl shipped out, did they? Whoever *they* were. You never could tell who started the ball rolling. It was like a chain letter. Tip the wink on the old-boy network, that was how these things were done.

The magistrate had replaced the telephone in some exasperation. The politicos never understood the necessity for following correct procedure, observing the proper form.

Left to his own devices, he set about observing that form.

'Will the arresting officer please approach the bench?'

Detective-Sergeant Blunt moved forward from the back of the court from where he had been observing the proceedings with unusual interest. He had reason to be interested. Not often orders came from the top as they had this time.

448

'Sir?'

The magistrate leaned forward. 'No previous convictions?'

'Nothing known, sir.'

'What do you intend?'

'Possession with intent to supply, sir. Possible links with known drug dealers.'

The magistrate sighed. The silly buggers always over-egged the pudding. Such a serious charge meant that he would have to recommend her for trial – judge and jury and all. He said quietly: 'I'm hard of hearing, officer.'

Sergeant Blunt hesitated. There was a hidden instruction here, reinforced by a small flick of the finger which proclaimed His Honour's membership of the same Masonic chapter. 'As you see fit, sir.'

The magistrate nodded. 'Most helpful, Officer. Please remain at the back of the court.'

He rubbed his spectacles thoughtfully. So far so good. At least the young woman had not had the wit to get herself a lawyer.

Better get it over with.

'Does the defendant plead guilty or not guilty?'

Marguerite hesitated, but Freda stepped forward quickly. 'Miss Leblanc speaks very little English, your Honour.' Out of the corner of her eye, Marguerite could see the flicker of surprise on Sergeant Blunt's face, but he did not intervene. Freda ploughed on. 'Miss Leblanc wishes to plead guilty to possession. Personal use only.'

'Are you in agreement, Miss Leblanc?'

Marguerite nodded. 'Oui, monsieur.'

'I see.' The magistrate glanced down at his notes, and then peered over his spectacles at Freda. 'I take it you are the proprietress of the Queen's Own Colonial Club of Beak Street, Soho, and that you are here to vouch for the defendant's good character?'

'I am, your Honour. If it pleases your Honour.'

'Continue.'

Freda tucked a stray hank of red hair back beneath her hat, took a deep breath and launched herself.

The magistrate listened impassively to the spirited speech in defence of an impressionable young girl who had fallen into questionable company. Marguerite winced while Freda explained that the defendant came from a family of unimpeachable virtue, pillars of the Church, and that she had been the recipient of the strictest of convent educations.

'I can assure you that Mademoiselle Leblanc's character is without stain. Whatever has happened is clearly no fault of hers. She is of the most respectable of families. Her parents are the closest possible friends of mine. She has been known to me since she was a child.' Freda warmed to her theme, dropping her voice conspiratorially. 'She's a French princess, you know. Lives in a château.'

'Very interesting, Miss Winogradsky, but scarcely relevant.'

That the young woman's apparel appeared more appropriate to a day's labour in the fields than to an afternoon at Versailles did nothing to convince the law's appointed representative.

At the end of the performance – and a performance it certainly was – the magistrate peered at the defendant. Young she certainly was – and could have been pretty if she had paid a little attention to herself. He wondered briefly about the minister's involvement. Maybe the old bastard had been doing a bit of moonlighting with the girl.

After savouring this thought, he brought his mind back to the discharge of his morning's obligations.

'Young woman, Miss Winogradsky's assurances that you have had the advantages of wealth and privilege make your appearance in this court all the more reprehensible. However, since I am informed that you have no previous convictions and have a perfectly good home to go to, the Bench is inclined to leniency.'

The gavel came down with a sharp tap. 'Fined ten pounds. Five pounds costs. The court will rise. Ten-minute recess.'

Out of the corner of her eye, Marguerite saw Freda's triumphant thumbs-up. But it was not over yet. The magistrate's voice rose above the general chatter and chair-scraping which followed this announcement.

'One moment, please. Will the defendant and the arresting officer please remain in court and approach the bench?'

'This way, miss.'

Marguerite found Sergeant Blunt's hand under her elbow. The magistrate did not glance up, busying himself with his notes until the court began to empty. Discretion; that was what he was there for.

Meanwhile Marguerite waited. A strong scent of lime aftershave emanated from the magistrate, and she was uncomfortably aware that she had not had a bath for two days. Just the same, Freda's strategy had clearly worked; she had been let off lightly, and she was beginning to feel all might not yet be lost.

The sting in the tail caught her by surprise.

'Young lady, a word of advice. Unless I have confirmation from the sergeant here that you have gone straight from this court to the Channel ports and boarded a ferry, I shall have no choice but to recommend you for deportation.'

He shuffled his papers together and stood up. 'In other words, Miss Leblanc, go home and stay home. Before you get yourself into further hot water. I can only hope that your parents will exert a greater degree of control over you in future.'

Marguerite opened her mouth to protest, and then thought better of it. She was about to explain that she had no home to go to, but it was clear that this would only lead to further trouble.

Had Marguerite had a good night's sleep, had she not entertained the wild hope that by some miracle Ben might turn up and rescue her, she might have put up some kind of defence. As it was, she felt miserable and lonely and very foreign indeed. All her plans seemed to have unravelled. Elsie Potter and George Flowers would certainly disown her after this.

When she looked round, even the battling doyenne of Queenie's had vanished, shooed out clucking like a recalcitrant mother-hen by a court official.

With Freda's departure, Marguerite was left with no option but to accept the return of her identification papers in exchange for a lift in an unmarked police vehicle down to the docks at Dover.

39

A Few Lies and Some Truths

Three days after Marguerite had been ignominiously shipped back to France, Mr Wilkins, the butler at Daisyford Hall, announced the arrival of a visitor.

'A female person to see you, madam. Most insistent. She said to give you this.'

The butler offered the silver salver to his mistress with the air of one who wished to convey his general disapproval of female persons who were most insistent, and most particularly of female persons who had to scribble their names on a scrap of paper, as opposed to ladies who presented their compliments on a calling-card.

Elsie Potter inspected the piece of paper. The name on the scrap of paper was Marguerite's.

'Is it Mademoiselle Marguerite?'

'Not exactly, madam. I believe an . . . *acquaintance*.' The butler's disapproval was clear in the hesitation. Elsie reflected that there was no-one more snobbish than servants.

'Show her in, Mr Wilkins.'

Elsie examined her visitor with interest. She had been waiting to hear from the child. In fact, she had been growing increasingly concerned.

Had she known in advance what Freda had to tell her, she would have been even more concerned.

After the hearing, Freda had waited for Marguerite

outside Chelsea police station. When she did not emerge immediately, she had gone round to Old Church Street to wait for her. Finding the place shuttered and dark, she had returned to Soho to take care of business.

The following day, she rang Ben.

'What the hell do you mean, she hasn't come home?'

'Just that, Freda. I don't know where she is.'

'What the fuck does that mean?'

'I think she's run away.' Ben's voice sounded miserable and contrite. 'I'm sorry Freda. A little misunderstanding.'

'Cunt,' said Freda. She knew exactly the nature of Ben's little misunderstandings. 'You fucked her, didn't you? And then you tried to wriggle out of it?'

Silence.

'Did you or didn't you?'

'Freda, I'm no good for her. I have nothing to offer. I'd only wreck her life.'

'You stupid bugger. She's worth more than that. Far more than that.'

'I know.'

'Then, what the hell did you think you were doing?'

'She's the best thing I've ever known. But I can't do anything about it. My godfather—'

'I hope it drops off, cunty.' Freda slammed the telephone down. She had never been so angry in her life. Nevertheless, none of this solved the mystery of what had happened to Marguerite.

Freda took a taxi to Chelsea police station. Here she learned the truth of what had happened from the desk sergeant.

'Bit unusual, isn't it?'

The desk sergeant agreed that it was.

'Know anything?'

The desk sergeant suggested that there had been a deal of toing and froing. 'Important people. Orders from the top.'

'*That* kind. I see. Thanks, Officer. See you right next time you come down the manor.'

This was bad news to Freda. Orders from the top meant powerful adversaries. Powerful adversaries could only be countered by powerful allies. Powerful allies were of no use if they were kept in the dark.

Freda caught the next train to Daisyford Halt and commandeered the only taxi to take her to the Hall.

She sent in Marguerite's name rather than her own because it seemed simpler. She was somewhat overawed by the size of the place, the superciliousness of the butler and – once she had gained admittance – the undoubted grandeur of her hostess.

Elsie finished her own inspection of her visitor.

'Since you are clearly not Mademoiselle Leblanc in person, I assume you bring news of her. Mrs . . .?'

'Miss. Winogradsky. Freda Winogradsky. Please call me Freda.'

'Indeed. Freda. I have to tell you that I have been most concerned about Marguerite. I had expected to hear from her by now.'

'You're not the only one, my old duck.' In her agitation, Freda slipped unconciously into her usual vocabulary. 'Silly cunt's got herself into a right pickle.'

Elsie received this information calmly.

'Tell me.'

Elsie listened to Freda's story with concern but without surprise. Marguerite had many things to learn; no-one learned anything unless they made mistakes. Clearly this was a catalogue of mistakes.

Freda was right: the girl had rushed in and made a fool of herself with Jimmy Jarman. As an old associate of the cardinal, Jimmy would have been on to him immediately.

She had compounded the foolishness by making an idiot of herself over Bobo Malvern's grandson Benjamin.

'Fuck me with a feather,' as Freda put it so graphically,

and Elsie could not help but admire the aptness of the allusion. Ben Catesby was a layabout, everyone knew that. The Lord only knew what she saw in him. But that, too, was to be expected.

She sighed. She, too, had made the same kind of mistakes in her youth. Her blood ran in Marguerite's veins. The girl was a chip off the old block, there was no doubt of that.

Elsie telephoned George's secretary as soon as Freda had been sent on her way, this time in chauffeur-driven style rather than in the rattle-bang taxi in which she had arrived.

The time had come to tell George what she no longer simply suspected. The only way to stop him galloping to the girl's rescue was to establish a prior claim of kinship. Then he would have to play it her way.

Elsie's way was the right way. She had never been more certain of anything in her life. For the first time for many years, her heart and mind were both engaged in Marguerite's survival – more than her survival, her success. She was like an old warhorse who scented battle.

She left a message for George to ring her as soon as he returned from Moscow.

'George, we've got a problem.'

George did not even return her call. He turned on his heel as soon as he read the message, and drove straight down to Daisyford.

'It's Marguerite. I knew it.'

'I'm afraid so.'

'Tell me. Don't leave anything out.'

Elsie told him.

'I'll go after her immediately.'

Elsie held up her hand. 'Dear George. Always so impetuous. I'm afraid you'll have to curb your desire to gallop to the rescue. There's more.'

'I'm waiting.'

'I have a prior claim. She's mine.'

George stared at his old friend, who was now toying absentmindedly with one of her orchids.

'For heaven's sake, Elsie, don't be so mysterious.'

'Not at all mysterious. She's Tom's bastard.'

George digested this cautiously. He knew that Tom Potter had been Elsie's nephew – her beloved brother's only child and her chosen heir. He sometimes wondered if Elsie's decision to remain childless had been because she did not want to disinherit the boy. And then he had been killed by a sniper's bullet in the last days of the war. He remembered, too, that it had been in southern France that the tragedy had happened. That fitted the story, but it was not proof.

'How can you be so sure?'

Elsie raised her head and looked at him steadily. 'She's flesh of my flesh, George. I know it in my bones, as surely as if Tom had told me himself. I'd stake my life on it.'

'You sound like a gypsy fortune-teller, Elsie. There must be something more.'

Elsie shrugged. 'For what it's worth, there is. A keepsake ring. A memento. She showed it to me. Said it was her father's gift to her mother.'

Elsie stretched out her hand to show George a heavy gold signet ring on her little finger. 'Just like that. Identical. My father gave us one each. My brother's went to Tom.'

George's gypsy instincts surfaced. 'What if it was a trick?'

Elsie's gaze was level. 'Unworthy of you, George.'

George stared at his old friend, then relaxed. 'You're right.'

'Of course I'm right. But it makes no difference. I know she's mine.'

'Have you told her?'

'No. And I have no intention of doing so.'

'For the love of heaven, Elsie, why ever not?'

The orchids received a little more attention while Elsie composed her thoughts.

'I believe she knows it anyway. Perhaps not the details – but I've reason to suppose she's guessed she's kith and kin. But it's her choice not to claim it. A matter of pride, I imagine.'

'Pride?'

Elsie nodded. 'She wants nothing she hasn't earned. I find that entirely admirable, and I don't intend to interfere with her decision.'

Elsie was silent for a long moment. Then she said slowly: 'I have enjoyed something all my life that I have not earned, and that has been a burden to me all my life. We who inherit are not simply hostages to fortune, we are prisoners of that fortune. We cannot choose our ancestors and we are at the mercy of our descendants. You may find that hard to understand, George, but I can assure you it's so.'

George put out his hand and touched her cheek gently.

'But what of Marguerite? She has a right to know.'

'None of us has a right to know anything – still less something as uncertain as the moment of our own conception. I know that I am not my own father's natural daughter, but yet my father is still my father. I have all I have, I am all I am, by right of birth. It changes nothing. You should know *that*, George.'

A shadow passed over George's face. Elsie knew him well – too well perhaps. He had confided everything in her, including those memories long buried in his heart. She was the only person in the world who knew his secret.

He said quietly: 'What do you want me to do, Elsie?'

'Do? Do nothing. Let the dust settle.'

'I can't accept that. I must at least go to her, reassure her of my – our – support.'

'You'll do nothing of the kind, George. Patience. I have faith in her. I expect no less of you.'

'Even so . . .'

'I absolutely forbid it. For the moment the situation suits our purposes admirably. It allows us – *you*, my dear George – to proceed with our plans without fear of attracting further and even more unwelcome attention. As things are now, the wolves will think they've won.'

'Wolves?'

'The ones in shepherd's clothing.'

'Ah. The devious Monsignor Melton. You think he's behind it?'

Elsie nodded. 'And behind him the cardinal – the whole thing has his teeth-marks all over it. Giuseppe's a Sicilian and proud of it. I imagine his methods are even less scrupulous than Charles's. It's my guess our little monsignor's having his tail tweaked.'

George grinned. 'The taller the hat, the bigger the bastard, as they say in the Vatican.'

'Your side of the fence, George. I never did hold with the left-footers.' Her expression grew thoughtful. 'I suppose it's inevitable the silly little goose should have jumped in with both feet. No doubt she wanted to prove herself. Probably to you, George. So you may feel in some measure responsible for encouraging her to imagine she could do it all on her own.'

'I did nothing of the kind,' protested George. 'All I did was suggest a few options. Let her know that she had my support.'

Elsie smiled fondly at her friend. 'I know you, George. You'll have tried to spoon-feed her. She's a baby, but not that much of a baby that she can't learn to toddle for herself. The young have to learn the hard way. Fall into a few potholes.'

She shook her head. 'I'm quite sure I'm right. We must leave our little Marguerite to work it all out for herself. She'll come to us when she's ready. If not, you'll have my permission to fetch her. But not until I tell you.'

459

'You drive a hard bargain, Elsie.'

'Not at all. You, too, must learn the value of patience, George.' She glanced at her watch. 'With that in mind, you'll stay to luncheon.'

After lunch, during which the presence of the servants dictated that intimate matters could not be discussed, George returned to the subject closest to both their hearts.

'What did you say the woman's name was? The one who told you the story?'

'I didn't. But I think it was Freda something. A club in Soho, I think she said. Although heaven knows how the child found her way there.'

'No! Not Freda? I wonder how she managed to get hold of old Freda.'

'You know the woman?'

'Indeed, I do. She runs Queenie's. It's rather famous, in an infamous kind of way. No doubt it was young Ben Malvern who took her there – Freda sometimes mentions him. She knew his parents – best friends in fact. Unlikely, I know, but something happened in the war, and wartime makes strange bedfellows. Freda's a foul-mouthed old harridan, but she has a good heart. I'm not surprised Marguerite turned to her when she was in trouble.'

'Why not to you? Or me?'

George looked at her, smiling. 'Under the circumstances, not the most sensible option. We had both expressed our willingness to help her. She wouldn't want to jeopardize that. You should be proud of her. I think she kept her head.'

Elsie considered this for a moment. 'And this woman – Freda whatever her name is—?'

'Winogradsky. A refugee from tyranny, like us all. Once a refugee, always a refugee. She used to run a soup kitchen for lonely immigrants like me. The food was terrible and the place was a rat-hole, but she'd managed to lay in a stock of perfectly drinkable Tokay and the company was stimulating. So when the lease of the Queen's Own Colonial came up I was fortunate to have made enough money to be able to help her.'

'You're a dark horse, George.'

'I don't always keep company with blonde thoroughbreds such as yourself.'

Elsie half-smiled at this, and found herself blushing. Dear George. Plenty of men still paid her compliments, but George was the only one who could make her blush like a girl.

She composed herself again. The sooner she got this romance on track the better. But the girl was still ridiculously young; she would have a long way to go before she could make George a wife.

For a brief instant, Elsie had an intimation of her own mortality. Men – and women – remained children until they were no longer someone's child.

She pulled her mind back to her earlier visitor.

'As I was saying, I rather took to Miss Freda Winogradsky. She's clearly lived an extraordinary life. Not the usual run of my acquaintance, but stimulating.'

'You never cease to astonish me, Elsie.'

'I shall disregard that, George. I have never been a snob. But I think Miss Freda could well be useful to us. From what you say, this interesting lady owes you a favour. Call it in.'

'How?'

'She can keep in touch with the child I didn't think it wise to bring the matter up myself. Tell her to do it discreetly and delicately – if your estimable friend has any notion of what those two words mean.'

'Freda will do anything I ask.'

'Good. Then, ask her.'

Part Five

1963-1964

40

Coming Home

Marguerite stood alone on the top of the ridge which commanded the familiar view. At that moment she felt nothing, expected nothing, understood nothing except that she had come home.

At first sight nothing had changed.

The Hermitage stood sentinel over the valley. The ancient citadel rose from its ochre precipice as it had for a thousand years, a monument to the pride and power of the Church. But now, in its isolation from the village and the valley which had once sustained its life, it served as a reminder of its indifference to that life.

Where once had been a village, with its Mairie and schoolhouse, its butcher's and baker's, its promenade for the matrons and *boules* court for the old men, was now a heap of grey stones with the purple heads of thistles nodding amongst the broken pavings.

The hillsides were scarred with the marks of a battle-ground, the debris of that fearful collaboration between heaven and earth which had destroyed the manmade terracings, smashed the irrigation channels, torn up the olive groves. With the summer's new growth frosting the blackened stumps of trees and the charred clumps of sage-brush, the valley looked much as it must have done in ancient times, when the soldier-monks burned the forest which had clothed the slopes, the better to keep watch against their enemies.

These things she saw with her eyes, but not yet in her heart.

The stream spread over the meadows in shallow pools which sparkled in the sunshine as she made her way down the ravine. The current was moving, sluggish and mud-laden, towards the wreck of the village below.

She increased her pace, splashing through the shallows and hurrying up the slope towards the heavy doors which stood, as always, on the latch alone.

She entered, calling Father Patrick's name. It seemed as if the place was deserted. She made her way up to the library – surely the old man would be there. The broken windows had been repaired, and the ledgers were still stacked in the bookcases, the rocking chair set ready to catch the last rays of the sun.

The place was dusted and swept, and there was a fresh ledger set out on the table. But of Father Patrick there was no sign.

Quiet as the grave, the silence frightened her. The fear – that cold clutch at the heart she knew only too well – led her to the graveyard.

Whether it was instinct, or that odd gift of under-standing which had been her mother's legacy, she did not pause among the sorrowing angels and smooth-faced madonnas. Instead, she made her way directly through the cemetery until she reached the iron gateway which led into a sunlit meadow beyond.

She struggled for a moment with the rusty latch of the gate. Then she glanced upwards. The branches of the peach tree which grew hard against the wall were loaded with downy fruit. Absentmindedly she reached up, selected and plucked a ripe fruit.

She cradled the fruit in her palm, feeling the warmth of the fur which veiled the flesh. Then, as so long ago, she bit into the ruby cheeks, allowing the juice to trickle down her chin, eating hungrily. After a moment she stopped.

Shaking her head, she dropped the half-eaten fruit to the ground, as if the sweet juice had turned bitter in her mouth.

She moved through into the meadow. Even though it was late summer, the daisies which were her name-flower were still in bloom – the snowy petals and smiling golden faces serving not only to bring her pleasure but also to remind her of what she had lost.

She gathered a handful and began to weave first one little wreath and then a second. The task did not take long, and it took no more than a moment to garland the pair of granite slabs which spoke of eternity. They were together now at last, side by side, companionable in death as they had been in life.

She made the sign of the cross and kneeled beside the newly turned earth.

'Holy Mary, Mother of God, pray for us sinners.'

She began the incantation as Father Patrick had taught her, and then fell silent. On this side of the wall, no Holy Mother might be invoked.

She had no tears for the dead. As always, she felt the rage – not against the dying, but against the crow-black thing which was neither angel nor devil but a mockery of both – a harbinger, a shadow, a mask of death.

There was a bitterness, a dark anger that she was once again cheated of that last farewell, never permitted to keep company on that last journey with those she loved.

The worms were the only reality. That was all there was. There were no candles to light the darkness, no stars, no moon, no sun.

'Marguerite?'

She raised her head at the sound of the well-loved voice.

'Tonin? Oh, Tonin, I've missed you so!'

It seemed that Tonin must always be there for her. His strong arms carried her back to the Hermitage. He argued with the new young resident over her right to its shelter. He, too, brought broth to strengthen her, flowers to cheer her. And finally, when she had gathered her strength again, news of the valley.

He did not ask her how she had fared on her travels. He knew her too well for that. She would tell him everything in her own good time. For the moment, he was eager to tell her what had happened in her absence.

He was eager, too, to tell her of the new plans he had made – but for this, too, he was wise enough to wait. He knew how headstrong she was. She would have to see for herself, understand for herself.

For the villagers, in the aftermath of the disaster, it had seemed to many that the only option was to accept what was offered, that the village and the valley could never be as they were, that nothing again would ever be the same.

Buses arrived for those who had accepted permanent relocation in the cities of Avignon and Lyons – some even as far away as Paris. For those who still refused to leave, temporary accommodation had been found in Valréas, and each day the people returned to their homes to salvage what they could from the ruins and see to their surviving livestock.

As the waters receded and the sun baked the mud to a hard crust which could be hacked and swept off the stoops and the cobblestones, opinion among the villagers began to polarize.

There were some among those whose property had not suffered as much damage as others who felt that the decision to abandon the place had been taken too hastily.

A week passed, and then another, and the memory of the disaster began to be replaced by hope, the flame fanned by Tonin's assurances that Marguerite was working on their behalf to raise the necessary funds.

Something might be done. This was closely followed by the conviction that something *had* to be done, and that Marguerite, with her newly earned reputation for miraculous intervention, was the one to do it.

The more stubborn of the villagers began to defy the evacuation order, and remained overnight in their homes. Among their number was Marie-Pascale.

Soon Tonin was most often to be found by her side, raking over and planting in the fertile sludge which had replaced the terracings, letting nature dictate how her garden should be sown.

The growing season was already well advanced, but the midsummer flood had brought a second spring to the valley, and the rich loam accumulated over the centuries behind the ramparts of the High Pool had spread over the parched and worked earth of the broken terracings in a thick blanket of fertility.

Marie-Pascale had green fingers; anything she set in the earth grew and flourished. To a herdsman such as Tonin accustomed to cropping rather than harvesting, this was a constant source of wonderment. What had begun as a practical alliance developed into a firm friendship, and from this friendship into love.

By the time Marguerite returned to the valley, Tonin and Marie-Pascale had already agreed they would be wed.

Marguerite knew nothing of this. And, knowing how much she needed his friendship, Tonin did not enlighten her.

Quite apart from Marie-Pascale, he had important matters to discuss with her – matters which he hoped would distract her from her sorrow over the loss of Father Patrick.

Tonin might be thought a simpleton, but he was a practical man. He put his trust in the sweat of the brow rather than in an all too careless Providence. This scepticism was confirmed when Marguerite gave him an account of what had happened in London.

Tonin looked into his friend's eyes as she talked. He realized with a pang of regret that the young girl he had known had vanished for ever. Whatever had happened to her while she was away, she was no longer a child. She was a woman now; it was to this that he must appeal. To her womanhood, her maturity, her ability to see to the heart of things – all these things were necessary for the success of his plans.

And Tonin had plans. Different plans from those which had been discussed with such eagerness with Father Patrick. Different from those which had taken Marguerite to London.

Revolutionary plans. Plans of which he was not certain that Marguerite was yet ready to hear.

Marguerite had more pressing matters to attend to.

The new young resident had allowed her temporary sanctuary, but he had made it clear that he had no intention of permitting this arrangement to become permanent. It was as much as his job was worth to do something of which the warden would disapprove. And something told him that this determined young woman fell into the category of things of which Monsignor Melton would not approve at all.

'Out of the question, mademoiselle. My superior—'

'Nonsense,' said Marguerite firmly.

Then she proceeded to explain exactly why the young priest should not bother his superior with such a trivial matter.

She had learned her lesson when she had confronted Sir James Jarman: to keep her temper, talk softly but carry a big stick.

It took the pressed daisies, one for each year, which had been found in the old man's hand as he lay where he had fallen, to convince him that there was good reason why the old man had chosen her mother's tombstone as the place to lay his bones.

'You cannot possible mean—?'

'That I am the natural daughter of a priest? Is that so shocking?'

'Mademoiselle, you know it is.'

'Judge not, that ye be not judged,' said Marguerite severely, in the certain knowledge that the young priest had just replaced Madame Blanchette with a younger and prettier housekeeper.

The priest hesitated. 'I shall have to consult my conscience.'

'Do that,' Marguerite agreed, smiling at the pink-cheeked girl hovering close by. The young priest coloured, and Marguerite knew that she had her knife in the hinge.

Fortunately the new resident had received instruction from the Jesuits. The brown-clad fathers were men of reason and compromise. He reasoned that, since the warden himself had been most insistent that he did not concern himself with the past, there might be room for compromise. What was this obstinate young woman but the living embodiment of what had gone before?

If the past was none of his business, he could safely ignore her presence in the present. This moral somersault completed, he consulted his conscience, as he had promised.

'Let him who is without sin cast the first stone?'

'Absolutely.'

Just so long as she kept well away from the guests.

'Nor hide nor hair,' Marguerite agreed cheerfully.

With this arrangement in place, she felt optimistic enough to send a short but dignified letter to each of her benefactors, Elsie Potter and George Flowers, to explain as best she could what might have seemed as if she had abandoned everything and literally run for the hills.

471

She had briefly debated with herself that she might use the death of Father Patrick as a convenient excuse for her abrupt departure – but immediately dismissed it. Father Patrick would never have tolerated her getting out of the consequences of her own mistakes with a lie. And most certainly not a lie in which he was personally, even if inadvertently, involved.

She gave no detail, simply explained that she had put herself in a situation for which she had only herself to blame, which had left her with no option but to leave for France. She would return as soon as possible, and meanwhile she was engaged in assessing the extent of the damage and finalizing plans for the work of restoration.

Barely a week later, a letter arrived from the bank in Valréas with the news that George's accountant had forwarded the proceeds of the cheque. The letter included a brief note from George – it must have crossed with hers – assuring her that the establishment of the Foundation was already under way, and that Elsie Potter sent her good wishes.

He also delicately implied that Freda had been in touch with Elsie, and he understood that there had been a little local difficulty. He was having the matter looked into by his lawyers, since it clearly would not do for her to have a criminal record which might prevent her return.

This had been a complication she had not thought of, and she was grateful. This assurance, and the arrival of the money, was a sign that her failure had not been absolute. And there was still some of Ben's winnings left – she had only Providence to thank that it had been safely tucked away in the pocket of her *bleu de travail*.

She made a quick calculation. They had enough in the bank account to restore the water-conduits, if the labour was free and all they had to buy was the materials.

*   *   *

She set off in search of Tonin to give him the good news, and found him at the borie village, where those villagers who had chosen to remain had pitched temporary camp.

Tonin listened quietly to Marguerite's excited talk of cement moulds and plastic pipes and electric pumps.

'We can start immediately, isn't it wonderful?' she enthused. 'We can replant all the crops. Not just what was lost in the storm, but the ones the monks planted in the old days, the ones in the records – the cherries and the strawberries and the melons and asparagus.'

Tonin said nothing, but his yellow-flecked eyes narrowed.

'We won't even need the monsignor,' she rushed on. 'I'll go to Rome – right over his head. *Make* them turn the Hermitage over to us.'

Tonin nodded thoughtfully. He was by no means convinced of the rightness of this plan. It seemed to him that the sooner the Hermitage was tumbled from its rocky precipice the better for everyone. But he did not tell Marguerite this; he knew how much it meant to her.

After all, she had been born there, she had lived there all her life, it *was* her life – all of her life that she had left. And now with Father Patrick gone, and the new young resident telling her what she could and could not do, it was no wonder that she felt so passionately about it.

'You'll see. We'll have our community centre, our land – all we need to make the whole thing work. All we've ever wanted. We can use the Hermitage to house everyone,' she finished triumphantly.

Tonin was startled by this Utopian vision. He might be only a goatboy, but he knew women liked to sit by their own hearth. Women in general, and Marie-Pascale in particular – although he knew perfectly well that this was not the right moment to broach the subject with Marguerite.

So all he said was: 'Not everyone will want to live all together, Marguerite.'

But there was no stopping her. She was like his bell-wether when she had caught a whiff of acacia blossom in a neighbouring ravine in spring.

'Don't worry, Tonin. We'll have plenty of money to rebuild the village – but all in good time. The *co-opératif* will employ everyone who wants to be employed, and the land can be owned by everyone. In a few years, we'll be the most prosperous valley in the *département*. They'll be queuing up to learn how we've done it.' She beamed at him happily. 'I'm – we – I'm certain we can raise the money.'

The thought of raising money gave her momentary pause. Next time she would have to be far more circumspect. Just the same, she knew she was right.

Tonin knew otherwise. All his instincts told him she was wrong.

He shook his head. 'It sounds so s-simple the way you tell it, Marguerite. But I'm not sure. I think there's another way.'

Marguerite was silenced in mid-flood. 'What on earth do you mean, Tonin? We've come too far together to give up now.'

'N-not give up. That's what not what I m-mean. Me and Marie-Pascale—'

He fell silent, knowing it was not the moment to broach a matter he knew she would see as a terrible betrayal.

Marguerite's green eyes were wide and dangerously bright.

'What about you and Marie-Pascale?'

'Marie-Pascale and m-me,' he said uncertainly. 'We've b-been thinking—'

'*You've* been thinking? What on earth about?' It was a rude thing to say, and rudely said.

Tonin's ears went red – reminding her poignantly of

that other time, a lifetime ago now, when she had sought him out at the bories.

The gold-flecked eyes narrowed, and the nostrils flared. She recognized his wolf-look. His cornered-wolf look.

'Tell me, Tonin.' Her voice was gentler now. You couldn't bully Tonin when he was wearing his wolf-look.

Tonin shook his head. He did not know where to begin.

Whether it should be with his friendship – more than his friendship, his love – for Marie-Pascale. Or – and this might well be a case of out of the frying pan into the fire – with his new ideas for the restoration of the valley's fertility.

They were not so much new ideas as the oldest ideas in the world. You could not find them in books. Unless it was those books which had long been familiar to him – the messages to be read in the scent of earth, the flavour of grass, the clarity of night sky, the colour of sunrise.

He was more and more convinced that the valley had to be given the freedom to bring forth her own fruits. That this alone was the way to create a future – for himself and for Marie-Pascale and for everyone else. Everyone, including Marguerite. Particularly for Marguerite, since she was the natural heir to those ideas.

Long before the Hermitage was built, the valley had sustained an ancient people, the people of the borie village. Their ways were the old ways, the gentle husbandry of a people to whom the earth was a mother, who believed that man and nature could work together in harmony and had no need to lock horns in an eternal battle for supremacy. The flood and the fire had revealed many of their secrets: the enclosures for domestic animals, the forest clearings where crops were grown, the middens where future fertility was stored, the copses which had been left as shelter for the wild creatures on which they depended for meat and clothing.

As for the borie village, that was living proof of their

skill as architects and builders: the domed dwellings had proved themselves far sturdier in the face of fire and flood than the mortared houses of the village below.

His observations of the altered contours of the valley and the pattern of regeneration which had emerged over the summer had taught him that the Hermitage and its dependants, far from bringing prosperity, had sucked it dry.

Tonin was enough of a *ravi* to recognize the light in the sky when he saw it, with or without a heavenly choir; enough of a simpleton to believe that what he could see others could be made to see.

The valley was already healing itself. If the valley had been a goat, he would have slapped its rump and sent it out to forage for itself.

Marguerite had respect for his instincts; she would – she must – listen.

Marguerite watched these thoughts flickering over his well-loved face.

What she understood – perhaps because it had always been Tonin's duty to show her the way – was that she must listen.

He had raised his head now, and was watching her intently.

'Marguerite . . .?'

'Tell me.'

With this gentle prompting, his increasing confidence demonstrated by the disappearance of the stutter, Tonin told her all his thoughts.

She listened with mounting excitement to his assessment that the disaster was no disaster at all, but a lesson to be learned. It was as if a celestial bulldozer had done all the work for them.

She did not, however, agree that the Hermitage was of no value to the enterprise. On the contrary, to her it was more of a talisman than ever.

Marguerite had always turned to Tonin for love and comfort. She thought it would be as before – that they would be good friends and daily companions, that she could take up their relationship where they had left off.

She needed him now, needed him more than ever. But there was an awkwardness between them. The awkwardness had a name: Marie-Pascale.

She had never been anything but direct in her dealings with her best friend. If he was not going to tell her of his own accord, she would have to coax it out of him.

'I know there's something troubling you, Tonin.'

Now he nodded, watching her anxiously.

'Is it Marie-Pascale?'

Again the anxious nod of the head.

'She's your woman?'

He hesitated for a moment. Then the words came tumbling out. 'I thought you had gone for ever – that I'd never get you back. I was so lonely. There was no-one left, and the work was so hard, and there were so many things to be done. And then she was so good to me, so kind. She really loves me – I know she does . . .' His voice trailed away uncertainly.

'And you, Tonin? Do you love her, too?'

'I do – I really do!' He raised his head, his face eager. 'And she loves me – she really does. It was you who told me she might be able to care for me – you remember, on the eve of the St Jean. And you were right.'

He hesitated, the eyes once again wary. 'We have . . . an agreement.'

'To be married?'

He nodded. 'Her parents have given their consent.'

Her heart lurched. She gazed at him, not knowing what she should say, how to cope with this new blow. Tonin, her Tonin, was to belong to another. For the first time in her life, she would be truly alone.

She reached inside herself for the strength that she needed. It was Tonin who now needed reassurance, her understanding, for his own happiness. He had not known how to tell her; it was she who had had to drag it out of him.

Her voice was gentle as she put her hand on his. 'I'm glad for you both. She'll make you a good wife.'

Tonin grinned joyfully and pushed his hand into his hair with the old gesture. The tousled hair and the slanting eyes once again belonged to the Tonin that she knew.

'I'm so happy you feel like that, Marguerite. She – I – I mean – we think we're going to have a baby. I didn't know how to explain to you.'

'What explaining is there?' She teased him, just as she always had. 'That you've discovered at last how babies are made? I think it may be a little late for that.'

Tonin's ears flamed scarlet.

'M-Marguerite, you're impossible!'

Marguerite laughed and blew a mocking kiss – but the gesture and the laughter masked a sharp stab of pain. Worse, a feeling of betrayal. Not Tonin's betrayal of the love she had borne him once, the friendship she bore him still – but the betrayal of the one man with whom she had shared the ultimate expression of love.

Marie-Pascale was not the only woman in the valley to find herself with child.

41

Love's Labours

If there was one thing of which Marguerite was absolutely certain in her uncertain world, it was that the child she carried would be born. And when it was born it would be hers alone, the first thing in her life which she could truly claim to have made. Now, at this moment, the sower of the seed was of little consequence – she was the earth which nurtured it. It would be flesh of her flesh, blood of her blood, bone of her bone. Hers for ever.

Marguerite told no-one about the baby at first – not even Tonin. And certainly not the young resident, who was flirting contentedly with his housekeeper.

Her own beginnings had been no more auspicious: whoever it was who had spawned her, it was her mother who had borne her. She was her mother's daughter. She, too, would have a daughter.

She would teach the child all that she knew. She, too, would run barefoot on the hills, feel the sharpness of stones beneath her feet, learn the secrets of the sweet-scented herbs which grew there. She, too, would have a tawny owl for company.

But what if she had a son? Ah, if the child was a boy, she would teach him to be wise and fearless, brave and free, and in time to choose his love and be for ever true.

All these things, the hopes and fears, the longings which nourish the soul, are those which mothers feel when the unborn infant quickens in the womb. All these thoughts had come to her on that first day, the moment she had felt that first fluttering, no more than the stirring of a butterfly's wings, which gave reality to what until then had been no more than a promise.

The days passed busily. Every evening, Marguerite would go up to the bories, where Marie-Pascale would have a *marmite* bubbling on the back of the stove, and there would be a savoury soup for supper.

Tonin was out all day on the hillside. There was no nook or cranny of the valley he did not know like the back of his hand, nowhere so overgrown in which he could not read the lineaments of the ancient cultivation – and every evening he spread out his charts.

As far as the day-to-day provisioning was concerned, the inhabitants of the bories settled down into a working partnership. There were already bees for honey, and the mountainside yielded plenty of wild greens. The baker and his family were among those who had chosen to take up residence, and the first thing the baker did was scrape out and light the ancient bread-oven. Marie-Pascale hoed and dug, and planted lines of carrots and potatoes, cabbage and leeks. Neat rows of chickpeas, beans and lentils waited to be dried and stored for winter. The vegetables attracted rabbits for Tonin's snares, and a young heifer would soon be ready to come into milk.

Marguerite resumed responsibility for curing the aches and pains of the little population, and began to teach her skills to the baker's youngest daughter. The settlement was tolerated by the authorities; but as yet it had no official recognition, and someone – usually Tonin – had to make regular trips to Avignon to argue with the officials to turn a blind eye to the formalities.

Visits to the library brought more information on earlier inhabitants of the bories. They had indeed served as a refuge for Marguerite's ancestors, the Cathar dissidents – a twelfth-century Leblanc was mentioned as a ringleader in an uprising against the papal tax collectors. Delighted with this, Marguerite found herself a new admirer – a young clerk in the *syndicat d'initiatives* who showed her how to apply for grants.

'Twenty acres for an apple orchard would attract a ten-per-cent premium, but if we plant apricots we get twenty. How about it?'

Tonin grinned and ruffled her hair. 'We can't get grants when we don't even own the land, *ma belle*.'

Marguerite considered the implications of this assessment. Tonin was perfectly right. There was a steady trickle of money from London, enough to finance the purchase of tools and simple machinery, but they needed to raise enough to buy the land.

There was always the threat that Paris would take a hard line – that they could find themselves evicted. And with winter closing down fast they would need all their slender resources if they were to survive until the spring. By the Christmas there were a dozen families in the borie village. The blacksmith from Pernes-les-Rochers had taken over the old forge, a weaver had brought up a spinning wheel and a loom. There were hens in the yard and pigs in the sty. To the inspector of rural dwellings sent out from Avignon, the bories could now be defined – as officialdom always needed to define such things – as a viable community.

A viable community required the attention of the men from Paris. The officials in Avignon, soothed by what they saw as the sanction of the Church since Marguerite was resident in the Hermitage, might be prepared to turn a blind eye to a few squatters, but a viable community was a matter for the big boys.

The big boys were not a matter which even Marguerite could tackle. The big boys were a matter for George

Flowers. It was time for the Foundation to flex its muscles. And so, in the fair round hand Father Patrick had taught her, Marguerite settled down to write to George.

George read the letter and got to work immediately. In George's philosophy, you never left till tomorrow what you could do today.

There was the small matter of her conviction for the possession of illegal substances. A criminal record was not a promising start to a career in fund-raising. He could fight it with lawyers, or he could fight it with cunning. For Gypsy George, the choice was easy.

Whoever had done her the wrong – whether the organ-grinder or his monkey – it was the pro-notary who had the power to put it right.

The cardinal's Sicilian habits, so rightly deplored by the monsignor, left him open to a little tactful persuasion. While Melton was devious – although George would go further than that – he was at least committed to working within the system.

If Melton was a crab, scuttling sideways at the first sign of trouble and only picking on those smaller than himself, Navarino was a shark. The cardinal swam in far deeper waters than even his masters knew.

George knew this because he trawled the same waters. It was not hard, through the more omnivorous of his associates, to come up with a list of His Eminence's unsavoury associates in the world of what could loosely be described as finance. These included launderers of Colombian drug money and profits from the Mafia's various enterprises in the New World.

This list, once compiled and edited, he discreetly pushed across the desk in exchange for a glass of the cardinal's excellent sherry. Just to show that he had done his home-work, this was followed by a file of xeroxed copies of bank accounts with post-restante addresses on various offshore islands.

His Eminence glanced down once. And then again. The only sign that this had disturbed him was the light drumming of his fingers on the desk.

'I imagine we have an agreement to reach, Mr Flowers.'

George nodded. He was a reasonable man. In business, there can always be areas of agreement.

'Your Eminence, far be it from me to interfere in the internal affairs of the Hermitage. However, I have to tell you that my Foundation is interested in the purchase of the land which, if my information is correct, has been turned over to the Département de l'Intérieur in Paris.'

'Your information is correct.' The cardinal's voice was wary.

'Inconvenient. Very. I am hoping you might use your influence.'

A pause. 'What have you in mind?'

'I've no doubt we'll encounter the usual difficulties. I imagine you have kept consultative rights? Rights of way and so on? Good. Then, you will be in an excellent position to be of assistance. Bureaucrats never understand practicalities. But they do understand the application of a little tactful persuasion.'

'Indeed.' A thoughtful pause. 'I can certainly use my influence. There are, as you suggest, reasons why I might hope to be successful.' A further pause. 'Any other requests, Mr Flowers?'

'One other. A personal matter. A certain young lady of whose identity I believe you are aware has suffered somewhat from – how shall I put it? – a campaign of harassment at the hands of your estimable warden. I'm sure you'll be distressed to hear that the worthy monsignor has been a little over-zealous. Some nonsense over a packet of – what's the legal phrase? – illegal substances.'

The pro-notary sighed. 'Dear Charles. As they say in this country, one's right hand never knows what one's left is doing.'

'All most unfortunate. There are circumstances in which one's left hand might consider it politic to undo what one's right hand has done.'

'E vero.' The cardinal sipped his sherry thoughtfully.

'It would be a pity to limit a young person's freedom of movement,' George continued smoothly. 'Travel does so broaden the mind; you are yourself an excellent example. I'm sure, for instance, that you yourself have had your mind broadened considerably on your travels?'

George waited. 'Excellent sherry, by the way.'

'Manzanilla. A common error.'

'Of course. Made in Sanlucar.' George named the little sea-port where the wine was made.

The cardinal smiled thinly.

'A case of mistaken identity. We are all vulnerable. Even your estimable monsignor.'

A pause. 'Charles is not always infallible.'

'Unlike His Holiness. That reminds me – please give my best to dear Giovanni when next you see him.'

This suggestion that his tiresome visitor was on first-name terms with the new Pontiff decided the matter.

'Leave it with me, Mr Flowers.'

'Good. Excellent. I leave it in your capable hands, your Eminence.'

As George bent his head to kiss the cardinal's ring, he observed that the proffered hand was as pale as laundered linen. And as he made his way out into the autumn sunshine he reflected that there might be some truth in the old gypsy saying, 'The whiter the hand, the blacker the soul'.

A thousand miles to the south, autumn had turned to winter in the valley, the scars of the battle vanished under a blanket of snow.

In the cemetery, icicles hung from the outstretched wings of the marble angels and the fallen leaves were frilled with frost.

Spring came. The ice on the angels' wings melted, to be replaced by snowy drifts of blackthorn blossom.

Spring was a time for renewal.

'A bun in the oven' was how Freda would describe her condition, and Marguerite realized how much she missed the old harridan's irreverent company.

So one day, when she had gone shopping in the market at Valréas and taken a little refreshment in the market bar, she telephoned Queenie's.

There was a long silence when Freda heard her news, then the line crackled back into life. 'Are you sure you want it, my duck? Because if not—'

'Of course I want it, Freda,' Marguerite cut her off before she could embark on a terrifying list of available options.

'Fucking nuisance, kids. But if you say so, girly. Are you all right? Got enough food, booze?'

Freda was nothing if not practical.

'All of that. All I need is a bit of advice. About Benjamin Catesby.' She hesitated, but Freda was too quick for her.

'Don't do it, darlin'. Let it be.'

She had known it anyway. For the first few weeks she checked the postbox, listened for the ring on the Hermitage's telephone which would tell her that he had changed his mind, that he truly loved her. When it had not come, she had gradually grown used to the thought that this baby was hers alone.

Freda had not finished.

'Besides, silly cunt's getting married on Saturday.' She cackled. 'Not that that ever prevented a girl turning up on the doorstep demanding her rights. But somehow I don't think you're the sort.'

No. She was not the sort. She never had been the sort,

and she certainly was not going to change the habit of her short lifetime.

She was not, however, in control of her own destiny.

The moment Elsie heard the news from Freda, she telephoned George at his office. Since it was still early and his secretary had not yet arrived, he picked up the telephone himself.

'Fig trees and fertility, George.'

'What the devil are you talking about, Elsie?'

'Freda describes it as "a bun in the oven".' Elsie waited. 'Are you still there, George? Good. You have my permission to fetch her home. At once.'

On the day Elsie gave George his freedom, Marguerite was already seven months with child.

As her pregnancy wore on, she had retreated to the safety of her old room at the Hermitage.

She was too wrapped up in her own being, and in the new being so soon to be born, to be of much use to Tonin. Not that he needed her. Marie-Pascale was expecting his child – due to be born at the same time as Marguerite's – and she had never seen him so content.

She no longer went up to share their supper each evening, but took a bowl of soup in a corner of the kitchen in the company of the rosy-cheeked young housekeeper – just as long as there were no visitors.

Every day, when the new young resident swung the bells to mark the noon angelus, Marguerite took her midday meal of bread and cheese to the heretics' graveyard.

She needed the tranquillity these daily visits brought her. Babies and dead people were safe – the first because they depended utterly, the second because they depended on no-one at all.

She was not alone on her daily pilgrimage. She had a familiar, a cold-blooded companion – a lizard, golden-bellied and turquoise-backed, known to the

486

country people as the Grim Reaper.

The name was partly for the faint skull etched into the smooth scales of its flat head, and partly for its habit of feeding on the insects attracted by the flowers placed on the graves.

Without moving its fine-patterned head, some sixth sense – perhaps because the young woman's daily visits at this time had accustomed it to her presence – told the reptile that no danger threatened.

Some women bloom in pregnancy, and Marguerite was one of those women. She carried herself with grace, barefoot even in winter – and now, in spring, she wore a loose robe, stitched out of some soft dark stuff she had found in the Hermitage's attics and which might, in that particular place, have been taken for the habit of a novice nun.

Had it been capable of such philosophical musings, the reptile would have found the presence of a pregnant woman in a boneyard no less appropriate.

Cemeteries are more full of life than of death, the one being fed by the other. Among the tumbling stones, kestrels hunt mice. Feral cats, tiger-striped, catch moles. Beneath the etched slabs, woodlice finish the debris the worms have left. In the high days of summer, swallowtail butterflies, patterned black and yellow as Chinese emperors, descend from the sky to sip sweat from the foreheads of the gravediggers who must sometimes do their work in the midday heat.

The Reaper, motionless and diamond-eyed, inspected its visitor. Had it been human, it would have appreciated the beauty her condition had brought her. The russet hair, cut short to frame the heart-shaped face, gleamed with golden lights. The skin glowed with the soft tints of a ripe apricot, the green eyes sparkled.

The lizard, either through curiosity or through force of habit, took up a new position on the top of the wall above the gateway, waiting for his companion to pass through.

Had he been aware of such things, the Reaper would have seen that there were tears in her eyes. But the cold-blooded reptile did not know the meaning of tears, had no knowledge of mortality, neither took thought for the future nor felt sorrow for the past.

Not so Marguerite. She leaned back against the warm stone of the wall beside the double grave, and lifted her face to the warmth of the sun.

Above her, the Reaper stood sentinel. He, too, needed the sun's rays to warm his cold blood. Although neither watcher nor watched yet knew it, today the lizard was not the only witness to her sorrow. There was an intruder in the cemetery, but he was in no hurry to make his presence known.

She carried a fatherless child. Yet even that was a lie: no child is ever fatherless. It would be truer to say that she, as her mother before her, carried a child whose father, through circumstance or choice, chose not to acknowledge his fatherhood.

The lizard stared beyond her, unblinking.

It was a matter of choice for the father, but not for the mother. She closed her eyes. Lulled by the hum of insects, the gurgle of the stream, the chatter of a fall of goldfinches feeding on the thistles, her mind drifted to thoughts of the men in her life. One belonged to the past, the other to the present, the third – although she did not yet understand this – to the future.

Benjamin Catesby, her childhood sweetheart Tonin, George Flowers. Each in his way had been – was – would be – as necessary to her as earth and water and air are to a young plant, still pushing down its roots and spreading its infant leaves before coming to the real business of living: the survival of its genes through the multiplication of the species.

Neither the reptile nor Marguerite herself heard the approaching footfalls. The Reaper, unblinking even in sleep, relied more on his keen eyesight than on his hearing.

The lizard did not need to move his flat-scaled head to know that an unfamiliar element had entered his private world. Nevertheless, he was in no hurry to yield his vantage point.

He waited until the human disturbance had broken his circle of territory before making his escape with a flick of his tail on the pebbles.

The rattle of the pebbles was the first Marguerite knew of the intruder's presence.

No intruder at all – but George Flowers, come to claim his woman.

42

New Life at Daisyford

Elsie flung open her house, her arms and her heart to Marguerite. And Marguerite, with the Hermitage a lonely place, and Tonin busy with his new wife and the practical affairs of the valley, was glad to be made welcome.

'You shall have everything money can buy, my dear – at least I can offer that. Think of it as a kindness to me. Indulge a selfish old woman. I shall be glad of your company – and you will most certainly need mine.'

George Flowers came and went without ceremony, always the dark face smiling, always with some new and wonderful stories of the glamorous world in which he moved. She never knew when the big blue Bentley would draw up in the drive, and Gypsy George would come to find her in the little sitting room Elsie Potter had given her for her use, his arms bulging with presents.

'You must be mistaking me for a fancy lady, George. And me no more than a simple country girl.'

'For the moment, perhaps.'

He laughed at her then, white teeth bright against the dark skin. She felt easy with him now, and secure. She had never felt secure with Tonin, still less so with Ben Catesby, fading now in her memory.

Gypsy George. Tinker George. One thing at least he shared with the father of her unborn child – he had excellent taste. She loved the luxury of the beautiful things he brought back from his travels. From India, saris made of gold-embroidered silks in jewel colours, and the finest cashmere shawls. A glorious Berber wedding garment made of thick black satin embroidered in scarlet – loose and romantic. Pure white pashmina shawls and tiny garments stitched by Spanish nuns for the child now stirring in her womb.

Marguerite sometimes wondered why George was so good to her. In return, she could offer so little. For certain there must be a thousand women much more rewarding than she to claim his attention.

'Are you sure, George?'

'Sure of what, my dear?'

'That you can be bothered with me. I think I've caused you nothing but trouble.'

He looked at her then in the strange gypsy way he had, as if he took infinite pride in her, as if she was the most precious thing in all the world.

At such moments, her heart lifted, and she wondered how she would ever have survived without him. Sometimes, when they were sitting by the fire in the library at Daisyford, with Elsie busy about her papers, he would sit on the floor beside her and put his hand against her belly, feeling the movement of the baby within, smiling to himself.

George was very firm that she should not tire herself out with Hermitage affairs.

'Tonin and I can manage very well without you at present, my dear. That young man has some excellent ideas; I'm having them analysed by the natural-resource people at Harvard. You chose your lieutenant well. You must relax. You've quite enough on your hands without worrying about what's going on in the outside world.'

'Just as soon as the babies are born—'

'Babies?'

'Two babies.'

George stared at her in bewilderment; then he threw his

head back and laughed aloud. There was such joy in the laughter that Marguerite could not help teasing him.

'George, if I didn't know I couldn't in all honesty pin the blame on you, I would!'

George stopped laughing immediately. His face suddenly serious, he took her hands in his.

'Marry me, then.'

'George, dear George, there's no need to make an honest woman of me. I'm well able to take care of myself – and the babies. Elsie's doing an excellent job of providing all the things I can't.'

'I know that perfectly well. And I am perfectly happy to wait. But I need you to know the offer's on the table.'

'Thank you, George. Dear George.'

Marguerite's voice held a tenderness which made him, not for the first time, long to be the gypsy he really was, to sweep her up in his arms and make her his woman, pregnant or not, marriage or not. George knew that she would one day be his, and with this – for the moment at least – he must be content.

Meanwhile Marguerite was cocooned in luxury at Daisyford.

Hilda Humphreys requested permission from Miss Potter to change the nature of her duties.

'Do I understand you're applying for the post of nursemaid, Humphreys?'

'I have that in mind, madam.'

'Do you indeed? And who will care for the old lady?'

'I have that all under control, madam, if you please.' Hilda's face was eager. 'There's my niece Mary has received her training at Monsieur Worth. I'm sure that if I keep a careful eye on her she'll find her feet in no time.'

'So it's a foregone conclusion?'

'Yes, madam,' said Hilda firmly, but only because her employer was smiling. Miss Potter seemed to do a great deal more smiling now that Marguerite was around.

Hilda took to her self-appointed role with gusto. She replaced her neat little black dress with a navy-blue uniform and a starched apron for wear around the nurseries.

She took her responsibilities to the expectant mother even more seriously, nagging Marguerite to have porridge for breakfast instead of her preferred croissant with *café au lait*, and making sure she got plenty of what she called fresh-air-and-exercise. This was a new notion for Marguerite, to whom the concept scarcely needed definition.

Hilda even found a pair of tattered land-girl overalls to match Marguerite's *bleu de travail* – she still found these comfortable country wear, particularly now that she had a swelling belly to carry – and the two women would take long walks through the leafy spring woods. For the rest of the time, Hilda fussed in the nurseries and hauled baby necessities down from the attics, stitching and knitting what she considered to be lacking.

Easter came, and the world was green and new. The babies were due in April, when the lambs were in the fields and all of nature was giving birth.

The first contraction was a mere tightening of the belly muscles – a warning, no more. Marguerite did not even call for Hilda, so sure was she that it was nothing at all.

After half an hour, with no further twinges, Marguerite was sure she had been mistaken. Then came another contraction. This time there could be no mistake. This time she went to find Elsie.

'I think we're on our way.'

Marguerite, midwife to so many both human and animal, knew everything and nothing about how babies are born. All life comes into being this way, in blood and pain, the agony forgotten in the joy of birth.

She knew that labour is never easy, harder still if it is the first time. And even harder if the labour is for twins.

The flesh is so fragile, the bones so brittle, the body must learn so quickly to bend to the inevitable.

But this, this was something she had never imagined. The pain came in waves, leaving her breathless. It was as if a thousand cannon balls were pressing down on the hard tunnel of bone.

She knew she must give in, let herself float on the waves of tightening muscles, breathing quickly and rhythmically to conserve her strength.

The babies were born on each side of midnight. First one, and then the other, five minutes between, one the last of the night, the other the first of the day. Two tiny infants to cradle in her arms, to sing the lullabies of her own babyhood. The language, even the song itself, is of no importance; it is the love alone which soothes – the mother as much as the infant.

Elsie stayed with her all through the labour, her back straight, her chin tilted as she ordered the hospital doctors and nurses around as if they were the below-stairs staff at Daisyford.

'Over here – come along now. No dawdling. Didn't Doctor tell you? Look sharp.'

For the childless Elsie, it was the closest she had ever come to the miracle of birth. And she knew it was a miracle, her miracle as well as Marguerite's.

The first cry of the newborn infant tears at the heartstrings, can never be forgotten. The birth-cry was familiar to Marguerite, exhausted after her labours. She had heard it many times before. The fear is there, and the pain, and the agony, too – but most of all, and last of all, the joy.

'Home tomorrow,' said Elsie firmly. 'Hospital is no place for the living.'

The day after their return to Daisyford – Elsie had forbidden him on pain of exile to come any earlier – George arrived from London with armfuls of lilies, his face wreathed in smiles.

494

'How're my beauties?' The dark curly head bent over each child in turn; the hands lifted the babies so gently, with such tenderness, that Marguerite felt her heart turn over, felt herself being swept up in the whirlwind of George's enthusiasm. Of all the infants ever born, the tiny girl was the most beautiful and brilliant, the baby boy the most handsome and clever.

If ever she could love George, she loved him then.

For George, Marguerite was the mother of his children. Strangely for one of his breeding, he was not a jealous man. Perhaps it was not in his nature; perhaps as a child he had seen too much of the misery it caused among his own people. The Romanies are a proud race, quick to take offence and even quicker with the knife, and quarrels over women always ended badly.

But there was another reason why George was glad, a darker reason which had to do with the experiments conducted on boy-children in Hitler's concentration camps. The gypsies no less than the Jews were considered vermin. George had always known that he would never hold a child of his own in his arms.

The only living person who knew of this was Elsie. And now the woman he loved had given him children. Had such a thing been possible, he would not have put it past the scheming old witch to set it up in the first place.

George had no need to enquire after the identity of the father of Marguerite's children. He knew because Freda had told him.

She had not meant to tell him, but it just slipped out one day when he had been plying her with her favourite tipple – *crème de menthe* with a chaser of Veuve Cliquot. Freda loved the Widow, but she never drank her own cellar unless someone else was paying for it.

The news that the biological father of Marguerite's children was the Earl of Malvern came as a considerable relief. George had seen the wedding pictures in the papers.

This at least indicated that Ben Catesby had no intention of laying claim to his bastard children.

The christening was in the chapel at the end of the garden, conducted by an amiable old vicar who held his living from the family. Hilda had looked out the family christening robes – there had been twins born at Daisyford before – miraculous drifts of lace and lawn.

'None of that papist nonsense,' said Elsie as she held up first one and then the other of the infants to the font.

Freda insisted on standing godmother to both, arriving in a huge Daimler commandeered from one of her bemused customers, and wearing an extraordinary hat with ostrich plumes. Naturally she drank far too much of Elsie Potter's best champagne.

'There's always a first time, my darlin' duck.'

George played the part of the proud father, and Marguerite realized that there was nothing she could do about it – that this was to be his chosen role.

Elsie had already made her plans.

'I intend to turn over the entire west wing to you and the babies, Marguerite. You will have your own establishment. Humphreys – I suppose I must call her Nanny now – will enjoy being queen of the roost. You will be perfectly independent. You may come and go about your business as you please. George will tell you that one of the joys of Daisyford has always been that it is so convenient for London.'

Elsie did not intend that Marguerite should turn over her life to her children. She was too valuable for that. There would be much to do if they were to succeed. Marguerite had the vision, George had the muscle, and under Tonin's direction the details were rapidly dropping into place.

Power and influence could only be wielded from a position of strength. Elsie meant to give her that.

What Marguerite did not yet know, lost in her dreamy

world of motherhood, was that she was already set on the path to power.

The twins, Rosie and Robert (named at Elsie's suggestion for her long-dead brother) were not in the least identical.

The physical differences were the most obvious. Robbie was as dark as Rosie was fair. Rosie's eyes were as blue as the sky, while Robbie's were a soulful brown. Robbie was of an even disposition, placid and sweet-natured, while Rosie clenched her little fists and yelled herself hoarse. was wakeful, Robbie slept through till morning. These differences became more apparent as they flourished under Hilda's care – Nanny Potter, as she had now become. Rosie's was the first tooth, while Robbie was the first to form a word – 'dada' or 'mama', no-one quite knew which, although George was perfectly certain it was the former.

Rosie could never be induced to stay in one place, while Robbie would spend hours in his playpen amusing himself. 'Stop that, Rosie. Come on, Robbie,' echoed down the corridors of Daisyford. Mrs Crabtree was enchanted with their appetites, and even the stern Mr Wilkins allowed them to play in the pantry, banging the silver spoons and rattling the ivory pepper mills.

When the babies had passed their first year – Mrs Crabtree's twin birthday cakes were a triumph – Elsie sought out Marguerite in the nurseries.

'We have matters to discuss, Marguerite. Come to me in the library when you've settled the children.'

Marguerite found the old woman in her usual place, perched on her high chair at the end of the orchid-laden table, in the beautiful room where they had first met.

Elsie waved Marguerite to a chair by the window.

'Sit there, Marguerite, where I can see you.'

Eighty years was long enough, and Elsie Potter was tired. Tired in the body and tired in the spirit. She had put her house in order, there were children in the nursery, and the two people she loved most in the world had found companionship in each other. She had wished it could have been more than that, but Marguerite was wary of any new entanglement. She had been too hurt, too much abandoned by those she loved to give her heart again.

'Let me tell you, child, some things I have learned in my life. As you know, I have no children of my own. Maternity is not something of which I have any direct experience, but I have watched others make the mistakes all women make. You are not all women, and I have no intention of permitting you to behave as other women. I have no doubt you will discharge your duty to your children with all the care your loving heart can bring. But I must warn you not to live your life through your children.'

She paused thoughtfully, her hands playing with one of the magnificent orchid blooms.

'You are who you are, Marguerite – and I intend you should remain so. I mean to give you the freedom to know that every day you can decide exactly what you wish, without the restrictions of money or the obligation to discharge your responsibility to your ancestors. That's something which has plagued me all my life. Perhaps I might have been more than I am had I learned that lesson sooner. But for you it will be different. You will have none of those obligations. Your duties lie elsewhere – to the vision you have.'

She raised her hand to indicate that she had not yet finished.

'That's the the reason I leave you my house, my lands, my fortune to do with what you will.'

Marguerite sat perfectly still. George had warned her that this might be Elsie's intention, but she had not believed him for a moment. Now, confronted with the reality, she felt many things – hope, joy and fear. Above all, the fear of what she was being asked to accept.

'Elsie—'

'No. Don't speak to me yet. I have no wish to know the first thoughts which rush into your head.'

She stopped, composed herself, and continued: 'You will be fearful; that's to be expected. And you will feel elation. And no doubt you will also feel gratitude. Please remember that I need no thanks. I expect no protestations of unworthiness. I am selfish enough to know exactly what I want – as I am fond of telling George.'

The old woman drummed her fingers on the table. 'And don't let any of my family persuade you that I've not left them well provided for. There's not one who hasn't had what's due in my own lifetime, and they can have no claim on my estate after I am dead. There'll be no need for lawyers to pick over my bones. I've had myself declared – what do they call it? – *of sound mind*, just to avoid trouble over the will.'

A smile lit her face. 'You can do that, you know. I had no idea, but it was George who arranged it. I think he found it rather amusing, since he has never considered me anything but a self-indulgent old madwoman.' The smile broadened. 'He's right of course. And because I don't trust you, any more than you should trust yourself, I have entrusted you to George. He will be your trustee. Sooner or later, he will make you his wife.'

'George? I—'

But Elsie's hand came up again to stop her protests. 'Treat him gently, Marguerite. He loves you, and I think you love him, too – although you're too foolish to know it yet. Either way, he's yours.'

The voice stopped, the head bowed, the face in shadow.

'Plant the seeds from my fig tree in the valley when your work is done. In a thousand years they will flourish.'

Marguerite started to her feet then, suddenly concerned

499

for the old woman. 'What are you saying, Elsie? There's so much to be done. Enough for a lifetime.'

'Your lifetime, child, not mine.'

Another pause. This time the old woman lifted her face to the light of the window so that Marguerite could clearly see that there were tears in her eyes.

'One other thing. I'd like orchids on my grave, just for old times' sake.'

'Elsie!' Marguerite's voice was choked with tears. 'I won't let you go!'

As if to give substance to her words, she seized the gnarled old hands in hers, gripping them tightly, her tears splashing on the fragile freckled skin.

But Elsie gently detached herself. 'This is not goodbye, my dear. Simply *au revoir*. I shall visit you when you need me. I'll be a benevolent ghost; you won't find me wailing in the attics at midnight. No closer than the fig tree. But there you'll find me. If you have patience, I will come to you.'

Marguerite shook her head. It was there now, in the corners of her mind, crow-black fear. She turned away, buried her face in her hands.

'No!'

But the voice would not let her go. 'There's another reason I can ask this of you, my child. We have not spoken of it, and I do not intend to speak of it now – unless it is to say that I would appreciate it if you would wear your mother's ring. You have earned the right to it, and I would not like to think that you were not aware that I knew of it.'

Marguerite raised her head, startled. 'How long have you known?'

Elsie smiled gently. 'From the first day, child.'

Marguerite hesitated. 'I never meant that you should suspect. Is that why—?'

'I have done what I have done? No!' Fiercely the old

woman shook her head. Then, more softly, added: 'Perhaps. Who knows? But I am glad of it. Content that it should be so – that there are the ties of blood which bind us.'

Marguerite's mind tumbled. So quick. So final. It was everything and yet it was nothing – this unknown father that her mother had not even acknowledged. A blank page which now had a name. The daisies. Was that the meaning of the daisies, her name-flower? No. That was a secret her mother shared with Father Patrick. Was there more? More. Far more. This had been his home. Her father's home, now hers. He would have been a grandfather to her children. She shook her head. That was fantasy. What was he like? Who had he loved? Why had it happened? What did he look like? There was so much she needed to know. So much that Elsie could tell her.

All this time, as the thoughts tumbled through her head, Elsie's hands held hers. There was gentleness there, the fingers light, as if she was caressing one of her beloved flowers. To Marguerite it seemed as if the old woman could see into her mind, had made the journey with her. Now a gnarled hand came up to Marguerite's cheek.

'What good would it do to know all those things, my dear? If you insist, Hilda will show you the old photograph albums; she's always been the one to keep them up to date. If I wanted to know which of my aged contemporaries had died, Hilda would always have clipped the obituary. I prefer the living; there's all eternity to keep company with the dead.' She shook her head. 'No, my dear, there is no need to search for the past; it is with you always in your children. They will teach you all you need to know. You have no need of archives and faded family portraits to tell you what you can feel in your own heart.'

The voice stopped; then continued: 'I can tell you all you need to know about the young man who fathered you, but I shall not. Had your mother wished it, had she known anything she wished you to know, she would surely have told you. You – and I – must respect her wishes. As for me, I can tell you that my nephew, your father, was kind, honourable and brave. All the things a woman admires in a man. I meant to make him my heir. You must accept that, had he known you, he would have loved you, as I do.'

She sighed. 'He was so young when he died, scarcely more than a child. And if you are wise, my dear, you will accept that that is all there is. That it is enough – more than enough. Your mother was right. She chose well. You are ample proof of that.'

'How can that ever be enough?'

'Believe me, child, it is enough. It is more than enough.'

When Elsie spoke again, her voice was low.

'You are your mother's daughter, Marguerite. She made you what you are. But I also have a claim. I have made you what you will become. I know you, daughter of my heart, better than you know yourself. I recognize myself in you.'

Elsie understood how hard it would be for Marguerite to let her go. But yet she knew that the girl must be there to bid her farewell. For her sake, not for Elsie's. That this was the only way to chase away the demons which still haunted her.

Elsie had learned all about the death of Thérèse in the tranquil days at Daisyford before the birth of the twins. Heaven only knew, after that event there had been little enough time for anything else; but at that time the two women had talked far into the night, and Elsie knew the anguish the young woman felt at being denied that last farewell, the knowledge that she had never been able to cradle her dying mother in her arms.

This was to be Elsie's last gift to Marguerite, the young woman who had brought her so much joy. She would have the gift so long denied, to be there at that last moment.

She said quietly: 'Death is not to be feared, child. It's

part of you always, in you when you're born, there to claim you at the end. You can no more escape it than you can escape yourself.'

'No!' The tears rose now in Marguerite. 'I won't let it happen! Not to you! Not to me!'

'Don't turn away. I need you to be with me, to take my hand, to go with me as far as you can.' The voice was low but unafraid. 'You can come with me to the edge. It's a journey I must complete, but you may return, carrying the knowledge in your heart. That's all it is. An easy thing.'

Marguerite nodded then, her face in shadow.

'I will do as you ask.'

For this reason, for the love she bore her, when the time came, when the truth could be denied no longer and the old woman was fading fast, Marguerite yielded.

She gave what was asked of her because she knew she must.

She cradled the old woman in her arms all through the night of her dying, watching and listening, until she knew the end had come. There was no agony there, no pain, just the gentleness of love so easily given and so easily taken. Until the last sigh, faint as a breeze, which told her it was done, and done with love and gentleness, a completeness in that final breath.

And then, for the first time since her mother died, the crow-black thing which had haunted her for so long turned its eyes on her and showed her its face.

No longer the face of death, but the face of life, of all living things that are born, and die, and will be born again.

43

A Visitor to Daisyford

'What big *teeth* you have, Grandma . . .'

Marguerite froze. She would have known that voice anywhere.

A silence, then two voices squealed in unison: 'All the better to eat you with, my dear!'

The remainder of the story was lost in a crescendo of histrionic growlings, crashing furniture and wild giggling.

She turned the handle of the night-nursery door and entered.

'What the devil are you doing here, Ben?'

The tangle of bodies separated into its component parts. The twins flew into her arms. Marguerite hugged them, glaring at the interrupted storyteller over the curly heads of his lost audience.

'I'm waiting for an explanation, Ben.'

'Really, Marguerite. That's no way to greet the father of your children.' The voice was mild, the lips curved into a smile, but the eyes were wary.

'Daddy, Daddy,' squealed the two little traitors, 'Mummy's home!'

That, at least, was true.

Marguerite stood there, rooted to the spot, trying to wrench her mind into focus. She had only been away for a couple of days. Surely Hilda wouldn't have—? Of course Hilda would. Benjamin Catesby could charm the birds off the trees if he had a mind.

George's fault. It was all George's fault that she had not been there to send him packing. George had suggested a few days in London to take away the sadness of the loss of Elsie. In George's view there had been quite enough funerals in Marguerite's life.

'No more moping. Time for the real world, my dear. I've booked you into the Ritz.'

The outing had been such a success that she had suggested that they drop in at Queenie's on the way home. She had regretted the decision almost immediately, in case she bumped into Ben Catesby, but by then they were on their way up the narrow stairs and Freda had spotted them.

She had nothing to fear. Freda confirmed that Ben had not been in for months.

There was a good reason why there was no chance of meeting Ben at Freda's. He was already at Daisyford.

She stood there, hand on hip. 'How long have you been here, Ben?'

'Time flies. When was it, children?' Ben ruffled the two heads – the one as dark as the other was fair. 'I can't remember exactly, my dear. Long enough for us all to get very well acquainted.'

'Ac-quain-ted,' repeated Robbie, rolling the word round his tongue. Her son had a magpie passion for words, bright scraps of tinsel once collected, never forgotten

'Monday, Tuesday, Wednesday,' offered the practical Rosie, counting on her fingers.

'Three days?' said Ben in mock astonishment. 'So long? You're a busy woman, Marguerite, for a mother.'

'Ben, I must insist—'

'On apologizing you were not here to greet me?' Ben cut in swiftly. 'Think no more of it, my dear. The estimable Hilda more than made up for your absence – once I had explained that you must have forgotten you'd invited me.'

'Outrageous. I did nothing of the kind.'

'But I'm sure you meant to. After all, you're a very busy woman. One can't remember everything.' He sighed, but his eyes were wary. 'Never mind. We've managed to amuse ourselves, haven't we, my dears?'

'Yes! Yes!' squealed the twins.

'We've been reading *Little Red Riding Hood*. We'd just got to the bit where the wolf gobbles her up.'

'I can imagine.'

'Look, Mummy, look! Daddy brought us lots of presents!'

The tiny traitors danced around the room, scattering boxes.

Marguerite's eyes flashed. 'You've no right to walk in here—'

'That's where you're wrong, my sweet. Children need a father – boys most of all.' The eyes glittered beneath the lids. 'Robbie and I have been having a wonderful time, haven't we, Robbie?'

'Bang, bang!' agreed Robbie happily, waving a toy machine-gun. 'Daddy says he'll take me hunting when I'm bigger.'

'Indeed?' said Marguerite angrily.

'Look, Mummy! I've got a dolly with proper hair!' shrieked Rosie, not to be outdone. 'She's got two sets of knickers and she pees,' she added with satisfaction.

'I don't need to tell you that my daughter and I have sworn eternal devotion. As you know, I adore blondes.'

'Blondie, blondie!' squealed the besotted Rosie, tugging at his hand.

Marguerite took a deep breath. 'We'll talk in a moment, Ben. Please. I have to settle the children.'

Ben grinned. 'Of course, my sweet. As sooner or later as you wish. I'll be in the library.'

He waved his hand at the twins. 'Sleepy time, darlings.'

At this opportune moment, Hilda appeared in the

doorway. Marguerite gathered her wits as best she could.

'Madam? I hope I did right, madam? His Lordship was most insistent. And I thought . . . well . . .'

'Of course you did, Hilda. We'll discuss it later.' She cast her a warning look and laid a finger on her lips.

She could not blame Hilda. She would not have stood a chance.

Marguerite went downstairs to the library. George – where the devil was George now that she needed him?

Ben had made himself very much at home. The chink of ice in the glass of whisky in his hand showed that even the reserved Mr Wilkins had been seduced by his charm.

When she entered, he rose to his feet, the long limbs unfolding gracefully. He smiled – the smile she remembered so well.

'Ah, the radiant young mother. Motherhood becomes you, Marguerite; if it were possible, you're more beautiful than ever.'

'As Freda would say, Benjamin – fuck off, cunty.'

'Dear Freda. Such a way with words.'

To her irritation, she felt a blush rise to her cheeks.

She looked him up and down slowly, telling herself that this man meant nothing to her. She could not be such a fool as to imagine that Ben – careless, indifferent Ben – had any hold over her now. Five years he had been gone from her life and in that time she had had no word from him at all.

Naturally, she had occasionally read of his doings in the gossip columns – usually at Hilda's prompting, since her preoccupation was not much with the world of high society. Charlotte's parents, it had been reported, had bought their daughter a handsome manor house close to their own. There had been a glossy feature in *House & Garden* detailing the refurbishment by a fashionable interior decorator.

She had not been entirely indifferent to what had happened to him. Soon after the twins were born, she had – purely out of curiosity, she told herself – passed by the house in Chelsea and seen that it was for sale.

George was another matter. George Flowers was all she had to protect her in the world – the man who gave her what Elsie had so shrewdly elected he should give her: advice, companionship, a strong shoulder to lean on.

To some, there was only one explanation of why a man like George Flowers, a man who had had half the eligible women in London after him – not to mention Paris, New York, probably Moscow and Peking as well – could allow himself to be led by the nose by a chit of a girl with a couple of bastard children whose father she refused to name. He was certainly her lover, and equally certainly the father of her children.

All this remained below-stairs gossip in the grand houses of the neighbourhood who welcomed the new young mistress of Daisyford with cautious curiosity. Money and possessions buy respect – even if they cannot always buy happiness. It was not happiness that Marguerite was searching for in those few men she chose to take to her bed. For happiness she had her babies, and she had George as her protector, she had Daisyford, she had her Foundation.

She could have had her pick among the neighbours – married or not, young or old. Even so, there had not been many – no more than could be counted on the fingers of one hand. None of them had lasted longer than a night or two. None of these brief entanglements convinced her that the game was worth the candle, and she was shrewd enough to make sure that no word of these adventures reached George. Not even Hilda knew of them, let alone the rest of the household. In this, she was no different from the uninvited visitor who had so inconveniently appeared in her absence.

'You've no business to be here, Ben. You're disrupting the household. You'll leave at once.'

'Not very gracious.' The grey eyes were hooded, but the mouth showed maddening traces of amusement. 'However, you are understandably confused. For this I forgive you.'

'*You* forgive *me*?'

'Of course.'

'What the devil for?'

'For everything. For not being here to greet me. But, above all, for your disregard of the conventions. Your lack of what I can only describe as good manners.' The lazy drawl – so irritating, so horribly familiar. 'It's only polite to tell a man when he is to be a father. Twins, too. The insult doubled. You had no right to deny me that.'

'That's outrageous!'

The cheek of the man made her blood boil – the notion that he could just walk into her life and claim what he had not even bothered to earn. It was completely absurd. The past was behind her. He could not hurt her now. There was no place for Benjamin Catesby in her life – or in her children's lives, either.

'Who told you where to find us?'

'You don't exactly hide your light under a bushel.' A shrug. 'As for fatherhood, blame Freda. The old baggage can never keep a secret for long.'

'Is that why you're here?'

'Not entirely. Let's say I missed you.' The grey eyes were watchful.

'Rubbish. You have a wife. You've got what you wanted.'

'Not true. I've got what I deserved.'

'You've no business to be here. I owe you nothing. You've given me nothing.'

'Such ingratitude, my dear. I gave you the adorable twins.'

'That was the limit of your generosity.'

'Scarcely my fault, as we've already established. You gave me no choice.'

'What was the point? What difference would it have made?'

Marguerite willed herself to keep calm. She walked over to the table where Elsie's orchids still shed their pale glow. She looked at Ben, telling herself that this man had no claim on her now.

'You told me you had no wish to breed,' her voice was harsh. 'You also told me that your fiancée could afford you, and I most certainly couldn't. I can't claim you didn't warn me.'

'Water under the bridge. I'm here to offer what I can.'

He was close to her now, his hands reaching for hers. His hands, the hands which knew so much. His lying hands. Even so, the heat of desire raced through her – everything forgotten in the sweetness of memory. Ridiculously, humiliatingly, she was once again the young girl she had been when they made love together – how long ago? So long. Too long.

She said wildly: 'I have a lover.'

'You're lying, my dear. From what Freda tells me, you have a man who loves you, but you keep him at arm's length. Interesting behaviour in a woman – and, in my experience, very rare.'

'What's that supposed to mean?'

'The word is that you have your little adventures. Adventures don't count.'

Her cheeks flamed scarlet. 'None of your business, Ben.' After a moment she added, unable to resist: 'Not so little, either.'

The edge of the lips curled into a smile. 'I'm delighted to hear it – for your sake.'

'As I said before, none of your business.'

He said quietly: 'There's no question of a divorce. Lottie's made that perfectly clear.'

'You've asked her? Why?'

'Why do you think?'

'I've no idea. Certainly not because of me – of us. I have no wish for anything from you.'

'Your choice, my sweet, not mine. But there are other considerations. Our children need a father. You're a busy woman. As you know, I've never had the slightest desire to busy myself. We could have a thoroughly satisfactory arrangement.'

'That's outrageous, Ben!'

'Not at all. We share so much. Most especially this.' His lips met hers – a touch, no more – and just as swiftly moved away. A promissory note of a kiss, the current coursing through her.

He said softly: 'Shall I swear eternal devotion?'

'No chance I'd believe you.'

Even as she spoke, the words denied what her body was telling her.

'You can't deny you loved me once. You can love me again.'

'No!' Her mind screamed of the danger she was in. Of the mistake she had made once and should never make again. But her heart leaped to hear his words. She could feel his hands on her, those hands which knew too much about her. None of her casual entanglements had made her feel like this.

That, too, was a betrayal. A betrayal that even, that one and only time, he had known exactly what she needed, known exactly how to make her skin shiver at his touch, the heat rise through her, the desire mount. She told herself it meant nothing. God alone knew if a thing like that came naturally, like being born with eyes of a certain colour, or being able to sing in tune. She did not even know if it was something that men like him could always do with the women they slept with. Or if men such as Ben Catesby even cared. She gathered herself. She told herself that this was lunacy, destructive lunacy. But yet – and yet – he looked at her with such longing that her heart turned over.

'Why? Why now? Why after all this time?'

'Too many questions.'

'To which you have no answers.'

'I never pretended I had.'

Such carelessness. Even so, knowing it all, still her arms ached for him. Her body did not judge him; her body could forgive him anything. His unfaithfulness, the carelessness with which he took others to his bed, his betrayal of her trust. She knew every inch of him still. The texture and smell of the angular body. How the muscles moved beneath the skin, the touch of flesh against flesh, the line of hipbone, the curve of the spine. The scent of him above all – a sweet fragrance of sandalwood and freshly laundered linen. Her body wanted him. She could feel it now, betraying her. Feel her body turn dewy at the thought of his touch, pink and luscious as hearts and roses – there, right there. Like any old maid, dried up after long abstinence, her body yearned for him.

She knew the absurdity of what she was feeling, willed her mind into the equation. Knew, too, that to her body it did not matter a damn what her mind told her. Right from the beginning, when she was no more than a child and she had hated him – and loved him – at first sight.

And, oh, the sweet seduction of the words that lovers use. He said – worse, he whispered in her ear – all the things all men say to all women. Nothing new – the old words. 'We were meant for each other – you know that as well as I.' And 'Only here. Only now. Only you.'

His hands held hers so tightly that the print of the fingers bruised her flesh. He drew her to him. His eyes were on her, his hands held hers, willing her to want him, needing to know it for himself.

'You never loved me, Ben. The truth is you never cared for me.'

Had these been questions, he might have answered; but, as it was, he dared not say what was in his heart. He had no right to answer.

Having no answer, he tried to make her understand.

'Truth is relative. Love is relative.'

She shook her head fiercely. 'Love is absolute.'

He drew back then. He could not contradict her. He had no right to do so. He did not tell her everything. Did not tell of the bargain he had made – of the price he was prepared to pay for her, for his children.

Had he been certain that what he had to offer was what she needed, even then he might have won. Had he known how close he was to winning her; had he understood that at that moment she was blind to all reason; had he known how much she wanted to believe, needed to believe; had he understood that at that moment all she saw was his lips, so sweet – the taste of his lips, so sweet, such sweet betrayal; had he known that she was no longer certain of anything, that she no longer cared about anything except that he was here – in that moment of abdication, anything might have happened.

Such possibilities – so easily destroyed.

Destroyed by footsteps in the passageway. A door opening. Voices.

A visitor to Daisyford. A visitor who had good reason to fear what he might find.

Voices in the hallway. One voice was all that mattered – unmistakable.

'George!'

Ben's hands released her instantly. There was guilt in the gesture, in the quick abdication of possession. He had not yet earned the right to love her. Did not know it was too late, already too late.

'I came as soon as I could, my dear.' George moved towards her, put his arm around her possessively, kissed her hand. He smiled into her eyes. 'As soon as I got your message.'

'The message?' It was on the tip of her tongue to say she had left no message, but something stopped her.

George's dark eyes took in the man he had long known to be his only rival. 'I trust I am not interrupting anything?'

'Not at all, George. Ben – Lord Malvern – Mr Flowers is my dearest friend and most trusted confidant. Please don't let me delay your departure.'

'As you well know, my sweet, I'm in no hurry to leave. Meanwhile, I'm delighted to meet Mr Flowers. I have heard so much about him.'

He held out his hand. 'Marguerite my dear, your visitor might care for refreshment. Shall I get the admirable Wilkins to bring him a whisky? Or – since I observe he knows his way around – he might prefer to get his own.'

'The last, I think.' The chink of ice in a clean glass. The scent of the whisky. The two men were looking at each other, sizing each other up. Marguerite glanced between them, irresistibly reminded of two cockerels in a barnyard.

George broke the silence first. 'I believe we have business to discuss, Lord Malvern.'

'Most unlikely, Mr Flowers. I never do business after lunch. And very rarely before.' Ben raised his glass. 'And certainly never with a drink in my hand.'

George glanced at Marguerite. 'I gather Lord Malvern has not yet revealed the reason for his visit.'

'Purely social, I assure you.' There was nothing – no guilt or hesitation – in Ben's voice which could have warned her of what was to come.

'Perhaps, and perhaps not.'

George had a thick sheet of blue paper in his hand. He laid it carefully on the polished surface of the table.

'Very distinctive, sir, your godfather – in all things, including his writing paper. I use the same supplier of stationery myself.'

Ben reached forward, picked up the paper, studied it for an instant, and set it back in the same spot. After a moment, he pushed the paper over to Marguerite.

'What do you make of that, my sweet?'

His voice was still the idle drawl – careless, unconcerned. She glanced down. There were only three words written on the paper. *Not another penny.*

A cold wave rushed over her. 'Ben? Is that why you came? For money?'

He did not reply immediately. Instead his eyes held hers with a look so intense that she had no choice but to glance away.

After a moment, without looking at him, she said: 'Is it true?'

Another silence. 'If you believe it, my sweet, it's most certainly true.'

She had no reply. Only a vast emptiness of unanswered questions. When he spoke again, it was to George.

'As a matter of interest, Mr Flowers, how did you get hold of the – shall we call it? – incriminating evidence?'

'Hand-delivered. Anonymous. But, as you can see, the sender took no trouble to disguise his identity.'

Ben sighed. 'As one might expect. My godfather enjoys his little games. So convenient, games. So easy to pull the strings which make us dance. We are all the victims of our natures, puppets in the hands of the eternal puppet-master, don't you agree, Mr Flowers?'

'No, Lord Malvern, I don't.' The dark eyes were watchful.

'Ah. A note of dissent. Then, perhaps you believe in fairy stories. Fair maidens, gallant knights, dragons. The adorable twins certainly do.' The hooded eyes flicked over to Marguerite. 'Do I gather that you wish to be rescued, my sweet?'

'You're talking in riddles, Ben.'

'Not at all. You have a choice. The dragon. Or the knight in shining armour.'

'How can I tell which is which?'

'Ah. A difficulty here. That you must decide for yourself.'

'And if I can't?'

'Then, you will have neither. A terrible fate – at least you must agree with that, Mr Flowers?'

George said evenly: 'Business first, pleasure later. How much?'

'Ah. A little horse-trading by the gypsy. A good judge of horse-flesh, our Mr Flowers. How do you feel about that, my sweet?' The hooded eyes were on her. 'Are you insulted? Naturally you are. My apologies as a gentleman. My sympathy as a horse-trader.'

'How much?' George repeated. He already had his chequebook in his hand.

Ben picked up a pen, scrawled a figure on the blue paper and pushed it over the table. George nodded, reached for the pen.

'What the devil do the two of you think you're doing?'

The two faces turned to her with mild curiosity – as if she was a stray piece of luggage, a parcel which might or might not have been delivered to the wrong address. Sign here, in the space provided, goods delivered in acceptable condition.

It was George who answered. 'This gentleman has something to sell. We have just agreed a price. I imagine it's a gambling debt.'

Ben said nothing, neither denying nor confirming. He simply watched expressionlessly as the pen scratched rhythmically over the paper.

Anger rose in her, a tight ball of rage in her throat. 'George, stop!'

'All in good time, my dear.' George did not even glance up.

She reached out to rip away the cheque. But Ben had moved towards her. His hand came down on hers, gripped it firmly.

'Don't.'

Complicity. The two men were bargaining over her. She could not believe it was happening – refused to believe it had happened.

When the signature was appended, Ben released her hand.

'Thank you.' With one smooth movement the cheque had vanished. Ben looked at her then, but she could not tell what message the grey eyes held.

'Don't blame the boyfriend, my sweet. Your gypsy horse-trader is only doing what comes most naturally. Doing the best he can. We all are. Even you, Marguerite. It's the way of the world.'

'What world?' She shook her head fiercely. 'Your world. Not mine.'

'Then, you deceive yourself, my dear. You, too, yield hostages to fortune. As I know only too well.'

He was by the door now. 'Which reminds me, my sweet – my love to the adorable twins and my undying admiration to the estimable Hilda. I commend Mr Flowers to your care. Don't waste him, my dear. Good men are hard to find – still harder to keep.'

He was gone. She started after him, but the door had already closed.

She gave hostages to no-one. The tears in her eyes, then, were not of sorrow, but of rage.

So foolish. So utterly foolish to think for a moment that it was she he wanted. To think that she could have been so vain, so stupid as to think that it was love for her, care for his children, which had drawn him here.

'Marguerite my dear . . .' It was George's turn to reach out for her, but with an angry cry she broke free. The tears fell in earnest now. She hated him then, hated her betrayer with all her heart – for the carelessness, the arrogance, the fool he had made of her.

George's powerful arms were around her, holding her.

George. George who had loved her and asked nothing in return. She wept then in his arms. This time her tears were of sorrow – for herself, for her children, for the loss of innocence, for the knowing that what she had once loved she had lost.

George held her close, knowing how near he had come to losing her.

Throw the bones, read the runes – the truth is not as it seems. There is nothing fixed, nothing which cannot be changed. Nothing unless it is that men are men and women are women and children need a father.

George knew this; Ben abandoned it; Marguerite had not yet learned it.

44

Sunlight and Moonlight

George Flowers took Benjamin Catesby's advice. He did not let Marguerite out of his sight for an instant. He cancelled appointments, curtailed trips – and when his business was so urgent that even he could not avoid it his absence was marked by a daily delivery of roses driven up from the City in the blue Bentley by a mystified chauffeur.

The time had come not to woo her but to win her. She needed to forget; needed to learn to love again. This was the only card he knew how to play.

Never was a siege laid with so much care. Never had George had to work so hard. Sweet words were not his way – he had too much passion for that – and until now they had never been needed. There had never been a woman he had not been able to captivate. All it took was a smouldering glance, a pressure of the hand, a snap of the fingers. What he lacked in words, he made up for in those small attentions which make a woman feel loved and desired.

It had all been so easy – until now. Until now it had all been a game.

Marguerite remained unmoved. Even Hilda was astonished at her mistress's casual acceptance of George's adoration.

'I think Mr George is trying to tell you something, madam.'

519

'Hilda, I think you may be right.'

But still she would not be wooed, let alone won. There was too much anger in her heart. That the anger was against herself made it no easier to bear.

It was Freda who gave George the idea which broke the deadlock. She poured herself a glass of champagne from the bottle he had ordered and glared at him irritably.

'What the fuck's the matter with you, Gypsy George?'

She never used his nickname. Now it echoed in his head.

The old harridan was right. He was who he was. The only thing he had not offered Marguerite was himself. And a gypsy was what he was. If she was ever to see him as a man, accept him as a lover, this was the only way.

To be anything other than who he was would be like fighting a war without any weapons. All that was strange was that he had not thought of it himself. Perhaps not so strange. Never before had he needed to open his heart to a woman, to show himself as he really was.

Now George knew exactly what he must do. The annual gathering of the *tabor*, the gypsy clan whose blood he shared, was only days away.

George did not warn Marguerite of his intentions; he simply made the necessary arrangements and drove straight down to Daisyford. He did not park as usual in the magnificent courtyard, but took the side road which led round to the stableyard. He used the servants' entrance to gain admittance.

He was quite sure that Hilda would be his willing accomplice; he wanted to make sure that Marguerite would have no chance to make excuses. When he was satisfied that all was ready, he went to find her in the library. As usual at this time of the morning, Marguerite was at her desk working through a pile of papers.

He stood in the doorway watching her for a moment, wondering if Freda's parting advice would work – or if Marguerite would simply send him packing.

'Listen, cunty. Just tell her you're sorry. Doesn't matter what for – she'll know. No woman can resist a man when he's apologizing for something. Then grab her.'

He hoped to God that Freda was right. He took a deep breath, held out his hand to her.

'Forgive me, Marguerite.'

She looked at him, and he could see the anger in her green eyes.

'For what, George?'

He waited, his heart sinking. The voice was polite, without warmth.

'There's nothing to forgive, George. It's you who should forgive *me*.'

'Done!'

He did not have to learn the lesson twice. In a moment he had swept her up as if she were no heavier than a feather.

'George! Put me down at once!'

In spite of her resistance, he sensed that she was glad to feel the warmth of him, the strength of him. For answer, he held her all the closer.

'No argument, my love. I have my trusty steed at the ready, the provisions are packed, the clothes bundled up in the pocket handkerchief, and I mean to carry you off to my gypsy lair.'

'George, don't be absurd! I can't possibly leave the children!'

She struggled in his embrace, but the laughter told him he might win.

'No pleases; no buts. Not even tomorrows. Now.' He held up his hand to forestall further protest. 'Hilda and the children are off to the seaside; it's all arranged. Daisyford can get on without you perfectly well. There's nothing to keep you here.'

She hesitated one second more. He had asked her to

forgive him. Why? Why should she need to forgive George? George who had never wronged her, had never done anything to hurt her, unless it was that he was not the man who had betrayed her – not once, but twice.

The man who deserved nothing from her was not George.

George. How could she not forgive him? How could she not grant him what he so passionately desired?

This was what she told herself. But the truth was that she was lonely. In spite of the company of the children, the busy life she led, she was lonely. She longed for love. Ben had known that. Ben who had wronged her had been right. Known how she longed to be swept off her feet and carried into the sunset, never mind if her abductor was a knight on a white steed or a fire-belching dragon.

The blue Bentley would have to do instead. With its top wound down and its boot piled with luggage, it was already purring at the door. There were no more protests, no arguments; she let herself be swept.

They were already driving on to the Dover ferry by the time Marguerite even bothered to ask where they were going.

But George just shook his head and laughed at her. 'All in good time, my love.'

The sun was setting by the time the ferry docked at the port of Calais, and still George refused to tell her where they were bound.

'We're nomads, my beauty. We ride with the wind. No sleep tonight. Tomorrow, when we reach our destination, then we will sleep in each other's arms.'

Her eyes sparkled as she listened. This was a new George, a George she had not seen before. 'Is it to be ravishment?' she asked.

'Of course.' The white teeth gleamed. 'Food first. Ravishing later. Now, reach in the back for dinner.'

George's notion of provisions was nothing dainty: great

hunks of meat and bread; figs, too – Elsie's blessing on the journey.

They turned off to picnic under the stars, eating hungrily, enjoying the robustness of the food, the coolness of the night air, the sounds of the night creatures. After the meal, they were on the road again, the powerful car like some silent chariot sweeping through the darkness.

To George the journey was far more than it seemed. A gypsy's heart is at its lightest on the open road, and a light heart is ready to shed its burdens.

This, too, was part of George's plan: that she should know him as he really was. She was his woman; she had a right to know all those things which were in his heart.

But now, as they drove south through the gathering night, she, too, was greedy to know all there was to be known about this man, so familiar, now so oddly changed.

What of his mother? his father? his childhood? He laughed at the eagerness of her questions.

'Not so fast, my love. A gypsy story is like a journey. First, where the journey begins. Last, where it ends.'

'Then, since you will not tell me where it ends, we must begin at the beginning.'

'With my father, then, and my mother. My father was a Magyar; his ancestors rode with the Mongolian horsemen who colonized the plains of Hungary. My mother was pure Romany, from the town of Braila – famous for its musicians – under protection of the boyar. Her clan was Kalderash, of the noble *tabor* of the coppersmiths.

'There were six of us children, but I was my mother's only son. I believed my mother the sweetest, the bravest, the kindest in all the world. Because my father died soon after I was born, I had always to be the man among so many women.' The white teeth flashed. 'Perhaps that's why I love them – expect them to love me in return.'

'All women?' she teased – but only half in jest. Already there were the first stirrings of possessiveness.

523

'All women. Women are the only thing worth fighting for, worth dying for.' There was a fierce anger in his voice. 'If it had been given to me to die for my mother and my sisters, I would willingly have done so.'

'Tell me.' Her voice was gentle.

'All in good time. My mother was beautiful. Almost as beautiful as you. Like you, she loved to dance. My father fell in love with her when she danced at the gypsy fair in Bucharesti – and she with him. For a gypsy woman to choose an outsider to be her man brings shame on all the clan. Worse, she was already betrothed. Among the Romany, a betrothal is sealed in blood. It cannot be severed except by the knife.'

The fierceness startled her. At that moment she understood how little she knew of him. She had not thought of George as a man of passion. He had always seemed so solid, reliable. Her protector – a strong shoulder to lean on in time of trouble. Not even Elsie's warning had been able to change that.

Now she was truly curious.

'And your mother? Did she have to leave her people because of what happened?'

'No. They forgave her because she was beautiful and wilful and of the blood – a descendant of the great Rasvan, prince of Moldavia. We of the Rom are a proud people. A race of kings and queens, we acknowledge no peer on this earth – and precious few in heaven. But the bloodlines are known. Much is given and much is expected of those who carry the line.'

'And you? Is much expected of you, George?'

'I am only half of the blood, but yes. Even though I have long ago left the Rom for my father's world.'

A long silence in the night, and then the voice began again.

'Birkenau was the name of the place where my mother and my sisters were killed. The soldiers came first for the women and the babies. Our mothers and sisters and grandmothers and the little children herded into the cattle trucks and taken away. They lied to us, the men and the boys. We were told no harm would come to our loved ones if we did what they wanted. We didn't know it then, but they were already dead. Taken into the woods and slaughtered like rats.'

She waited, knowing that she could not reach him in the place where he had gone.

'I was fifteen and already a man. To my eternal shame, I could do nothing to save them. To the men with guns we were *zigeuner* – lower than the Jews, lower than vermin. They hated us because we understood them. We knew why they were doing what they were doing. We knew better than anyone the truth of what men will do for riches and power, the terrible things which can be excused in the name of duty. Among the Rom, all property is theft, possessions poison the heart, and duty corrupts the mind. We believe this because we know where it leads. That was the knowledge for which my people paid the price.'

His knuckles were white on the wheel. 'Among the Rom the thing is known as the *porraimos* – the devouring.'

'And you – the husbands and the sons?'

'They took us to a place called Marzahn, for what they called the cleansing of the bloodlines. Even now I cannot speak the words to tell you what they did to us. I can only tell you that that is the reason I will never hold my own children in my arms.'

She caught her breath. So that was the secret – the secret George had held to himself for so long. Had Elsie known it, too? Had the old woman planned this all along?

Marguerite dared not move or speak, knowing that the only thing she could never show was pity.

George's voice was firmer now. As if he had said the worst thing which could be said.

'Those of pure blood were simply killed. But we of

mixed blood were given a choice. Submit to their knives and impose their will on others – or death. An ugly death. Not a brave death. Not even a death like the terrible thing suffered by our mothers and sisters. They made sure that we knew the ways in which we might die. The subtlety was to make us choose to live, to make us know that we had chosen.'

The night wind whipped his hair into a dark cloud around his head.

'The surgeon was a woman. I know her name, but I would never keep her memory alive by speaking it. God knows, what they did to me was nothing to what they did to others. Although there were many times when I would gladly have chosen to die.'

There were tears. Marguerite knew there must be tears. She did not know what to say – how to bring him comfort.

The moon was fading in the sky when the voice began again.

'Afterwards I was ashamed. Because of what they had done to me, in the eyes of the Rom I was no longer a man. So I joined the *gadjikane*, the world that is not of the Rom. Now, when I return, because of the money I've made among the *gadje*, I'm treated with respect. I have *bakst*, luck; and luck is very important to us. But what I've done is also a betrayal. There's a saying among the Romany, "sau laci, eck vadra", which means "like crabs in a bucket". If one escapes, the others must drag him back.'

'But still you return?'

'For the sake of the *porraimos*. For the sake of my mother and my sisters. But – even if I had wanted to – because my father was not of the blood, I know I could not live as they do. For those of the full blood, it's very simple: the way of life is not a choice. If you cage a swallow, he dies.'

He fell silent at last.

He had told the woman he loved all those things he had

never spoken of before – all the things buried deepest in his heart – and in the telling he had given her his soul.

The soul of a gypsy once given can never be reclaimed.

All night long, Marguerite's head resting on George's shoulder, they followed the banks of the Rhône, and he felt the warmth of her cheek against his. His soul reached out to her to share her dreams. Troubled dreams or dreams of happiness – he would bear all burdens.

She was his woman – that was his choice. If she could love him, he would be content. Whatever choice she made for herself, she would always be his woman; he could no more alter that than fly to the moon, now fading in the light of approaching day.

She woke as the big blue car, with its polished chrome and pearly paint, joined a motley procession of people and vehicles winding through a walled city on a wide plain.

Marguerite pushed her hair back from her eyes. She was no longer sleepy, but bright with curiosity.

'No secrets now. Where are we going?'

He put his hand to her shining hair. Smiled at her curiosity. He always forgot how young she was – scarcely more than a child.

'The place is called Les-Saintes-Maries-de-la-Mer.'

'And why are we going there?'

'To dip a lady in the sea.'

'A lady?'

'The Blessed Sara. Black Sara. Our patroness, goddess – whatever you will. She lives in the crypt beneath the church. The *gadje* say she was the handmaiden to the three Marys who escaped from the Holy Land after the Crucifixion. We know otherwise. Her real name is Kali, the Hindu goddess of death, the guardian of the underworld.'

Marguerite shivered, a cold hand at her heart. 'A strange patron.'

'Not at all. She comes to us all. Far better to know her face. She's a welcome guest at the feast.'

'The feast?'

'We do nothing without feasting. But there's business, too: we make deals, celebrate births, mourn deaths.' The white teeth flashed. 'But, above all, we choose our brides.'

Mischievously she asked: 'What if the bride chooses not to be chosen?'

George's dark eyes smiled back. 'No chance of that; it's the women who make the deals.'

'And are you so sure I'll choose you?'

'Of course.'

Her eyes sparkled. 'Sure an' it's a terrible risk you'll be taking, Mr Flowers – and me a wilful young colleen with no more sense than a leprechaun after a night on the poteen.'

He laughed at the mock-Irishness. 'True.'

'What if I pick myself a fine young man with flashing eyes and a knife in his teeth?'

'He would find himself a use for the knife.'

'Would you fight for me?'

'To the death.'

She was startled by the fierceness of the reply. He had often said she was his woman. But not until this moment had she thought of him as her man.

The long night, the solitary journey with its storytelling, had been unreal, dream-like, but the morning was reality.

And then, as the sun rose over the marshes, for the first time she knew that she could love him in return.

The warmth of the breeze against her face, the bright river of people among whom the powerful car was only one of many, all came together to bring her a new certainty.

By now the stony plateau pastured by flocks of grey-fleeced sheep had given way to the shimmering lagoons and reed-beds of the delta. Around them now, all of nature rejoiced in the spring. In the reed-beds, bitterns boomed and herons snaked their slate-grey necks. The scattered stands of goat-willow released a snowy flock of white-plumed egrets to billow skywards as the procession passed.

She realized how little she had known of him. But now, after he had opened his heart to her, she was hungry for everything about him. Curious about his life, about the strangeness of the Romany – about how they might see her.

'Will your people welcome me, George?'

'There's a gypsy saying: "Purse in hand, bride on horse, welcome the wanderer."'

'Very practical.'

'We're certainly that – menders and patchers of other men's goods.' He waved at the throng. 'Did you ever see such a people for weaving straw into gold?'

The crowd was surging all around them now – some on foot, but most in a motley variety of wheeled transport. Every kind of vehicle had been commandeered for the journey: mule-carts loaded with clattering pots and pans, horse-drawn wagons topped with canvas sails, battered vans, wheezing saloon cars – all fringed and draped and painted in the bright gypsy livery. The colours were as exotic as tropical butterflies – scarlet on black, emerald on violet, yellow on blue.

The river had now divided into many little tributaries, echoing the spreading waters of the delta. Each tributary had its own particular character, no two the same. Here a gang of urchins, brown-limbed infants clamped to their backs like tiny monkeys, churned among piebald ponies. Over there a troupe of muscular acrobats, bulging bundles carried carelessly on broad shoulders. There a line of donkeys laden with tight-bound faggots of firewood and led by children.

Most exotic of all, a sprawling procession of

Amazonian women, full-breasted, broad hips swinging beneath layers of billowing bright-patterned petticoats, trudged alongside bullock-carts laden with goods and chattels on which their men sprawled, slender and wiry and all in black – like so many starlings settled to roost.

'Latvians – from the shores of the Baltic,' George explained. 'They speak an ancient language. They call themselves *tzigane* – the old word for tinker. Not a word we care to use; it's insulting, like "nigger" among the *gadje*. Their women are considered a catch. But their men are quick with the knife.'

'They fight over their women?'

George laughed. 'What else is worth fighting for? If it wasn't for the Blessed Sara, there'd be a bloodbath every night.'

'I'll mind my manners.'

'No need. I'll not let you out of my sight.' The passion was there, the promise. 'You are my woman.'

'But I still have to claim you for my man.' Her eyes sparkled mischievously. 'There's a bargain to be struck. A choice to be made.'

'Soon. First we must find the *patrin*. The sign – the Romany writing. A knot in a blade of grass, a cross woven of leaves, a forked twig. It tells you where to go and what you will find. I learned to read it long before I could walk.'

When they reached the shore, the river of people spread out and vanished among the dunes which dwarfed the little white-walled port.

Each clan pitched its own camp, each camp was marked by a trail of the little *patrins*.

George's people were only one of many such clans – all equal, all kings and queens. Even so, as George explained to her with pride, the Romanians were considered a cut above the others – true gypsies, holding to the old ways.

A cluster of hoop-sailed wagons looped with garlands,

a clutch of brightly painted covered carts had been drawn up in a wide circle round a blazing fire where there was much bustle and evidence that a feast was in preparation.

George slipped the vehicle deftly into a gap between a mule and a piebald horse – a flourish greeted by a delighted round of applause from those who had turned to inspect the new arrivals.

There were people all around them now, touching and questioning, greeting, laughing. George translated for Marguerite in brief bursts – news of the clan, of births and deaths, betrothals and love-pledges.

After the initial bustle, the men returned to their conferences, while older women went back to preparing the food. Free as a flock of bright-winged birds, the girls flouted and flounced among the young men.

Marguerite hesitated to join the throng, feeling as out of place as a drab peahen among all the peacock finery. Seeing her smooth her crumpled clothes, George walked round to the boot of the car and pulled out a battered leather suitcase.

'Wait here with this. Don't wander.'

He disappeared, to return almost immediately with a tall, brown-faced woman, bright-eyed and graceful in her patterned flounces.

'This is Mara. Mara – my woman.'

The bright-eyed woman smiled and nodded, took the suitcase in one hand and held out the other to Marguerite. 'Come, daughter. We have women's business.'

The voice was surprisingly deep, the accent indefinable – mirroring George's own, but more guttural and less comfortable in the unfamiliar English.

Tugging Marguerite behind her, Mara pushed her way through the crowd towards the motley circle of vehicles, of which George's sparkling monster was now drawing admiring crowds of the brown-limbed urchins.

Bright eyes peered curiously from beneath fringed curtains. There were flowers everywhere, painted and swagged, tucked behind ears, nestling in dark hair.

The curtains on one of the wagons parted to admit them. Eager pairs of hands drew her inside. Within was like an Aladdin's cave filled with chattering women preparing themselves for the festival.

Mara flipped open the lid of the suitcase to reveal a froth of flower-sprigged skirts and scarlet petticoats, a snowy-white blouse trimmed with exquisite lace, a fringed shawl embroidered with golden-centred daisies. Mara set to work with a will. Bright cottons fluttered, silk ribbons were tied and retied, hair plaited and pinned and curled.

The last item, a small leather box tucked away at the bottom of the suitcase, drew admiring gasps.

Mara held up glittering handfuls of jewellery: gold chains shimmering with tiny coins, to garland wrists and throat; jewelled combs to slip in the hair; shining hoops for the ears.

'The *balibasha* sets a high price on his woman.'

'*Balibasha*?'

'Your man. *Balibasha* means "leader".' There was awe in Mara's voice.

A mirror was held for her inspection. Marguerite smiled into the glass; a gypsy woman smiled back.

'Good?'

'Better than good. Wonderful.'

Mara nodded, then held out her hand again. 'Come.'

Back in the firelit circle, the rich scent of roasting meat rose from the fire, and Marguerite suddenly realized that she was ravenous.

It was not yet time for the feast. Mara clapped her hands for attention. When she had it, she raised her arms, the bangles glittering.

'Brothers and sisters, who speaks for this woman?'

'I speak for the woman.'

There was a stir and a murmur, and for an instant Marguerite was confused by the handsome Romany who came forward to take her hand.

Mara's voice rose again. 'The *balibasha* speaks for the woman. Does the *tabor* consent?'

A murmur of voices rose, swelled and fell away.

'The *tabor* consents.'

She set her finger lightly on Marguerite's forehead.

'Welcome to the *tabor*, daughter of the Kalderash.'

She kissed her on both cheeks, then spun her towards the firelight.

'Accept your woman, *balibasha*.'

Mara took George's hands and set them on Marguerite's waist.

'Woman, take your man.'

George smiled into her eyes, and she knew that he was no longer Gypsy George but a true Romany, a king among kings. It was as if he had shed an unwanted skin and his body – so thickset, almost clumsy, in his formal pin-striped suits – now seemed perfectly proportioned in its narrowness of hip, flatness of stomach, breadth of shoulder. He wore the clothes with easy grace – the snowy full-sleeved shirt tucked into a broad belt, the scarlet hand-kerchief round the throat, the narrow black trousers thrust into leather boots ornately stitched and tasselled with silver.

Now truly she saw him not only as a man but also as a mate. Anticipated how that body would feel in her arms, what scent of skin; how limbs might enlace and bodies join.

These thoughts in her head, Marguerite spun in her flounces, coquettish, her green eyes sparkling.

The white teeth flashed in answer. 'Mara did well.'

'That's all?'

'Hush, or Sara will hear us.'

'She's jealous, then, the goddess?'

'She's a woman. She doesn't take kindly to rivals.'

Marguerite laughed. 'Cross my palm with silver, give me your hand, let me tell your fortune. Here—'

Quickly, without thinking of what he had told her of the things of which he had spoken, she turned his hand palm-upwards, tracing the vigorous lifeline, looking for the tiny wrinkles which number children, finding none.

And then her heart turned over.

He put out his hand to her cheek, caressed it gently.

'My woman chose to give me children. Two reasons to love her more – if that were possible.'

She looked at him in wonder. 'Do we mean so much to you?'

'What more proof can I give? My heart and my life have long been laid at your feet. Last night I gave you my soul. You strike a hard bargain, Marguerite.'

For answer came laughter, full-throated and joyous, setting the coins at her throat tinkling like little bells. He caught her and pulled her to him, cupped her chin in his hand.

'I love you, Marguerite. How many times must I tell you before you hear me?'

Her green eyes were steady, holding his. She said: 'I hear you now.'

She took his hand and brought it to her lips, kissing the tips of the fingers, lightly, sweetly – and in the gesture sealed the promise.

With the gathering of dusk, in the low slow twilight, the feasting began.

The meat was speared on the end of one of the curved knives which every Romany kept close to his hand – George's now glittered on the broad-buckled belt which circled his waist. There was wine to be drunk from

534

goatskins – held high and poured down open throats, so that the liquid spurted in a wide arc which glittered in the firelight.

There was music all around – but it was a strange music, obeying no rules. Having no rhythms to soothe the ear, it spoke of deeper things, things of the soul and not of the body – the sound of sea-birds, the rustle of leaves in the forest, the wailing of wolves in the mountains at full moon. If the music was strange, the instruments were even stranger – gourds stretched with the skins of fishes to make drums, fiddles fashioned from turtle shells, pipes of narwhal horn – the sea-creature whose single spur spawned the legend of the unicorn.

The bridal couples watched from an open wagon draped with carpets and piled with silk-embroidered cushions. Children darted between, bringing them meat and drink.

Marguerite went to find him then – the king among kings, George among his people.

'I, too,' she said.

Proudly he led her forward to join the others, her right hand in his left, turned over at the wrist. A knife-blade flashed. A rivulet of blood sprang on the white skin. An old woman stepped forward with a ribbon of red rag, bound the two wrists, his left to her right, the blood mingling.

'You are my sister, I your brother, for ever.'

George kissed her then, a lingering kiss in which was all the longing of the past and the promise of the future. And she laughed, and they parted, to kiss again, this time deeply, his strength around her.

The music changed, and the dancing began. And for the first time Marguerite heard the true Romany music, a language which for her needed no learning. As she danced she knew that she, too, belonged to these people, that there was something in her heart which understood the songs of the wanderers, which felt as they did, which invaded her body and soul.

She danced with such grace it made his heart sing to see her – as if she was a bird on the wing, floating on thistle-down, light as a swallow.

'George, sweet George, dance with me, George.'

The gypsy wedding dance is formal, neither touching nor parting, each bride at arm's distance from her bride-groom, women linking arms with women and men with men as the spinning circles spin. George, his face shining with love for her, had no need to guide her.

Dusk brought the fetching of the dark saint from the crypt beneath the chapel by the seashore, the great crowd jostling and pushing for the privilege of carrying the little wooden statue through the foam. Three times they advanced and retreated, bodies licked with salt and crusted with the sea-spray, their song rising among the crashing of the waves, glittering under the moon.

They stole away then, deep into the dunes, hand in hand.

'Dear George, sweet George.'

'My love, my woman, my life.'

He took her in his arms, laid her down on the soft carpet of sweet grasses. She turned to him, her lips hungry for his kisses. Sweet kisses, so soft. She felt his hands on her, urgent now with the waiting and the longing. The first act of their lovemaking was as wild as the morning skies, filled with passion, her body his at last, her legs wound round him, her hair spread in the sand, her lips parted to meet his, the green eyes as dark as cloudy emeralds. So quick, too quick, that first lovemaking.

The second was slower, more lingering, a shared pleasure, that leisurely exploration which is only possible when first hunger is satisfied – hers as well as his. She was eager to taste, touch, feel – everything about him was surprising. This was what she had waited for. The rosy

536

bloom of skin under the touch of fingertips, the delicate tracery of veins, the pulse-points, the measure of limb against limb, the scent of hair, the sweetness of breath, the taste of mouth on mouth. Lips that only touch, no more, lip on lip.

She loved his body – the beauty of it evident in the gypsy clothes – now revealed for her pleasure. She loved the strength in the brown limbs, the broad back, the deep chest, the way the muscles knotted down the spine. She wanted to possess him, know all of him, as greedy as a child for forbidden sweets. Here and here – and there? How does that feel, George? Dear George, sweet George, her gypsy prince – tell me everything. Tell me where and what and how. This was her time – not his – and he was content to let her make love to him. Her pale body shadowed his in the moonlight, the breasts so round and soft under his hands, she was like some wild creature – no more real than a mermaid, a dancing faun, a creature of sunshine and rainbows.

The third time was the best. She loved him then as she had never known it could be, with truth and gentleness and passion. The truth which knows the thing is right, the gentleness which comes from the heart, the passion which comes of long waiting for the moment of fulfilment. She did not know it could be like this, that a man could love a woman so, could make a woman feel so much beloved.

She was greedy now for words.

'Say you love me. Say the words.'

'I love you, Marguerite.'

'And again.'

Laughing, he gave her what she asked. He, wiser than she, did not ask for them in return. How strange it was that they came so easily to his lips, but not to hers. Just behind the joy, the fear was there, the fear of the reckoning – she had been too hurt, too lost, to set that final seal.

But still she loved him in her heart, and in her body

537

– and in her soul. All that was lacking was the words. Small words, three words. Three hostages to fortune – and she had given too many of those in her time.

George had no need to hear the words. He knew what was in her heart. Marguerite asked no more questions. Sweet George, beloved George, father to her children in every way but one. He was her gypsy lover and she a bird borne upwards on the wind, a bird which has learned at last to fly.

Three days and three nights was the limit of the Romany gathering. For George, there were deals to be made – he was not the only son of the Rom who had made good money among the *gadje*. For Marguerite there was the companionship of Mara – her sponsor in the *tabor* – a thousand new things to be learned from the women and girls who, as George had promised, made her welcome among them.

Each evening they joined the festivities and the feasting, but each night-time was their own. Marguerite lost count of the times and the places they made love – half-drowning at the edge of the waves, with stifled laughter in Mara's borrowed caravan, serenaded by nightingales in a thicket. Most perfect of all, an abandoned cabin in the marshes – a circular hut thatched with reeds, hidden behind a curtain of yellow irises, so cunningly camouflaged that no-one but George would ever have known it was there.

Each morning, Mara braided her hair with new ribbons, ironed her flounces and tucked fresh flowers in her hair. Mara was happy to see the *gadje*'s eyes so shiny and bright.

'The *balibasha* pleases you?'

'Oh, yes, Mara. Yes!'

Mara smiled, thinking to herself how little they knew, these *gadje* women – nothing of the gypsy ways. But, still, this one seemed to know more than most. There was something of the ancient line there – some wise woman in the lineage. She did not question the *balibasha*'s choice of woman. She was content to take pleasure in the happiness of the woman who made the *balibasha* glad.

At the end of the allotted time, Mara did not bid her farewell. The encampment simply vanished in the grey light of dawn of the last day, leaving the buried embers of the fire and the tracks of the motley vehicles in the dunes.

The estuary of people separated into its different tributaries, sucked back into the mother river as swiftly as it had formed. There were no farewells, no leave-takings – like migrating birds, the Romanies simply vanished.

Later, in years to come, to Marguerite the time spent among the people of the Rom was like a stolen jewel, a glittering necklace of separate joys – each moment perfect and distinct, but joined by the golden chain of George's love.

45

The Practicalities of Life

If Marguerite dealt in dreams, George dealt in reality. His concern for his woman had always been practical as well as romantic.

On the way home from the gathering at Les-Saintes-Maries, he swung the big car away from the broad river basin of the Rhône and wound through the hills of Upper Provence till they reached the valley of the Hermitage.

'Just to make sure the boy Tonin's keeping his head above water.'

With the exception of the time he came to fetch her back to Daisyford five years earlier, it was the first visit George and Marguerite had paid to the valley together.

His enthusiasm for her project had never faltered. He used his own wheeling and dealing to further her cause, and dropped in on Tonin whenever he had business in France.

The two men had forged a firm friendship. To an outsider, it might have seemed that Tonin and George were a surprising alliance. To Marguerite who knew them best, it was not surprising at all. There was enough of the gypsy in Tonin, enough of the nomad in George, for each to have an instinctive understanding of the other. It was almost as if they were members of the same clan, with their own language and ways of communicating.

Because of this, Marguerite felt free to leave the two men together and disappear on her own forays, her feet bare as always, just as she had in the old days.

She was happy to see that the land was already responding to Tonin's gentle husbandry. A young forest had sprung up along the ravine down which the waters of the High Pool had plunged. Careful coppicing provided shelter for a herd of deer, and there was lush green pasture now where once had been stony hillside.

It seemed his instincts had been right – the fire and flood had indeed been a blessing in disguise. It was as if nature, chained for so long, had been waiting for just such an opportunity to throw off her shackles.

Each evening Marguerite joined the two men and Marie-Pascale as they pored over the plans for the future. Tonin's wife had green fingers – anything she planted was sure to flourish. Her special care was the fertile inby land where the vegetables were grown. Now, in early May, the young seedlings promised abundant harvest.

Over the five years since the storm had carried away the walls of the High Pool, Tonin's revolutionary theories had already yielded practical dividends. A nursery had been established for the cultivation of ancient strains of wheat and barley which were resistant to modern diseases, and the French government had provided grants for research into the properties of the herbs and flowering plants which sprang up from seeds which must have lain dormant for centuries.

Tonin's view that it had been the intensive cultivation necessary to support the Hermitage which had rendered the land infertile now had the cautious support of George's eco-scientists at Harvard. The Harvard team came down to the valley, took measurements and samples, and published their findings in *Nature*. This brought in a flood of donations to the Foundation – and gave George the idea that the system could be marketed to governments through a sister company in which shares could be issued and profits declared. This was already proving so popular a service that there were plans to float the company publicly.

Plans for the rebuilding of the village had been shelved in favour of the valley's natural centre, the cluster of domed bories. The design of these, although primitive, was as near perfect as nature and man could make it. There was even a natural cesspit with rudimentary plumbing.

'We need a school,' said George thoughtfully, and called a meeting to discuss the employment of a teacher.

Each family kept a pig and a cow, there were hens and geese in the stone-walled yards, and plans were being made for a watermill to bring power and light. Under the mulberry tree of a warm evening there was talk of silk-worms as a way of making a few francs.

'Corner-of-the-apron money,' said Marguerite with a smile, remembering the daydreams of her youth.

Seeing how well it was all working, she felt a pang of regret that her life had taken such a different path from Tonin's. But nevertheless she knew that the part she played was vital not only to the valley, but also to the whole future of her burgeoning Foundation. Their experience must be shared with others – and Marguerite's energies were, as George had advised her, employed in the wider world.

Over the five years since the twins were born, even while Elsie was alive, Daisyford, magnificent as it was, had served as a focus for the powerful men and women who supported the scheme – and would support all those planned for the future.

With the future in mind, George had helped her set up a committee composed, as had originally been planned, of those who had reason to be grateful to the Hermitage for sanctuary. That, at least, had been a contribution Marguerite could make even when the babies were still occupying most of her time, fitting all the pieces of the jigsaw puzzle together, remembering names and faces and events triggered by scraps of information gleaned from the society and business pages of magazines and newspapers, continuing to consult Freda.

Not all those approached were co-operative; and these, it was perfectly clear, were the warden's special-category guests – the ones which had so upset Father Patrick. Nothing could be done about these, except to hope that their complaints would not trigger further action from the monsignor. This was always a risk, and Marguerite was careful that her preliminary approaches were as tactful as possible.

In this, Daisyford was invaluable. No-one turned down a weekend invitation to Daisyford, and there was always some moment when Marguerite could take her target aside and put her proposition. In fact, her manoeuvrings had become something of a weekend entertainment in themselves, and those who were not included began to wish that they were.

The Foundation now had a core group of supporters, a monthly newsletter, and money in the bank for future projects. These future projects – the creation of similar enterprises in other countries – were the main subject of their evening discussions in the borie village.

The half-dozen families who had established the bridgehead had by now swollen to a settlement of more than fifty souls, not counting infants in arms. Tonin and Marie-Pascal now had not one but two sturdy little boys, the eldest of whom, called for Father Patrick, was already showing signs that he had inherited his father's skills. Marguerite resolved that next time she would bring the twins – Hilda was inclined to fuss over them, but the manicured lawns of Daisyford were no substitute for the hills of her own childhood.

The Hermitage brooded over the valley as always. Tonin confirmed that the people of the bories had little contact with the new young priest or his guests. Not even the market at Valréas had his custom, but every month he drove his housekeeper to shop for supplies in Avignon. With the destruction of the village and the loss of its inhabitants – many of whom had moved up to the bories – the ties which bound the Hermitage to the valley had been severed at last. And with this the obligation to its people.

A kind of armed neutrality had been established. Rights of way were debated when necessary, but it was clear that the Hermitage had no longer any interest in anything except the provision of a service to those who paid for it.

Since Marguerite had no wish to claim her old room in the turret, it was not until the last day of her visit that she paid a courtesy visit to the young priest – more mischievously than with any serious intent, knowing how nervous he would be. To her delight, she nearly frightened him out of his wits when she surprised him stealing a kiss from the pretty young housekeeper.

'Mademoiselle – such a pleasant surprise.' His flustered hands flapped like frightened pigeons. 'I – we – didn't hear you arrive.'

'I can imagine, *mon père*,' she offered gravely.

'I – we—'

'No need to explain, *mon père*. A hundred Hail Marys will suffice.'

The story of the pink face of the priest and the stifled giggles of the girl caused George considerable merriment when she told him later. If the tale got back to the warden, it would take more than an education by the Jesuits to get the young priest out of that particular hole.

However, the visit did produce an interesting piece of news. Not news so much as a promissory note. A letter had arrived for her, care of the young priest. He had set it aside, meaning to forward it; and then, having no forwarding address, had forgotten all about it.

He hoped that his confession of this sin of omission

would distract attention from his embarrassment at being discovered in such a compromising position.

The letter was interesting enough to do just that. The handwriting was scholarly, the translation into French a courtesy, the provenance the Bishop's Palace in Venice.

Beloved daughter in Christ,
Forgive what may well be an intrusion on a life which may well have taken another course, but I would like you to know that I was aware of the affection in which your mother and yourself were held by my good friend Patrick O'Donovan, my brother in Christ. I have no doubt that his loss will have brought you great sorrow, and I pray that God will give you strength to bear the burden.

I would like you to know that I held my brother Patrick in high esteem. He was a good man, and an honest man – qualities which are all too rare in these days, as I have had good cause to learn over the years. Be assured I shall continue to pray for you as I have since the day I first learned from my beloved brother of the manner and circumstances of your birth. Pray for me, as I pray for you.

I would also like you to know that if there is any way in which I can be of use to you, I shall expect you to call on me without hesitation.

By the grace of God and in the expectation of His mercy, I remain your humble servant and father in Christ,

ALBINO LUCIANI
Bishop of Vittorio Veneto

Part Six

1978

46

Striking a Deal

'Deo gratias! Habeamus Papam!'

At precisely eighteen minutes past seven of a warm summer evening in the year of our Lord nineteen hundred and seventy-eight, the waiting thousands in St Peter's Square raised the cry which welcomed the election of a new pope.

If it was a surprise to many that Albino Luciani was chosen to fill the shoes of the Fisherman, to the patriarch of Venice it was nothing short of astounding. 'This dough won't make gnocchi' had been the patriarch's down-to-earth comment to those who fancied his chances as he entered the Conclave.

The cardinals, charged with electing a successor to Paul VI – a man whose closest adviser was Michel Sindona, mafioso, murderer, blackmailer, fraudster, Freemason – chose a good man, an honest man, a simple man. The choice proved a mistake – at least as far as many of the Conclave were concerned.

The poor, however, were overjoyed. The patriarch was already the people's choice – and the people do not often get what they want. Their enthusiasm was not misplaced. There were many who expected much. Among these, Marguerite. She had never met the man now known as John Paul I, but she knew him to be her friend.

Until the moment the news came of Albino Luciani's unexpected elevation, Marguerite had set the letter from

549

the bishop aside, along with the few mementoes and small treasures she had kept from the days of her girlhood in the Hermitage.

It was not until the puff of white smoke rose from the Vatican's chimneys that she showed the letter to George.

She had never given up on her dream – she had simply set it aside until the right moment came. Now she did not hesitate. The capture of the citadel was within her grasp at last.

As soon as George had read the letter, he made a telephone call to his lawyer and requested the delivery of certain documents, cancelled his appointments and flew immediately to Rome.

The pontiff was a busy man, but not so busy that he could not share his supper with a man like George Flowers.

'Benvenuto al mio umile domicilio, signor Flowers.'

The greeting, modestly welcoming the visitor to his humble home, made George smile as he bent his head to kiss the papal ring. But it served its purpose – a reminder that the Vicar of Christ might live in a palace, but at heart he was still a peasant.

'Per favore. Sederse, sederse.'

The beringed hand came out in the peasant ritual of dusting the chair. In the magnificent surroundings of the papal apartments, the gesture served at once to put his visitor at ease and to underline his humble origins.

Albino Luciani chose his native tongue to communicate whenever his guest was, as now, conversant in the language. This was another way of subtly reminding his visitors that he was a man of the people.

'La piace un dolce?'

Beaming happily at George's acceptance of the offer of a spoonful of sweetmeats to sweeten the encounter – a ritual among all peasants everywhere – the small, round, white-clad figure rang a little bell.

A solemn young novice nun entered immediately bearing a silver tray on which were set two exquisite Sèvres dishes of preserved cherries and two cut-crystal glasses of iced water.

'Bene. Bene.'

The small ritual completed, the two men sat back and studied each other. Luciani examined George with particular interest. He had already known all about George Flowers long before he had taken the telephone call which led to the invitation to share his supper.

He knew that George had a formidable reputation as an astute businessman who drove a hard bargain. He knew also that he was the *éminence grise* behind the Foundation which had done such excellent work among the poor and dispossessed who were the pontiff's special crusade. And that for many years he had served as protector and – presumably, since the pontiff had a down-to-earth view of such matters – long-time lover to Marguerite Dieudonnée Leblanc.

Marguerite was the real reason that George had been able to reach him so easily, and she was also the reason that Albino Luciani had taken an interest in George. Luciani was a man of conscience, and the girl who had meant so much to his old friend was always on his conscience.

A peasant, he had a peasant's cunning. He needed to test the waters. Discover exactly where his visitor stood on the issues close to his heart.

'Do you know Venice, signor Flowers?'

'Indeed, I do – a beautiful city.'

'Indeed, she is. But with much poverty hidden beneath the beauty. The Queen of the Adriatic does not like to soil her silken skirts.'

'I gather you gave as good as you got, Holiness.' The ex-patriarch's long-standing battle with Venice's patrician fathers over the city's homeless had attracted attention in the Italian press – and George made it his business to know such things. 'I greatly admired your stand over the Albanian refugees.'

'It was the least we could do.'

'Indeed.' George's voice was dry. The Albanian gypsies were a source of much controversy, and the patriarch had been a steady champion of their cause.

'I realize you have particular reason to be concerned. I know well enough of your people's sufferings.'

'That, too.'

'I'm afraid the Holy See has much to answer for. We have failed too many times in our duty to protect the weak.' The pontiff sighed. 'I'm well aware that the hopes of many lie heavy on my shoulders.'

'We look to the future, Holiness.'

The pontiff smiled at his guest. The conversation had been oblique but satisfactory.

'You have had a long and tiring journey, signor. You must be hungry. No business on an empty stomach. First we eat. Then we talk. I have asked my dear housekeeper Maria Josefa to prepare a *pancotto*; she makes the best in the Veneto.'

The dish was indeed simple but excellent – a bread soup made with strong meat broth spiced in the Venetian manner with nutmeg and cinnamon.

The pontiff ate with relish, spooning in the thick soup in silence until his appetite was satisfied. When he had finished, he pushed his plate away, returned his glasses to his nose, and turned his attention to his guest.

'Now I shall pour you a glass of *vin santo*, and we will talk of the *risotto nero* of the Veneto, and of the fishermen coming into the lagoon at dawn, and perhaps touch lightly on the pretty girls who take their evening *passegiatta* in the Square of San Marco.'

He glanced mischievously at his guest.

'Does that shock you, *mio amico*? I think not. From what I have heard, you are the first to appreciate a beautiful woman.' The pontiff leaned back in the gold-tooled leather chair with its thickly encrusted papal coat of arms and laughed – an exuberant gurgle of merriment quite at odds with the solemnity and dignity of his position.

'The sins of the flesh have always seemed to me the most excusable of human weaknesses,' continued the pontiff thoughtfully. 'The love of God can light a fire in a man's heart, but it cannot warm his body on a winter night, nor rub his aching muscles when he's tired, nor feed him a steaming bowl of soup when he's hungry.'

The smile was full of unpontifical mischief, and for an instant George wondered whether the excellent *pancotta* was the only reason that the housekeeper had followed her master to Rome. Albino Luciani, it occurred to him, should never have been a priest at all – there was too much warm blood in his veins for a man of the cloth.

The small figure in white sighed. 'We were good friends, Patrick O'Donovan and I. We shared much. I knew his weakness because it was my own.' A pause. 'I knew of the child of course. Patrick loved the mother, I'm sure of that – and her child was the dearest thing in all the world to him. I have thought of her often, as I have prayed for her. Until now there has not been an opportunity to be of assistance.'

'But now?'

'My novice master once explained the vow of celibacy as a necessary evil which had to do with property and inheritance. Men who are forbidden legitimate heirs have no claim on the Church's material goods. Simple but brutal.'

'Among my people, all property is theft,' George said quietly.

The pontiff nodded. 'Our Lord would certainly agree. Yet we are mortal men and subject to mortal laws.'

'Mortal laws can bend.'

'But they cannot be broken.' A pause while the spectacles were adjusted. 'Which brings us to our business. I believe I already know why you're here.'

George nodded, his face expressionless. He was enjoying himself enormously. Whatever was at stake – and in this case it was no more or less than the happiness of the woman he loved – George relished a deal above all.

'Name your price, Holiness.'

'Make me an offer, signor.' The reply was swift – the classic reply of the horse-trader.

George laughed. This was a language he understood – a language to which he was born.

'I take it we can do business?'

'Perhaps.' The pontiff's voice was curious. 'I think I betray no secrets when I say that I have long been uneasy about the use to which the Hermitage has been put in recent years. Father Patrick was good enough to keep me informed. I gather the current resident is considerably more complacent. I have called for the accounts – although there seems to be some difficulty in locating them. I believe large sums are involved.'

'So I understand.'

The spectacles slipped down the nose. 'Is it such common knowledge?'

'Uncommon. But certainly known.'

The glasses were removed and polished vigorously. 'I can tell you, signor, if I give you what you ask, it may well prove to be the poisoned chalice.'

George spread his hands. 'I have a strong stomach.'

The pontiff shook his head. 'You'll need it, my friend. You will be making dangerous enemies. Do not make the mistake of thinking they cannot reach you. They are dangerous, such men. Unscrupulous, without the law. Even I, with so much love to sustain me, so many prayers rising to intercede for me, know that I can count on no-one. At this very moment I have already embarked on a course which will set those same cardinals who voted me into office baying for my blood – and could well lead to my death.'

George was silent. Then he said: 'Why should that be?'

The pontiff shook his head. 'I am no longer an unknown quantity. They already understand I cannot be bought.'

The two men looked at each other for a long moment. It was the pontiff who broke the silence.

'You're right, my friend. All property is theft.'

George smiled. 'In an imperfect world, we must find imperfect solutions.'

'You have a solution?'

'A suggestion. The Hermitage is a liability – and as an investor one should always divest oneself of liabilities. It's an embarrassment, it's expensive, and it has served its purpose.' George waited for a moment. 'But most particularly because you have no choice.'

'Speak plainly.' The eyes narrowed.

'The warden of the Hermitage answers to Cardinal Giuseppe Navarino, your pro-notary in London, as I am no doubt you are aware. The cardinal is a close friend of Archbishop Macinkus. I imagine you are also aware of that.'

'Indeed, I am.' The voice was thoughtful. The Archbishop of Chicago was the main thorn in his side, the main reason why progress in setting the Lord's house in order was so slow. The archbishop was to all intents and purposes the Vatican Bank. The Vatican Bank – at least in the view of the people's pope – had become a den of thieves, a sink of iniquity.

The spectacles received a further energetic polishing. 'You must understand my limitations, signor.'

'I think I am aware, Holiness.'

'You will also understand', the pontiff continued carefully, 'that I am not unaware that there have been certain . . . let us call them *irregularities*, which have come to light in our financial institutions. Of these, you may perhaps be better-informed than I.'

'There have been rumours,' George answered carefully.

'Something of an understatement, if my information is correct. It seems that his Eminence has not been exactly discreet.' A small smile. 'Although it seems no-one knows anything about anything. One might almost say the law of *omertà* has been applied. However, those are my own problems.'

The pontiff leaned back in his chair and set his napkin on the table.

'There are certain things which are within my power.'

'And the Hermitage might fall into that category?'

'Possibly.'

'How might it become more possible?'

'I shall need good reason to divest myself of what is a considerable asset. Proof positive of wrongdoing.'

George relaxed. This was exactly as he had planned.

'I anticipated your interest, Holiness. Should the supreme pontiff request to inspect the internal accounts of the Hermitage for the last ten years, he will find its earnings have been channelled into a limited-liability company claiming tax-exemption under the Vatican's lease.'

He paused and then continued: 'He will find that the company is the sole shareholder in an investment fund which now totals around a hundred million dollars.' He paused for an instant to allow the pontiff to assimilate the size of the sum. 'As you might expect, the fund is a major presence on the stock markets of London, Tokyo and New York. Quite a little cash cow, as long as no-one's particular who does the milking. Unfortunately it is currently under investigation in all three countries for alleged involvement in the laundering of drug and other illegal moneys.'

'The records will prove this?'

'So I have reason to believe.'

The pontiff's eyes narrowed. 'Belief is a matter for the faithful, my friend. I shall need something more concrete.'

'Let's say I've taken a personal interest over the years. If, as I suspect will be the case, you have difficulty in obtaining the accounts from your own sources, I can provide you with copies.' He reached into his briefcase and laid a file on the desk.

'Have you indeed? May I ask how?'

'The supreme pontiff scarcely needs me to point out that those human weaknesses we were discussing earlier are not confined to the clergy. One of the fund managers has a very expensive mistress.'

'I see.' The prelate was silent for a long time. 'And how would the disposal – let us call it – of the Hermitage affect the cash cow, as you so colourfully describe it?'

'No stable, no cow.'

'Indeed.'

Another pause. Then a bubble of merriment. 'What do you say, signor? This woman, this daughter of my old friend that you seem to care for so much – if you give her what she wants, will she make an honest man of you?'

George grinned. 'I am already an honest man. She won't have me.'

'And you think that if you do this deal with us you will win her?'

'Perhaps. But it is more than that. She's a remarkable woman, capable of greatness. I trust her – and I believe in her.'

'And you think that I, too, should put my trust in her?'

'It would not be misplaced.'

'Good. Today, I think, good will come out of evil. Make your woman a faithful husband, signor. I trust you to do God's work where the Church has failed.'

The longest pause of all. Then: 'How much would you say your interest was worth? Would you put it as high as one dollar, American?'

557

George reached into his pocket, his face still expression-less, and laid the note on top of the file of documents.

The dollar bill was picked up, examined, and then tucked into the papal pocket.

'You're very persuasive, my friend.'

'We have it, my dear. The place is ours.'

'George, I don't believe it!'

George reached into his pocket with a smile. A letter with the papal seal was laid in Marguerite's hand.

Marguerite stared down at it for a moment, and then threw her arms round George's neck and kissed him thoroughly.

They had an easy, unself-conscious physical relation-ship with each other – ever since the pilgrimage, when she had seen her lover as he really was.

Usually George came and went without ceremony – they both lived busy independent lives – but this time Marguerite, anxious to know the result of his visit, had driven from Daisyford to the airport to fetch him herself.

When George walked through Customs, she was standing there waiting for him. As always, his heart lifted when he saw her.

'You look delicious, my darling.' This was an under-statement. To George – quite apart from the opinion of others – she was, had always been the most beautiful woman, the most desirable woman in the world.

She smiled and put her hand to his cheek. She had taken particular care with her appearance today, and George could always be relied upon to notice. The Givenchy suit had been his choice from the latest collection. The new hairstyle, upswept and sophisticated, had been chosen to set off the purity of the profile and the fineness of the bone-structure.

She was extraordinary – far more extraordinary than he had ever imagined. Not that he had ever imagined anything. He had quite simply fallen in love, hopelessly and helplessly, for the first time in his life on the first day he had met her, and he had never been able to deny her anything.

Now, fifteen years later, as she manoeuvred the gleaming BMW convertible into the traffic streaming out of the airport, he adored her more than ever – if such a thing were possible. He showered her with gifts – one of the few ways in which he was able to express his Romany adoration.

The vehicle itself had been a present to her the previous Christmas – given with his usual casual generosity, as if it was no more than a bottle of scent or a bar of soap.

'George, it's the most extravagantly beautiful thing I've ever seen. Are you sure?'

'Of course I'm sure. I worry when you're on the road. I want my woman returned safely to my arms.'

Freda, who had been spending the holiday at Daisyford, christened it the 'tart-mobile', and the twins demanded to be taken for a spin round the village immediately, insisting on winding the top down even though it was snowing heavily.

But it was true that she spent long days on the road. She travelled frequently to the valley – it was the closest to her heart of all their projects, but there were several similar now in various parts of the world. A new one had been planned for Romania, another in Latvia, a third in Estonia. The interest in the east was George's doing. He could see that there would come a time when the Iron Curtain would fall, and such seedlings planted early could afford shelter in the coming storm.

The Foundation was probably the most important initiative ever undertaken in its field – the provision of community centres and communal landholdings, training and expertise. The guiding philosophy was Tonin's: the application of ancient principles of natural husbandry.

Volunteers had been easy to find: there were plenty willing to share their skills. Each centre was tailor-made for its location, and each had been set up in response to some disaster, whether manmade or natural, which had left the inhabitants dispossessed.

Although it was certainly George's extraordinary financial expertise which had made each separate undertaking viable, and Tonin's energies which had set the organization in place, it was undoubtedly Marguerite's vision which had brought each project to fruition.

One thing had still remained. A matter of pride. Marguerite's pride. The Hermitage itself, the place for which the organization had first come into being, had been her only failure. Until now.

'It's wonderful,' she breathed. 'When do we begin?'

'As soon as his Holiness has countersigned the documents.'

'George, you're a genius. How can I thank you?'

'You know very well how. Marry me.' His deep voice tugged at her heartstrings. He asked for so little and he had given so much.

Marguerite glanced at him quickly and smiled. 'You're so patient with me, George. I don't know how I would have survived without you.'

He smiled. 'Somehow, my darling. I think you would.' He paused for a moment; then he said: 'How are the children?'

'Thriving.' Her face lit up. 'Rosie's decided she's heading for a place at Oxford, and I think Robbie's in love. It's the only possible explanation for the size of my telephone bill and his sudden interest in the Romantic poets.'

George laughed. 'I shall have to give him the benefit of my advice. But I have infinite sympathy with his predicament.'

The voice was light, but the sentiment was there. George

had never given up hope. Never once lost patience with her refusal to accept his hand.

She said equally lightly: 'He's waiting for you – stored it all up for you. You know how much he values your advice. It was all I could do to stop him coming with me to fetch you.'

They fell silent, each lost in their own thoughts. But it was a companionable silence, the silence of two people who knew each other so well that words were unnecessary.

Fifteen years it had been now, Marguerite thought with surprise. Fifteen years since George had moved with gentle firmness into her life. Ten years since they had first become lovers.

He had such patience, George, such love. And now the Hermitage was hers.

They were already back at Daisyford, sitting by the fire after supper making plans for the conversion of the Hermitage, when she thought to ask him the price.

'How much?'

For answer, George reached in his pocket.

'A dollar? *One dollar?*'

George nodded, his face as expressionless as when he had concluded the deal.

'But . . . why? How on earth . . .?'

But George just shrugged and smiled. A Romany will never tell how he does his deals. Not to anyone, but most particularly not to the woman he loves.

And still less to the woman who – although she did not yet know it – was just about to consent to become his wife.

47

A Wedding and a Funeral

Finally, after ten long years, Marguerite agreed to crown her hair with orange blossom and wear a white gown to please the man who had given her what she wanted most in all the world.

What had amazed everyone was that she had not consented before.

'Really, Mother, and about time, too,' said Robbie with mock disapproval, and Marguerite laughed with him. Robbie could always say anything he liked to her. She loved both her children equally, but they had never been anything but very different. The practical Rosie was all that Marguerite had ever wanted in a daughter, but the romantic Robbie held a special place in her heart.

Both the children promised physical beauty, but it would have been hard to see them as brother and sister, let alone twins. Rosie had Thérèse's raven-black hair and olive skin, but her eyes were as blue as Elsie's had once been. Robbie favoured his father in looks at least: he was tall and fair-haired, and even now the girls were falling at his feet. But, unlike his father, there was a firmness of purpose in him, a steadfastness in all he did. A son to be proud of, as George was fond of reminding Marguerite – as if for a moment she might forget it.

The twins' education had been liberal, multilingual and – if you were to ask any of the neighbours who found the doings of the folk at Daisyford inexplicable – unsuitably eccentric. Sometimes their scholastic year was spent in France and sometimes in England, with holidays spent wherever Marguerite's work took her, but always with the security of Daisyford to come home to.

It was obvious to everyone that George was the best father to her children anyone could have ever wished for. Never mind what the neighbours thought of the unconventional arrangement, the twins adored him. There was never a time when the four of them were parted for long, and certainly neither she nor George would have considered for an instant sending either of the children to the boarding schools Daisyford's neighbours so eagerly recommended.

Over the years the memory had faded of the visit of the man their mother confirmed was indeed their father. He was never a physical presence in their lives but, somewhat to Marguerite's surprise, Ben never lost touch completely. There were Christmas presents each year, with impersonal little notes in a hand other than Ben's own, as if someone else had been delegated the task of choosing them. A twelve-bore shotgun with vouchers for the Holland & Holland shooting school arrived to mark Rob's fourteenth year, and that same year Rosie received a vanity case from Asprey with a string of pearls tucked inside.

'His Lordship has taste, you can say that for him,' said Hilda approvingly, but bit her tongue as soon as she saw Marguerite's frown. She and her mistress had never discussed Ben's abortive visit; it was the one subject which was strictly out of bounds.

At intervals, too, there were occasional postcards from Verbier, or Bermuda, or Bali – or one of the other places where the rich and idle passed their time. The scribbled message on the reverse gave nothing away: 'We're here for a few days. Weather wonderful.' Marguerite told herself that she neither knew nor cared if the 'we' was his own wife or some other woman who could afford his charm.

It was not so much old scores to be settled, Marguerite told herself, as unfinished business. If she was finally to be wed, there were attics to clear, cobwebs to dust. She owed it to George; she owed it to the children; above all, she told herself, she owed it to herself.

The reality was far simpler. Physical wounds may heal in time; wounded pride is an open sore for ever.

Ben had not sounded in the least surprised by her telephone call. He had agreed to her suggestion without hesitation. Lunch? Claridges naturally. His usual table of course.

He had his back to her as she entered, but she would have known him anywhere. She would have known him by the set of the shoulders, the way the hair curled on the back of the neck, the thick mop of blond hair, greying now to a silvery sheen.

She caught a glimpse of her own reflection in the mirrored walls. She was no longer a girl, but she had matured into what the newspaper profiles of her called a timeless beauty. She had never understood the phrase, unless it was to underline that time passes and beauty fades.

'Marguerite my dear.'

He rose to greet her, delivered the obligatory social kiss.

'Very good of you, Ben – at such short notice.'

They talked with stiff politeness until the meal was ordered and served and the waiters had left them in peace.

'Now, my dear, to what do I owe this unexpected pleasure?'

The familiar face, the lids lowered over the sardonic grey eyes were suddenly too much for her.

'The hell with you, Ben!'

She listened in horror to her own words. Everything – the carefully planned speech, the tempered reminders of what they had once shared, the hidden reproaches – flew out of the window.

'What's this? Old scores? Surely not.' The eyes flicked over her in amusement. 'Do I take it you bear resentment? And after all this time? I can't imagine why. I've been a model of absentee fatherhood. Never embarrassed you for an instant.'

'Rubbish! You came to my house, humiliated me. George had to buy you off.'

'I see.' He sighed. 'You mean the gambling debt. I hope you're ashamed of yourself. An uncharitable conclusion, too easily jumped to. I can't blame your gypsy horse-trader. It was neatly done. My godfather has a way of putting his finger on the weak link in any chain – in this case, my well-known profligacy.'

'What do you mean? You wanted money. You said so.'

'I said nothing of the kind. There *was* money involved – but not that kind of trifling sum, and certainly not from you.'

'I don't understand.'

'My dear girl, of course you don't. My saintly godfather specializes in half-truths – never outright lies. In this case that note did indeed refer to a refusal to give me what I had asked for. But it had absolutely nothing to do with gambling. You may remember, my dear, that I never gamble. With one exception.' The eyelids flicked up.

To her irritation, Marguerite could feel a girlish blush mount to her cheeks. She did indeed remember the night he had pressed his winnings into her hand. Flustered, she pushed her hand into the short crop of russet hair, and then said evenly: 'So what *did* you need the money for, Ben?'

'You may find this hard to believe, my dear, but for you. For us. To buy my freedom. Lottie had already agreed to a divorce. I asked her for one as soon as Freda told me about the babies.'

'Freda told you? When?'

'She took her time. But she told me. And then I did the

only thing I could. The gentlemanly thing. I explained the situation to Lottie. She was angry naturally, but she's always a practical girl. She named her price – which, as it happened, was about all there was left in my particular kitty. She didn't need the money. As she sees it, she likes to get a full refund on faulty goods.' He grinned. 'And there's no doubt she had ample proof the goods were faulty.'

'So why did you go to the monsignor?'

Ben said quietly: 'My godfather is my trustee. He has absolute discretion over my family trust. Does exactly what he wants. He refused my request. Quoted his Catholic conscience, the old bastard. He knew perfectly well that Charlotte and I could have got an annulment – neither of us had made any secret of not wanting to breed. There was nothing I could do. Lottie was quite adamant about the money. A full refund or no dice. She added it all up, believe it or not – gave me the bill. Unfortunately I couldn't pay it.'

'So you did nothing?'

The grey eyes held hers. 'I did what was possible. I came to offer what I could – half-shares in my life. I didn't think for a moment you'd accept – but I wanted, needed to make the offer. I had no idea if you'd even consent to see me – which was why I gave you no warning. And then, to my eternal confusion, you weren't there, and I had a chance to fall in love with my own children. Absurd.'

She glanced down, unsure of herself for the first time. Then she said: 'But why not tell me? Why let me think you wanted money?'

'You *wanted* to believe it.' He shrugged. 'I have my own pride, Marguerite. Anyway, I saw which way the wind blew. It was perfectly clear you didn't need me. If you can believe it of me, it was an act of generosity.'

'You walked out, Ben. No problem at all. It was just as easy as that.'

566

Ben shook his head fiercely. 'Nothing easy about it. Giving you up was the hardest thing I've ever done in my life. Giving up my children was the most honourable thing I've ever done. Possibly the only honourable thing I've ever done.'

'Honourable! Abandoning your children was honourable!'

'Of course.'

Marguerite's eyes widened. Still she did not understand. Humiliatingly, terribly, she needed to ask the question.

'What about me?'

The grey eyes were steady. 'You might equally say what about me? What about us? You may remember a moment when I told you that I loved you. It happened to be true. At the time. Had you for an instant—' The voice stopped abruptly.

'Had I what, Ben?' Marguerite's voice was low. She had never thought to hear this from Ben. Always thought that it was she who had suffered, not that she had caused Ben to suffer.

'Had you for an instant—'

But the moment had passed. Ben's face had regained its familiar sardonic expression. 'What about *you*, Marguerite? You're beautiful, rich, successful; you have your children, your good works. You lack nothing, need no-one.'

'Rubbish!'

'Is it? I doubt if old George would agree. According to Freda, you've led him a terrible dance.'

The green eyes flashed. 'George has nothing to do with this.'

'Don't be such a goose. George has everything to do with it. He was – is – the one you need. He's capable of loving you – that was perfectly obvious even to me. I'm not capable of loving anyone. Never have been. You wouldn't have been able to change me. I gave you George instead.'

'*You* gave me George?'

'Of course. We made a deal. George knows all about deals.'

There was laughter in the grey eyes. 'Didn't he tell you how the gypsies choose their brides?'

'What the hell is that supposed to mean?'

'My dear girl, until I walked back into your life, you'd never even considered George as a lover. As a friend certainly, but not as a lover. You have cause to be grateful to me – both of you.'

'Really, Ben!' She began to laugh in spite of herself. 'What makes you so sure it was you who convinced me?'

'Of course it was.' After a moment, lightly: 'I served my purpose, my dear. The twins have as much of my blood in their veins as yours. A couple of little cuckoos in a comfortable nest. No sense in tipping them out. I couldn't have feathered their nest. There was nothing I could do for any of you.'

She stared at him. 'Very considerate.' Then she added quietly: 'You know perfectly well you didn't ask me.'

'Didn't I?' For answer, Ben trailed a finger down her arm, letting the fingertip rest on the pulse at the wrist, feeling the beat of the blood beneath the skin. Knowing that, even now, she would not be able to resist him. In that at least they were evenly matched. Strange that in so many things they were so different, but in that one thing alone . . .

No. He shook his head. What was done could not be undone. He said lightly: 'That's all water under the bridge now, my dear. Be thankful. I'm a lousy husband. A good lover, but a terrible husband. You wouldn't have been able to change that. Women always think they can. But they're wrong.'

She held his gaze. Looked at him long and hard.

But he shook his head, smiled, kissed his fingertips, touched them to her lips. 'That's what I'm good for, my dear. And it's all I'm good for. You know it, too. You're like me. We're two of a kind. If you hadn't been a woman, we'd have been good friends – fucked a lot of girls.'

'Benjamin Catesby, that's outrageous!'

And then, finally, Marguerite, too, began to laugh – quietly at first, but then a peal of joyous appreciation which turned every head in the room.

Ben watched her. He had lied when he said that he was not capable of love. He had loved her once; he loved her still – particularly now, with the sparkle in her eyes and the flushed cheeks to remind him of the girl she had been before she had taken the cares of the world on her shoulders. That was one of many things on which they differed. Perhaps it had always been the attraction of opposites. Ridiculous that the old saws should always hold true.

When the laughter died down, he put out his hand to her again.

'Friends?'

She stopped laughing then.

'Friends,' she repeated as if the word itself was unfamiliar.

It came to her then, the reality. It was as if she had walked into the icy waters of the High Pool in winter. What had once been – what in the far reaches of her heart she had thought might be again – was never to be.

Ben knew it, too. He said: 'No regrets, my sweet. Your man has been a far better father to my children than I would ever have been.' The lids dipped, but the voice continued quietly: 'I love them, you know. I think of them often. In spite of it all. I wish I knew them better.'

'Perhaps you should tell them that yourself.'

'With your permission, my dear, I will. I'm proud of them – what I know of them. Perhaps now – now they're no longer children – they'll find some way in which I can be of use to them.'

There was silence between them. A necessary silence. It was almost as if they were a quarrelling married couple who had at last agreed to a truce. It was a silence in which each came to terms with what each believed to be the truth.

It was Marguerite who broke the silence. She said: 'Will you come to the wedding?'

'I don't think so, my dear.' The smile was back on the lips. 'Consider me there in spirit.'

The spirits were there in force on the day of the wedding at Daisyford. As was only to be expected of a benevolent Providence, the morning dawned fine and sunny.

The wedding present from Lord Malvern mystified everyone but the bride. A huge box of chocolates wrapped up in gold paper. No note accompanied it, and none – at least as far as the bride was concerned – was necessary.

Freda had claimed the role of matron of honour – rummaging in the attics of Daisyford for a suitable costume and emerging in triumph dressed up as a Russian babushka with fully embroidered bodice and ten layers of petticoats.

'Just the thing, my darling duck,' she cackled, pushing the scarlet helmet of hair into an improbably flower-embroidered bonnet.

Rose, after a great many closetings with Hilda, selected a 1920s evening shift in blue silk, bead-fringed, as the appropriate attire for a grown-up bridesmaid.

'Don't wriggle, Rosie,' scolded Hilda as she dropped the dress over the young girl's curves. A buxom fifteen-year-old, Rose had not yet quite shed her puppy plumpness; but, as Hilda said as she pinned and tucked, at least the bumps were all in the right places.

Robbie's choice – his duty was to give his mother away – was an Edwardian frock coat rescued from a steamer trunk. The garment, slightly mildewed and moth-eaten, proved a perfect fit – and the overworked Hilda, assisted by her niece, with many protests of unsuitability, was persuaded to brush and mend it.

The entire household was in a lather of excitement for weeks beforehand – no-one could remember how long it had been since the last wedding at Daisyford. Mrs Crabtree came out of retirement to push the boat out over the wedding feast. There was a boiling of hams and a beating of cakes and a baking of pies such as had never been seen before – or at least, as Mrs Crabtree explained with satisfaction, since the wedding of Elsie's mother the year the old queen died. Mrs Crabtree had not been there in person, but her mother, a scullery-maid at that time, had told her all about it. The recipe was brought out and dusted down. Forty pounds of fruit and two whole bottles of the best brandy went into the wedding cake – three tiers, with columns.

Bassett, who had succeeded to the post of butler on the retirement of Mr Wilkins, polished up the Victorian silver and raided the cellar for the last of the 1945 vintage champagne. Hilda flitted anxiously between the fittings for the wedding gown – Norman Hartnell, ivory organdie with a train of old Brussels lace – and the laundry room where the two under-housemaids were set to work on the starching and blue-bagging of the linen for the tables.

On the day itself a whole oxen was roasted for the estate workers and villagers, and a whole yardful of chickens turned on spits for the guests. For anyone who might still have a little corner to fill, there were baskets of raspberries from the fruit garden and basins of clotted cream from the estate's own herd.

So it was that finally, in the little church where the twins were christened and Elsie had rested on her last journey, Marguerite became Mrs George Flowers.

The press turned up in force. Beauty allied to power was

always good copy – and particularly if there was a touch of mystery, even a touch of the exotic, about the central players.

George was waiting for her at the altar, impeccable in a dove-grey morning suit from his tailor in Savile Row. Rosie had tried to persuade him to appear in his gypsy finery – he had taken the pretty teenager to Les-Saintes-Maries the previous year, and she had fallen for a handsome young gypsy lad with a gold tooth and a persuasive way with a violin.

'Go on, George – you'll look terrific.'

But George refused. In the *gadje* world he played by *gadje* rules. The only concession he made to his own people was the ring he slipped on Marguerite's finger on the morning of the wedding. The ruby centrepiece had once formed the clasp on the necklace of Queen Marie of Romania. George was gypsy enough to want his woman to be a queen.

'George, it's beautiful, but I can't possibly wear it. It must have cost a fortune,' she protested, laughing. 'It'll look terribly extravagant.'

'Nonsense, my dear.' The white teeth flashed. 'Tomorrow, if you wish, you can trade it in for three sink-wells in Bangladesh, a whole village in Latvia, a hundred square miles of rainforest. For today, it's the cross you'll have to bear.'

'If you're sure . . .' Marguerite was still doubtful.

'I am. And not for me alone, my dear. Wear it as a compliment to all those who expect so much of you – of us. The poorer the people, the greater their appetite for splendour. Believe me. I know my own.'

She had no choice but to do as he asked – and not just with a good grace, but with the love and laughter George always brought her.

In the wedding photographs which flashed all over the world, the ruby could clearly be seen, as large and incongruous as a ripe cherry, beside the wedding band on the fourth finger of Marguerite's left hand.

So it was that Marguerite Dieudonnée Leblanc became Daisy Flowers – as the headlines trumpeted with glee. Everyone loved a fairy story with a happy ending.

And George had been perfectly right about the ring. It became a kind of talisman, an earnest of hope, a sign that if she could do what she had done others could do the same.

One wedding guest alone was missing from the feast. After the ceremony, Marguerite took her bridegroom by the hand and walked with him down to the last garden. Together they laid the wedding bouquet of orchids under Elsie's fig tree.

The wind rustled in the leaves, although the air was clear and calm.

'What took you so long?' was the whisper in the breeze.

And then George, as he had done that first moment of his coming to her, swept his bride up in his arms.

Now, as then, she struggled to free herself, laughing. 'George, George, put me down!'

That there was answering laughter, clear and silvery, could not be attributed to the bursts of merriment which rose from the distant wedding guests.

It was too close at hand, too sweet and full of joy:

48

The Roll of the Dice

For the second time that year the white smoke rose from the Vatican's chimneys, and the cry went up of 'Habeamus Papam'.

The death of Albino Luciani, His Holiness Pope John Paul I, came as almost as much of a shock to the congregation of the faithful as his election had to the men in the Holy City's corridor of power.

Thirty-three days was all that was allotted the people's pope. But in that time he had managed to scare the wits out of those whose wits were not accustomed to being scared.

A heart attack was blamed, but the body was hustled away too quickly for a proper autopsy to be performed. That a man in the best of health should die so suddenly, and after a mere twenty-eight days on the papal throne, and in the most tragic and curious of circumstances, gave rise to rumours.

These rumours included the links of the Vatican with the Banco Ambrosiano and the mysterious suicide of banker Roberto Calvi, found hanging under a London bridge. The connections between the Curia, the Mafia and a certain Masonic chapter were already under investigation by Interpol. The rumours of church-funded companies in Panama which serviced the drug barons of South America bubbled and boiled. Millions of dollars were said to be at stake.

The Catholic world was plunged into the turmoil which follows in the aftermath of battle. Turmoil favours the wolves. All reforms were halted, all investigations ceased, all decisions revoked on the death of the man who had declared his intention to open the business dealings of the Holy See to public inspection. All but those few to which the pontiff had already given his personal seal.

His Holiness had appended his signature to no more than a handful of documents on that final fatal evening. But these included the transference of the deeds of the Hermitage of the Rock to a charitable foundation which listed as its executive director Marguerite Dieudonnée Leblanc.

The price was one dollar, paid in full.

'Jesus Christ!'

Monsignor Charles Melton very rarely took the the name of his Lord in vain, but this time he was ready to pay homage to the devil himself if it would undo what had been done. It meant nothing less than discovery and disgrace.

The Hermitage's real value to the Holy See now far outstripped the income the monsignor's manoeuvrings had succeeded in securing from his 'special category' guests. Just as in the old days when kings ruled over nations, the real value to the Vatican lay outside the avowed purpose – the provision of sanctuary – and was to be found in the bloodlines recorded in the confessions. These days the guest list alone was enough to serve as proof of residence in what had effectively become an offshore tax haven under the protection of the most powerful organization in Christendom.

George had been perfectly correct in his assessment of the funds available through this lucrative trade, although even he had somewhat underestimated their value.

Latin American money – no names, no pack drill – provided the bulk of the moneys which went into the highly efficient laundering operation. There were plenty of good Catholics among the cartels, just as there were plenty of the faithful who held the Mafia's family values. A little faith oiled the wheels of commerce.

After the initial shock had worn off, Monsignor Melton began to gather his wits. All might not yet be lost – there were ways and ways.

A dollar indeed. The pontiff must have been out of his mind.

'Giuseppe? A word in your ear.'

The warden of the Hermitage was a devious man, a ruthless man. He was certainly not a man to see his life's work vanish in a puff of white smoke.

Roll the dice, rattle the bones. When in doubt, look for a miracle.

Where better to look for a miracle than at the Hermitage of the Rock?

The first shot was a warning.

Tonin sent news from the valley that the warden of the Hermitage had lodged an affidavit with the prefecture in Valréas. The affidavit, signed by Cardinal Giuseppe Navarino, alleged that a mistake had been made. The Foundation had no right to take possession of the Hermitage – whatever the price.

At issue was not the building itself, but the inalienable duty of the Hermitage to house the ledgers.

To the monsignor it was a holding operation – but to Marguerite it was an attempt to defraud her of what was rightfully hers.

The legal fees mounted daily. There were times when both George and Tonin pleaded with Marguerite to give up her dream.

'We can do without the damn thing,' growled George.

'Let them keep it, *ma belle*,' urged Tonin.

But Marguerite was adamant. She simply refused to

discuss it. 'The place is ours. Bought and paid for.'

The practical Rosie agreed with George and Tonin. 'Let it go, Mother. The game's not worth the candle.'

Robbie was her only ally – the only one who defended her stubbornness. There was something in him which understood why she had to battle so hard. 'It's a talisman, isn't it, Mother? Like capturing the enemy's standard.'

'Perhaps.'

But in truth she was not even sure herself why she felt as she did; it was as if she could not help herself, as if there was some force greater than herself which urged her on. Something above and beyond the promise she had made to Father Patrick.

Sometimes she thought it might be the spirits of her ancestors, the ancient people of the borie village, and that there had to be some other reason why she felt as she did.

Robbie was right. She would not sleep easy until she had captured the citadel. Whatever the reason, she stubbornly refused to concede defeat.

For three long years the battle raged; it became something of a *cause célèbre*, a matter for thundering from pulpits, the cause of the resignation of at least one functionary of the French civil service.

The delay suited the warden. He had no desire for the ledgers to be rehoused, as they must surely be. Meanwhile the Hermitage became a kind of no-man's-land, barricaded against the enemy.

Eventually the long-running dispute came to the attention of Luciani's successor. The Polish pope was a pragmatist. He had learned the art of diplomacy in a hard school. Give with one hand, take away with the other.

On the death of Giuseppe Navarino under circumstances which led the coroner to record an open verdict, His Holiness elevated Monsignor Charles Melton to a cardinal's scarlet, prior to appointing him to the vacant post of pro-notary in London.

The only matter which was taken out of the cardinal's hands was the management of the Hermitage's affairs.

'Enough is enough, my son.'

'The hell it is,' said His newly elevated Eminence under his breath.

The one thing which he would not be able to prevent was the moving of the ledgers to the Vatican as soon as the Hermitage was handed over to its new incumbents. It could be delayed until the opening ceremony of the centre. But then would come the reckoning.

Within a day or two of their arrival under the care of the librarians of the Holy See, the damage would be discovered.

The housing of the guests was no longer an issue; he had already established a new sanctuary in a Dominican seminary on the French Canadian border – handy for the American clients who were now providing the bulk of his business.

Charles Melton kept a careful eye on proceedings. It was not in His Eminence's nature to take chances. When the word went out that the Holy See was ready to reach a compromise on the Hermitage, he made sure that he had marked His Holiness's card.

Once more it was George who did the dealing. Once again, he bent his head to kiss the papal ring.

'Mr Flowers. A pleasure to meet you at last. I have admired your work and noted the success of your enterprises in my own poor country. You have stored up much treasure in heaven.'

The language of capitalism came easily to the man who had diplomatically chosen the same name as his predecessor, but was considered a safe pair of hands by his peers. The College of Cardinals was careful not to make the same mistake twice.

Once again, George found himself bargaining with the Vicar of Christ – but this time the price was very different.

578

Unfortunately His Holiness's admiration was not negotiable on earth.

'A million dollars, Mr Flowers.'

George withdrew with as much grace as he could muster. It was scarcely a price; *blackmail* would have been closer to the mark. Perhaps now Marguerite would give up her dream. A million dollars was far too high a price to pay for a pile of old stones. The Foundation was answerable to its governing committee. Such expenditure could never be justified.

George counted without Marguerite herself. She borrowed the money on the open market on a thirty-day promissory note backed by the deeds to Daisyford, and paid it over in cash.

What Marguerite did not know – what George could have told her if she had asked him – was the way the markets worked. He could have warned her that she might well not know to whom she would end up owing the money. That lenders buy and sell their debts as if they were banknotes.

The deeds to Daisyford changed hands several times on the day that Marguerite raised her loan. The result of this was that the papers finally came to rest in the vaults of a Swiss bank which held them on behalf of a mutual fund based in Panama. The controlling shares in the mutual fund were held by a nominee company with a post restante in Liechtenstein. The only shareholder in the company in Liechtenstein was a London subsidiary of the Vatican Bank.

The single nominated representative of the London subsidiary was none other than His newly elected Eminence, Cardinal Charles Melton.

49

The End Game

In the great hall of the Hermitage on the day of the inauguration, Marguerite's gaze moved down the length of the laden table, seeing not the double line of guests but a dozen tiny reflections in the glistening silver, refracted portraits in the bowls of spoons, blurred images in the mirrored surfaces of the gilt serving-dishes. The gathering was indeed gold-plated – if that was the name you gave to that particular brand of legalized piracy which had permitted them to make their fortune.

She paused at the end of her speech, the green eyes bright, raising her head so that the chestnut hair gleamed in the light of the sun streaming through the window of the room which had once been the crusaders' refectory.

'Our achievements – and, make no mistake, they are yours as much as mine – speak for themselves. The results you see before you, the evidence is all around.'

Everything has its price – in kind or in money.

The purpose of the inaugural gathering, according to the press release, was to cover the purchase price of the Hermitage demanded by the Holy See. The guest of honour no less a person than Cardinal Charles Melton. His Eminence, it was reported, was ready to bury the hatchet. The date of the inauguration had been adjusted at His Eminence's request to take place a week later than originally planned – to give the cardinal time, his secretary explained, to make the necessary arrangements for the removal of the ledgers. In her anxiety to comply with whatever made things easier, Marguerite overlooked a few details – such as that the ceremony was now on the very day that the promissory note fell due.

The press took note of this change of heart in high places – the story of how the ancient sanctuary came to be handed over to what was now known as the Green Foundation was a matter of public interest.

Marguerite's gaze swept the room and then travelled on to the lush valley visible through the tall refectory window. She had no doubt that Robbie would be out there with Tonin as soon as they could slip away.

Just as the St Jean had marked the greatest tragedy which had befallen the valley, so it would mark its moment of triumph.

There were little posies of marguerites down the middle of the table – George's idea naturally. Outside, the heat hung heavy over the valley, the scent of lavender filled the air, and the sun had already ripened the green fruit on the olive trees to a bruised violet. Later, a walk on the hills was planned. As was to be expected on the St Jean, there would be no rain.

She smiled at her audience, then bowed, the applause rippling and swelling as voices were added.

George had risen to his feet.

'Gentlemen, a toast. To the future – ours and yours.'

Glasses rose obediently to lips. The murmur of voices confirmed the toast. Comfortable bottoms shifted on rented chairs, and the guests returned to their port.

'A triumph, my dear.' George's voice in her ear.

Marguerite glanced at her husband, grateful as always for his reassuring presence. 'I'll be glad when His Eminence has had his say.'

On the surface, all was optimism and bonhomie. On the surface, it was all so smooth – as if this was a club that everyone was anxious to join. She knew that the reverse was true, knew exactly how hard it was to persuade men like this to support an enterprise such as hers. But now, after all this time, here they all were. The men who had provided the impetus behind the Foundation.

She hoped that by the end of the day George's briefcase would contain pledges for a million dollars – the money which would redeem Daisyford.

Marguerite told herself that there was no reason for her unease. Told herself that the cardinal's presence indicated that he no longer had any interest in the place. That he had simply come, as he had already explained, to escort the ledgers to their new home in the Vatican library.

George had told her that there was a new sanctuary established in a Dominican seminary in the wastes of Canada. Protection – whether from earthly or divine retribution – had always been for sale.

George was on his feet now, raising his hands for silence, a broad smile of pride on his tanned face.

'It is my personal privilege to express the Foundation's gratitude to our esteemed colleagues, without whom none of this would have been possible . . .' The list of sponsors flowed over the debris of the meal like warm treacle through cream.

Marguerite's gaze swept briefly over the gathering, her spirits unexpectedly dipping. None of these men cared. To them, charity was public relations.

'It only remains to express my heartfelt thanks in anticipation of your generosity – and, with her permission, add to them those of my beloved wife.'

George dropped his voice conspiratorially. 'This is all my wife's doing, you know. She is' – he glanced around, timing his delivery – 'more man than any of us.'

A few of the men laughed politely. But most were sensitive enough – or politically aware enough – to wince at a remark that would in these times be taken as sexist. But, then, George, everyone knew, had always been a law unto himself.

For the moment it was over. Later, after the guests had inspected the work which had been done in the valley, paid a visit to the bories, admired the hardy breeds of sheep and cattle in the byres, the cardinal would have his say. And then pledges would be counted. George had no doubt at all that they would raise far more than Marguerite had borrowed.

She had not told George that she had pledged Daisyford as security. She knew only too well that he would have immediately tried to redeem the pledge. He could have done it, too – she knew that well enough. But that was not what she wanted. This was her business; it had to be hers and hers alone.

The men began to chatter among themselves, their shared concerns surfacing. Charity was the window-dressing. These men made money. That, above all, was why they were here. Decisions were made over caviar and *fraises de bois* and the good wine of Burgundy. Commodities. The Singapore stock market. Politics – always politics. The price of oil.

These men did not fear war. Violent death was big bucks; huge fortunes were made from the production and replacement of weapons.

Disease was even more profitable – the largest fortunes were made from those drugs which pedalled hope, but which were scarcely less lethal than the ills they were supposed to cure.

Marguerite turned away. She had finished her task. Now it was up to others – the professionals. The thing already had a momentum of its own. The pebble had broken the surface. The ripples were spreading fast. Soon the Hermitage would only be a symbol – a powerful symbol, a symbol of hope for millions, but it was nothing unless those hopes were met.

The Eastern Europeans stood to benefit more than anyone from the Foundation. George was proud of their work east of the Danube. His voice rose above the chatter – recommending his own pet project, a homeland for the Romany people, to the assistant director of the World Bank.

Tonin's voice reached her ears, extolling the virtues of a new system of crop rotation – a favourite hobbyhorse. 'You must see the results for yourself, Herr Viener. You'll be astonished.' She smiled to herself, briefly elated. He had – they both had – come a long way since those days on the hillside when Sarriette had kicked over the bucket of milk and there had been one fewer cheese for market. Tonin – the *ravi*, the simpleton, the goatherd – was lecturing the German Minister for Eastern European Development on how to tackle the special problems left by the withdrawal of the Russian colonizers.

Yet there was something wrong; something had been lost. An innocence perhaps. It no longer felt as if this was a movement by the people, for the people. The Foundation was big business now, a franchising operation.

On the surface, all was bonhomie. The omens were good. The pledges were already rolling in. In spite of this, of her confidence that the gamble had paid off, Daisyford would be redeemed, the future assured. Marguerite shivered, drawing her shawl around her. Not even George's reassuring squeeze of the hand could dispel her feeling of impending disaster.

Strange that the fruits of success had so bitter an aftertaste.

She walked over to the window, the tall narrow window at which Father Patrick had loved to sit in companionable silence with her mother. So much sorrow here. So much loss.

Her feet were silent on the cold stones. She had kicked off her high heels under the long mahogany table, just as always. George liked her to wear heels, the higher the better. They were a symbol of power.

But, in this place above all, she needed to feel the coldness, the familiarity of the stone beneath her feet. She leaned against the casement and gazed out through the panes, noticing first the delicate shimmer which the hand-pressed glass gave to the reflections – the glass had been replaced with scrupulous accuracy – and then, almost automatically since she knew it so well, the view beyond.

Her dress felt smooth and soft against her body. It was made of gossamer fine cashmere – not black, but the colour of the darkest rubies, reflecting the stone on her finger. The lining was of pure silk taffeta, which rustled softly as she moved. As always, George had seen to it that her clothes suited her to perfection – choosing the cloth on his travels, having the stuff made up for her in Paris or London or New York or Rome. She found the fittings boring, unnecessary, but she did not argue with him. George supplied all the things in her life which she lacked – or almost all.

Behind her the voices rose and fell, the shared vocabulary confirming their maleness, their membership of the same club.

Marguerite knew all about the club, even enjoyed its chauvinism which could so easily be turned to her advantage. But now, at this moment, the sounds were meaningless. Her heart was beating so hard that she was certain everyone could hear it.

A familiar figure – so familiar there could be absolutely no mistake – was moving down the far side of the ravine, following the old path which led across the stream.

It could not possibly be him. And yet – as always – there could be no mistake. For a second he hesitated, and then vanished in the direction of the cemetery. She waited, hearing the beating of her own heart above the noise of chatter. Hating herself for the feeling she could still get when she saw him.

She had thought the lunch at Claridges had been the end of it. That she was immune from such feelings. But still, still . . . She shook her head. Such absurd thoughts, so unworthy of a woman in her position.

After a time the figure reappeared, hesitated, stared up at the window. Instinctively guilty, she drew back. Too late. He raised his hand, beckoned, and turned and vanished from sight. She already knew where she would find him. Already knew that she would go to him. That she would not tell George that he was here.

Dear heaven, as always it caught her by surprise, this feeling of helplessness, the abdication of reason which was the start of desire. It was a betrayal that she could still feel that quickening of the pulse, that churning of the stomach, that melting of the bones and liquefying of the flesh which is both longed for and distrusted by women who have chosen to exert power not through their sexuality, their weakness, but through strength.

'Marguerite?'

George was always sensitive to her moods. Now he was by her side, his hand on her arm to draw her back to the gathering. She shook her head, moving quickly away from the window, suddenly fearful that he would notice the intensity of her interest – and understand.

'No, George. Let it be. I'm fine.'

But George knew his woman. He looked at her now with eyes which were almost topaz, the dark pupils with a feline narrowness, glittering. She always forgot that he had the instincts of a hunting cat. That he was a dangerous man. Dangerous to others – never to her. She was his one weakness – he had always told her that.

This time he did not understand. Misunderstanding her preoccupation, he said gently: 'It'll soon be over, my dear. There'll be other challenges. It's like a child, this organization of ours; it must learn to walk for itself.'

She smiled at him, making her face cheerful, her voice light. 'I know, my darling. Look after business. I think I'll get some air.'

George nodded. But the look he gave her was troubled.

There was nothing she could hide from George. She moved back to the window, stared down again at the place where he had vanished from view. Why had he come? What did he want?

Seeing him there, the familiarity of him, the long, easy movement which carried him down the steep slope and up the path – her heart beat faster.

She must go to him, and go to him without delay. Nodding and smiling, she moved through the gathering till she reached the curtain which still hid the writing room. She slipped through.

Eagerly her fingers searched for the iron handle which gave access to the secret staircase, the staircase which led to the cave where the well-spring rose.

50

The Cave of the Well-spring

'Ben?'

It was dark in the cavern. A single candle lit the little shrine by the well-spring. Beyond, in the shadows, leaning against the damp wall, she could just make out the familiar figure.

She stood there, her bare feet cold on the damp stone. Uncertainly she said: 'What is it, Ben? Why have you come?'

'I need your help. I think you need mine.'

She waited.

'Old Freda's dead.' The voice was flat, unemotional. 'Fell off her stool. Heart attack.' A silence. 'It was quick. Didn't even finish the champagne. I should know. I paid for it.'

'Ben, I'm so sorry.'

Marguerite began to move towards him, but there was no answering movement from Ben.

Marguerite hesitated, tears starting to her eyes. 'I loved her, too.'

Silence. Then: 'Yes.'

'Talk to me, Ben.'

'Ask me why I bought her the bottle.'

'Tell me.'

She did not know what to say, how to comfort him.

He moved forward into the light, and Marguerite could see that his face was very white.

'It was a reward. No – an incentive. She decided to come clean with me about what really happened here all those years ago. She told me because I asked her.' He shrugged. 'It was the first time I had ever really wanted to know. It was the first time she had ever wanted to tell me.'

She stared at him, the smile vanishing from her lips.

'Why? Why now?'

'Who knows? Maybe she saw the old man with the sickle. Maybe she wanted to lay a few ghosts. She said she'd had it on her conscience all these years, wanted to transfer it to mine.'

His eyes were hooded, but the familiar drawl had returned.

'Remember many years ago you tried to tell me that the ledgers did not always tell the truth? You were right – although I didn't think anyone would imagine there might be downright lies. According to Freda, my mother's confession was a fabrication from start to finish. She knew all about it. It appears my godfather had a few sins of his own to cover up, which is why he took responsibility for me. Apparently looking after my spiritual and physical welfare is no more than the equivalent of forty years of Hail Marys. Practical payment for a moral debt. Or worse.'

'Worse?'

'I can't be sure, but I have my suspicions. All I know for the present is what Freda told me. She started at the beginning, when my parents fell in love. Then it was the old trouble – Romeo-and-Juliet stuff. Capulets and Montagues. My mother was a Cuthbert – a Catholic. My father a Catesby – a Protestant. Not just any old defector, but the ancient enemy.' Ben sighed. 'It may sound absurd, but a seventeenth-century Catesby denounced a seventeenth-century Cuthbert. My ancestor on one side was hanged at Tyburn because my ancestor on the other side shopped him. Something to do with the Gunpowder Plot.'

Ben shook his head. 'You'd think they'd have forgotten by now. But no. According to Freda, it was a red rag to a bull. There was a family row. My mother dug her heels in and threatened to elope to Gretna Green. The Cuthberts put their heads together. Clearly a job for their father confessor. Who just happened to be a young and ambitious Charles Melton. Told him: Get it fixed or lose the job.

'Unfortunately my mother, naturally egged on by her best friend Freda, proved rather hard to fix. He had more success with my father. Spun him some story about proving himself worthy of a good woman's love, suggested he enlist in the Red Brigade and fight the good fight in Spain. The silly bugger headed off for death or glory – although how slaughtering a few Blackshirts could prove love for a woman is a mystery to me.'

Ben paused. 'With the coast clear, he gets back to work on my mother. By this time she realizes she has a bastard on the way. Me. My dear godfather explains to her that her young man's abandoned her. My mother quite calmly tells him she doesn't believe a word of it; furthermore will he oblige her by conveying the happy news to her beloved?'

'And?'

'Nothing. Apparently he never tried. The plan never really changed. The Catholic solution applied: jolly the mother along until there's another little Catholic in the world, and then persuade her to give it up for adoption.'

Marguerite shuddered. There were things about this religion she would never understand. 'Terrible.'

'My mother would have agreed with you, it seems. She *did* agree to come here, as long as she had Freda to keep her company. Neither of them had any doubts that my father would soon join his sweetheart. There are always excuses. He's on his way, the frontier's closed – that kind of thing. The nine months go by, and I pop out. The father confessor appears, all ready with the adoption papers. No dice. My mother's quite happy with her little bastard, and more than content to wait for her beloved to roll up and make an honest woman of her when he's ready.'

A long silence, then the voice resumed.

'Then something very unfortunate happens. Word comes through to the Hermitage on the Catholic grapevine that my father's got himself inconveniently slaughtered on the walls of Avila. Nothing official, but the priests always know – it's their business. Now things really began to go wrong. Under normal circumstances, marriage wouldn't matter. It could always be fudged. The trouble is that in my case there's a peerage to be inherited. An only son dead, and now an illegitimate grandson. Peers of the realm can be madmen or mass-murderers, but they must be born in wedlock. No question. Even if it's only a few days on the right side of the blanket. Melton needed time to work out a story. He's made a mess, and he knows it. And that's when Freda steps in.'

'She told the family?'

'She told *both* families. Felt responsible, she said.'

'They didn't know about the child?'

'Not until she told them. The Cuthberts had already thought something might be wrong, although they didn't suspect the pregnancy. But they *did* think their errant daughter seemed to be taking rather a long time to recover from her love affair. They'd already paid a call on the father confessor's boss, the bishop or the cardinal – or whatever he was at the time – and it all came out. Horror of horrors. And a very untidy loose end. Me.'

'Why not just keep quiet? Ship you off for adoption and not tell anyone anything?'

'The Catesbys wouldn't have any of it. They had a grandson. Someone to carry on the family name. Something to salvage out of the wreck.'

'And then?'

'Someone or other stepped in. I imagine the late unlamented Cardinal Navarino. Tells his man to tidy it all up. And then something very strange happens. Strange and tragic. Suddenly we have a suicide on our hands. Or what looks like suicide.'

'You don't think that's what it was?'

'It looked fine on paper. Tragic accident while deranged with grief over the loss of the father – buried in the heretics' graveyard, just to make sure there was no record of the dates. The dates were the trouble. There was a marriage certificate of course. Properly witnessed and dated well before the birth. Neat. Tidy. No blame.'

'How did they do that?'

'All in the timing. Fix the dates, resurrect the dead. A marriage took place – there's the entry in the register in Valréas to prove it. But not when it's supposed to have done, and not between the two people named. Freda stood in for my mother as the bride; some tramp stood in for the groom.'

Marguerite stared at him. 'But why? Why did Freda agree?'

Ben's face darkened. 'Scared. She's lost both of her protectors – my father and mother. She was an immigrant. A Jew. She thought that if she stepped out of line she'd have been on the next boat to Siberia. She may well have been right. It was a bad time.'

'So why tell you now?'

Ben shrugged. 'Intimations of mortality, my sweet. Guilt. She knew she'd had a part in something wicked. Had had it on her conscience all these years. Wanted to transfer it to mine. She probably knew she was about to hit the trail for the pearly gates.'

She said quietly: 'You could have asked the questions.'

He was very still, like a lizard waiting for the warmth of the sun. After a moment he said: 'I didn't want to.'

She watched him in silence. 'But you knew where your mother was buried. You knew there was something wrong with the dates.'

He shook his head, and there was anguish in the lines of his face. 'I knew and I didn't want to know. I was still only a child. My grandparents found me a painful reminder of something they would rather forget. My godfather was all I had. If I crossed him, I had everything to lose and nothing to gain.'

Ben was silent for a moment. Then he said: 'The marks on the gravestone – they're the proof. And now the damn thing's gone.'

Marguerite swung round on her heel and went over to the little shrine above the well-spring where a small statue of Mary Magdalene stood.

'You mean this?' She held out the corner of stone with the markings still visible. 'Your godfather made Tonin break it up with a pickaxe. He thought he'd tipped the whole thing into the river, but he hadn't. Tonin saved the bit with the initials and the date; he thought it might matter to someone. He brought it here for safe-keeping. There are superstitions about the shrine. Old stories of miracles. Bones. The country people believe in things like that. Father Patrick didn't approve. But people still come. They leave small offerings. Curls of hair, photographs – moles' paws for luck.'

'A mole's paw. Yes.'

Ben reached out and took the corner of stone with great gentleness. In that moment Marguerite knew how much he cared. How much he had always cared. She should know well enough what the loss of a mother meant to a child. How terrible it must have been to grow up with nothing, with no-one.

'I understand, Ben. I really do,' she said gently.

His face was still in shadow, and it took him a long time to reply.

'I don't think you do, my sweet. You knew – you wanted to know – about your mother's death: the how and the wherefore and the when. I knew nothing of mine because I never wanted to know. It was easier to believe she'd betrayed me – and that my father was the cause of that betrayal. Even now, I'm only here because of you.'

'Because of me?' She was startled.

'Because of you. To protect you from what Melton means to do.'

'What can he possibly do?'

'You don't know my godfather as I do. He's ruthless. He does whatever it takes. There's only one way to stop him. The confession. The date on the stone proves that it's a fabrication. I brought the key to the ledgers – must have slipped it into my pocket on the day I read the entry. Kept it on my watch-chain ever since. Now I mean to use it.'

She said quietly: 'Why now? What difference can it make now?'

He shook his head. 'It's better if you know nothing. He'll make his move – and when he does I'll be there.' He put his hand to hers, squeezed it reassuringly. 'Get back to your guests. They'll be wondering where you are. Trust me. Just behave as if you know nothing.'

'But—'

'No buts. Just for once, trust me.'

Marguerite started to protest, and then was stopped by the pressure of his hand.

She nodded. 'You can listen in the writing room without being seen. Use the secret staircase – the one I showed you when you read the ledger. Count the doors: it's the fifth on the line. Whatever you do, don't go right to the top. There's a door there, too. It's always kept locked, but you can open it if you push hard enough. There used to be a wooden platform outside which led on to the roof. Abelard liked to use the broken bits as a perch.'

'A perch?'

594

'That's all it's good for. There's a thousand-foot drop.'

She could hear the breath catch in his throat. 'Is there indeed? So I was right about the blood and the brains.'

'You're talking in riddles, Ben.'

'I was never more clear about anything in my life. The final piece of the puzzle has just fallen into place.'

'The puzzle?'

'Something Freda told me. That day, the day my mother died, Freda said there was a terrible argument. Some nuns had arrived under the impression that they were to take me away. My mother was furious. Later that evening my godfather arrived with a note. My mother read it. She rushed out, and that was the last that anyone saw of her.'

Marguerite stared at him. 'What was in the note?'

The candlelight flickered over his face. 'Whatever it was, it came as a wonderful surprise. Freda said she was positively glowing.'

Now it was Marguerite who had been holding her breath. She released it with a sigh. 'Like a woman on her way to her lover?'

'Like a woman who believes her lover to be in the next room.' The voice was flat, expressionless. 'That she has only to open a door and fall into his arms.'

'Surely—? Surely not that? He's a priest. Something like that would be far more than a mortal sin.'

Ben looked at her, the grey eyes steely. 'I think my godfather's capable of anything. Including murder.'

Something in the Woodwork

'A word in private with our estimable chairwoman.'

Marguerite hesitated, glancing at George, seeking reassurance. And then, irritated with herself at this display of feminine dependence, met the cardinal's gaze.

'Of course, Eminence.'

The gathering had broken up while Marguerite had been in the cavern. Tonin and Robbie had taken the German delegation to inspect the plantings around the bories. Rosie had slipped off to pay a quick visit to Marie-Pascale; she loved the sturdy countrywoman who had served as surrogate mother to both the twins in earlier years.

George pressed Marguerite's hand reassuringly. 'Don't worry, my dear; I'll be here if you need me.'

Marguerite smiled at her husband. Usually she consulted him on everything. But the Hermitage was hers; she knew perfectly well he would never have approved of the price she had been prepared to pay to fulfil her dream.

The red-robed figure had already vanished into the writing room – still lined with the scarlet ledgers, but empty now of its paraphernalia of ink, pens and sand. The young priest who had replaced Father Patrick had excellent eyesight and no need of anyone to take dictation.

Marguerite followed.

'Eminence? You have something to say to me?'

'Indeed, I have, daughter. A proposal. On a delicate matter – personal.'

Marguerite looked at him coolly, scarcely able to mask her dislike.

'I shall be interested to hear it, Eminence.'

'A matter, let's say, of *discretion*. An offer I hope you will be too sensible to refuse.'

She waited.

The cardinal's voice continued smoothly: 'You will announce your decision to withdraw from the arrangement you have made with His Holiness. You will do this gracefully and with your customary dignity, but without offering any explanation beyond the constraints of finance.'

Marguerite stared at him in astonishment. 'Eminence, with the greatest respect—'

The cardinal held up a bony hand. 'Hear me out. I am not offering you a choice. I am simply informing you of my requirements. You may decide for yourself if you will meet them. To make your decision a little easier, I took the precaution of bringing these.'

He laid a briefcase on the sloping surface of the writing shelf and carefully removed a bundle of papers. These he handed over for Marguerite's inspection, although there was scarcely any need.

'In the name of all that's holy—'

Margaret stared down at the deeds to Daisyford.

'A very apt comment under the circumstances.' The cardinal smiled – a thin twitch of the lips lacking mirth or warmth. 'I'd forgotten dear old Father Patrick was an Irishman. Charming to hear him commemorated in such a manner.'

He considered her in silence for a moment. 'Yes, indeed. Poor old Patrick. A good man, but a little – shall we say – *impetuous*? To return to our discussion. Your property is mortgaged, as I'm sure you're aware, on a thirty-day promissory note. The document expired' – he glanced at his watch – 'an hour ago. I hold the deeds, although I don't intend to explain the hows and wherefores of how I came by them. It's enough that I have them, that you know I have them, and that I can do what I wish with them.'

Marguerite watched him in stunned silence. How could she have been so careless as to think that there had been no ulterior motive in his delaying of the date of the fund-raising weekend? Worse, how could she have been so stupid as not to know that, in money matters, twenty-four hours made the difference between success and disaster. She had always left details like that to George.

And now? What now? What choice was he offering?

The stooped scarlet-clad figure walked over to the stacked ledgers, put out an absentminded hand to caress them, then turned to face her.

'Possessions. They make us so vulnerable, do they not, Mrs Flowers? I know how much you value your beautiful home and how seriously you take your responsibilities to your late benefactress. Let alone to your children. And one even has responsibilities to one's husband, does one not? I cannot imagine how dear George let you put yourself in this unfortunate situation. But, then, one doesn't necess-arily tell one's nearest and dearest everything, does one? I may be an unworldly prelate, but I'm well aware of the ways of the world.'

Marguerite was calm now. She could see that the cardinal was enjoying himself; he was like a cat playing with a mouse.

'There's nothing personal in this, Mrs Flowers. Please believe me. I am merely protecting the Church's interests.' The cardinal watched her with his pale eyes. 'I think we understand each other. I shall keep the deeds naturally. As a guarantee of your good behaviour.' He sighed and rubbed his forehead theatrically. He allowed himself a few theatrical gestures on his elevation to the scarlet.

The people liked their senior prelates a little larger than life.

'Rolling acres are not to my taste, I must confess. I'm a simple man; city pavements are all I ask. But perhaps when one has commitments, heirs, dependants to consider – no doubt they have their uses.'

Marguerite looked at him, the green eyes like emerald fire. 'As you say, you leave me no choice, Eminence.'

'Very wise, daughter. In that case, I would be grateful for a little help with these.'

The old man began to pull the locked ledgers from the shelves. 'I think . . . I think all of them. It looks so much more persuasive.'

The curtains were drawn. Candlelight blazed, casting its light on the silent audience, illuminating the figure in scarlet robes.

Cardinal Charles Melton, his hand on the pyramid of scarlet-bound ledgers, faced the room.

To Ben, watching from the shadows of the writing room, the gathering looked like a conference of gangsters.

When the cardinal spoke, his voice was quiet, each word distinct, dropping like a small pebble into the dark pool of his silent audience.

'Blackmail, gentlemen; I make no secret of it. Should these ledgers fall into the wrong hands . . .'

The cardinal waited for his words to sink in. As they did so, a murmur rose from the gathering, a murmur of fear and apprehension, followed by bewilderment.

The cardinal held up his hand. 'Just my little game, gentlemen. My little joke. But it serves to illustrate my point. We have here a valuable resource – far too valuable to be allowed to leave its natural resting place.'

A collective sigh rose – a sigh of relief, quickly followed by curiosity. They all knew that the old bastard must have had an ace up his sleeve, that he would not have come here for nothing. This was no more or less than might be expected of the man who had contributed so much – so very much – to the well-being and promotion of his friends. His Eminence, a man without scruples, a man to whom the end always justified the means.

'Friends – and I know I am among friends – all of us are aware of the charitable purpose for which we have gathered here. Charity, gentlemen, stores up treasure in heaven. As we are equally well aware, treasure on earth is harder to accumulate. Gentlemen—'

Attention suddenly switched to the secret door as it swung on silent hinges. Ben moved forward swiftly, reaching out for the pyramid of stacked volumes, the key in his hand.

In a moment he had unlocked the first, the second, the third of the ledgers. The next instant the pages were spread wide on the polished oak. Another and another, until the shimmering surface was covered with the open pages, the snowy vellum fluttering like white doves as they settled on the dark wood.

With a cry of anger, the cardinal reached forward to gather up the spread volumes, the scarlet robe flapping around his outstretched arms.

The company craned forward, inspected, leaned back to digest what was there. Eyes flicked up and down from the cardinal's face to the debris on the table. There was not a man there who did not know exactly what the consequences would be if he had found himself in the same position. In a politician, it would mean impeachment. In a banker, it would mean the sack. But in a cardinal?

There in the candlelight for all to see were the virgin pages – as clean and new as the day they were pressed.

All the witnesses later agreed that, if it had not been for his Eminence's unwise decision to gather up the evidence, the disaster would never have happened.

The bright silk of the cardinal's robe fluttered in and out of the candle flames, scattering tiny sparks. The sparks became small flames. The little flames took hold rapidly, fed as they were by so much dry paper – bounced and licked along the snowy volumes, and still the audience watched as if bewitched.

Disaster might even have been averted if the audience had been in full possession of its senses. Put it down to the effect of brandy and liqueurs, or an understandable enthusiasm at the prospect of unlimited access to other people's secrets, or a natural disappointment when the possibility so swiftly vanished, that the assembled company did nothing to save the day.

Marguerite was the first to come to her senses, the first to realize that the unthinkable was happening. 'For God's sake!'

As the spell was broken, hands began to beat at the little dancing tongues. Stimulated by these attentions, the flames spread cheerfully in blackened pools and smouldering patches, but it was not until a few sparks leaped upwards and took hold in the thick fold of velvet curtaining that the people panicked.

It was George's voice which calmed the churning throng, his guttural commands rising above the clamour. As the room emptied of people, the fire took hold with feverish rapidity. The wooden panelling and ancient beams served as tinder to a furnace.

That there was not loss of life was because of the secret stairwell which offered an escape route into the cavern where the wellspring rose, and from there into the safety of the bories high on the ridge.

Even so, it was a miracle that there were no casualties.

George himself was the last to leave, knowing that there was no hope of extinguishing the flames.

Not quite the last. One man still remained. In the middle of the furnace, the cardinal spun in his scarlet robes, high priest of the sacred fire which consumed a thousand years of Catholic guilt. A whirling dervish among the flames, feeding the fire, coaxing it to ever greater heights with fistfuls of the tell-tale vellum, the cardinal destroyed the evidence.

No casualties, that is, but one.

The only casualty, God rest his soul, was His Eminence Cardinal Charles Melton. No-one could understand why he had not followed the others, why he had chosen to turn upwards rather than downwards to safety. Or why the door which had once led on to the battlements but now led only into the void, always so securely locked, had been so easily opened.

The most dramatic pictures which appeared in the press were of the flaming figure in scarlet, arms open like the devil himself, as the body bounced and broke on the jagged walls of the Hermitage of the Rock.

As he tumbled downwards, the cardinal's scarlet soutane – a garment of great magnificence, lined, interlined, braided, piped – billowed out like the sails of a ship, or the wings of some exotic bird. The silk – so beautiful, so well made, so securely stitched – ballooned around the frail body at its heart.

The warm breath of the fire met the cool air which rose from the earth, causing a little whirling wind which playfully tossed the balloon upwards for an instant, then let it fall, and rise a little and fall again, until it deposited its broken burden on the earth, rolling down the slope of the hill, over and over, until it finally came to rest – incongruously, miraculously – in the soft green pasture of the heretics' graveyard.

Throw the bones, read the runes, death comes to us all in the end.

Coda

The fire blazed for days, smouldering among the ruins, licking and cracking and consuming everything there was to consume.

The Hermitage had had its time. Never again would the confessions be written down in the ledgers, or the ancient walls hold the secrets of a thousand years of sin. The slate was wiped clean at last, a millennium of Catholic guilt buried under the smouldering rubble.

It was a miracle that the fireball did not set light to the hillside and bring death and destruction to the borie village. Even though it never rains on the night of the St Jean in the valleys of Upper Provence, for the second time that century the heavens opened and the rain fell from what had been only moments earlier a clear and starlit sky. Some legends live on; some die.

The ochre ramparts, denuded now of their citadel, still soar towards the sky – no longer a monument to the pride of man, but a symbol of the power of nature, the indestructibility of the earth from which they spring.

In time the naked rocks brought forth new growth. Mosses grew on the lip of the blackened crater, saplings rose among the blistered stones, hummocks of grass took hold in the crevices. In time, the fullness of time, the wild creatures of the valley reclaimed their own.

And in time, the gentleness of time, no-one would have known that the secret place had ever existed. Except for those who could trace the outlines of what had once been the citadel in what to others would have seemed no more than a trick of the light.

The borie village continues to thrive, living proof of what can be done when the will is strong and the heart rules the head. On the ramparts of what once had been the High Pool, a fig tree flourishes. Marguerite and George return each year to visit Tonin and his grand-children, bringing their own grandchildren to play in what had once been and is again the herb garden of the Cathar women.

And in time, too, in the secret place which had once been the Hermitage of the Rock, birds nest, bees swarm, the cold-blooded lizards take strength from the sun.

In the meadows the daisies still bloom each spring. And every year, say the country people, a young woman sets down her burden and looks across the valley to where the Hermitage once stood.

Some legends die and some are born. One legend which persists is the story of the bones, the inconvenient bones of the Mother of God. Beneath the tumbling stones the cavern lies buried. The shrine is still held to be holy. Call it superstition, but miracles are still known to happen there. And still the country people come to lay their gifts beside the well-spring.

On their silver wedding anniversary, on the day of the Eve of the St Jean, Marguerite Dieudonnée Leblanc took her beloved husband to watch the sunset over the valley.

She turned to him then, now they were alone in the place she loved best in the world, and told him the thing she had never told him before.

'Husband George,' she said, 'did I ever tell you that I love you?'

'No, my darling,' his answer came softly. 'But, then, you never had to.'

It is a secret place, the Hermitage of the Rock. It keeps its secret still.

THE END

EMERALD
by Elisabeth Luard

When Edward VIII married Mrs Simpson, he gave up his crown, his kingdom . . . and his child. *Emerald* is her story. The story of a King's daughter the world never knew.

From the moment of her birth in her mother's secret hideaway in the South of France, to the Hebridean island which became her childhood refuge, to the jungles of Mexico where she found first passion, to the glittering catwalks of New York and Paris, to the strange circumstances of the birth of her own child, Emerald was always too brilliant a jewel to blaze unseen. With no inheritance but her mother's beauty and her father's charm, Emerald has no option but to fight for her own – in life, in love, and in the final choice . . . whether or not to accept her birthright.

'A romantic and glamorous story'
Daily Mirror

'Intriguingly plausible'
Living

0 552 13737 5

FAMILY LIFE
Birth, Death and the Whole Damn Thing
by Elisabeth Luard

'Unspeakably moving . . . She deserves a medal'
Libby Purves, *The Times*

Not everyone goes to school on a donkey, keeps an eagle owl in the spare bedroom cupboard, or plays chess for the French Foreign Legion. But for the four Luard children, all this was perfectly normal. As normal as taking the scrap bucket across the stream to feed the household pig, or knowing how to hitch up a mulecart.

Elisabeth Luard's not-so-simple tale captures the spirit of bringing up four children as they travel across Europe, their lives a series of old-fashioned adventures. Littered with anecdotes and a scattering of their favourite recipes, this book is a celebration of family life. But no family is immune from tragedy – still less one which lives life to the full. In Francesca, the eldest of the three daughters, we find a true heroine. Passionate, honest, perceptive, she tells her own story – until that moment when she can tell it no more.

Ultimately, however, *Family Life* is a mother's tale of love without regret. A tale of laughter and tears, of joy and sorrow, of life and death. It is a story you will never forget.

'Some of the most poignant and moving writing this year'
Daily Express

'Writing with admirable courage, she contributes memorably to the literature of family life'
Elizabeth Buchan, *Mail on Sunday*

'Books can be good, bad or patchy, but there are some that you will never forget. Elisabeth Luard's belongs in the last category'
Sue Gaisford, *Independent*

0 552 14544 0

A SELECTED LIST OF FINE NOVELS
AVAILABLE FROM CORGI BOOKS

14060 0	MERSEY BLUES	Lyn Andrews	£4.99
14049 X	THE JERICHO YEARS	Aileen Armitage	£4.99
14514 9	BLONDE WITH ATTITUDE	Virginia Blackburn	£5.99
14309 X	THE KERRY DANCE	Louise Brindley	£5.99
12887 2	SHAKE DOWN THE STARS	Frances Donnelly	£5.99
13266 7	A GLIMPSE OF STOCKING	Elizabeth Gage	£5.99
14232 8	LILIAN	Jill Gascoine	£4.99
14382 0	THE TREACHERY OF TIME	Anna Gilbert	£4.99
13992 0	LIGHT ME THE MOON	Angela Arney	£4.99
14097 X	SEA MISTRESS	Iris Gower	£5.99
14141 0	PARADISE LANE	Ruth Hamilton	£5.99
14529 7	LEAVES FROM THE VALLEY	Caroline Harvey	£5.99
14297 2	ROSY SMITH	Janet Haslam	£4.99
14486 X	MARSH LIGHT	Kate Hatfield	£6.66
14220 4	CAPEL BELLS	Joan Hessayon	£4.99
14207 7	DADDY'S GIRL	Janet Inglis	£4.99
14390 1	THE SPLENDOUR FALLS	Susanna Kearsley	£4.99
14045 7	THE SUGAR PAVILION	Rosalind Laker	£5.99
14332 4	THE WINTER HOUSE	Judith Lennox	£5.99
14332 3	FOOL'S CURTAIN	Claire Lorrimer	£4.99
13737 5	EMERALD	Elisabeth Luard	£5.99
14544 0	FAMILY LIFE	Elisabeth Luard	£6.99
13910 6	BLUEBIRDS	Margaret Mayhew	£5.99
10375 6	CSARDAS	Diane Pearson	£5.99
14124 0	MAGNOLIA SQUARE	Margaret Pemberton	£4.99
14400 2	THE MOUNTAIN	Elvi Rhodes	£5.99
14298 0	THE LADY OF KYNACHAN		
		James Irvine Robertson	£5.99
14466 5	TOUCHED BY ANGELS	Susan Sallis	£5.99
14154 2	A FAMILY AFFAIR	Mary Jane Staples	£4.99
14118 6	THE LAND OF NIGHTINGALES	Sally Stewart	£4.99
14118 6	THE HUNGRY TIDE	Valerie Wood	£4.99